I'LL KNOW YOU
BY YOUR HEART

I'LL KNOW YOU
BY YOUR HEART
Part 1

A novel by
TONI DEMAIO

TATE PUBLISHING
AND ENTERPRISES, LLC

Published by Tate Publishing & Enterprises, LLC
127 E. Trade Center Terrace | Mustang, Oklahoma 73064 USA
1.888.361.9473 | www.tatepublishing.com

Tate Publishing is committed to excellence in the publishing industry. The company reflects the philosophy established by the founders, based on Psalm 68:11,
"The Lord gave the word and great was the company of those who published it."

Book design copyright © 2014 by Tate Publishing, LLC. All rights reserved.
Cover design by Anne Gatillo
Interior design by Caypeeline Casas

Published in the United States of America

ISBN: 978-1-62902-543-8
1. Fiction / Humorous
2. Fiction / General
13.12.09

I'LL KNOW YOU BY YOUR HEART

The best and most beautiful things in this world cannot be seen or even heard, but must be felt by the heart.

—Helen Keller

THIS NOVEL IS DEDICATED TO:

Nancy Gagliardi Ferris, the little sister of my heart, who was the first reader of my first draft, those many years ago, and the last reader of my final draft. With deep love and gratitude for a lifetime of friendship, love and support, and most of all for the cheerleading that finally got me over the finish line.

ACKNOWLEDGEMENTS

I want to thank all the characters in my novel, both those based in reality and those who are products of my imagination for the inspiration to tell our stories. I want to thank the Lord for his gifts and his guidance always. Kasey Gardner at Tate deserves a huge thank you for seeing something special in my manuscript and for being such a wonderful, vibrant, welcoming soul and a complete joy to work with. The entire experience with Tate Publishing has been a privilege and I thank Lauren Perkins, and all of the talented team for your creativity and hard work.

I want to thank my family, Gram, Mah, Dad, my brother, John, Nanny and Pop, and my beautiful fun and funny daughter, Samantha, who are all in Heaven now for their support and love eternally. I want to thank the family who is with me on earth as well for their love, encouragement and acceptance: my son Will, his wife, Sheri, and my daughter, Tiffany, and Redd, the grandkids; Amber, Killian, Mikey, Gabriel, Demetrius and Graziana, and the great-grandkids; Kayley Jeanne and Kaden Hunter. I love you all and am grateful to be your Gramy and Grandma. My niece, Katie DeMaio, deserves a special acknowledgement as she is very talented and the newest writer in our family with her first book set to be published this year. I know John is bursting with pride and telling the guys all about it up there in the greatest rock and roll band in the universe. I have special love and deep gratitude for Dean Ridgway, my younger half-brother for caring enough to find me again, and for putting me back in touch with Bill and Bob Ridgway, my twin half-brothers. I know all three of you make Dad very proud.

I have tremendous love and gratitude for my hugely talented author friends, Sherry and Nancy for their deep, constant and enduring friendship, unconditional love and support always and most of all for teaching me invaluable lessons and raising me up always. They are two of the finest women on this earth. Marianne Michaels deserves my deepest gratitude as well. From my soul to yours I thank you for your gentle guidance and for curing me of being 'a walking Ouigi board.'

Two incredibly generous and talented teachers deserve my deepest thanks and love. The late Walter James Miller, award-winning poet and professor, taught, encouraged and mentored me for years and I will never forget him and his lovely, Mary. The supremely talented screenwriter, Christopher McCabe, lent his knowledge along with his support, friendship and guidance in helping me to do my best work.

I need to acknowledge Jane Gagliardo for many years of generous support and friendship. You are in my prayers always. And for my spiritual family at Unity, in the Reiki Circle, and in the church, I thank you for providing the final piece in my spiritual puzzle and for embracing me as you embrace every living soul, and our beautiful planet

I want to give special thanks to my guardian angels who saved the best for this last act in my life and who sent my fiancé Joe Reynolds, my way; so much better late than never!! And I am grateful to Joe for being perfect for me in every way and so willing to join my circus!

FOREWORD

This book is a novelization of both events in my lifetimes that have occurred along with events that are fictitious. Some of the characters in both of the lifetimes depicted are real, while some characters are fictitious. All of the names have been changed to protect the not-so-innocent, with the single exception of Hazel Alice Shively Sheldon, aka Gram…the most real character I have ever known, and the first one to introduce me to the idea of oneness with all humanity, and all religions, united in God's love, and taught so beautifully by Unity.

Many of the scenes depicted in this novel come straight from my dreams. And many years ago while doing research on Ohio history at Princeton Library in N.J., I was shocked to discover that some of the characters I had dreamed about had actually lived and done the things I was writing about. Have I been dreaming about a past life for most of this one? I think so, and believing this has helped me to understand the lessons my soul most needed to learn in this lifetime.

CHAPTER 1

In the loony bin they say, "For every patient who walks through the front door there is someone crazier on the outside who helped to drive them there."

Actually, when my turn came, I drove myself.

But my husband did help me to get there in his own way. Bull Harris was always too good looking and charming to be one of those steady, reliable husbands you think you want at thirty. Women chased him and he tripped and fell on a regular basis.

Unfortunately being susceptible to charm, I'd allowed him to manipulate me into marrying him fourteen years before I was ready to see and face the truth about him…the truth about us. I guess actually, the truth about myself.

My years of attempting to turn myself upside down and inside out in order to win his complete love had finally ended in my self-induced nervous collapse. One day I had just decided to try 'crazy' since coping well hadn't done a thing to improve the situation.

It took fourteen years to get to crazy because Bull was so slick and I was hell-bent on 'turning the other cheek'. He came on like a brown-eyed puppy boy in need of adoption, but was really a viper on the prowl capable of conducting love affairs in the early morning hours before work while the kids and I slept peacefully, impressed with his commitment to his career and his superior work ethic. I didn't know any other hairdressers who would take clients at 6:30 A.M. just to provide a good life for the family.

Actually, for years I had been tortured with the inner knowing that my husband was an unfaithful liar. Bull always insisted I was crazy, and imagining his infidelities. I tried to give him the benefit of the doubt and believe in him, but this ultimately led to the day I would look in the mirror and face a complete naïve fool.

And not only was Bull a creative womanizer, but his latest girlfriend, Teri-the-Bitch, had made certain I find out not only about her, but the fact that he was also secretly involved in organized crime. Suddenly all my nagging, agonizing suspicions were a reality I couldn't ignore or tolerate.

Bad enough he cheated, but joining the Mafia and selling drugs was a bit much even for Bull. As a couple we'd always been anti-drug, which of course meant he was also a hypocrite. And if there's one thing I can't stand, it's a hypocrite.

I had stayed in the marriage too long as it was, due to a stupid promise I had made to the kids, Ben and Gillian. "There will never be a divorce in this family!" I'd said, nearly killing myself in the attempt to live up to that one.

Oh, but it wasn't easy to get away from Bull. He was crazy…and half Italian too, and not about to give up his virgin/wife/mother-of-his-children figure. He was the type of guy who felt entitled to his stuffed shells at home, all the while secretly savoring his occasional piece of apple pie on the side.

Toward the end, there were days Bull would almost convince me he really did love me, and that there might be hope for our little family. "I'll never love any girl the way I love you, Sunny," he vowed passionately…after a spectacularly creative sexual episode. Predictably, we did have the best sex during that final year. I'd do anything to keep him away from *her*.

Then I found out he was still seeing Teri-the-Bitch after vowing never to even speak to her again. Funny how, when finally faced with the fact that I knew everything, the truth suddenly began to come out of his mouth.

"Give me a break, Sunny! I've been faithful to you…sometimes for months at a time!" "But what I'll miss most, Honey…if you do give up on me," he said as I escaped into the bathroom, "Is our not growing old together. I was counting on that. Hell, that's why I married you! Because you, Sunny, are the girl I want to grow old with."

Flatter me, Asshole! So back in Junior High, I stuck out to him as the one girl he envisioned 'growing old' with. Talk about planning ahead.

"You're gonna get old and die long before I do, Bull Harris," I muttered, checking for non-existent crow's feet in the mirror, "And if God has a sense of humor, your dick will die first."

"Whatdya say?" he called from the bedroom. "Talk to me, Honey. You're always nagging at me to talk. So how come now, after bugging me for the truth, you don't want to try to work this little misunderstanding out? This truth thing isn't doing a fucking thing for me."

"Our first misunderstanding, Bull, is that your lying and cheating is a 'little misunderstanding.'" And at this point in my life, I wouldn't recognize the truth if it flew by on little pink wings."

"Come on, Sun, lighten up," he pleaded as he came through the doorway and sat on the toilet lid. "I told you I gave Teri up! It was a stupid mistake. That broad doesn't mean shit to me. It's you I love."

And that love was worth what, maybe a nickel, if that?

I watched his smug face, all satisfied with himself, in the reflection of the mirror while he shifted his gaze up and down my body; looking me over as if I were suddenly a new conquest instead of his wife of fourteen years. I was seething with confusion, anger, and heartbreak.

In some ways Bull was a drama queen; a real romance junkie. And the sad truth was that not even Marilyn Monroe could have kept up that 'first kiss' excitement for fourteen years.

"Calm down, Honey," he coaxed in his silky hairdresser's voice, "Don't get all crazy on me now."

"Don't you dare tell me how to feel," I shot back, brushing my long, dark-auburn hair and liking the crackle of the static electricity. "I turned myself into freaking Italian Barbie for you and it never made one bit of difference. Do you have any idea how hard it is for an Italian American woman over the age of thirty to maintain a weight of 110 pounds? It's been a nightmare of starvation and it's never made one stinking little iota of difference. Ooh, how I tried to believe your lies…how I prayed for the bliss of stupidity…and even while trying to look the other way, I caught you in three affairs. They may not have meant shit to you, Bull, but they did to me. I swear, Bull, if you do it again…if you see that bitch, Teri, again…I will call you out on the third strike! You little bastard! I will!"

He stood and shifted his weight from one foot to the other, pulling his pudgy stomach in so his chest would appear even broader. He played with one of the buttons on his opened shirt. Under the harsh bathroom light, his gold chains twinkled at me from where they nestled in his black, curly chest hair. "I'm only human, Sunny," he said, sighing loudly over my shoulder while he checked himself out in the mirror. "And I explained to you how each of those girls was relentless. They chased me, Sunny…wouldn't give me any peace…threw themselves at me!" He rolled his expressive eyes toward the ceiling, "I'm a guy, Sunny!"

"That is…so true," I sighed as he took a step toward me and I breathed in his familiar scent of cologne and hot man. The only man I'd ever been with, hot or not.

He pulled at his neatly trimmed black beard. "But no other girl does it for me, Sunny, not the way you do…And I know I make you happy, at least in bed I do." His smile was confident again. He was on familiar ground now. "You can't deny it, Baby."

He looked so cocky I couldn't resist playing with him a little. He certainly deserved it. "We're happy in bed, Bull…I guess…but really you have to admit I'm at a disadvantage, being your virgin and all. I have no one to compare you with."

He was on top of me in an instant. "So that's what this is all about. You want to be free to screw around. Teach me a lesson and turn into a slut!"

"You mean like Teri? How many men has she had?" I turned away from him and rubbed at the fresh bruises forming on my arms from his viselike grip. All the while, I felt strangely reassured. If Bull could get this upset at the thought of losing me to another man, if the idea of anyone else making love to me could inspire this much passion and violence in him, then he must still love me. I was right, wasn't I? Well, at the time I thought I was right, using a twisted sense of Italian logic.

Of course I knew I'd eventually have to leave him. I couldn't imagine going through this drama crap at sixty or God forbid, seventy! And there was the matter of his 'secret' business, which Teri had made sure I'd find out about, thinking that would be the last straw for me.

Whenever I'd tried to discuss the rumors I'd heard about his involvement in selling drugs, he'd tell me to mind my own business…for my own good.

One thing was obvious to me, though; he was under tremendous stress and not feeling good about what he had gotten himself into. But when I cried and offered to pack up the kids, shut down my business, and run away with him to Canada or Mexico, he refused to even consider it, and urged me to be patient.

"I've given Teri up and soon I'll be getting out of this whole mess. She's in it with me, and it wasn't my choice," he insisted, "I can't tell you anything specific for your own good. Just trust me, Sunny. It'll be over soon. And forget this nonsense about the Mafia…there is no Mafia…"

He spoke convincingly, but he looked scared. For the first time in our lives together, Bull Harris looked scared shitless.

And due to our history, trust was the one thing I could never do again. The battle for Bull's soul raged on for months. My new nickname became Columbo as I grew into a gifted detective. Bull was obviously very confused as I tripped him up on so many of his lies.

Some days after I would threaten to leave him, he swore he would never let me go. "You're like a cancer in my heart and mind, Sunny. A sickness I'll never be able to live without."

His words weren't very flattering, but pretty good imagery; at least from a guy who never read fiction or watched the soaps.

Worst of all, Teri turned out to be a surprisingly vicious little blonde Terrier. She had him by the leg, actually by the balls, and she wasn't about to let him go. She engineered a program of torture including threatening phone calls from strange men, and random gunshots that would whiz out of the woods behind my antique shop and slam into the sides or back of the cabin walls. Off season hunters? Kids shooting targets? An assassin?

Bull and I had moved the family to the Poconos from New Jersey four years earlier when I'd discovered his second affair. He had sworn to be faithful then and had managed to convince me he wanted to make a new start in a new place. It turned out I was good at running the antique shop we created on the front acre of our two acres of lawn out by the main road, and Bull was free to give his attention to his hair-styling shop in the next small town.

But when Teri began her campaign to get Bull away from me, I began to dissolve slowly and steadily. Not only was I a nervous wreck from those bullets that would come at me without any warning, but I had to endure the threatening visits by intimidating strangers who would hint broadly that I should 'keep my mouth shut' about things that didn't concern me.

And for the first time in my life, I was deeply frightened. I told Bull about the gunshots knowing beyond a doubt they couldn't be a coincidence since they only seemed to come out of the woods when I was walking up the path to the shop.

Actually, Bull looked frightened too, when I told him, but he would never have admitted it. "Sunny, that's just nuts. Why would someone try to kill you? I've looked over every inch of the back of the shop and I just don't see any bullets in the logs. You've got to get hold of yourself. You're acting crazy." Then he roared out of the driveway in his truck and didn't come back for several hours. When he finally returned and refused to discuss it any further beyond his muttered reply to my questions, "There won't be any more problems around here so just forget about it."

Lonely, scared, and racked with anxiety as I watched my marriage, my life, crumbling around me, I took a chance and asked my neighbor over for tea one morning. Cynthia was home most mornings now since she had recently moved her sick mom into their home in order to care for her. Bull was never one to encourage friendships with the neighbors, or anyone else for that matter, but I knew, if given a chance, Cynthia and I could become real friends.

We talked for a while about our kids and then I drew a deep breath and asked her if she had heard the gunshots on the various days when they had nearly missed hitting me on my way up from the house to the antique shop.

She stared at me for a moment; then grasped my hand, "Are you all right, Sunny? You're awfully thin."

I smiled at her with trembling lips, "I'm fine, I just wondered if you were aware of the problem we seem to be having with off-season hunters…I mean, it just isn't right to have to worry about this sort of thing. What if our kids were playing out back by the woods and a stray bullet…"

Cynthia looked down at her hands, obviously uncomfortable and I immediately wondered if Bull had already spoken to her about this. Maybe he'd done some damage control and suggested I was imagining things. I felt more helpless and isolated than ever before. "No," she finally said, I haven't heard anything, but really, lately mom and I have spent more time at the doctor than we have here at home."

She raised her eyes to mine and I could read pity there. "You know, Bull is very worried about you. He came by last Sunday, and I was really impressed with how much he cares about you." She smiled hopefully at me.

So finally, in this confused state of mind, weighing ninety eight pounds fully clothed, and shaking and crying uncontrollably after a particularly demoralizing encounter with Bull, I drove myself to the nearest hospital to hide and re-group, asking to be admitted to the optimistically named mental health ward.

Just like in the movies, the people there were very nice to me. I was hungry for friendship since Bull had slowly been forcing me to break contact with my family and friends over the past four years since we'd moved to the Poconos.

"Tell us what happened to make you come here, Sunny," one of the nurses urged. So I did.

"Well, Bull was in the shower at the time. He had just told me he'd decided that although he loved me, he also loved Teri, and he was better off 'business wise' living with her since they both had the same desire for money. And they didn't much care how they got it. *But*…and it was a big but…he still wanted to come and 'visit' me and the kids a few times a week." Wink. Wink.

"The real truth, Sunny," Bull said (as if there were an unreal truth), "Is that I'll do anything for money. I know you don't know that about me because I wanted you to love me, but I'm sick of not having things. I can't take it anymore."

I looked around at our nice home, then out the window at our two vehicles. "We have plenty of things, Bull. What more do we need?"

"That's just it, Sunny, you have no clue. You're just not greedy enough for me…and I'm getting sick of your drinking."

My drinking! Now that was something Bull had talked me into starting, bringing home bottles of wine, uncorking them, pouring a glass, or two, or three, for me; probably because he didn't want me to have too clear of a head, given his hobbies. Recently, I had to admit, though, I was a gung-ho wino all on my own. Over the past year, Chablis had slowly become my best, and only, friend.

I began shaking again as I absorbed his heartless matter-of-fact words, and reached for my wine glass which at the moment was an art deco vase…my medication of choice, my tranquilizer in a socially acceptable bottle. My head spun, throbbing with confusion. Bull had always loved me, now suddenly it looked as if he didn't. If he continued with his recent patterns, tomorrow he would again. I couldn't take another minute of it.

"Bull," I sobbed, "I don't even know who I am anymore. I'm a mess and I'm ashamed. I don't think…I don't think I want to live, or even know how to, if you leave me."

"Then die." His eyes were as hard as cold, dark stones. He turned away from me and walked into the bathroom. I heard the water pound full force against the tiles.

I waited until I was certain Bull was good and wet; then selected the three-fifty-seven magnum pistol from his gun collection. I loaded it, and sat on the bed, staring down the barrel of the gun for what must have been a full, dramatic minute, before muttering, "Screw this," and firing above my head and into the ceiling of our one-hundred-year-old home."

"What were you feeling at the time?" asked the grim-faced woman in white who was writing things down on a chart.

"I was…I guess I was feeling pretty stupid since I was covered in plaster, and I was angry at myself for being such a fool; for wasting my whole life. I couldn't face disappointing the kids with a divorce and for a moment I thought my kids would actually be better off without me as a role model but I fired at the ceiling instead. And then I came here so you could help me."

The woman looked sympathetic and not at all shocked. She'd most likely heard some even sadder stories than mine, "What was your husband's reaction to the gunshot?" she asked, pencil poised over the chart.

I took a shaky breath and cleared my dry throat, "I heard him scream my name. It was like a roar from his gut. He tore out of the shower and just stood staring at me, wild-eyed and naked as he dripped soapy water into the carpet. I've never cared much for that carpet anyway it's a nasty shade of green, so I didn't say anything. I just sat on the bed and stared back at him."

"You're fuckin' crazy, Sunny!" he said.

"You might be right about that. I feel a little crazy," I answered, combing the plaster out of my hair with my hands and forming my plans for the day…I would use this day to find out just how crazy I actually was. I figured this was the perfect day to do it since the kids were spending the weekend with Bull's mother, my husband was leaving me, and I suddenly had nothing better to do anyway…so what the hell?"

"Bull left. I stared at the ceiling for a while and tried to stop crying. I'd always wanted a skylight over the bed, but this was definitely not the way to go about it. Then I drank most of a bottle of Chablis, showered, dressed in my best black dress, applied my make-up which immediately ran down my cheeks in muddy, rainbow rivers, set my hair in hot rollers, combed, styled, sprayed; re-did my makeup, then packed a bag with mostly black clothes, though unintentionally, and the unfinished manuscript of the novel I'd been writing."

For the past several years I had been writing a novel based on the dreams I was continually having about a girl named, Jessamyn. Although in my dreams she existed in 1797, I recognized her as the sister of my heart. She was the only person I knew of whose life was more screwed up than my own.

For years, for all my years really, the dreams had been having an impact on me because in these dreams I was her. I knew what it was like to walk the world in her skin. And as the years passed, the book turned into the 'novel from hell' that had no apparent end.

Then my teacher from night school insisted I research Ohio history to check my historical facts and I found out many of my main characters had actually lived. Jessamyn had been a real person, and I had no logical idea of where I was getting my information about her life. Was I remembering my own past life? My gram thought that was it, and I kind of did, too.

Or was Jessamyn the real me before I lost myself in marriage to Bull? Not as likely, because the dreams and visions had begun back when I was a small child.

"Sunny?" The nurse brought me back to the moment with a jolt. Lately, it was harder to stay focused on the miserable mess of my real life. "I have to bring your paperwork up to the nurse on duty and in a few minutes someone will come to get you. Do you want a magazine, or a glass of juice while you wait?"

I shook my head. I had enough to think about while I waited. Maybe here I would finally learn why I was constantly dreaming about Jessamyn. Even the night before, as my life crumbled around me, I had dreamed I was Jessamyn wrestling with a nightmare.

The man she wanted, Bruin Mahoney, looked enough like my own husband, Bull, to be his twin. But that was where the resemblance stopped. If they were twins, Bull was the 'evil' twin and Bruin was everything a woman could hope for in a man.

In Jessamyn's dream, within my dream (pretty confusing, huh?) she searched for Bruin as I had considered searching for Bull on those lonely nights toward the end when he would disappear for hours and not bother to call or make up a creative lie I could try to believe, when he did eventually show up.

Deep in sleep, Jessamyn dreamed she was in the forest very late at night. She leaned back against the hard bark of a tree trunk and caught her breath. The shapes in the woods were shades of black on gray and she imagined the woman with Bruin held fast to his leather vest as they inched their way down the narrow path behind the church. She heard a giggle when Bruin stopped short and the woman bumped against his broad muscular back.

The sounds of the fair grew faint in the distance and Jessamyn guessed they had come far enough when Bruin turned and pulled the woman into his arms. When he kissed her, Jessamyn felt pain in her heart and she hid her face in her hands and stifled her sobs.

Behind her closed eyelids, Jessamyn fancied she could see and sense exactly what was happening. The young woman trembled as Bruin's hands closed around her breasts, and as he pulled at her bodice and ran hot kisses down her neck and into the scented hollow of her cleavage, she clawed impatiently at his shirt. This was the kind of forbidden adventure that fired her young hot blood.

"Don't make me wait any longer," she whispered in a soft, breathless voice, "I want you, Bruin...now."

It was good to be wanted. Bruin threw his vest aside, pulled his shirt off and spread it on the grassy knoll. Then he undid his boot laces and removed his boots and trousers.

It was a warm night and the only sounds were the shrill tune of a katydid, the screech of a bat. There was mystery behind each tree, and the danger of uncertainty.

The slender young girl stepped out of her dress and under garments. She spread her arms as if they were fairy wings and spun naked, laughing, savoring the delicious feeling of warm night air moving over her lush body.

Her graceful flesh took on an iridescent glow in the dim light of the crescent moon above, while the perfection of her body and the youthful exuberance of her dance stirred Bruin's senses.

He wanted her but he did not love her and he knew he probably never would. As an honorable man he had done his best to make this clear to her, but nothing he did seemed to discourage her. She wanted him as much as he wanted her with no thought to the future or the possible consequences. He reached for her and pulled her down upon his shirt. She squealed and tried to roll playfully away from him.

"That's enough teasing." Bruin pulled her back to him and covered her body with his own. She slowly ran her hands over the muscles of his arms and shoulders before drawing his face down to kiss his lips with surprising strength and passion in one so young.

He pulled away when she bit his lip, and then, closed his eyes and buried his face in the fragrant flesh of her neck and shoulders. He surrendered to the comfort and release from tension he found in the warm, soft, secret places of a woman's body. For a brief time, an hour or two, he could forget his disappointments and live in his dreams.

As she writhed beneath him like a jungle cat, he explored her body with his hands then traced the same paths with his mouth, breathing deeply of the scent of a woman and all it meant to him. She moaned and he was glad he could please her so well. It made him feel good, almost powerful, and when he entered her body, he moved for his own pleasure, but in such a way as to drive her into a deeper frenzy.

It wasn't long before she lost control and shrieked into the dark of the trees, her back bowed, her eyes bright and dark at the same time with pure ecstasy. This only made him feel more in control and he adjusted his rhythm to the slow, teasing thrust and grind he loved; then closed his eyes and, God help his soul, he pretended she was Jessamyn, the one woman he could never have now, and that what he felt in those magical moments was love.

Shattered inside, Jessamyn stumbled back along the path toward the light in the church window up ahead. Blinded by her tears, she cursed herself for caring...for allowing her heart to be broken...again and again by her best friend on earth.

*   *   *

J ust as Jessamyn awoke in the dim light of the church to find it had all been a dream, I awoke as well to face what would turn out to be the worst day of my relatively short life...

So, an hour after 'checking into' the infamous sixth floor of The Pocono View Hospital, Stroudsburg, Pa., I stood in my new room, marveling at how closely the place resembled an unimaginative Howard Johnson's, decorated in tired shades of turquoise and orange, all the while hating myself for having to come here. I chose the bed nearest to the door and handed my basic black frock and personal belongings to Kathy, the nice, young mental health aide who was assigned to orient me to my new home, at least home for the next two weeks.

For the moment I had run out of tears and my mouth felt dry and sticky. I gulped the water Kathy handed me in a paper cup; then gazed quickly away from my puffy-eyed reflection in the mirror over the dresser. Bull has always described me as looking like a sexy librarian since I have big Italian brown eyes from Dad's side of the family, and long, dark auburn hair from Mah's Irish ancestors, and I wear glasses. But today I looked too pitiful to face the mirror with a smile. Poor Kathy had to stand by and watch me dress in the regulation P.J.'s and despite my own embarrassment, I felt sorry for her. It couldn't have been any more comfortable for her to have to watch a naked stranger put on a pair of faded pajamas.

My emaciated state well hidden within the droopy folds of blue flannel, I padded down the hall in my hospital issue slippers. Kathy walked along beside me. "It's best for you, Sunny, if you mix right in with the group when you first get here," she said, "You're supposed to share your problems with the other patients, and then the healing process can begin."

She smiled encouragingly at me.

"You mean," I said, clearing my parched throat, "That I'm supposed to just walk up to some stranger in a pair of these P.J.'s and spill my guts to them...just like that?"

She blinked at me. "Well, yes. That's pretty much how the program works. And it does work, Sunny. You'll be surprised at how much better you'll feel."

At least I was walking into this room of strangers as a fashionably thin woman. There were no lumps or bulges beneath my blue flannel tent. Due to stress and anxiety I hadn't been able to eat in weeks and it was ironic; the greatest tragedy of my life so far, had brought me one of my fondest wishes. I was finally thin enough to please even Bull and for the first time ever, I couldn't have cared less.

We rounded the corner and I stared back at a roomful of others who wore the telling blue flannel, yet I couldn't help feeling particularly exposed, as if I were trapped in one of those dreams where I make a grand entrance at a very important party and suddenly realize I'm stark naked, or wearing a tiny bikini, or…maybe even a pair of blue flannel crazy pants pajamas.

The eyes of the other patients made me feel like a bug in a jar, and I knew what Sylvia Plath had experienced and described in her book, *The Bell Jar*. I remembered being fascinated by the way she had fictionalized her mental problems, her time spent in a place something like this.

At first I thought the others were being rude to stare at me like that, and then I remembered this was no party. We had all apparently left our party manners outside of this building on the other side of these very thick walls. We were misfits, united in our differences. We hadn't quite measured up to what was expected of each of us on the outside…at that very real party I imagined was going on out there without us. I figured we were playing by another set of rules here, but I felt left out because I didn't even know what game we were playing yet. I'd never been a misfit before. I'd never fallen out of step, stepped out of line, and I felt panic grab me by the gut.

Suddenly I was burning up. The sweat ran down my back and I caught the scent of a wild animal; a frightened animal. It took another moment to realize it was me.

I craved cool, clean, fresh air. I turned toward the exit sign and stopped. When I had wandered in here for help I had actually signed away my right to free choice, at least for a while, my very right to breathe fresh air at will. The panic rose with a mind of its own. I had to get out of there.

I raced down the nearest narrow hallway toward a large door. Kathy called out to me, "Sunny please calm down. Take some deep breaths. You're making it harder on yourself."

I threw myself against the door, my heart beating in my ears, skipping beats, thrashing. The hair on my body stood electrically on end as

I strained on tip-toes to see through the tiny window just above me. I could see a piece of sky! Just a little piece through the windows out in the hallway, but at least I knew it was still out there.

And I could see a bank of elevators; small, steel prisons that could carry me back down to the freedom outside of this hateful place, this place where I would be forced to face myself, to examine myself like that bug in a jar I felt such a kinship with. I clawed at the door handle and pulled with all that was left within me, but of course the door was locked. They couldn't allow the crazy people to wander the halls, breathing the fresh air. Was I really crazy too?

For the rest of my life, people would assume so. They would whisper behind their hands about me just because I had come here on a very bad day and asked for help. I had shown weakness. I had given up, given in, and I would pay for it for the rest of my life.

Someone placed a hand on my shoulder and I spun around, careening madly, reflexively back into a corner. Someone was moaning. I could hear it as I slid down the wall and screamed.

The last thing I remember thinking before they gave me the shot and I lost consciousness was that the zoo would be ruined for me now.

I had always loved the zoo, walking along the flowered paths, and laughing at the monkeys on a sunny day with Bull…and Ben…and little Gillian. But that part of my life was over now. I could never visit the zoo again without aching to set all of the animals free.

CHAPTER 2

For no good reason I was all alone in the dark somewhere in the suburbs of New Jersey. I walked tree-lined streets in my night-gown, searching for my home when the ground under my feet began to tremble with the crashing footsteps and the huge roar of what I imagined to be a monster. I crawled under a big lilac bush on someone's lawn; then peered up through the purple flowers at the biggest angry ape I had ever seen.

He was looking around and I just knew he was looking for me. I figured he had to be since this was my dream, so I kept still and waited for him to move on down the street; then I darted out from my hiding place and ran across the yards. I ran for my life and even though I could hear him coming behind me, I still felt I could outrun him, or outwit him if it came to that, because I knew I would survive. I knew it because that's what I do. I'm a survivor.

"If you think I'm scary, Sunny," he bellowed, "just wait until Bull finds out about this hospital bill!"

The big ape had a very good point. I could only imagine Bull's reaction when he found out I had checked into this very expensive 'mental health' ward.

Then I pulled myself back to consciousness, and as I opened my eyes to the hard reality of my hospital room, my head began to throb and ring like an alarm clock and I remembered Bull had left me. I had decided to go crazy, gotten roaring drunk drinking wine out of a silly art deco vase, shot a hole in the bedroom ceiling, drove here, *drunk*, hoping to find a safe place to get my head back on straight, and I didn't even know if my children knew where I was. I could only hope they didn't know everything that had happened.

What would Ben and Gillian think when they found out their mother was on the sixth floor? I never intended to hurt them, to shake the foundation of their world which is pretty much all I had accomplished so far. How could I have lost myself to the point where I thought my own children would be better off without me? Even for two weeks?

Disgusted with myself I rolled over to face the door. A huge young man grinned at me from his seat by the bed, and I jumped a little. He had been watching over me like Nana the dog standing watch over the kids in Peter Pan, my favorite children's book. He had bushy dark hair and kind eyes that put me immediately at ease.

"Hi, Sunny," he said, "Are you feeling any better now?"

"Not really. I've got a killer headache," I croaked in my froggy new voice.

"If you feel well enough to stand and walk down to the nurse's station we can get you some Tylenol and a cold glass of juice."

That juice sounded great. "O.K. thanks…What's your name?"

"Everybody calls me Big Jake."

"I can see why," I said, taking the hand he offered to me as I rose slowly to my feet.

"Use our slippers, at least until you get your own back."

Unbidden, my tears began to rise up again with a mind of their own, as Big Jake handed me a pair of paper slippers with smiley faces on them. This had always been my logo. I even had a smiley sun peeking out from under a rainbow on the sign of my antique shop. But these smiley faces made me feel even more like an imposter. How had the stubborn optimist I had always been deteriorate into the pitiful wreck I was today?"

After swallowing the Tylenol and draining two cups of juice, Big Jake suggested I try to eat a little something. I nodded reluctantly, and he led me to a table where three women sat staring at trays of roast turkey, gravy, watery corn, and sticky looking mashed potatoes, with ice cream for dessert.

He put my tray down and pulled my chair out for me. "I see we're watching our weight this evening, Ladies," I said, to no reaction from any of the other three. "I'm Sunny Harris. I came in yesterday."

The oldest woman stared at me blankly, "Are you going to eat that ice cream?" she asked. I handed it to her and she took it without another word.

The youngest one, bent toward her food and hugging herself, spoke next, "Hi, Sunny. I'm Jessie. I'm here because my mother doesn't want me." She stared down at her plate for a moment and I noticed her fork was shaking in her hand. "She doesn't have a clue what to do with me. My…stepfather…has been…getting after me…for years now." She took a ragged breath as tears welled up in her lovely hazel eyes and her pink lips began to quiver like a small child's.

I reached across the table and touched her shoulder. "I'm so sorry," I said, feeling totally helpless. "Where is your father? Can't he help you?"

She smirked, a hard look narrowing her eyes. He ran off when I was two or something." She shrugged. "It's not so bad here. I just hope they let me stay...I don't want to go to a foster home. You don't know. It could be a lot worse there."

I stared at the bandage on her right wrist and wondered if...

"I cut myself this time so I could get back in here." She smiled a smile older than her years. "I didn't go that deep, just deep enough to land me in here so I could be safe for a while."

I nodded at her as if I could possibly understand her situation.

I glanced at the woman to the right of Jessie and smiled encouragingly. "What's your name," I asked.

"Helen. You can call me Hel if you want...most people do after they get to know me. I'm what you'd call nuts. I mean really nuts." She made the crazy sign next to her ear and laughed, clearly amused at my wary expression. "And that, My Dear, is my one and only problem. But it's a doozy."

I smiled back, glad to see none of us had knives and forks at this table.

When Helen laughed I could see her teeth were greenish with a mossy build-up. When I had been admitted earlier, it was mentioned several times to the various personnel involved in the process that I was still brushing my teeth, so I guess they thought that meant I wasn't all that crazy based on my level of personal hygiene.

I swallowed a mouthful of lukewarm turkey and attempted to make conversation. "So, Helen," I said, "How crazy are you? I mean, I guess we wouldn't be here if we weren't all a little bit crazy."

"But I'm big-time crazy. Psychotic; sometimes dangerous to myself as well as to others." Her mouth curved into an impish grin and she winked at me. "I'm in and out of these places, and the sixth floor is better than the State Hospital. When welfare's decided they've paid enough this time, they'll kick me out, pretend I'm cured, but I'll be back."

Helen bent over her tray and picked at her mashed potatoes. Her straight, dull, brown hair fell forward into the gravy and she hooked the hair back behind both ears, sighing loudly. "I hate the slop they feed us here."

"What kind of work do you do when you're not in a place like this?" I asked.

"I used to be a secretary, but now I'm nothing. I'm on permanent disability. I live with my brother. We hate each other."

I took a few forkfuls of food, but I was full quickly and I sipped at my juice instead, then decided to plunge in and 'share my problem."

"I guess this is when I tell you my problem. I was told that's what I'm supposed to do," I began, already feeling the sweat begin to slide down my back. My cheeks were burning and I felt like a fool. "It's hard to know where to start, but here goes; my husband got involved with his third major girlfriend in the past several years. Of course he kept denying the whole thing and telling me I was crazy and totally wrong. I stuck it out because I promised my two kids we'd never get a divorce, but his girlfriend made sure I found out about her and the others, and the fact that he's involved in something very illegal and dangerous." The tears started again, along with an overwhelming feeling of weary helplessness, and Helen and the old lady just stared at me as if I just had to be kidding.

Jessie reached across the table and squeezed my shoulder this time in support.

"I'm just so sick of the whole mess. For a few minutes this morning I felt like I didn't want to live anymore. I felt like such an ass...such a complete failure. I've devoted fourteen years of my life to a marriage that probably was never meant to be. It just hurts so much to try to end it."

"I really hate breaking up," Jessie said in a dreamy little voice, "It really sucks."

I heard Big Jake call my name and I jumped. My nerves were tighter than guitar strings.

Big Jake bent down over me and spoke near my ear. "Your husband is here, Sunny. We had to call him to let him know." He put a large, heavy reassuring hand on my shoulder. "Are you up to seeing him? You don't have to if you don't want to."

I started to tremble, anticipating how angry Bull would be to find me here. We'd had to let our hospitalization insurance lapse this past winter and we hadn't gotten far enough ahead to be able to renew it yet.

"Don't be scared of him, Sunny." Big Jake said in a voice no one would argue with, "He won't hurt you as long as I'm around."

His concern touched me, and tears sprang back into my eyes. I was so sick of crying, but couldn't seem to control it. Why couldn't I have been destined to sit next to someone like Big Jake in eighth-grade English instead of Bull? "O.K.," I said, "I might as well see him and get it over with."

"Are you finished with your tray?"

I nodded. "I can't eat any more."

Big Jake took my tray away while I stood and crossed my arms over blue flannel. The others were staring at me again and I turned toward the big heavy door, unsure whether I wanted to go through with facing Bull or just stay here and feel like a moron with this group of curious strangers.

The door opened, deciding for me, and there stood Bull, looking appropriately concerned. He carried a huge box of candy in one hand and in the crook of his other arm rode a very large teddy bear. For a moment I lost by breath. He was still my Bull and I always felt happy to see him, no matter what he may have done. Not even God could help me; my heart always leaped up and waved at the first glimpse of this rotten little bastardo.

Immediately he found me with his eyes. As far back as Junior High, it had been this way with us. But why, when we were so deeply connected, did he feel the need for a girlfriend?

I walked slowly toward him and he came quickly forward to greet me. Big Jake took a few steps toward us and Bull glared as if to warn him away.

"How are the kids?"

"They're still at my mother's. Come on, Sunny, get dressed and let's get out of here. That guy is pissing me off. What did you tell these people?"

"I can't just leave, Bull. I've signed myself in here for observation... at least a two-week stay."

Bull's eyes hit my face like a fist. "And how am I supposed to pay for that?"

Big Jake lowered his bulk into a chair a few feet away and sighed loudly.

"Don't you have anything else to do, Buddy?" Bull asked, staring at him like a Doberman, crouched and dangerous.

"I'm doing my job, Buddy, that's all," Big Jake returned, along with an effective stare of his own.

I watched Bull flex his wide hand into an angry fist. I touched his arm and he jerked away from me. "Please, Bull," I whispered, "Let's sit down and talk."

He hesitated; then followed me to the sofa farthest away from Big Jake.

Bull's eyes darted nervously about the room. "Sunny," he said, "I'm sorry things got out of hand at the house this morning. I really didn't mean what I said. You know me…I do love you and I know we can work things out if you'll just come home with me. I ca…I don't want to be alone. I need to have you with me."

My stomach churned at his familiar words…at the 360-degree turn. He never meant anything he said. "Bull, look at it this way, maybe it will do you good to be on your own for a few weeks."

His eyes turned cold again. "I'm telling you, Sunny, I won't be alone."

I felt the tears building up again, but I swallowed hard, determined not to let him see me crumble. I hated denying Bull anything, but if I was ever going to work out my problems, it would have to be with the help of a professional, and away from Bull's influence. "I'm not well, Bull. Don't you realize that? I'm worn out…this is the best place for me right now."

His fingers dug into my arm and Big Jake was on his feet in a heartbeat. "I know what you need, Sunny," Bull hissed near my ear. "You need to come home with me where you belong."

Big Jake towered over the both of us and Bull dropped my arm, sprang up and faced him. "I'm not gonna hurt her," he said through clenched teeth, "She's my wife, Man."

"If you touch her again, Bull, I'll have to ask you to leave."

The eyes of the two men locked fiercely while I spoke soothingly, trying to ease the tension. "Bull, please try to understand I need to be here. I'm so hurt and depressed right now I'm not sure I have the energy to give anything to the kids, or to you."

"That's bullshit, Sunny. You're too sensitive, you let things get to you. We need you at home. It's where you belong."

I drew a shaky breath. "Bull, I've had some kind of a breakdown. I feel all shattered inside, and I can't feel anything but the pain."

"Suit yourself. But remember I warned you."

"Warned me?"

"I won't live alone, and if you get any ideas about talking too much to these people about me and my business, just remember you're in a nut ward now and nobody will ever believe anything you have to say again. Keep your mouth shut, Sunny, about whatever you think you know; if you know what's good for you."

I began to laugh. I couldn't help myself, but there was no humor in it. "I think you're crazier than I am, Bull," I gasped. "You can't frighten a suicidal woman with death threats."

There were tears streaming down my cheeks, blurring my vision, yet for once I was seeing Bull clearly. "Punish me, Bull!" I squeaked, trying to catch my breath, "Kill me! Put me out of my goddamned misery!"

Bull looked confused as he stood there blinking at me. "You are crazy, Sunny."

"Maybe I am right now." I said, some of my spunk coming back in a rush of healthy anger. "But I won't be for much longer, because no matter what you say, I am going to stay right here until I get well enough to raise my kids. That's all I care about now."

He looked wounded and not at all pleased with being displaced as my main reason for living. "Oh, yeah, we'll see about that. You've turned weak, Sunny; too weak to raise my kids by yourself."

I held his eyes with my own. "Maybe coming here and asking for help shows I have a kind of strength you can't begin to understand."

"Ha!" I hated that mocking laugh of his. We faced each other in silence. Then Bull stepped toward me and shoved the teddy bear into my arms. Next, very slowly, he placed the candy on the coffee table between us as if it were Valentine's Day. I couldn't thank him for the gifts. They seemed so sad in the face of what we were going through; symbols of all that was wrong with our crippled marriage.

Bull just stood there glaring at me, clenching his hands into fists I could almost feel tearing into me. Big Jake stood again and walked toward us this time.

"So that's your decision, is it? You're going to stay here." Bull stared past me…it was as if I didn't exist for him anymore. "It's a real shame you don't want to come home. The kids will be upset when they find out their mother doesn't care about them anymore. What kind of a mother tries to kill herself?"

"Oh my God! Please don't tell them that, Bull," I pleaded, "I shot the ceiling, not myself. And I'm only staying here long enough to get well. So I can be a better mother to them. Please don't hurt them like that, Bull, just to get back at me."

His smile was cruel. "You can't deny you fired that gun, Sunny. I'm just going by the facts and the fact is if you loved us you wouldn't want to die."

I was sobbing now. "Please! Please don't hurt them! I don't want to die, and I know I'll get better if I stay here. I'll never do anything like this again. I swear it!"

"You'd better go now, Bull," Big Jake said, "You're upsetting Sunny."

"Well, I wouldn't want to get little Sunny all upset now, would I? She'd better get some rest here in this four-hundred-dollar-a-day-home-for-retards, and not worry at all how her husband's going to pay for it!"

Bull strode to the big locked door and hit it with both hands in a loud boom that went right through me.

"Come on," he snarled, "Open up! I've got to get out of this crazy house before I go nuts too!"

I threw myself forward onto the sofa cushions and sobbed until I had no tears left.

"Does that asshole always treat you like this?"

I shrugged, and struggled to a sitting position, swiping at my tears. "Sometimes he treats me like a queen, but he's very jealous and I think he was mad because you were so nice to me. He's always been crazy about things like that."

Big Jake shook his head. "I wouldn't make excuses for him anymore, Sunny. You deserve to be treated with respect all the time."

I nodded, but I didn't feel it. Big Jake's words sounded good to me, but I didn't fully believe I had the right to a happy life. I was so used to taking responsibility for anything bad that happened in our lives together. Bull had done a good job of convincing me I deserved everything I got.

"You can turn in early if you want," Big Jake suggested. "You've had a full day."

I agreed. The hot shower felt good on my aching back, but I was as limp as the soapy cloth I moved over my bony body, and later, when I slipped into my strange bed, I was too tired to sleep.

Huge waves of sadness swept over me and no matter how hard I tried, I couldn't stop the tears and the guilt. What would I tell Ben and Gillian? How could I tell them I was almost certain I would have to divorce their father in order to save my own life?

I was grateful not to have a room-mate. Finally, I sat up in bed and switched on the bedside lamp. It was only ten o'clock and I had another hour until 'lights out'. The night nurse had allowed me to have my books and manuscript from my suitcase and I had been allowed to hang my clothes in the small cubby of a closet.

I'd been told wearing street clothes was a privilege along with winning back the use of a knife and fork at meals. All the patients voted on who should receive privileges at the weekly community meetings. The next meeting was two days away.

I stacked my books on the nightstand; then leafed through the manuscript I had titled, *Reach For The Sun*. I began to read, and immediately felt peaceful. Jessamyn was as close to me as a sister would have been. It seemed as if the clues necessary to an understanding of my own life were somehow hidden in the novel I was writing about this girl from the past.

And the very act of writing her story gave me a sense of identity that even Bull couldn't destroy. Over the years he had found a way to stop me from acting and singing. He had even found a way to keep me away from my closest friends and family by moving me to the mountains and buying a business I had to run each day all year round, but damn it, he couldn't stop me from writing. No one, not even Bull, could control the direction of my pen on paper.

I snatched up my pen and opened my blank notebook. I wanted to escape from this terrible day and go back to a time when I didn't know Bull existed. I wanted to be a child again, even if it was only for an hour or so, and only in my imagination. I closed my eyes and my mind raced back over several decades.

I was about four and the family was living in Newark, New Jersey, when I had my first vision, or flashback, into another time and place.

I think the episode was triggered by the music coming from our radio. I was eating dinner with the family at the red and gray formica and chrome kitchen table when it first hit me. "I was burned by the Indians in a covered wagon," I blurted out. "But I lived. Some of the others died that day, but I lived."

My parents froze in mid-chew and turned to stare at me, heads swiveling like vaudevillians practicing their double takes. My little brother, Joe-Joe was too busy smearing strained peas somewhere near his mouth to bother to react…and anyway, he was used to me.

"What did you say, Sunny?" My mother asked, glancing nervously at my father.

I could see the flames leaping all around me and I could actually smell the feral odor of the shrieking painted Indians as they surrounded the wagon train. The canvas at the top of the wagon was burning, and I was scared beyond any fear I'd yet known…beyond pure terror. I wanted my father. He was somewhere close by, fighting the Indians, and I prayed nothing would happen to him. I thought of my mother who had died more than a year before and wondered if this was to be the day we would meet again in Heaven.

My mind raced to grasp at a way to turn this situation around. I was a survivor, but even to me, it appeared hopeless. Then I felt a soaring up of my spirit and my hidden reserves of strength surged to the surface. I got angry. The anger triggered me into action and as I grew angrier, I grew less afraid.

If I was going to die, I'd die fighting mad, and so I sprang forward and concentrated on pulling the body of the woman who was with me in the burning wagon, toward the opening. I knew she wasn't dead yet, but she was as heavy as only dead weight can be, and I grunted aloud as I pulled and heaved her back; back and then out the opening toward the tall weeds and grasses; toward the sunlight.

My emotions had numbed and I was working purely on instinct, when a young boy of about twelve darted over from the next wagon and helped me to lower her to the ground. He peered up at me from under the floppy brim of an old stained leather hat that was much too big for him. His watery blue eyes were clearly appalled by all he had witnessed on this day; a day that had started out to be so exceptional in beauty.

The boy composed himself enough to speak to me and asked, "Where is Mrs. Boothe's little girl, Miss Jessamyn? She isn't with the rest of the kids hiding in the bushes."

My heart lurched and I felt dizzy for a moment. The wagon was filled with black smoke now, but I knew I had to go back inside, and as if being led, I leaped in, rushed forward and groped around under the seat up front. Words ran though my head in a sing-song chant, "Little children hide from fire. Little children hide from fire."

I heard the horses screech and the wagon jarred down with a metallic clatter to rock on its' wheel base. The horses bucked away to safety and I was glad someone had let them loose.

I continued to hold my breath and I closed my eyes too, against the acrid, stinging smoke and then I felt a soft arm, a small, limp body. I snatched the child up against my breast and escaped out the back again, lungs bursting, aching sharply for a cleansing breath of fresh air, mere seconds before the frame of the wagon could collapse around us. Sparks and cinders flew, stinging my back as I hit the ground and skittered over to the shelter of the next wagon. I felt relief as I checked the child over. She wasn't burned and she was still breathing, but in a raspy, choking gasp, and she was ghostly white.

Then I shuddered and jumped like I had the time I'd shoved one of Mah's bobby pins into the light socket in the living room. My eyes returned to their normal focus and I was back in the kitchen. I must have looked as strange as I felt because even Joe-Joe was staring at me as if I had a cat sitting on the top of my head.

I took a deep breath, relieved there was no smoke in the air beyond that of my parent's cigarettes, and asked, "Do you think we've all been here before? Do any of you remember the wagon train?"

My father turned away, twirling the dial on the radio in search of a change of mood, while my mother stood to clear the table, "You really must eat your beets, Sunny," she said, scraping plates over the garbage pail, "How do you expect to grow tall and strong enough to settle into a long life on earth if you don't eat your vegetables?"

"I hate beets," I said.

My father decided to ignore my bizarre behavior and I could see the unspoken message in my mother's eyes that this was something we'd be discussing later on. My father didn't have much patience with any evidence of psychic gifts. The psychics were all on Mah's side of the family and he wouldn't have had it any other way.

CHAPTER 3

I slumped down as low in the over-stuffed leather chair as I could manage. I raised my knees up and hugged them, finding comfort in the worn blue flannel. Dr. Carroll sat behind the desk and studied me; his clear blue eyes made bigger through tortoise-rimmed glasses. He certainly looked the part of a psychiatrist. His face wore a pleasant expression and his clothes were tasteful; all the hues of restful blue, in his dress and the décor of his office. Two students of whatever sat on straight-backed chairs near the door, with kind though slightly panicky expressions on their faces, clutching pencils held in readiness over twin notebooks.

I blew my nose hard into a tissue and tried to force my tears to stop. I was truly sick of crying, yet powerless to stop the annoying sobbing which overtook me at least once an hour. I accepted the paper cup of water one of the students rushed to offer me, and drained it quickly, asking for more. I was being checked regularly for dehydration.

I had just finished telling my 'story' to these people and the fact that I could condense the sad tale of my life into a few sentences, made me feel a bit less depressed and anxious, but only a bit. I mean, how bad could it really be if I could tell you about it in under five minutes?

"So, Sunny," Dr. Carroll said, clasping his hands before him on the blotter of his shiny desk. "What do you think you should do when you get out of here?"

"I have absolutely no idea. If I knew what it was I should be doing, I wouldn't have needed to come here."

One of the students giggled and Dr. Carroll gave her a blank look. I grinned at her, grateful for a sign of spontaneous life somewhere in the room. "I guess I need to know if I'm crazy before I make any plans. Can you tell me if I'm crazy, Dr. Carroll?"

He smiled at me for a moment. "The term crazy is hardly in our clinical vocabulary. Not many people qualify for what you mean when you say crazy, Sunny, but I can schedule a day of psychiatric testing for you. We'll know more then, and can outline the best course of treatment for your particular problem."

I nodded. "Good. That makes sense. I've always known I'm different, but I really don't feel crazy. Even though my husband has been calling me that for as long as I can remember."

"Do you think your husband would agree to come in for a few sessions? It would help me to treat you if I could get some idea of how you interact with each other. And I'd like to assess your husband's mental state as well."

"He might cooperate; if you ask him. He's pretty upset with me right now. But he'll probably come in if you ask him."

"I'll give him a call as soon as we're finished. So is there anything else you'd like to share with us, Sunny, before our time is up?"

"How much time do we have left?"

He checked his watch. "Twenty minutes."

"You're a psychiatrist, right, Doctor?"

"Yes. Why?"

"That means you do analysis; beginning with the childhood?"

He nodded vigorously. "To the extent that it will help in each particular case."

"So I should begin by telling you my story, starting at the beginning."

Dr. Carroll grinned again. "You seem to relish the idea."

I smiled back. "In a way I do. I'm a writer, Doctor, and I've done a lot of self-analysis. I had to do it for acting classes years ago, and I kind of got into the habit. I'd like a second opinion, though, if you're willing to listen to me. I'd like some insight into the 'character' I've become."

"Go ahead, Sunny, but I warn you, with your creative personality it would probably take about twenty-five years or so to do a complete analysis of you."

"Should I be offended, or flattered, or does that have more to do with repeat business and sending all of your kids through college?"

He laughed. "Just begin wherever you want to, and we'll make the most of the time we have during your stay here."

I took a deep breath and glanced away from the curious students to the painting on the wall over the doctor's head; a grassy meadow with sheep grazing on a blue-sky day. I took a moment to gather my thoughts then I just dove in.

"Dr. Carroll, have you ever heard of a person remembering their own birth?"

He raised his eyebrows and the students scribbled like crazy in their notebooks. "I read an article about that a few months ago, I think it said about two percent of the population claim to have such early memories."

"I'm used to being in the minority. But do you think it's possible to remember that far back?"

"What do you think?"

"The memory seems real. I remember there was a lot of pain. I've had two children myself and I know what it's like for the mother, but the baby has pain, too. At least I did."

"So they say."

"I could hear my mother screaming and begging for the ether, and all I wanted was for it to be over for the both of us. Then I was pushed down a tunnel and yanked out into a white world filled with a blinding light that hurt my eyes. It had been safe in the warm, dark place where my mother's heartbeat let me know I wasn't alone, but the cold delivery room was loud and frightening."

"Didn't they place you in your mother's arms?"

I shook my head. "It turned out my mother had grabbed the ether mask and taken huge breaths of it before they could get it away from her. She passed out just before I was born and the doctor had to pull me out at the last minute. He was yelling at her and the nurse snatched me away to squirt drops in my eyes which made me feel even worse."

"Finally they washed me and then dressed me in a stiff diaper and a white shirt. And every time they moved me from one place to another, I was terrified of falling. When Ben and Gillian were babies, I was always careful to hold them close to me when I carried them so they wouldn't be afraid. I wanted them to feel safe."

Dr. Carroll wrinkled his brow and leaned toward me. "So you actually remember all of this? You're certain no one described your birth to you?"

"Who could have told me? My mother was out cold for hours. And while all this was going on I was hoping to be given to my mother. I knew the hands that were working on me weren't hers. I know it's hard to believe, but even at five minutes old I knew the difference."

I checked the faces of the others in the room. They were totally absorbed in what I was saying. I recalled my sister-in-law once saying,

"Sunny could sell ice to the Eskimos." And I wondered what the doctor was really thinking; what judgments he might be making about me.

"This seems to be a particularly painful memory," Dr. Carroll interrupted, "You understand now, as an adult, why you weren't given to your mother right away, so why do you think it still bothers you after all these years?"

"I was completely vulnerable. I was still hurting from the birth. At the moment of birth a baby expects to meet the person behind the voice they've been hearing for months. They already love and trust that voice and as humans they long for a loving human touch. It's essential to life.

I know this from experience. When the mother isn't there, it's devastating."

"Have you discussed this with your mother?" I could hear real concern in the doctor's voice.

I shrugged. "Of course: but things happen. If you're a parent and a psychiatrist you know the kind of unconscious damage we all do to our children. I'm no better than my mother, or anybody else. We're all left to deal with the imperfections of life in the best way we can."

"Anyway, I hated the nursery which was a big part of the problem early on. Angry babies crying for love, and when one of the nurses did change me, or change my position from one side to the other, I felt as if I were being arranged like a doll in January; forgotten on a toy store shelf."

Dr. Carroll swiveled back and forth in his chair. He grinned at me as he tilted his head to one side. "You don't have any problem expressing yourself, Sunny, that's for sure. And that's a good thing. I think you were born to be in therapy; no pun intended."

I grinned back. "Thanks, I think."

"Tell me about your father. You haven't mentioned him yet."

"Well, things improved a lot when I went home. In those days men didn't often hold their children until it was time to go home. When my father first held me I felt instant love and I knew I was, indeed, in the right place."

"Were you always close to your father?"

"Yes. He died when I was twenty-three and I had trouble making sentences for a few months. My mother misses him too, although they were divorced at the time he died. She's never remarried and I don't think she ever will. She's a strong woman; very independent. She raised me by the first edition of Dr. Spock."

Dr. Carroll laughed. "That takes a strong woman."

I laughed too, surprised I still could. I threw my crumpled tissues in the wastebasket. "It does. You know, I recently saw him on a talk show and I was amazed to see the old guy is still alive, but I was glad to hear him apologize to all of the 'old babies' like me, who, because of him and his lousy book, had been fed only on a rigid schedule, and, worse still, were left to cry alone so we wouldn't grow up spoiled; just damaged, with low self-esteem, or maybe a little bit crazy."

I drew in a deep breath and settled back into the chair. "So, as I waited in my bassinet, learning the power of the printed word, I remember feeling bored most of the time. Trapped in a useless little body; I remember crying because I was hungry all the time, and wet way too often, and every day I longed to be cuddled and held for no good reason. It's a shame Dr. Spock didn't think to include love in the schedule."

"I spoiled my kids, Doctor, if loving them is spoiling them. And I'm proud of it."

I glanced up and checked on the two students. They each had tears in their eyes, but Dr. Carroll was tougher than that, and I knew I wouldn't be able to avoid dealing with my real issues by telling him my stories at each meeting. He did look interested, though, and so I continued.

"One day I remember feeling especially alone and I must have carried on for a long time because I remember hearing my father's voice from the other room. He wanted to come in and get me, but my mother stopped him. It wasn't time to pick me up, according to her schedule. She came into the room instead and hung her dress on the closet door where I could see it. It had a white background with a print of little blue flowers. The collar was round and trimmed with lace.

"This is a little tip I read about in a magazine, Joey," she said to Dad, "The baby will think she's not alone in the room."

"I stared at the limp housedress for the longest time. I couldn't believe my mother would think I could be so easily fooled. Obviously she didn't know me yet."

Dr. Carroll shifted in his seat and shook his head as if to clear it. "You're quite a story teller, Sunny. You've got me curious about that novel you've been writing."

"How do you know about my novel?" I asked, wondering if there were hidden cameras in the walls around us. I made a resolution to be careful of whatever I did write when I was in my room late at night.

"I have a list here of everything you brought with you when you came in; the mostly black wardrobe; wonderfully symbolic, and the novel, as well as some other books. I especially like *The Power of Positive Thinking* by Dr. Norman Vincent Peale.

We smiled at each other and I shrugged. "I try to keep my spirits up. I've always thought of myself as a positive thinker; at least when I'm not considering suicide." I stared down at my hands. My nails were split and broken and I wished for a nail file; and no, it didn't appear.

Dr. Carroll's deep, soothing voice brought me back to the moment. "We're going to help you, Sunny, and it will be easier if you try not to worry about appearing crazy to me or anyone else while you're here. Already I can tell you aren't the kind of crazy you fear."

I looked into his eyes. "Are you sure?"

He laughed. "We won't know for sure until we do the tests, but I'm reasonably certain you're primarily a creative person who has undergone an unusual amount of stress and who is quite understandably suffering from extreme anxiety and depression.

I nodded. "That sounds about right to me, too, Doctor."

He looked amused again, but resisted another smile. "So if you'd please try to relax with your various therapy programs I'm sure you'll benefit from your time here."

The two students beamed at me as if I'd gotten straight A's on my report card and I beamed back at them feeling exactly as if I had.

* * *

I stepped out into the hallway and as I walked back toward the community room, I smelled the strong odor of what they call flop sweat in the theatre. I checked as nonchalantly as one can when attempting to catch a whiff of one's own armpits, and then decided to detour into my room to wash and re-apply deodorant. They allowed me to have deodorant in a plastic container, so apparently I wasn't sufficiently crazed to attempt suicide by ingesting my Mennon's Speed Stick.

I stared at my blotchy face in the mirror and repaired my smeared mascara with a wet washcloth. I was only allowed to use my makeup once in the morning to the great annoyance of the nurse at the front desk who mumbled, "People who care so much about makeup can't be all that sick, if you ask me!"

I couldn't believe it had never occurred to her that 'needing' make-up as desperately as I did was pretty nutty in itself.

I had hidden a lipstick inside of my pillowcase, and so I retrieved it and used it both to brighten my lips and my pale cheeks. As soon as I thought I looked better, I felt better.

I stood up straight and strode down the hall toward the dreaded community room. I didn't mean to be unfriendly but there weren't many, if any, people here who made me feel comfortable, and it was exhausting to pour my heart out to a bunch of weird strangers who really didn't give a shit.

The generation gaps were huge here. I could hardly speak to Harry S., a senior citizen who drooled and leered at one and all, regardless of sex, and who usually answered any shared confidence with an invitation to make whoopie in the broom closet at midnight. There was Helen, the closest to my age, but she was so screwed up I felt bad burdening her with any of my problems. The same went for Jessie who was a little doll and much too young to have to worry about me and my adult problems.

I fixed a hopeful smile on my face out of force of habit and walked into the room and straight under the spell of Alexander Grandy.

Nearly seven feet tall and well built, he looked like a very handsome Native American, with true blue-black hair, and deep blue-green eyes like still pond water on a sunny day. Alexander noticed me immediately, too.

I wanted to go right over to him, but I felt shy and decided to sit in front of the T.V. and wait to see what would happen next. It took only a few minutes of suffering through an inane game show before Alexander stood to his full impressive height and ambled toward me like an arrow in search of its' target. His straight backed, stiff gait reminded me of Ichabod Crane in that Disney cartoon of The Legend of Sleepy Hollow, but Lord knows it's difficult to make a good first impression in a pair of blue flannel P.J.'s.

My first impression of Alexander Grandy was that this was a troubled man. But it didn't take a genius to figure that one out since we were all presently residents of the local loony bin.

My next impression was that this man was definitely a Leo; a sign very compatible with me.

He stopped in front of me and I had to bend my head way back in order to look up into his face. He was standing in front of the wall of huge windows and since it was such a bright day, the back-lighting darkened his face and outlined his entire form in an aura of golden light. It took my breath away.

"Hello," he said formally, in a voice both gentle and deep with just enough of a rough edge to make it interesting.

I tried to look casual and friendly, "Hi," I said, and then couldn't think of another single thing to say.

"May I sit here?" he asked.

"Oh, of course!" I scooted over to the far corner of the sofa.

He sat down slowly. He seemed to do everything slowly and deliberately and I wondered if he was on medication. "I couldn't help noticing you a moment ago," he continued, "You're new, aren't you? I haven't been out of my room in a few days so I'm only guessing."

His eyes were incredibly gorgeous. So far he hadn't smiled at me, but he still gave off pleasant vibrations. "Lucky guess," I said, smiling briefly. I really had no good reason to smile and I felt foolish putting on a cheerful face.

"You're a Leo, aren't you?" I blurted out without thinking.

He stared at me for a full minute. He was 'reading' me. Finally he spoke, leaning closer and dropping his voice to a near whisper. "You're psychic, aren't you?"

"Yes…actually; you, too?"

He nodded gravely staring down at his big hands. "Be careful. The psychiatric community doesn't acknowledge the existence of such gifts. They feel the need to categorize us and I'm afraid we all get filed under the big C. for crazy.

I didn't know how to take this bit of information. "But Dr. Carroll just went out of his way to assure me I'm not crazy. And I did tell him a little bit about myself. About how different I've always been."

Alexander frowned and shook his head from side to side. "Don't trust him. You'll be making a huge mistake if you do."

This wasn't at all what I wanted to hear. I had been looking forward to my treatment; to getting better. I sat in silence for a few moments trying to decide just who I should trust around here.

Alexander chose this moment to introduce himself : and then it was my turn to tell him my name and give him a quick sketch of 'my problem'. Once again I accomplished all of this in under five.

Alexander waited until I had finished and then he reached for my hand and gave it a quick squeeze. "It sounds like all you need is a divorce. And the belief you can be strong enough to survive on your own and to raise your children."

I nodded slowly, staring at the beautiful, long fingers of his hand as he held mine so reassuringly. His touch was warm and welcoming. His nails were clean and squarely trimmed and he wore no rings. I wondered if he was married too.

As if reading my mind, he smiled slightly. "I've never been married before and I have no children, but I can imagine how difficult it must be to decide to divorce when children are involved."

I nodded; then asked, "What kind of work do you do, Alexander?"

"I've been working as a chef in various resorts around here for the past five years, but before that I was studying for my P.H.D. in Psychology." His eyes grew brighter and more alive. "I was a counselor, Sunny, studying at Yale, when I had my break."

"Break?"

"Psychotic break: I was in intensive therapy, which is the procedure all psychiatrists and psychologists go through, an important part of our training. But sometimes it can result in a psychotic break...with reality."

He seemed rather unconcerned and matter of fact about this startling information and I wondered if it had been as serious as it sounded to me. "What did you say is wrong with you?" I asked hesitantly.

He smiled and paused as if to say something ironic. "They think I'm paranoid schizophrenic. But I'm not. No family history of it: I just made the mistake of telling them some of my psychic experiences. Don't you make the same mistake."

I sighed. "So how did you get here from Yale?"

Alexander frowned and rubbed his chin. "I didn't actually. I got here from Bellevue."

"Bellevue Hospital in New York City?"

He nodded. "And if you're ever going to go crazy again, Sunny, I wouldn't recommend doing it in New York."

I laughed. "Why?"

"Bellevue is as close to Bedlam as you can get in this century. It's a living hell. I was lucky my sister found me because I didn't even remember my name or know where I belonged for a good couple of weeks there."

I was amazed. "What happened to you?"

"I had a car accident," he said, and I immediately felt better about him figuring he must have suffered a serious head injury and not a true breakdown. "I was on my way to Central Park," he continued, "when my car was grazed by a tractor trailer and I got smashed against the wall of the Lincoln Tunnel."

"Wow," I breathed.

"The next thing I remember is standing in the men's room of The Plaza Hotel stark naked and trying to clean the blood off my face, and well, everywhere, really."

"Scalp wounds bleed a lot," I volunteered.

He nodded. And it was only a scratch," he explained, "but the worst part was missing the full moon meditation meeting. That's where I was headed. The Children of Earth hold one each month and I never like to miss it."

"Tell me about it. What do they do? What do they meditate about?"

"It's a form of white magic. We collectively join hands and send up our prayers for world peace, and a clean and healthy planet."

"Sounds fascinating; I'd love to go sometime."

He took a moment to think this over. "Do you have a car?"

I nodded.

"O.K., if we're both out of here and neither one of us gets committed to the state mental hospital; we'll definitely make the next meeting."

"That's a deal, as long as I can drive."

I grinned at him and finally he gave me a full and honest smile. His smile was worthy of a movie star. His eyes grew soft and he looked much younger and slightly vulnerable.

"How old are you, Sunny?"

"I'm thirty-three. How old are you?"

"Forty-three this August: you were right, I'm a Leo."

"And a young looking one at that!" He looked maybe thirty-seven tops...

It was at this point the entire floor staff trooped over to stand in front of us and to stare, a few with mouths hanging open.

Alexander gave each one of them a long look and then he smiled as if once he'd decided to try it, he found he rather liked it and wanted to keep on practicing at every opportunity.

"You're feeling better, Alexander. We're glad you decided to come out of your room and join the group." A young man with thick glasses said. I checked his nameplate and made a mental note: Dave.

Alexander nodded at Dave and said, "I have someone interesting to talk to now."

CHAPTER 4

I loved art therapy. Each morning directly after breakfast a strange little woman who resembled a humorless Dr. Ruth with mean little eyes hidden behind huge pink plastic-framed glasses and too much makeup caked into the wrinkles on her face, directed us to express our supposedly true feelings in art created on cheap paper plates.

With a bad attitude and thinning over-processed hair, she presided over the long table of patients. Her name was Mrs. Hollander and she was obsessive/compulsive about keeping a pristine art table. After we'd finished our mandatory two pictures in chalk or oil crayons, we were each expected to wash our work area with paper towels and soap and water. Mrs. Hollander would actually lean down, her aged bones creaking, to examine the table at first hand, growing strangely crazed with misplaced anger if we dared to leave any streaks, water marks, or God forbid, any actual vestige of our colorful morning's work.

I found her odd behavior reassuring. I was still capable of recognizing a crazy person when I saw one and this lady was definitely sitting on the wrong side of the table. I vowed not to give her any ammunition when she got around to analyzing my mental state as reflected in my art work.

I never ever reached for the black crayon, knowing this would be interpreted in a negative way. In fact, I drew lush, colorful pictures of flowers, rainbows, and butterflies, and she took it very badly.

"A woman who isn't sure if she wants to live can hardly be in the mood for spring flowers and all that jazz," she'd say accusingly, as if disappointed in my cheerful outlook, and fix me with an x-ray eye.

I decided to try the truth and explain myself. "Actually, Mrs. Hollander," I said, "I prefer drawing happier pictures because they help to lift my spirits."

I guess she'd never heard of 'fake it 'til you make it' because this earned me an angry scowl; but I wasn't worried. Surely Dr. Carroll wouldn't give her opinion much weight in any decisions that had to be made in regard to my mental state.

So despite the disruptive presence of Mrs. Hollander, I enjoyed working with the colors; creating something pretty, and innocent.

One morning I decided to give Mrs. Hollander exactly what she wanted since I was in an especially foul mood and I felt like reflecting these feelings honestly in my art; just once.

I selected the deepest blue crayon, which was as close to black as I dared go, and I colored in the night sky all around a huge crescent moon. In the distance floated three stars growing dimmer in the distance. Mrs. Hollander loved it, relishing the sense of loss and isolation it immediately brought to mind. God, she was a sick woman.

She was downright contemptuous of little Jessie. I suspected this was because she was so young and pretty, and Mrs. Hollander was not, and perhaps had never been either one of those things.

"Do you call that art?" she snapped when Jessie presented her with a child-like, though charming drawing of a family of three having a picnic in the woods. "Don't you dare try to play games with me, Little Girl. What do you know about a happy family life? This picture has nothing to do with the reality of your life."

Jessie burst into tears and I reached out to comfort her.

"I just tried to draw what I wished would happen," Jessie sobbed against my shoulder.

"Give the kid a break, Mrs. Hollander. We're not all Picasso's, you know," Bob said, flinging his paper plate in her direction with a show of disgust.

"Don't I know that!" she snarled, gathering up our supplies.

"What about you, Mrs. Hollander? We haven't seen you draw anything yet," I blurted before I could stop myself. "I'd like to analyze one of your drawings. I bet you'd draw the devil himself." I had no trouble lashing out to defend Jessie, but I would never have said it to defend myself.

Helen let out a loud peal of laughter bordering on hysteria. "I bet they'd lock her up and lose the key if Dr. Carroll ever got her into therapy.

For a moment I thought Mrs. Hollander might slap Helen or throw the oil crayons at us all, but instead she threw them down on the table and stormed out of the room.

"Who hired that crazy bitch?" Bob asked. "She must have something really freaky on Dr. Carroll…naked drunk pictures, or maybe worse."

*   *   *

Group therapy was my second favorite activity of the day. Dr. Vincent was a young Italian hunk with big, kind brown eyes. He was great at getting even the most shy patient to speak out, but whenever there was a lull during the hour he'd give me a grin and ask me a question and off I'd go. I had absolutely no problem sharing my stories in group.

Even Alexander became more talkative and soon we were sitting together dispensing advice and sympathy as if we drew a weekly paycheck from the place.

The more I listened to the stories of the others, the more I remembered from my own life. I shared much of these memories with the group and soon it was obvious I was entertaining the others. That was fine with me and I always tried to tell each story with enough flair to hold the attention of my audience. In a way I was searching for answers in my past as to why I had gotten myself into the mess I was in now.

"I'm bored," Helen complained, yawning loudly, when no one felt much like talking. "Tell us one of your earliest memories, Sunny. That shit really cracks me up. I don't know what I'm gonna do for fun around here when they send you home."

I grinned at her. I had grown to like Helen and I enjoyed making her smile. "Well, let's see. You all know I remember being a baby. We'll it was shortly after birth that I began to develop a sense that sooner or later in this lifetime I was going to have to pay some pretty heavy dues. Gram had told Joe-Joe and me about karma, and I was pretty sure I had some paying back to do.

One by one the circle of heads bobbed their understanding back to me. So I was a serious child right from the start. My given name is Donna DeAngelo, but my father called me Sunny, hoping I would live up to the name."

Alexander laughed loudly and squeezed my hand.

"Even as a baby I had the ability to understand what was being said around me. It was awful not to be able to form understandable sentences to express ideas I had no trouble coming up with, and crying angrily became my main form of communication for many months."

"Once I remember sitting in my high chair while my mother carried on a conversation with our best friend, Ba. I had named her Ba, yelling it out the moment I first watched her enter our apartment. It was as if

I'd been waiting for her to show up. I took one look at her and a vision sprang into my mind of shifting sands, palms waving in a hot breeze and huge pyramids calling to us in the distance."

"Cool," said Jessie.

"The name sounded strangely right to Ba, too, because she stared into my eyes and said, "So you've named me Ba. I think that's what you should call me from now on.""

"And that's exactly what we all did. She may be Eleanor to the rest of the world, but to our family she has always been Ba. She has twinkly indigo eyes, a deep throaty laugh and a witty sense of humor. So on this particular day, as I sat in my high chair, and Mah and Ba discussed their various relatives and local gossip, I sat quietly and pretended to play with a rubber frog while eavesdropping happily. Then I noticed my mother approach the cupboard where my baby food was kept."

"I grinned at her and spoke in my infant babble, hoping to encourage her to feed me since I was getting hungry. But things didn't turn out the way I'd hoped. I saw her reach in and pull out the glass jar of Gerber's with the light yellow gunk in it. I hated that crap. I didn't have a name for it yet, but I began to yell anyway. "No, Mah, please! Help me Ba!""

"Of course all that actually came out of my mouth were garbled baby sounds. Mah and Ba laughed at the cute noises I was making and I got mad. "No!" I shrieked, "I'm not being cute, I'm serious. I'm starving and I want something good for lunch!""

"By this time I was nearly hysterical with frustration and I heard my mother remark, "Sunny must be really hungry today. She can't wait for me to get her squash heated up. Maybe I'll just give it to her cold.""

"SQUASH!" So it was called squash. I decided to stop crying and try a different approach. When she spooned the dreaded squash into my mouth, I spit back at her until she decided I must be sick and we had to make an unnecessary trip to see Dr. Valerio. But I never forgot my enemy was named squash and as soon as I could talk, which was pretty soon, one of my first sentences was, "I hate squash!"

Total silence; I looked around the room and the group stared back at me with stricken eyes. Alexander took my hand in his and I was grateful for his firm grip. I had hoped to make everyone laugh but I should have known better. These people were too sensitive to laugh at my remembered frustrations. They identified with the baby I had been and that child had their complete sympathy and support. For the first time in a long time, I had a feeling of homecoming.

*   *   *

I got a better reaction with the story of how my parents met. They were both in show business and it was before W.W.II. My mother was a model from Chicago and my father was a jazz drummer from Hoboken when they met in a show in Atlantic City, New Jersey.

My mother was dressed as Miss Rhine Wine in a flowing, white Grecian-style chiffon gown with a huge headdress of white grapes arranged upon her head of bleached blonde curls. My father had joined the company of the show late, and it was as she was doing her dance solo in this get-up that he first set eyes on her and nearly dropped his drumsticks. He went into an impromptu drum solo and my mother turned her regal head to see who was messing up her solo when their eyes locked in a symphony of love at first sight and my little star in Heaven glowed brighter.

My mother really looked great in that dress. She resembled Greta Garbo and had even won a look-alike contest. I always loved the gown too, in fact it proved to be lucky for me as well, when years later, in a cut-down version, I won a grammar school Halloween contest as a Grecian Goddess.

My mother thought my father was the cutest thing she'd ever seen, even though he was four inches shorter than she was when she wore her high heels. He looked a lot like Perry Como, but he had a volatile, dynamic personality all his own.

When the show in Atlantic City closed they took off together, traveling the country in shows, even performing on a Mississippi River boat. They had a fine, free-wheeling wild party of a life, doing exactly as they pleased; raising hell and breaking all the popular rules of the day, as unmarried people in the late nineteen-thirties didn't live together. Then two things happened; World War II., and soon after that, me. The war gave my father a great adventure as a Second Lieutenant in the Air Force. How he loved flying over that war. He dragged us to every new war movie for the next ten years.

They married in February of 1940, and then my father enlisted in the Air Force and took off for Europe. My mother waited patiently at home for her lively little Italian to return, working at office jobs now. She was ready to retire from show business and start a family.

When the war ended, my father brought my mother home with him to meet his parents who lived at the family home in Newark, New Jersey in the Italian section across the street from Branchbrook Park.

At their first meeting, Dad's little native Neopolitan Italian parents criticized my ignorant, Presbyterian wasp mother for not insisting on helping with the dinner dishes. She'd offered her help once, been turned down, and didn't have a clue she was supposed to fight her way back into the kitchen, ignoring all of their shrieks of protest, thus gaining their respect in the process.

Their next order of business after the introductory battle, was to sit my father down for a serious talk about his future.

I can imagine how it went... "You're almost thirty years old, Joey," Pop began.

My father clammed up at this point.

"You've had your fun." Nana chimed in, "Playing music all over the country is a life for a kid...child's play. Now it's time to grow up."

"Yeah, Joey, grow up!" Pop echoed.

I can imagine my father staring down at the immaculate beige carpeting still bearing the runner marks of the daily vacuum cleaning it endured.

"The world is a different place, now, Joey," Nana said using her hands to make her point and gazing entreatingly up toward God as if he could influence dad any more than she could.

"Yeah, Joey, listen to your mother. The world is a different place now. The war sobered it up," Pop muttered under his garlic breath.

My mother sat with her arms crossed, her long, show girl legs crossed too, her foot tapping an impatient tempo against the highly polished mahogany leg of the coffee table. I know for certain her mouth was drawn into a tight-lipped grimace.

"You've got to face reality, Joey," Nana said, down on her knees in front of his chair. "It's time to stop having fun now. It's time to come home to Newark and live like the rest of the family."

I wish my father had laughed, but he remembered Pop's razor strap still hung on the back of the bathroom door.

"Why don't you take up photography, Joey?" Pop suggested next. "You always liked to take pictures. You could use your G.I. Bill to pay for the school. Maybe take some college business courses too for when you open your own studio."

Finally Dad spoke. "I could do that, Pop," he said, "But listen, I've got an offer to go to Hollywood and play in the N.B.C. orchestra. I think I'd like that better."

"An offer, you say," Nana questioned, zeroing in on him. "And how did you get this offer since you just got home today? Is this a firm offer? What is the name of this person who made you this wonderful offer and how much would he be paying you?"

It turned out the offer was passed on to Dad by one of his buddies, a sax player from Cincinnati. He'd been the one to tell Dad most of the guys he'd played with before the war were already there and would vouch for Dad if he wanted to move there."

"You know, Ma, I can always work for the airlines. I've been offered a firm commitment for a job as a pilot on a run from New York to Paris. The only catch is I spend two weeks in Paris, then two weeks here."

This bit of information galvanized my mother into action. "Oh, no, Joey DeAngelo; I absolutely refuse to allow you to consider a job that will take you away from home for that length of time. Knowing you, it won't be any time at all before you have a family on both sides of the Atlantic."

Now everyone stared at my mother and she blushed.

Nana spoke first. People who don't do dishes shouldn't have a lot to say in private family conversations after dinner. But Jeannine, I do have to say I happen to agree with you."

Then Nana adjusted her hairnet. Her iron-black permanent waved hair was trapped and held immobile by a nasty looking spider-web-like hairnet. She always looked to me as if she were on her way to a job as a kitchen commando in Mussolini's old army.

My mother ignored the first part of her statement and was grateful for the unexpected support, so she returned the favor. "I think Pop had a good idea when he mentioned photography. You really are gifted at it, Joey."

Pop beamed at my mother. But then he always beamed at my mother, because like most Italian men, he had an inherited appreciation for tall, good-looking, green-eyed blondes.

And I think that's why my father chose photography as his new career. He was in love with my mother and ready to settle down and start a family.

He turned out to be an excellent photographer. He was an artist who took pride in his work and was successful at it, but we all paid the price for whatever it was inside of him that withered and died when he gave up his music.

I saw him play the drums a few times. Whenever we were out at a club, or a wedding and he happened to see one of his musician friends from the past, playing in the band, they always insisted on calling him up on the stage for a solo.

I was stunned by how wonderful he was behind the drums. He came alive with a vitality so electric he was transformed into a human sparkler, a roman candle, a man riding the swell of a wave of happiness so great and complete it was beyond the scope of my experience.

I understood my father best when I watched him play the drums and I forgave him for all the temperament and the occasional cruelty of his frightening temper; for all the times he beat us in a rage we couldn't imagine causing in our childish innocence. Each one of us paid a price for the privilege of being a member of his family.

He was a dynamic, charismatic performer, larger than life, and not to be expected to conform to the mundane, sane, behavior of the other parents who acted like Ozzie and Harriet clones. Joey DeAngelo owned any room in which he played and all of our hearts beat along with the rhythm of his flying sticks, his driving beat, his expertise and total involvement in the music.

I always suspected he'd given up show business for me. He really loved me and when I was born he wanted to be certain I would have a stable, conservative up-bringing. Instinctively, I tried to make it up to him. So during the years when I was a baby, a toddler, and then a little girl, I would sing and dance, and act out scenes from the old movies I saw on T.V., to fill the void left in my father's heart when he cut the music out of his soul, sacrificing himself and his personal happiness, and in a way, the happiness of the entire family, in the name of love and responsibility.

The saddest part of all is that he never allowed himself to own a set of drums after he chose photography as his new career. I wonder sometimes if the temptation would have been too great for him to bear if he'd had the drums there in the house, calling to him, reminding him of who he really was and what he was born to do...and be.

CHAPTER 5

Alexander and I just naturally began to spend all of our time together. It was great having someone to talk to, and since we both loved to walk, several times a day, we took the long walk. Around the nurse's station we would go, past the laundry room, and the patient's rooms and then we'd take a quick right down the hallway with the large wall of windows that showcased a perfect view of the mountains in the distance, facing westward. This is where we watched the sun set each evening. Our last right turn brought us around again past the patient rooms reserved for those most dangerous among us who had to be under constant observation.

We laughed together as we walked, ignoring the curious stares of the staff who wondered, as our conversation grew more intimate, just what was going on between us.

Neither Alexander nor I had many visitors since only family members were allowed and both of our families lived in New Jersey. Bull wouldn't allow the kids to come and visit me, yet, but I did speak to them on the phone each day, and hearing their voices was the high point of my day. They hadn't asked me what had actually happened on the day I came here, and I was saving that discussion for our first meeting, hopefully with Dr. Carroll present.

It was natural that Alexander and I would fall into the pleasant habit of spending each evening together. I was amazed to discover Alexander and I had grown up in neighboring towns, yet had never met, despite all we had in common. Alexander said it was because of the ten year difference in our ages.

I liked talking to him. He listened as well as any woman friend I'd ever had. We discussed our common beliefs and our heartbreaks. Our psychic and spiritual selves: our love of books and the theatre. For the first time in my life I had a willing and enthusiastic male audience.

"I want to know you, Sunny, really know you," Alexander insisted.

"You know me, Alexander," I said, staring at the carpet.

"Look at me, Sunny."

I considered bolting for my room, but instead I looked up into his very blue eyes. "O.K., Alexander. I'll read my novel to you, but are you really sure you want to hear it?"

He nodded firmly.

REACH FOR THE SUN

CHAPTER 1
1797

Art and life are blended as one for me, irrevocably. I can't imagine trying to live without my art lessons and my time spent creating art. This is why I expect I'll die very soon now that Papa has taken my life away from me.

And the dust! With every breath I take, the dust chokes my nose and rubs my throat raw! I hate this dust monster that swells and grows with each clattering turn of the wagon wheels. It streaks my face and arms with dirt and blackens my calico dress.

I am stuck traveling through a hell called Pennsylvania, trapped by my recently widowed father into leaving my true life behind and seeking the folly of a 'new start' I have no need for, in a god-forsaken wilderness called Beaver Valley, Ohio: a small settlement just west of Marietta.

I take refuge in my sketching pads and charcoal, yet I do long for color. I find it hard to express myself fully in scratches of black upon a gray sheet of paper. I am a painter.

At least I am until the day in the not too distant future when I will be joining Mama in Heaven, for surely I won't survive the pain of my broken heart. To have suffered so by the age of fifteen seems hardly fair, but Papa takes pleasure in reminding me daily no one ever promised us life would be fair and it is not at all fair that Mama died last year of the consumption when she was still so young and beautiful.

This, of course, is why he felt compelled to run away from Boston, and I counter by reminding him how Mama loved Boston and how she always encouraged me in my art studies. In fact Mama believed I had an unusual talent for painting and she expected me to become quite famous one day. She would take both of my hands in her small cold ones and say, "Jessamyn, Ma Cherie, you must continue to paint! You will be known all over the world as a great painter, despite being born a female. It is your destiny."

Papa only laughs at me and although I am grateful to finally see his mood lighten as we continue on this foolish adventure, I am not at all glad it is at my expense. Papa just never has appreciated art in any form and he finds my lessons and my time spent painting to be a terrible waste of time. In fact he considers me to be practically an old maid at the age of sixteen and he laments I shall never catch a husband if I don't abandon my foolishness before I begin to lose the girlish looks with which to bait the trap.

I say, "Too bad, Papa. I shall paint happily on into my old age. And when I've grown too decrepit to venture from my home, I'll give art lessons to other people's children. And I'll die a happy woman!"

"You'll die a stubborn woman, that's for sure." Papa says, as he stomps out of the wagon muttering words I'm not supposed to hear.

I cry all the time now without any warning. I cry for Mama who would never have let this happen to me, and I cry for myself. It is a terrible fate to be a victim of my papa's mourning. It is so unfair that my wishes mean nothing to him and that he controls the course my life shall take.

The wagon bounces down over another stone and I feel the shock in my spine. I have been shaken so relentlessly and so viciously since our departure from home a few weeks ago, I fear I'll never hold a brush steadily in my hand again.

And day after day, Papa sits upon the wagon seat, riding it as if it were an angry bronco, whistling happily as he steers the horses up and down, but seldom around, the many furrows in the abominably deteriorated National Road along which we travel as members of a wagon train made up of our friends and neighbors from Boston.

I swear most of the people I've known all of my life, have suddenly and collectively lost the sense they were born with! Why would anyone think it a jolly adventure to drop meaningful lives and set off for the unknown horrors awaiting us in the west? How can they ignore the stories we've all heard concerning the wagon trains unlucky enough to be raided by the bands of renegade Indians who still attack unsuspecting travelers who have nothing to do with the treaty violations made by those already living in settlements in places they shouldn't be in the first place.

I clutch at my long, dark chestnut hair and shudder, imagining the hot cruel slice of a tomahawk across my skull.

Oh, Mama, how I miss you! I scramble on all fours over to the part of the wagon where a few of my oil paintings are packed away in brown paper. I have to see Mama's face. I have to lose myself in the memory of our life in Boston; of a happier time and place.

I tear away the paper and Mama smiles at me through the paint and I will myself not to cry, but instead to find my comfort in the memory of the day I finished this painting.

I had begun this portrait in early spring, hoping to have completed it by Papa's birthday on the fourteenth of August. Mr. Whitfield, the art teacher, was due to come directly after lunch for my lesson, but I needed to make one last trip to The Old Feather Store for paint; cobalt blue, cadmium yellow, white and vermillion. I also needed a new wide sable brush for the bold strokes of the background, so I threw on a bonnet, snatched up my purse, and told the housekeeper, Mrs. James, to inform Mama of my whereabouts should she awaken from her nap before my return.

I had closed the heavy oaken door behind me before I realized I hadn't bothered to pin my hair up. I was sixteen and knew full well that when a girl reached the age of fourteen she was expected to dress more maturely and to wear her hair piled up on top of her head when venturing out into public.

I went ahead anyway. Mama would never scold me about it since she had been known to commit the same faux pas on numerous occasions. Mama had been born in France and she often laughed at the silly conventions of Boston society.

The peonies lining our front walk were wilting in the sun and I made a mental note to water them upon my return as I opened the front gate and stepped out onto the brick road.

Not many horses and carriages were about at this time of day and so I walked on quickly to the corner and turned left onto Spruce, past the quaint town homes with their neat picket fences embracing fragrant gardens, remembering how often Mama and I had walked this same road together on our way to the store before the consumption took so much of her strength.

Often, in those days, we would head toward town in search of material for matching dresses. Mama would always let me choose first and I always favored the brighter colors which complimented our dark coloring.

Whenever Mama laughed in public, everyone would look up and smile. "Jessamyn, mon petit chou! We do think alike, n'est pas?" She would say as I hugged her. Mama always smelled of roses on a hot night.

Since Mama's lungs had gotten worse, we hadn't walked to town in months. So I decided to run the rest of the way, for Mama, who always loved the feel of the wind fingering through her long, ebony curls, as, in years past, we both defied convention, and ran together, full out like young boys, our hair falling below our waists, tickling our hips through thin muslin summer frocks.

As I turned the next corner down Elm, my own hair whipped around into my face, and I laughed knowing I'd never make it past old Mrs. Marner's house without hearing some unpleasant remark.

Predictably, I could see her up ahead, an old prune of a woman in dull gray, rocking on her porch, afraid to miss anything that would be of interest to the Wednesday Afternoon Ladies' Quilting Group.

Her sad daughter, Beatrice, came out the front door and handed her a tall glass of summer tea, decorated gaily with a sprig of mint leaf.

I didn't bother to slow down for a full dosage of venom and instead called out politely. "Good Afternoon, Ladies!"

Beatrice and I caught each other's eye and shared a brief smile before the hawk-nosed hag began voicing her reprimand in a high pitched squeal that darted quickly through the spring air: "This, My Dear," she said to Beatrice, wagging a finger at me and fairly shouting, "is the kind of behavior that comes from having a French mother, an aristocrat, they say, but I doubt it, and a spawn of the devil drunken Irishman for a father!"

I stopped dead in my tracks and faced her fully from the sidewalk. Before I opened my mouth to speak, her mouth dropped open and I saw a bit of panic in her squinty, mean eyes, as a good bully never expects to be confronted head on. "And may God bless you as well, Mrs. Marner," I shot back. "The devil's spawn and I will see you in church this Sunday. Unfortunately, my sainted mother isn't well enough to attend services. But I will tell her you have sent her your best wishes, as pitifully inadequate as they might be!"

Then I sped off past a horse and buggy clomping leisurely along, and off around to Main Street and blessed peace and quiet. I wouldn't bother to repeat this bit of garbage to either one of my parents. Mama was too weakened, and there was no telling what Papa, with his temper, would do about it. Anyway, I'd always known my parents were an unlikely, though very happy couple, and the target of much speculation locally. Still, I cared little for the opinions of sad, dark souls like Mrs. Marner.

From the first day my parents met on the steps of The Old State House, there had been opposition to their union.

Mama was the beautiful only daughter of Henri Bouchard, the wealthy French importer, and Papa was the handsome, wild-at-heart, only son of Zeke and Mary Miles. Mama stood to inherit a fortune, but Papa's only inheritance was an over-abundance of charm and a talent for blacksmithing. Born of a lively Irish mother and an English father from the London streets, George was an unusual mix of carefree soul and hard worker who made friends on a daily basis and managed to build his business into a quick and growing success.

Although Papa never did get rich enough to please Mama's father, my mother claimed she knew she would marry him the moment their eyes met. And Papa swore he nearly fell backward down the steps of The State House, so overwhelmed was he by her extreme beauty.

"I swear Marie looked just like a china doll in ruffles and lace the color of summer sky," he said, "But my heart was lost to her for good when she ordered me to get out of her way. It's a good thing I didn't listen to her, but teased her back instead until she let me see that sparkle of mischief she has in those dark as night eyes of hers, or maybe you'd never been born."

I believed my parents when they spoke of their love. And although I didn't want to be within a hundred miles of them when they were in the middle of a disagreement, I knew my luck in having been born to two people who were crazy in love forever.

I had never met Grandfather Bouchard since he went home to France and died just before I was born, yet I felt as unconcerned as

Mama did when she explained he had left his entire fortune to char-ity, so distressed was he by my parent's marriage. Mama was right to choose love over money. It was the only choice a woman with a heart could make.

As I streaked past The Old Brick Meeting House I thought again of my childhood wish to one day be married there and almost laughed. I'd rather be an artist than a wife and intended to avoid marriage indefi-nitely. Although I'd been raised in my father's Presbyterian religion, I still loved the fairy-tale-like belfry of this magical place.

I let the wind carry me ahead and soon The Old Feather Store appeared in the distance and I was glad since I was now nearly out of breath. One hundred years in the same location. I'd often heard it said that you knew you really didn't need it if you couldn't find it at The Old Feather Store and I'd found that to be true.

I composed myself before entering and I considered tucking my hair up under my bonnet, but I was feeling defiant today and so I allowed it to go on curling naturally down over my shoulders.

I hurried up and down the many aisles, disciplining myself not to pause too often to examine the interesting and colorful items lining each shelf, and soon I had my paints and brush and was heading toward the front of the store to settle my account.

"Little Mite!" What are you doing here?" Papa's voice boomed out to me from the aisle I'd just rushed past and I stopped dead in my tracks. "Come and see who I've found."

"I'm buying paints, Papa," I called, turning back to greet him. Papa scowled at the paints but still I entered his powerful arms for a quick hug. Then I noticed a man standing next to him. He looked vaguely familiar, a tall man, with shoulders as broad as Papa's straining against the cloth of his suit coat, and he was extremely good looking in a rug-ged way with dark hair and eyes and a neatly trimmed black beard. My heart was suddenly beating a bit faster than normal and I hoped I wouldn't blush. I wasn't at all used to meeting handsome young men. Since Mama had grown so ill, I hadn't done much socializing. I pre-ferred working at my painting.

"Can you guess who this young fella is, Jessamyn?" Papa asked as if this 'young fella' were someone very special indeed. "I haven't set eyes on him in years."

I stared up into eyes like those of a young buck waiting in the forest; noble, gentle and strong all at the same time. First, I saw surprise register in his gaze, and then I saw something deeper and more mysterious. A look I couldn't name, but wanted to learn more about. I felt a stirring deep inside me in a place I couldn't name, and suddenly I felt my cheeks threaten to flame crimson, and I was grateful when he smiled first, easing some of the tension. "I'm Bruin," Jessamyn, Bruin Mahoney. I see we've both changed a great deal, and might I say for the better in your case, since we last played together in your mother's garden."

"Bruin! My friend, Bruin! How you've grown!" I said as we both laughed. I hadn't seen him in at least ten years. Not since his mother's death ended the friendship our mother's had shared.

"May I say you have grown nicely yourself," he said kindly, "It's amazing the changes a decade can bring." I thought I saw a flash of admiration in Bruin's eyes and I blushed at myself for wondering.

"Papa," I said quickly, "I must hurry home now. Mama will be up soon and Mr. Whitfield will be along at one to give me my art lesson. Bruin, it was good to see you again."

Papa rolled his eyes and sighed, but I chose to ignore his disapproval.

Bruin nodded, "Yes, and please give your mother my best, Jessamyn," Bruin said in a soft voice. "I hope to hear she's feeling better soon."

"You may deliver that message in person, Young Fella." Papa said impulsively, "Come for dinner tonight; be there at seven sharp as I like to eat my dinner when it's hot."

Bruin eagerly accepted the invitation, stealing glances at me the entire time, and I felt my cheeks begin to heat up again as I fought the feelings that were beginning to give me sharp, sudden sensations in my abdomen. I would not act like a foolish child! I knew Bruin Mahoney would always think of me as a child, and I also knew full well a man as handsome as this would surely be used to the complete attention of all females within range of his considerable charm. And with my art studies I really had no time at all for any thought of romance, especially an unrequited one, as I knew Bruin could command the attention of any girl he wanted in this entire city. I was no match for him.

Yet I remembered how sweet he had been to me when I was nearly five and he was at least twelve and the possessor of infinite patience with my constant chatter and childish games. I had always admired him and the thought of renewing our friendship was intriguing.

For the rest of the afternoon I found it hard to think of anything else. I hadn't realized how starved I was for the company of people closer to my own age, but now I had Bruin's visit to look forward to, and I felt excited for the first time since Mama had taken ill.

The last time I had been this interested in anything was upon the occasion of my first visit to The Boston Art Gallery and Museum. How I loved the hallowed air, the reverent quiet I found there. No church would ever compare with the art museum as a temple for the celebration of life; at least not for me. I need only to wander the halls to know there is so much more I must learn about artistic expression.

My happiest times, especially during Mama's illness, have been when I've had unlimited time to assemble my oils, breathing deeply of their seductive scent, to take my brush in hand, and stroke the myriad colors boldly, joyously, across the canvas that for a time feels like my true home.

*   *   *

I was proud of my portrait of Mama. We sat under an elm tree in the garden; I, at my easel, she reclining upon a chaise longue that the housekeeper and I had dragged out through the French doors that opened from her room onto the patio. The light filtered through the lush green leaves of the tree branches spreading far above us, and the birds sang cheerfully, celebrating the beauty of this glorious spring day, just as I did, immortalizing it with my paints on canvas.

Mama was lovely in a brilliant frock of pink silk with lush roses embroidered across the bodice and along each sleeve. Her shining curls were arranged in an upswept style with many tendrils spiraling down about her shoulders.

I had to ask her to keep still nearly once a minute as she bobbed her head about afraid she might miss some small pleasure on this incredible afternoon. "Look, Ma Petite," she cried out, pointing behind me, and completely dropping the pose. "Butterflies!"

I sighed and was asking her to at least try to be still for one full minute when Mr. Whitfield interrupted me.

"Let your mother relax for a while. You are fussing too much as it is."

He and Mama exchanged smiles and then he was all business once again as he peered at the painting through wire-rimmed spectacles that cut straight through the heart and soul of any painting to lay bare the mechanics, or lack thereof. His wispy, gray hair moved in the breeze, revealing a spot of baldness, and I held my breath, waiting for his verdict.

"If you fuss with your mother's eyes any longer you will risk completely missing the look you desire to capture. You must learn to stop making changes; to trust your talent. Move on to the background, now, My Dear; quite good."

"Good?" Mama asked, looking as if she had just smelled sour milk. "My Jessamyn is brilliant, Monsieur Whitfield. Surely a man with your education and sensibilities can recognize this."

Mr. Whitfield looked away and sniffed as if he didn't at all enjoy being corrected, especially by a woman, although I suspected Mama was beautiful enough to get away with it. "She is learning and developing, Marie," he murmured, shrugging.

Mama ignored him and focused on me. "Listen to me, Cherie, someday success will find you. I am sure of it. One day you will remember my words and know it was me who was right."

And then a fit of deep, racking coughing overtook Mama and she turned away to muffle the violent spasms in a dainty lace handkerchief. Her face grew red and damp with perspiration as she leaned back into the cushions and closed her eyes, one white hand lay upon her breast. It trembled slightly.

Frightened, I threw my brush down on the pallet and ran to her side, taking her hand in mine. It was cold and moist. "Rest now, and don't talk for a while. I will always remember the things you tell me, Mama, I promise."

Mr. Whitfield looked uncomfortable as he said his goodbyes and slipped away, my lesson forgotten. I stood before my painting, admiring Mama, amazed I had been able to capture not only her outward beauty, but the essence of her incredible spirit as well.

No matter what Mr. Whitfield or Papa, or any other man offended by my impertinence in seeking a career in the field of art, might say, I had done my best; for myself and for Mama. I had captured her luminous face. It was now frozen in time to shine forth against an eternal background of blue sky and deep pink roses climbing the wrought iron fence behind her. She would indeed live forever here upon this canvas. Surely Papa would come to value this painting. Surely he would finally be pleased and proud that I was born an artist.

*   *   *

While Mama napped Mrs. James and I worked for the rest of the afternoon to prepare a feast fit for our dinner guest. She kept sending me back to the garden to gather vegetables since she wanted them to be as fresh as possible. Endive, tomatoes, asparagus, red onions, peppers in shades of red, green, and orange were snatched from my hands as she thrust a basket at me and told me it was time to pick the strawberries for dessert.

At four-thirty Mama came into the kitchen looking fresh and well rested from her nap. She insisted on preparing her famous vinaigrette dressing. Then she added the wine to the delicate sauce to grace the roast and lastly, she chose the wines for each course.

"And now, Jessamyn," she said, "We must select the frock you will wear to impress our handsome guest."

I blushed. "How do you know he is handsome, Mama?"

"He was handsome even as a boy. He did not grow up to be ugly, eh? He is perhaps even better looking now, n'est pas, since you blush at the very mention of him?"

After trying on several ensembles we decided I should wear my white eyelet lace and linen with the yellow sash and slippers. Since we were dining at home, I didn't have to worry about pinning my hair up so Mama helped me to style it with sides pulled back and held fast by a yellow ribbon. The rest of my hair was left free to flow down my back. With hair as thick as mine, the pins I had to use to hold it up upon my head often gave me a terrible headache. I much preferred the freedom of this style, and I knew it suited me well.

"Tres jolie!" Mama complimented me as I checked on my appearance in the long looking glass in her bedroom. "Young Bruin will be enchanted."

"He is very polite. I'm certain he will act the proper gentleman and say all of the right things whether he is enchanted or not. How old is Bruin now, Mama?" I opened her jewelry box and explored the contents.

"Let me think." She sat down on her bed and gazed into space for a moment. "I think he would be twenty-three or four at the most. I've heard good things about him from the women at church with eligible young daughters. He has no noticeable vices and is a hard worker in his father's business. They own the Golden Crown Inn down by the wharf, you know."

"Actually, I didn't think to ask him what he did for a living. But I am surprised to hear he is a businessman." I held a silver chain up to the light and peered through the topaz that dangled there. Mama peered back at me through the golden light of the jewel. "Somehow that life doesn't suit him. I had the impression today Bruin is more a man of the outdoors; more like Papa."

"Ha! That would explain why your Papa invited him with such little notice to us. Sometimes I pity him, the only man in this feminine household." Her eyes sparkled as she smoothed the covers on his side of the bed. "But he never seems to complain, does he?"

Mama let me wear the topaz and although I felt more grown-up and ready to face Bruin, still I moved from room to room in a restless flurry of activity; arranging daisies, black-eyed susans, and queen anne's lace in a low centerpiece that wouldn't interfere with dinner conversation. I jumped and nearly dropped the crystal bowl when I heard Bruin's knock at the door.

"Jessamyn, let him in," Papa called from where he sat in the garden, and I hurried off to do it.

I opened the door for Bruin and we stared at each other for a moment too long just as we had in the Old Feather Store earlier that day. He was so much better looking than I remembered him to be as a boy; despite Mama's insistence he had been handsome even then, and I wondered if he thought I was pretty.

He had already removed his hat, revealing a fine, thick head of gentle curls, and I reached for the hat as I opened the door wider to accommodate his broad shoulders so he could enter the foyer, and without thinking, I commented, "You seem to be in exceptionally fine physical condition for a man who goes to business in town every day."

He arched one eyebrow at me as a slow smile spread across his face. I blushed, but tried to hide it, returning his gaze steadily. "I only meant," I said quickly, "that you appear to be a man more at home in the outdoors than at home in the confinement of an Inn."

"Very perceptive, Jessie."

This did not sit well with me. "Please don't call me Jessie. Jessamyn is the name I go by."

He laughed outright, and I wasn't sure I liked the sound of it. I didn't enjoy being baited.

"That Jessamyn is exactly what you used to say to me when you were a tiny little thing tagging along after me as we played in the garden. Remember the games we played? You always wanted to be an Indian warrior or a soldier on the battlefield; no nurse, or Indian maiden with a papoose for you. It was so charming how you had no idea how feminine you were. There was always this huge, spirit inside of you. That's who you knew you really were, despite what the rest of us could see."

His eyes were warm with memories and I found the wrinkles crinkling in their corners quite charming. I decided to tease him back a bit. "And I remember you as a kinder fellow, Bruin," I said, "You never laughed at me then. You made me feel grown up and your equal in all of our games."

His expression returned quickly to that of the polite guest. "I didn't mean to laugh at you, Jessamyn, but I was carried away with joy at the pleasant remembrance of our past time together. Those were my happiest days with my mother and I have thought of that time very often during these last years at the Inn."

"As I remember it, Bruin, the boy who was my friend, would never have chosen a life confined to the running of a business establishment. That young rascal planned to travel west and farm for a living."

His eyes grew sad. He nodded slowly. "You remember well. But my father is getting on in years and he needs me. At least has needed me until a few months ago when my younger brother, Paul, finished at school and declared a career in the family business would suit him just fine. So you can see I will soon be free of my family obligations."

I took a step nearer to him. "And what will you do then?"

He stared down into my eyes for the length of a heartbeat. "I haven't decided yet." He touched the tip of my nose with his finger.

"Cherie!" Mama called from the doorway to the dining room. "Do you plan to entertain Bruin out there in the hall all evening? Come along now, dinner is nearly ready and we have yet to offer our guest a cool drink."

We turned quickly toward Mama like guilty children, and hurried to join her. The dining room was lovely in candle glow, all the silver gleaming, the flowers, the linen and lace, so perfect.

Bruin handed Mama the package he'd been holding. "I hope a Chardonnay will compliment your menu, Mrs. Miles."

"Tres bien," she said, reaching up on tip-toes to kiss his cheek. "I am so glad George had the idea to invite you this evening. It has been much too long."

"Many years have passed, but why is it, Madam, you are lovelier now than I remembered?"

Mama laughed, coughed for a brief moment then winked at me. "Be on your toes with that one, Jessamyn. He is a charmer! Now let us join Papa before he turns grumpy and begins to complain."

Bruin and I laughed as we followed Mama out the French doors to the garden. Papa sat on a wrought iron chair, looking out of place in so delicate a setting. "Bruin!" he called eagerly, rising and moving to meet him. In one hand Papa held a mug.

"Would you like some stout?" he asked, placing a hand on Bruin's shoulder.

"Does the sun shine?"

"Ha! It surely does and tomorrow morning, I doubt I'll welcome the intrusion through our bedroom window!" Papa laughed his Irish laugh and set off for the kitchen and the stout.

Mama sat in the chair closest to Papa's and gestured for us to sit as well.

We sat together on the remaining choice, the wrought iron love-seat. Bruin's broad shoulder brushed against mine and a sudden shiver passed though me.

"Do you enjoy the theater, Bruin?" Mama asked, "Your dear mother did so enjoy a good play."

"Yes. She used to take me with her to the matinee and I am sorry to say I haven't had the opportunity to go in years. I've been occupied with the Inn. We've been expanding along with the growth of the city, but since my brother, Paul, is joining the business, I expect to be able to find time for such pastimes in the very near future."

"I love the theater, too, "I whispered, remembering the times Mama and I had gone to The Federal Street Theater. "Especially Shakespeare; he is our favorite."

"Would you two ladies allow me to escort you to a performance next week? You may name the evening and I'll arrange to be excused from my work."

"Oh, yes! We'd love it!" I said, appalled as I watched Mama shake her head.

"With my persistent cough I wouldn't be comfortable sitting through an evening's entertainment, but it would please me if you would take Jessamyn. She doesn't get out nearly enough."

Bruin looked me full in the eye. "Will you honor me?"

My cheeks were burning. Why had Mama done this to me? I glared at her. "I'm sure Bruin can find any number of girls to take to the theater. We mustn't impose on him, Mama."

Bruin laughed at me. "Don't be silly, Jessamyn. We've been friends forever. I would enjoy it very much."

"Then it's settled," Mama said, beaming at me even as I wrinkled my nose at her.

*   *   *

Mama was more excited about my going to the theater than I was. She nearly drove me to leap into Boston Bay in search of some peace and quiet.

"Most of the girls begin accepting the attentions of a suitor at fourteen, Ma Amour!" Mama teased, as she rummaged about in her wardrobe. "Look at you: fifteen and nearly an old maid! And to think you have a French mother!"

"Mama!" I wailed. "No man would ever be seriously interested in having an artist for a wife and I don't see the point of wanting something I will never have."

"Try this one on, Cherie," Mama coaxed, thrusting a silk gown at me with large roses in shades of red and pink crowded into a bold pattern. "Too bad you must wear your hair all piled upon your head, but society does demand...such foolishness. I know we'll get around it by allowing lots of tendrils to fall about your neck and shoulders. It will be lovely, you'll see."

She slipped the gown over my head and as it settled about my tightly laced corset, she pulled it together in back and we studied my reflection in the long mirror. "The colors suit you, but I prefer you in a solid fabric. I want nothing to distract from your beauty."

Together we decided upon an aquamarine silk trimmed with peach satin piping. Tiny peach pearl buttons closed the frock down the entire length of the back. The neckline was lower than the ones I usually wore and I wasn't used to baring my shoulders, but the puff of the long sleeves accentuated my waist making it appear even tinier.

Mama insisted on making an elaborate hat to match as the piece de resistance, and a wrap as well. I already had peach satin slippers of my own, so Mama declared me ready to greet Boston's nightlife.

*   *   *

"I wouldn't put myself through this ordeal if it wasn't to see Romeo and Juliet," I grumbled, as I dressed on the evening of the play. "I doubt if Bruin is suffering any over what he shall wear tonight! Sometimes I resent being female!"

"Hush," Mama said, "Don't be silly. Your looks give you an advantage over most people...especially men."

"That's why I like being an artist. I am accepted or rejected on the strength of my talent and abilities. I could be a trained gorilla and no one would know, or care, if they liked my paintings. In fact, I've decided to always sign my work with only my first initial and my last name so no one will be troubled, or influenced by the fact that I am female!"

Later, as Bruin and I walked toward the theater, I felt the excitement all around us. There was a breeze and I was grateful for it because every time I gazed at Bruin, I felt the heat of the brick walkway rise up under my long skirts, though not too unpleasantly. It had been a hot day and after commenting upon the weather, Bruin grew quiet.

Soon the walkway was crowded with other couples all moving toward the theater, and the street was jammed with carriages and impatient horses, all snorting and neighing and vying for position in front of The Federal Street Theater.

I touched his arm lightly and he reacted as if I'd burned him. "Thank you, Bruin, for taking pity on me and bringing me along tonight. I don't often go out in the evenings and I shall never forget this special night."

"Nor shall I," Bruin said with a look I couldn't quite interpret. His eyes were dark and intense this evening. Quickly he looked away from me and scanned the crowd all around us. Was he looking for someone? Someone he'd rather be with tonight?"

We stopped in front of the huge gilt-edged sign to the right of the theater entrance and Bruin read aloud: Playing tonight: Romeo and Juliet, by Mr. William Shakespeare, staring Miss Maude Lockridge and Mr. Robert Wallingham.

I was suddenly so excited my hands grew damp with perspiration and I felt light-headed as if I might trip on my own feet and fall. "I've heard they are quite wonderful together in this play." I whispered, just for something to say.

Bruin bent closer and I felt his warm breath tickle my ear. "I've heard the same thing, but I doubt it's a secret so you needn't whisper."

My hand few to cover my mouth and I tried to stifle a giggle as Bruin placed a hand against the curve of my back and guided me through the doors and into the theater. He handed the tickets to the usher, collected our programs, and steered me toward the stairway leading up to the box seats.

I was impressed. "You needn't have gone to such an expense," I said, "I appreciate just being here."

Bruin laughed. "You're a sweet girl to worry about the state of my finances, but I can well afford the tickets and if I couldn't I would find a way to do so for a girl as pretty and charming as you are."

His words brought Mama's playful warning to mind, but I resisted the urge to giggle, saying instead, "Mama was right about you, Mr. Mahoney." We began our ascent up the narrow staircase to our seats, so I spoke back over my shoulder, "You are definitely a charmer."

We entered our box, the one closest to the stage. With Bruin defending his sincerity, we sat together on carved walnut chairs upholstered in a rich royal blue velvet. The same velvet, with deep red trimmings, was repeated in the draperies around our box and in the heavily draped curtain down on the stage. A huge chandelier hung from the center of the theater alight with hundreds of smoky fairy candles glowing with a soft brilliance.

Then I noticed the effect the candle wax was having on the people below. "Look, Bruin," I whispered, "The candle wax is dripping all over the poor people down there in the pit."

Bruin looked pleased with himself. "I was warned about that when I purchased the tickets. I would hate to see wax stains on that exquisite gown of yours."

"I guess box seats are the best idea," I said, impressed all over again with his thoughtfulness. "Papa always got them for Mama and me."

I pointed to the gallery. "I'm glad we aren't sitting there. Those people aren't dressed very well and they're awfully noisy. Why some of them are staring at us, Bruin. And some are even making faces; how rude!"

Bruin's hand closed over mine and the sudden warmth of his touch affected me more than I wanted him to know. I snatched my hand back and fussed with the program, then turned my attention to the stage grateful the play was about to begin.

Following a brief introduction by the stage manager, the luminous velvet curtain began to slowly open. I held my breath and, leaning forward, clutched my program to my breast. The stage was a dream-like vision: an enchanting re-creation of Verona, so many years ago. I had read this play many times before, but I'd never seen it done and as the story unfolded, I became completely absorbed in the tragedy of the fated lovers from feuding families, one a Montague, one a Capulet.

When Romeo killed Juliet's cousin, Tybalt, the tears ran freely down my cheeks. Sympathy for these doomed young lovers washed over me in waves of despair and I nearly cried out when the last words of this beautiful, sad play were spoken.

There were five curtain calls to a standing ovation and as we left our seats, I was amused to see tears in Bruin's eyes as well.

We walked slowly away from the theater, and I was so moved by what we had just seen, I couldn't stop my chattering. "Never before have I appreciated the beauty of mere words, Bruin! They came alive when the actors spoke them aloud. It was magical and so much better than when I read the play by myself."

"I like seeing things through your eyes, Jessamyn. For one so young, you have a unique way of expressing yourself."

I sighed and gazed up at the moon, a perfect, pale, half a melon in the night sky. 'For one so young.' Would he ever see me as the young woman I had grown to become?"

"The city is nice when you can see a play like the one we've just enjoyed, or visit a museum," he said, "But I honestly find the beauty and peacefulness of the forest and the open countryside far outweighs any amusement the city can provide for me."

"I like the country too, Bruin," I said, but I could never live anywhere but here in Boston. I value my art lessons too much. And Papa and Mama are here."

Bruin seemed to hesitate for a moment as if re-thinking something he wanted very much to say. "Have you ever been out in the cool, green forest just after dawn when the animals are either waking up or heading home to rest. When everything seems fresh and new as if that day were the very first day on earth?"

There was a passion in Bruin's voice I couldn't help but respond to. "You sound like me when I speak of my art. I do know that time of day and I would love to capture it on canvas."

Bruin's grin held relief as if he were glad to finally speak to someone who knew what he was talking about. "So you are a bit of a country girl. Does your Papa take you out into the forest?"

"Yes; ever since I was little. And I'm a pretty good shot with a rifle too. At least if it's a target that's not moving."

"Do you think your Papa would mind if I came along with you next time?"

"Papa would love it. I'm a pretty poor substitute for a son, though he'd never admit it."

"I admire a woman who can handle a firearm: comes in very handy in the wilderness. Sometimes it can mean all the difference to her family's survival."

We paused under the softly glowing street lamp on the corner of elm. I grabbed the pole and swung around in a wide circle, laughing. "But since I intend to grow old right here in Boston, I guess my talent with a rifle will be forever wasted."

"Don't be so certain," Bruin said, stepping in front of me and placing his hand over mine, where it rested on the lamp post. He was standing in front of the moon and I wished I could see the expression on his face, but it was hidden in dark shadows and I could only guess at what he meant.

*   *   *

The buzzer sounded twice signaling it was time for the patients to go to bed, and I was jolted back to reality. The harsh sounds of the buzzer assaulted my ears and I leaped to my feet in confusion. I could get so deeply involved in Jessamyn's world, it was sometimes hard to come back to my own ruined life.

Alexander had a faraway look in his eyes. When he finally faced me his smile was sweet and sad all at the same time. "I think you really were her. It sounds so real when you read it to me, but,…who do you think I was?"

CHAPTER 6

Helen sat all huddled up in a ball on a folding chair sobbing so hard it was impossible to get through to her.

This was my first community meeting and both Alexander and I, along with Helen, Jessie, and Mark, a young man with a drinking problem who had been brought in the night before last, were granted clothing privileges. We were all relieved to retire our blue flannel, but the next vote didn't go as well. Alexander, Jessie, Mark, and I won the right to be allowed the use of a knife and fork. Unfortunately, there were still some patients who believed Helen was too much of a risk and she was voted down.

I couldn't stand to see Helen suffer so terribly and I tried my best to cheer her up, but her sobs grew louder and more pitiful, and soon Big Jake had to step in and escort her back to one of the rooms where they watched you constantly. She stumbled and moaned as they approached the hall; so Big Jake had to lift and carry her the rest of the way to an observation room.

I'd been feeling so much better lately that I'd assumed Helen was getting better, too. She had been laughing at my stories and talking more often and I had grown hopeful.

But now I felt only helpless, and I started to cry for her. Alexander put his arm around the back of my chair and whispered into my ear in his deep, silky voice, "Sunny, you can't take on other people's problems. You aren't strong enough right now for that. You have to concentrate on re-building your own life. Your children need you healthy and strong.

His arm felt as comforting to me as a fur coat in February and his breath was warm and ticklish against my ear and face. I looked up into his kind, blue eyes, so filled with complete understanding and empathy, and I started to fall in love, or into deep like. Perhaps it was only beginning lust. But whatever it was, it was the deepest and the most positive emotion I was capable of feeling at the time.

Alexander was the nicest man I had ever known. It didn't matter at all to me that he was probably crazy as a hoot owl because I was probably crazy too, and of course we were living in a crazy world anyway, so there was a good chance we might find a place in it together.

Usually after the community meetings we all voted to send out for pizza providing enough of us had spending money, but tonight most of us had lost our appetites over Helen's grief.

The others wandered back into the main room, while Alexander and I volunteered to straighten the conference room and re-arrange the chairs for tomorrow's group therapy session.

The sun had gone down during the meeting so the staff had left the deep-blue drapes open. I'd never been with a group of people who valued the sunset as much as we all did here.

Alexander and I stood together in front of the wall of glass. They weren't really windows because they didn't open, but they gave us the illusion of windows: the illusion of a normal room.

The night sky was clear and the stars shone as they only can over rolling mountains that spread out in all directions. Alexander was just behind me and I felt his arm slide shyly, hesitantly, around me as if he expected me to turn away at any second. It felt so right at that moment and I instinctively leaned back against him. And then it didn't feel right because he was so much taller than Bull. The contours of this male body were angular and unfamiliar. His arms were longer and my heart suddenly ached for the loss of my only love.

Still, I forced myself not to move away. I would have to learn to live without Bull and his familiar body. I would have to get used to someone else's arms or to no arms at all, ever again.

I concentrated on the beauty of the night: the sliver of a moon, the luminous stars. "You know what Gillian always says when the stars are this bright?"

"What?"

"She says the stars are winkling at her."

I turned toward him and he stared down at me with great intensity. My heart began to race and I considered running away, but his hands were suddenly pulling me closer to him and I knew I couldn't get away unless he let me go willingly. He was much stronger than I'd ever imagined.

"That's very charming," he said in a hoarse whisper, and then his face came down toward mine and I closed my eyes as he drew me into an amazing deep kiss that seemed to last...and last...and at the very last, he lifted me into the air. I could barely breathe: my heart beat in my ears, and when I opened my eyes I was staring straight into the eyes of this dear friend who had suddenly turned into a very passionate man.

"I love you, Sunny," he said.

*   *   *

Love! Alexander was talking about love already and I hadn't even begun to get over loving Bull. I tried to find a comfortable spot in my bed and soon gave up. I was wide awake now. Alexander thought he loved me and he barely knew me. I had never considered getting involved with anyone else. I hadn't considered it as an option for me. I had felt so completely bonded to Bull in marriage I had never even fantasized about being with another man. But now my imagination was taking off on flights to rival those of a teenage boy.

When Alexander had set me back down on my feet, he had brushed my body firmly against his on the entire trip down the full length of his torso. I had blushed to feel a certain unmistakably long and large bulge against me. Mr. Alexander Grandy was apparently gifted in many and varied ways.

I had never wondered about the size of a man's penis before. I had only been acquainted with Bull's penis and as far as I knew, they were all roughly the same. But the length and the width of Alexander's bulge had certainly made me curious. I wondered what it would feel like to make love with another man. I wondered if I'd keep thinking about Bull, or forget all about him. Apparently he was able to forget about me to the extent that he could fall into bed with any attractive girl who caught his fancy.

Still, I didn't believe I'd be able to actually go through with it. There was no doubt Bull deserved it, but I had always known the one advantage I had over his girlfriends was the fact that I had been his virgin. Bull loved knowing this, and I wasn't sure if I was ready to give up my advantage. Also, I knew there was a good possibility he might kill me and the man I made love with, if I ever did and he found out about it. And wasn't his finding out about it most of the reason for doing it?

I decided I had to find a way to relax and get some sleep or I would pay for it in the morning. I lay on my back and imagined a great glowing silver cord coming out of the Heavens and down through the hospital roof and into the top of my head. With each deep breath I took I imagined a cleansing white light was moving down my body, relaxing my every muscle and filling my heart and soul with a sense of peace and calm. In no time at all, I was sound asleep and back in Beaver Valley.

*   *   *

I never wanted to hate anyone, but I found I was beginning to hate Papa as the days passed slowly and painfully. The only comfort I had was the sketch book and box of charcoal I had managed to pack after Papa declared there wasn't room in the wagon for my easel and canvases and oils. He, of course, promised to replace them in Marietta before we got all the way to Beaver Valley, but there was nothing he could say to make it up to me.

During the endless days of dust and heat I comforted myself by looking through my sketch book and remembering my lost life in Boston. And as the days passed, I vowed to find a way back to that life. I would do everything in my power to persuade Papa to give up on Beaver Valley and move us back to Boston on the first available wagon train heading in that direction.

As I leafed through the drawings, I paused before the one I had done of myself in my dark-red velvet and Chantilly lace gown. This dress had been the first one I had made after Mama's death, after the ten lonely months of grief during which I could paint only the cold barren winter landscape.

Early last March, in this dress, I had gone to the last winter ball with that traitor, Bruin Mahoney, the man I considered in large part responsible for Papa's folly. The man who got him interested in joining this stupid wagon train.

Still, my memory of the Ball was a mixture of happy and sad. It had been nearly a year since I'd been out anywhere for fun. At first Papa refused to go with us although we tried our best to persuade him. Then, at the last minute, he decided to go along, and I remember being so glad he was finally coming around, attempting to deal with Mama's death. I had loved her too, but Papa couldn't see beyond his own heartbreak and I felt as if I'd lost both parents when Mama died.

I was ready to leave for the Ball long before Bruin was due to come for us, and I had to remind Papa to get dressed several times before he finally heaved himself up from his chair and his paper and, like a much older man, ambled up the stairs to his room to change into his Sunday best. As I watched Papa climb the stairs I felt a wave of terrible longing for Mama, dead nearly a year. Knowing she was safe in Jesus' arms helped some, but not enough to overcome my grief at her loss. If I still cried nearly every day for her, I could only guess at the depth of Papa's suffering. They had been like twin souls.

Bruin finally did come and Papa was ready just moments before he rang the bell. Bruin looked very handsome in a new suit of clothes, sporting a ruffled shirt front and black tie. His hat was made of lush Beaver and his cloak appeared new as well. Even Papa commented on his striking appearance and I could tell by the flush on Bruin's cheeks when he complimented me on my gown, he truly felt I looked my best as well.

Mama had always said, "Cheri, dark-red velvet was made with you in mind. No one else can wear it as well."

It began to snow lightly as we made our way down the walk toward Bruin's carriage, but I didn't mind since my hair was naturally curly and would only curl more so from the moisture. I threw my head back and tried to catch the frosty flakes on the tip of my tongue. Bruin helped Papa into the carriage then turned back to help me and laughed at what I imagine was the ridiculous picture I made standing there waving my tongue at the night sky.

"I love the snow!" I explained, wishing I'd acted with more thought to the effect I was creating.

"You always did," Bruin said, "Remember how we slid down old Potter's Hill on my sled?"

"Do I remember? I wouldn't be surprised to find my backside still carries a few bruises from that ill thought out adventure!"

Bruin and I grinned into each other's eyes, then he put his huge hands around my waist and as I uttered a tiny, "Oh," he lifted me effortlessly into the air and into the carriage beside Papa. Bruin climbed in beside me, and I found I was quite squashed between the broad shoulders of the two men. In fact, I wasn't certain I'd be able to breathe at all.

Luckily Papa moved across from us before I had to find out I was right and I inched over enough so we were both comfortable. Still, Bruin's shoulder and thigh were pressed firmly against mine and I wondered if this closeness was having any effect upon him. My own heart was tripping along at a great rate and for once I couldn't think of a thing to say.

Since Papa was in a better mood than usual, he rattled on about mutual acquaintances, about his business, about Bruin's father's business, and I was spared.

The dance was to be held in the ballroom of The Boston Hotel just down the street from The Federal Street Theater. The street was jammed with carriages and people hurrying toward the brilliantly lit hotel. The excitement in the air was impossible to miss and I suddenly felt very lucky to be on my way to the biggest event of the social season.

The snow was still falling softly and it twinkled in the light of the many colored lanterns hanging about the outside of the building. Papa watched happy couples caught up in the merriment, and his smile faded away. My papa had always been the jolliest man in any room, and the first to lend a helping hand to anyone who needed it, but tonight my papa was a sad and quiet man. He seemed to have diminished in size so curved was the posture of his once mighty back.

I reached across the carriage to touch his hand. "Try to enjoy yourself tonight, Papa. I know Mama would want you to enjoy your life."

He nodded absently, as if he barely heard me. Bruin took charge as soon as the carriage stopped in front of the door. He said something close to Papa's ear and had him laughing as he exited the carriage.

Then Bruin turned his attention to me. His eyes were dark and kind as he reached in to help me from my seat. My small hands were lost in his firm grip and again I admired his strength as he encircled my waist with his arm and guided me safely down to the walkway.

"You are very lovely tonight, Jessamyn," he said.

"Thank you," I returned, "You look very fine yourself."

*　*　*

The ballroom was everything I had imagined. The ceiling was ablaze with rainbows all reflected from the exquisite crystal chandeliers, European in design and aglow with a haunting brilliance.

A scrumptious feast topped each sleek, long, mahogany sideboard. Couples twirled and spun, laughing and talking as they danced across the floor, as smooth and reflective as ice.

The harpist slid his hands along the strings in a silky arpeggio just as Bruin asked me to dance. I quickly checked about to see if Papa had someone to talk with, and then, I said, yes.

I felt safe in Bruin's arms and I wasn't surprised to find he was a good, strong dancer. Many large men are surprisingly graceful on a dance floor. Papa had always been when he swept Mama off in a raucous bounding dance.

The music changed and Bruin led me smoothly on in a lively, swirling motion as we waltzed to Mozart. Over our heads the crystal prisms of the chandelier appeared to twirl along with us as he bore me off in a great swish of velvet and perfume. I wished this night could go on forever.

Bruin's eyes held mine fast and I dared not attempt to speak, so short of breath was I at all the excitement. I willed myself to look away and so I watched Kathleen Brady, an old friend of mine from school, twirl by in the arms of Jeremiah Winston, her ice-blue gown a shimmering flash of satin and lace. Carolyn Tompkins and Ralph Johnson were close beside them and they danced nearer to greet us.

Even Adelaide Sullivan, my last teacher at school, was here in a high-necked cream- colored gown, looking as demure as I remembered. We waved to each other and I thought she'd never looked lovelier with her dull light-red hair arranged in curls. She was not plain this evening, but delicately pretty as she danced by in the arms of her older brother.

Bruin and I stopped to catch our breath and soon Daniel Morton asked me to dance. Bruin said he'd welcome a moment to sit and rest his feet, so off we went.

"It's good to see you out and having fun, Jessamyn," Daniel said, and we had barely completed one turn around the floor before I heard a familiar shrill laugh echo across the room. I closed my eyes for a moment, steeling myself in preparation for the inevitable meeting with Cassie Taylor.

Cassie Taylor was an irritating little troublemaker. She had the knack for setting other women on their guard whenever she was around. There wasn't a woman in town who would trust Cassie alone with her husband, or her son, despite the fact that she was only seventeen years old and unmarried. The scent of musky nights and secrets never to be known followed Cassie wherever she walked.

Her best feature was her thick, cascade of auburn hair. Many a man had been dazzled by the sparkle of reflecting sunlight, or, as more often the case, moonlight, on Cassie Taylor's famous hair. She also possessed green eyes, the beauty of which was diminished only by the cold hard look she gave the world.

I had to admit that in certain lights her eyes could deepen to emerald, but of course Cassie perpetuated that illusion by dressing in shades of green. Although considered pretty, I'd always thought her tall, lean body and thin-featured face were too gaunt to be considered beautiful.

Still, I had seen Papa admire her from a distance, and at that very moment she was advancing on Bruin and I was certain she was up to no good.

There had been a time when I'd tried to like Cassie, but for some reason Cassie just didn't like me, and I had given up trying, since it was a feeble attempt at best, and I had decided to avoid her as much as possible.

"Do you mind, Daniel," I asked, "if we go back to Bruin? I'm terribly thirsty and could use a cool cup of punch."

Daniel didn't mind and so we joined Bruin and his admirer, Cassie, who stood too close to him, gazing up into his eyes with an inappropriately bold look. Her poor escort, young William Woods, stood to her left, looking as uncomfortable as I was beginning to feel.

"So, William," I said, touching his shoulder, "I see you're the lucky fellow who escorted Cassie tonight."

William's blonde hair fell appealingly across his forehead as he rolled his blue eyes toward the crystal above and grinned. "Yes," he said in a small voice.

Cassie spun and glared at me. "Jessamyn," she said, practically spitting the word out as if it tasted bad, "How could you go off and leave this big handsome fellow all alone?"

"I've always thought Bruin could take care of himself, Cassie."

"Indeed, I can," Bruin said dryly, extending a hand to me.

I smiled at him and allowed him to guide me to his side. "Would you like a cup of punch, Jessamyn?" he asked.

"Yes, I would," I returned as sweetly as I could, hoping he'd leave me alone with Cassie so I could find out what she was up to.

As soon as Cassie and I were alone, she turned on me in a rustle of dark-green taffeta. She was taller than me and as she stepped nearer I had a perfect view of her cleavage. Such a skinny witch would never have so full a bosom and I knew she just had to have stuffed some cotton batting down the front of her bodice.

Her smile was full of malice. "Bruin is too kind," she began, "he always was one to have an affinity for the less popular girls."

"What do you mean by that?" I asked, my cheeks going hot.

"Nothing." Her smile was wide and irritating. "He just mentioned to me how sad you've been since your mother's death and that he was glad to see you dancing and having a good time. I am sorry about your mother, Jessamyn."

My heart was pounding hard in my ears and I wanted nothing more than to feel Cassie's hair between my clenched fists. I wished I'd given her a good tarring when we were both in diapers because then I could have gotten away with it without causing a public scandal.

It was my Papa who saved Cassie by coming up to us. "Why aren't you two girls dancing? Haven't these young men eyes to see with? How can they ignore such sweet young flowers?"

Cassie turned her charm on Papa and then annoyed me even further by coaxing him into dancing with her.

Bruin came back with my punch and as we stood together, sipping and nibbling at the dainty pastries served to us by butlers bearing silver trays, I noticed an unusually tall, pale man standing near the door. He looked very much out of place in dark unfashionable clothing with a clerical collar visible beneath his long, strong chin.

The man stared back at me and I pretended to fix my attention elsewhere, but was drawn back to meet his gaze by the force of his strange, pale-gray eyes. They had an unearthly quality as if they could see into a person's soul. His hair was pale-blonde, wispy, and rather longish at the back, and although I felt drawn to wonder about him, it wasn't because I found him the least bit attractive.

"Who is that man, Bruin? I've never seen him before."

Bruin's eyes followed mine. "Oh, that's the Reverend Charles Putnam. He's come a long way; all the way from his settlement outside of Marietta, Ohio. It appears they need tradesmen and others interested in farming to come out and join their community. He's forming a wagon train due to leave in the spring."

My eyes flew back to Bruin's face. "Are you considering joining with him?" I asked, hoping it wasn't true.

Bruin's smile was a slow tease. "I'm thinking about it, and I wouldn't be surprised if your father wasn't prone to consider the same thing."

"What? You can't be serious. Why on earth would anyone wish to live in a place like that stuck out in the middle of nowhere?"

Bruin laughed at my alarm. "For the adventure; for the thrill of being in on the birth of a new city in a new and fertile land."

My heart was racketing about like a crazed thing. It couldn't be true. It was bad enough to think I might lose Bruin's friendship now that we'd re-connected, but it was totally unthinkable that I might lose my happy life in the bargain too.

I turned quickly back toward the reverend and to my dismay found my papa was now standing beside him, chattering away.

"Introduce me to this Reverend Putnam, Bruin," I suggested, clutching at Bruin's sleeve. "You've made me curious."

Reverend Charles Putnam stood several inches above both Papa and Bruin, but he was so thin and pale, his height wasn't as impressive as it might have been. He stared at me for a full minute then looked quickly away and blushed.

Bruin made the proper introductions while Papa beamed at me as if I were his prize pet colt. I shook the reverend's hand and tried to face his unusual gray eyes directly, but he could only hold my gaze for a few seconds before he began to fidget and a deep flush spread across his cheeks again.

"Bruin tells me you are here to persuade others to follow you back into the wilderness. As a man of God how do you justify promoting such foolishness?" I demanded to know.

Papa choked on his punch and Bruin chuckled then coughed, as he pounded Papa upon the back. My bold words apparently got the reverend's full attention for he met my gaze with raised eyebrows. "I'm afraid I don't understand your questions, Miss M-Miles."

"You must excuse my daughter, Reverend," Papa said quickly. "Jessamyn has been indulged since birth. She is an only child and I'm afraid my wife and I both encouraged her to speak out, perhaps without having fully explained that it is sometimes inappropriate."

I glared at Papa. "I have the right to question this man, Papa, since Bruin tells me you are considering following him into the bowels of hell, and I would imagine dragging me right along with you!"

Papa's eyes darted around the room as if looking for help. "Well, I, of course, was going to speak to you about it, Little Mite...should I decide..."

I suddenly felt faint. How could this be happening? Papa couldn't possibly be seriously considering such a foolhardy move.

"Miss Miles," Reverend Putnam intervened, "I...I hardly think it accurate to characterize Beaver Valley as being located in the actual 'bowels of hell'". A slight smile played about his lips.

"Hell or Ohio, it's all the same to me."

Bruin burst out laughing and I gave him my most withering look which made him laugh all the harder.

"Jessamyn, he said, "why don't you at least listen to the reverend before you pass judgment on his settlement. It's only fair."

"True enough" I conceded. "So tell me, Reverend, about this Beaver Valley, Ohio."

The reverend's smile was kind and I had to fight the inclination to respond to it. I stared back at him with a sober face, challenging him to explain himself.

"Let's see..." he began, scratching his pale cheek and staring deeply into my eyes. "The story of Beaver Valley really begins with the establishment of Marietta as the first freeborn city in that part of the world." His voice grew stronger with pride. "Back in 1786, here in Boston, there was a meeting at The Bunch of Grapes Tavern to discuss the development of Ohio. A few people you know, Mr. Miles, may have been there."

"They didn't waste any time in forming their plans for action, since by 1788, the first New England Pilgrims, as they were called, had crossed the mountains in covered wagons and drifted down the Ohio River in what came to be known as the 'second Mayflower' and they'd named their landing place, Marietta."

"Several years later some of the original families as well as the next newcomers from Boston had decided to farm the land a few miles farther west and it was there they formed the new settlement of Beaver Valley."

The reverend paused, with a dreamy look in his intense eyes, "I wish I could find the words to describe to you just how beautiful Ohio really is... The game is plentiful in the hills and on the plains, and we even have a herd of giant Buffalo seven feet tall. They're really something to see, Miss Miles."

I resisted the impulse to make a snide comment and glared at Bruin instead. He smiled benignly back at me.

"The rivers are all filled with fish; huge bass and pike and trout in all the streams. And the untouched forests of hickory, maple, oak, poplar, ash, walnut, sycamore and elm are an untapped natural resource."

Papa stood spellbound. I could almost hear the wheels in his head turning with renewed vigor. In truth, Papa looked like a new man. "How long will it take for your wagon train to reach Beaver Valley, Reverend?" he asked.

"Just short of three months, George. And I hope you'll consider coming with us; we desperately need a man with your skills. The closest blacksmith is the better part of a day's ride into Marietta."

I grasped Papa's arm and with my eyes, pleaded with him. He touched my cheek and smiled, unconcerned. "It would be good to accept such a challenge; to leave all my memories behind and begin a new adventure."

"But Papa, you can't leave memories behind. They follow you wherever you go." I could see that my words had no effect on him. He was already miles away caught up in the romantic notion of a new life in a wild new country. I felt the reverend's eyes upon me once again and I glanced at him. He looked quickly away and began trying to persuade Bruin to join his wagon train as well.

"I know of a farm you can take over, Bruin, if you are so inclined. Jeremiah Ralston is definitely going to sell out at the first opportunity and move back to Marietta with his sister and her family. He's fighting a serious illness and can't take another season of hard farm work."

"You can count on me, Reverend," Bruin said, as soon as I clear it with my father. My brother is learning the business fast and I really don't think they will need me much longer at the inn.

What fools. They were all fools to want to leave this happy civilized life behind in our beloved city of Boston. How could they?

I felt light-headed again and was about to go outside in search of fresh air when the reverend stopped me in my path. It was a bold move for one so obviously socially awkward.

"I…I'm sorry you don't feel enthusiastic about joining our community, Miss Miles," he said in a surprisingly shy voice for a man used to commanding the attention of many from a pulpit on Sunday mornings.

"You could say I lack enthusiasm," I said. "In fact if my father agrees to join you, Reverend Putnam, I shall consider it the end of life as I know it. I am an artist and I intend to paint. Boston is the perfect place for me to study and to display my work in the galleries."

He looked sympathetic. "I'm sorry…I d-d-didn't know. Perhaps if your father insists on resettling in Beaver Valley you could consider it an opportunity to paint the magnificent landscape of Ohio; to immortalize it, as it were. I'm certain you will agree once you see the intense beauty of the countryside."

I stared into his slightly startled light-gray eyes. "Somehow, Reverend, that fails to interest or to comfort me. Now if you will excuse me," I said, pushing past Papa and Bruin.

At that moment Adelaide Sullivan and her brother, Cecil, came toward us and the reverend called out to invite them to join our group. I could hardly be rude and run outside without at least greeting my former teacher in a proper manner, so I was trapped for the time being.

"Miss Sullivan," the reverend called, "Do you know Miss Miles? Why don't you two speak for a bit. It looks as though Miss Miles and her father will be joining our party."

I was shocked. "Miss Sullivan, are you truly considering traveling west in a covered wagon? Why on earth!"

She stood before me grinning like a free spirit. Her eyes shone at the reverend and it was obvious how reluctant she was to turn her attention toward the sound of my voice. "Oh, Jessamyn," she whispered, in a small, breathless voice, while fussing at the damp curls that had escaped her curly bun, "Why not indeed! I've never had a real adventure in all my life! I've lived in the front of a classroom, teaching and caring for other people's beloved children, and now I can't help but think it might be my turn to live a life that matters."

I could barely hide my shock. "But surely teaching matters, Miss Sullivan."

She waved my words away as if they were so many flies. "It matters in that someone has to do it, I suppose. And call me Adelaide, we aren't in a classroom anymore!" Her eyes danced with promise as if the entire world lay at her feet.

I'd never seen Miss Sullivan, or Adelaide, acting so young and girl-ish and I could only assume this sudden change was due to the presence of the new man in town, this strange Reverend Putnam. Whenever she caught his eye she flushed most becomingly and there was a touch of true prettiness in her face tonight, a blossoming beauty that had never been there before.

She giggled behind her hand. "I have no reason to stay here in Boston, Jessamyn," she confided, "My mother and I are both delighted to be embarking on so worthy a mission.

Reverend Putnam has asked for my assistance, and I will be help-ing him in his work. The children of Beaver Valley don't have a proper teacher and the reverend has been called upon to perform teaching duties for the entire town's children in addition to his duties as pastor."

She was dazzled and be-dazzled beyond hope and it was evident she would be no help to me in convincing Papa to stay in Boston, so I mumbled something suitable and then escaped outside for some blessed fresh air.

The cold night air was a welcome touch of reality to a night that had quickly become surreal as my worst nightmare was threatening to become my fate. I stepped into the falling snow where flakes melted quickly against my hot cheeks. I felt as if the whole world had gone mad tonight. And poor Adelaide Sullivan so obviously fancied the reverend while he barely gave her a second look; but he had stared at me overly long and so often I had found it most embarrassing.

*   *   *

I awoke in my bed at the hospital and shivered as if it were truly win-ter and not the middle of June. I could still feel the snow on my face and I trembled half from the imagined cold and half from empathy for Jessamyn. The poor girl was about to lose everything she cared for… and I knew exactly how that felt and my heart ached for the both of us.

I crept from my bed and opened the door to the hall a few more inches to let a shaft of bright light fall across the bed. I would record my latest dream and then I knew I'd sleep peacefully until morning. That was the way it always worked and it was one of the few things I could still count on.

I finished writing the dream sometime around 4 A.M., but my hand kept going. I kept on writing and this time I knew what every one of the characters was thinking and feeling. As if I were watching a movie, my hand moved to record the drama playing inside of my head.

*   *   *

Cassie Taylor had her paws all over Bruin again and she stood on tip-toe as she laughed up into his face, leaning forward, and hanging on his arms as if she'd faint at all the clever and funny things he said. "I'm glad we got rid of that stuck-up little baggage. It was kind of you to escort her this evening, but then you are a friend of the family."

Bruin looked surprised. "Why do you say such things about Jessamyn? Didn't you girls attend Miss Parson's School for Young Ladies together? I always thought of the two of you as being friends."

Cassie wrinkled her small, sharp nose at Bruin. "She's not so bad, I guess. It's just that I don't think she appreciates you properly."

Bruin frowned at her. "In what way do you mean that, Cassie?"

Her eyes narrowed slyly. "Take this evening for instance. Where is she right now?" Cassie scanned the crowd and pointed across a sea of brightly clad dancers. "There she goes now, dancing and laughing and flirting, no doubt, with Willy Woods."

Bruin looked amused. "Now Cassie, that wouldn't be jealousy I hear in your voice, would it?"

She flushed and her eyes flashed green fire at him. "Jealous? Me? What would I have to be jealous about? Jessamyn Miles? I just have no patience with girls who don't know when they're lucky...and who don't appreciate their good fortune. Any girl would be flattered to receive as much of your attention as you've wasted on Jessamyn this evening!" She took another step toward him and leaned back to gaze seductively into his eyes. "I know I would be most particularly flattered..."

Bruin turned away. "Cassie, you flatter me...And I think you're much too hard on Jessamyn. It's been a long time since she's had any fun." He waved to her as she spun gaily by.

"Dance with me, Bruin," Cassie whispered as she raised her arms and pressed her body against him. "Spin me around until I can't think anymore."

Surprised by Cassie's boldness, Bruin pulled back a few inches from her. Cassie laughed at him, mocking him, challenging him with her incredible eyes.

* * *

The ball ended long after midnight. George Miles had gone for the punch bowl with the 'extra something' in it, a few too many times, and he was the last to leave the dance floor. He'd thrown his confining top coat off onto a chair some hours before, and he coaxed Amanda Masters, the wife of his friend, Ben into one last wild romp around the dance floor. Jessamyn put a hand on Bruin's arm and watched with concern as George let go of Amanda at last and spun away by himself careening into several empty chairs.

"We'd better collect Papa now, Bruin," Jessamyn said, "And head for home before he passes out here. He looks exhausted, doesn't he? Of course he hasn't danced in a very long time."

Bruin thought George didn't look at all well. He sat slumped forward, his hair plastered to his damp forehead as he rubbed his left arm. Although there was a smile on his lips, it failed to reach his eyes.

"Is your arm bothering you, Mr. Miles?" Bruin asked gently, squatting next to the chair and rubbing his back.

It took George a moment to focus his eyes. "Young Bruin!" he croaked, "Young Bruin, have you been dancing?"

Bruin laughed. "Yes, sir. I have been dancing but not as splendidly as you have. Did you bump your arm, Sir?"

"No!" George scowled and tried to stand, but tumbled back down into the chair. "Just stiff muscles. Not used to the revelry."

* * *

George snored in the corner of the coach. He reeked of spirits and Jessamyn wished it were warm enough to crack open a window. "Papa had fun," she said, smiling at Bruin.

Bruin's arm rested along the back of the seat. He gave her a quick hug. "So did I," he said. He could barely think, so moved was he by the beauty of her small, perfect face. He sat listening to her chatter on about the dance, absorbing the light from her warm, brown eyes. He thought, at that moment, he could live happily forever within the glow of Jessamyn's big doe-eyes.

After helping George into the house, he returned to help Jessamyn from the coach and to walk her up to the front door.

"Thank you, Bruin," she said, opening the door of the coach, "It was a lovely evening, except for the unpleasant meeting with that Reverend Putnam person. I do hope you and Papa will come to your senses and give up the crazy idea of joining his wagon train." Her throat ached in reaction to the ugly thought.

"I don't think he's unpleasant. He's quite a nice enough fellow. It's obvious Adelaide Sullivan thinks so!"

Jessamyn giggled into her hands. "She was very obvious in her admiration of the man. I've never seen her so animated, so excited about… anything really."

"I found it sweet. They make a perfect couple, don't you think?" Bruin asked as he drew Jessamyn out from the coach and into the safety of his arms. He held her for a moment longer than necessary before placing her on the ground.

Her lashes fluttered as she fought to breathe normally. "I-I guess so," she stammered remembering how the man had stared at her and she wondered if Adelaide was the type of woman he admired, or if perhaps he preferred younger women…small dark-haired women with headstrong ways?"

In spite of Reverend Putnam, I did have a lovely evening, Bruin, and I thank you."

His dark, kind eyes had suddenly gone darker and a bit mysterious. He placed a finger against her lips and stepped nearer. "You needn't ever thank me, Jessamyn," he said, his voice low and intense. "Spending time with you is a pure pleasure."

His finger tingled where it had touched her luscious lips so briefly. His arms, his entire body ached with the desire to hold her, to crush her against his chest, to never let her go again. He shuddered at his impure thoughts and scanned the night sky for stars. The snow had stopped. It was clear and very cold.

Jessamyn mistook his shudder for a shiver and said, "It is much too cold a night to stand out here and talk, and since I must get Papa settled in his bed, I'll say goodnight right here, Bruin."

The darkness hid the look of disappointment on his face. "Thank you, Jessamyn, for being my lady tonight. I'll be calling again very soon."

Jessamyn giggled at the formal manner of his speech. "Oh, do call again soon! You silly old bear! You're the very best friend a girl and her papa could ever hope to have. I don't know how I would have gotten Papa home and up the stairs without you. Goodnight!" She waved over her shoulder and zipped quickly up the steps and into the warm and inviting house.

Bruin walked slowly back to his carriage thinking a slap in the face would have been far easier to take than the chilling finality of her light hearted words; thoughtless words relegating him forever to the cruel position of 'very best family friend.'

That night in his bed, her perfume lingered all around him, teasing him, and then torturing him, as he spent a fitful night where over and over he would take her face in his hands and savor the sight of her wide, innocent eyes, her smooth high cheekbones, her delicate nose and Cupid's bow lips. For all the hours until dawn he would imagine kissing those lips, possessing the perfection of her young body while she moaned beneath him and whispered his name only. With the hot breath of a woman in love she whispered his name...but only in his dreams.

CHAPTER 7

"Don't do it Sunny," Alexander warned; a stubborn dark look on his Leo face. "Please listen to me. I know what I'm talking about, and if you tell Dr. Carroll some of the things you've confided in me, they're going to lock you up and lose the key."

I was pouting in the corner of our favorite sofa. I curled a long strand of hair around my finger and drew my legs up under me. I hoped I looked appealing and that Alexander would give up the fight.

"And stop flirting!" he said, "Those little tricks of yours won't work on me."

I laughed and relaxed. "You're so smart, Alexander," I said, "And you know me well. It's kind of scary."

"Forget the flattery. That won't work either. Sunny, this is serious business. You are dealing with a mind lacking in imagination. This guy wouldn't believe he was born of woman if he hadn't met his own mother and seen the pictures to prove it."

Alexander looked very attractive when he was passionate about something, but I didn't bother telling him so since he would only have accused me of further flattery.

"Alexander," I said instead, "I really want to get better. And I really need to know if I'm crazy-crazy, or just creative-crazy. I have to know this for myself. I can't believe that if I'm functioning reasonably well Dr. Carroll will bother to commit me to the state hospital. That just doesn't seem logical, and one thing Dr. Carroll is, is logical. At the very worst, he'll probably recommend a lifetime of out-patient therapy, very expensive out-patient therapy. That seems more like the direction he'd be inclined to go in."

Alexander continued to scowl at the carpet. His large hands twitched where they rested on his knees.

I put my hand tentatively on the back of his neck and then massaged the tense muscles gently. His face softened. "Thanks for caring, Alexander," I whispered, "It means a lot to me. But don't worry. I'm not stupid. I won't say anything that will get me sent away. I promise."

"Then promise me you won't tell him about the fairies."

"Oh, the fairies. Well, lots of little kids think they see fairies."

"But when they grow up into big kids they have the sense not to share that particular memory with their therapists. Especially Freudian trained psychiatrists like Dr. Carroll who have the power to commit them to the real loony bin."

Alexander had a point. I stood up and wandered over to stare out the window. The fairies had started to visit me when I was about three and a half. In those days I was lonely for playmates and I spent too much time living in my imagination.

Three fairies came to visit, a blonde, a brunette, and a redhead. They always came to me late at night, usually after I'd had a long, boring day, and most often when I'd gotten myself into trouble by doing something to anger or disappoint my mother, which happened way too often.

They were each less than eight inches tall and they always wore vibrant sparkling gowns. They would ask me how my day had gone, and I felt comfortable telling them the truth about what I was really thinking and feeling. For what seemed like a long time, they helped me by listening to me and giving me their sympathy when I felt I was being treated unfairly by my parents who expected perfection from me at all times.

They stopped coming right around the time my baby brother, Joe-Joe learned to talk. But I knew why they'd left me. It was because of something I did to one of them.

The blonde fairy had come alone to see me that night and she was in a strange mood. As I told her my troubles she flew around the room and mocked me, belittling me, making fun of everything I'd told her.

At first I was disappointed and then a huge rage came over me, and I snatched the little fairy up in my hands and ran down the hall to the bathroom. It was late at night and I was the only one still up.

I filled the sink with water and threw the fairy into the swirling water. Her wings got wet and she couldn't fly away, so she screamed in her tiny fairy voice that wasn't loud enough to wake anyone up, and she struggled and begged me to save her since she claimed not to be able to swim.

I don't know what came over me, but I just stood there staring at her as she struggled to climb up the slippery sides. I felt a feeling of power for the first time in my life, and then I began to cry in shame. How could I do such a thing? How could I let myself get this mad?

Sometimes my mother said I was a monster when I disobeyed her and now I was that monster. For a few moments I had become the monster my mother imagined me to be.

I pulled the plug and dried the fairy off with a wash cloth, apologizing as I brought her back to my room and made a bed for her in my pink bunny slipper. Sick and light-headed I vowed to never let the monster of my anger out again. I finally went to sleep promising myself I would work hard to become the perfect good girl my parents wanted me to be no matter how hard it was to do. And to this day I don't know if I was dreaming. That's the crazy part. I think the fairies were real.

And I guess I wanted to tell Dr. Carroll about the fairies because I had failed again and maybe I wanted him to punish me in some way. When I had stared down the barrel of that gun and considered ending my life because I was so damn mad at myself for being Bull's fool, I had failed not only the unreasonable expectations of my parents, but my own resolve never to let the anger monster out again. The tragedy was that I had failed my children in the biggest way possible. For that I deserved to be punished.

"If I had more confidence in Dr. Carroll, I could assume he will recognize the fairies as a child-like coping mechanism for attempting to handle the justified anger you weren't allowed to express as a child, but under the circumstances I don't think you should risk it," Alexander said, breaking into my thoughts and touching my arm. "I just wish you wouldn't chance it, Sunny. It's too much information."

We looked into each other's eyes and I couldn't remember the last time a man had been so 'there' for me. Alexander had my back and I suspected he always would no matter what direction our friendship might take in the roller coaster I called my life.

"O.K.," I said, "You win. I won't mention the fairies."

Alexander looked shocked. "I won?" he said, I actually won?"

*   *   *

Despite Alexander's repeated warnings to be cautious with Dr. Carroll, whenever I stepped into his office, I always felt I was in a safe place. It was as if I'd left the hospital and returned to normal life.

"Dr. Carroll," I said, "Have you ever had an out-of-body experience? Or have you ever known anyone who did?"

Dr. Carroll stared at me through his thick glasses. His eyes looked even larger than usual, but they didn't give any of his opinions away. "I haven't. I've done some reading on the subject, though, why do you ask?"

"Do you think it's possible?"

"Do you?"

I tried not to, but I couldn't help laughing at him. "Doctor, I can't believe you get paid such big bucks to sit there and ask me what I think. It's either the greatest job in the world, or the lousiest. I can't decide."

He grinned at me; a real grin. "I can't either," he said, and we laughed together.

"That was a genuine smile, Doctor. You're making progress. Every time I come in here to chat with you, you get more real."

"Do I?" he asked, suddenly serious, as if it mattered at all to him, then he cleared his throat. "So what do you want to tell me today, Sunny? What's on your mind?"

I took an especially deep breath and began: "I was about three when I got very sick with a severe case of measles and strep throat. So sick I nearly died alone late one night. I wasn't alone in the house, but I was too weak to call out for my parents, who had no idea I had suddenly gotten worse. I was burning with fever and then, wishing with all my energy just to feel better, I found myself floating up and out of my body."

I glanced over at Dr. Carroll who was studying me with an expression I couldn't read, which was probably just as well.

"The top of the ceiling was glowing and all the colors in the room were brighter. Up here my room smelled musty and I was surprised to see a coating of dust on the fat cherubs who held hands and grinned at me from the molding, just under the ceiling. I knew my father wouldn't like it if he knew. He was into cleaning."

"I was free of my body and I wasn't sick anymore. I'd never felt so wonderful. I did a few somersaults around the room, and I even buzzed Joe-Joe, as he lay sleeping in his crib. Then I shot toward the ceiling again just because I could."

"It was then I noticed the group of shadowy figures surrounding my bed. They were watching me. I could sense this even though they didn't have much shape or substance. I felt I knew them but I couldn't place how, like when you happen to meet a kid you once played with for an hour in the park, but in a different setting this time, like on line at the Saturday matinee, and no matter how hard you try to think, the kid's name just won't come to you."

"But I knew these figures had authority over me and I thought... teacher."

"Teacher?" Dr. Carroll interrupted. "Do you mean you recognized one as a teacher from school? But you were only three so you hadn't been to school yet." He looked thoughtful.

"That's right. It was more as if I knew them from somewhere, yet I can't say where. Mostly, I just knew they had a lot to teach me if I was willing to learn it. And I knew they weren't going to be pleased with me now, so I considered flying away when their voices surrounded me, as if they were inside my own head and anchored me to the spot."

"Then a deep voice asked, 'What are you doing outside of your body, Sunny?'"

Dr. Carroll shivered slightly, but made no comment, so I continued.

"Leave me alone!" I said to whoever had spoken. "I don't want to be here. I don't want to hurt anymore."

"But Sunny," the voice said, "you know life isn't easy, still, you must keep at it. You agreed to do your best. If you go now you won't be pleased with yourself and you'll only end up coming back anyway. You know how it works."

They fell silent and as if they were willing it to happen, my mind began to fill with thoughts of my parents, my gram who was and is my favorite person, and my baby brother, Joe-Joe, who runs a close second. Joe-Joe chose this moment to wake up with a start. With wide, frightened eyes he peered out from between the crib slats at my too still body, and I think he might have been able to see the figures too because he started screaming, "Shishy! Shishy! Wake up!" He was trying his best to say, Sissy, but Joe-Joe was cursed with a slushy S. early in life."

The doctor snorted once with laughter then regained control of himself and I continued.

"My arms and legs grew heavy and useless, and as Joe-Joe's screams got louder, I sank down closer to the bed. "Oh, all right," I grumbled, "I'll stay, but I'd better get everything straightened out this time because I don't ever want to come back.""

"And so the figures floated up to meet me and I could feel their approval as they encouraged me along the way with a kind of angelic pep talk, then pushed me back down into my body."

"My mother came rushing into the room in answer to Joe-Joe's cries and when she saw me soaked in sweat and looking nearly dead, she shrieked for my father. "Joey, come quick! Sunny looks terrible.""

"I felt a little bit better since my fever had broken, but I sulked while my mother fluttered around me, changing my damp nightie and bedding. I remember feeling relieved I wasn't so sick anymore, but I know I held the thought in the back of my mind that if things got too tough down here, I could always get sick and simply float away.

"Not very good thinking, Sunny," Dr. Carroll interrupted, "That's what you wanted to do when Bull tried to leave you. Wasn't it? Well, wasn't it?"

My throat grew suddenly dry and my back felt slick with sweat. I didn't want to talk about Bull. I didn't want to think about Bull. Dr. Carroll stared me down and I nodded reluctantly at him and wiped my tears away with the Kleenex he pressed into my hand. I sat quietly for a moment and watched the sheep graze on the grassy hill in the painting over Dr. Carroll's desk.

"Was I delirious, Doctor? Or was I dreaming? What do you think?"

He shrugged. "Probably a combination of both. It makes a hell of a story the way you tell it though, doesn't it?"

I nodded again. "I always did love a good story."

Dr. Carroll leaned back in his chair and drew a deep breath. "You've mentioned your gram several times now as a positive influence. Why don't you tell me about her?"

I grinned at him and relaxed. I was on familiar ground now. "I have to warn you," I said. "I can talk about Gram all day."

"So what was Gram like?"

"You mean what is she like? She's my mother's mother, and she's still with us. Gram and I are actually quite a bit alike. We're both Sagittarius, and we're very in tune with each other." "She was a flapper in the roaring twenties, which is exactly what I would have done if I'd been there, and she's lived in almost all of the fifty states. She had one husband, but three marriages. It's confusing unless you know her."

"Well, I'm getting to know you," Dr. Carroll said. "So I have some idea."

"Right. You see, Gram married my mother's father, who happened to be a rogue and a bigamist passing through Iowa on his way to Chicago. She thought he was exciting and a little dangerous so she married him in 1920 and that's how she got to fulfill her number one dream of becoming a flapper in Chicago."

"The reason Gram kept divorcing her husband was because he got into a lot of mischief. Not unlike my husband. But the reason she kept re-marrying him is more interesting. He was born on Lincoln's birthday and she kept expecting him to become more Lincolnesque with time. Abraham Lincoln has always been Gram's favorite man."

"But when she found out her husband was a bigamist she decided to give up on him and that was the last divorce. She made friends with his other wife and kids and his two sisters, all fine people, and she keeps up with them to this very day. That's Gram."

"Do you share her interest in Astrology?"

"Yes, is that crazy? Oh, I don't care anymore. I'm just me. Anyway, she's also into foot reflexology, which is a healing form of massage, and Graphology, the analysis of handwriting. In fact she was the Eastern President of the American Graphological Society for many years and she was also born a psychic medium."

"Are you psychic?"

"Do I look psychic?" He didn't laugh so I continued, "I don't know. Sometimes I think so. I know things before they happen and I pick up information when I first meet people, sense things about them that turn out to be true later. I suppose you don't believe in any of that stuff."

He smiled, but didn't comment.

"Can you guess how I learned to add?"

"Tell me."

"Gram taught me and Joe-Joe to play Blackjack. She loved Reno, Nevada, which she discovered while getting her last divorce and she goes there for a couple of months out of each year. She works as a shill for the house, playing with the casino's money at slow tables because people don't like to gamble alone and she's allowed to keep all of her winnings. She makes a decent living at it, too."

"She sounds like quite a colorful character."

"She's definitely an original. During the forties she performed as a mind reader on the stage in Atlantic City, New Jersey, under the stage name of Princess Anthia, and at various times during her travels she's been a waitress in New Orleans and a bar girl in Chicago during prohibition."

"Do you mean a bar maid?"

"No, it's different. As a bar girl, after her first divorce, she was paid to drink weak tea and coax the club patrons to order more drinks. It paid well so she did that until she became the girlfriend of a mobster. His sweet Italian mother had arranged their first date hoping he would marry Gram and eventually settle down."

"Gram had no idea who he really was until one night when he suddenly pushed her down onto the floor of his car, pulled a Tommy gun out of a secret compartment behind the front seat and machine gunned a speakeasy because they had refused to buy his bootlegged gin. Poor Gram had a terrible time getting away from him and staying alive because she knew too much."

"She had to hide my mother with her family back on the farm in Iowa while she went on the run, dyeing her hair red and calling herself Kimberly Alexander or Helen Sinclair."

Dr. Carroll snorted again with suppressed laughter. "Where did she come up with those names?"

"I don't know about both of them, but she got Kimberly from the Kimberly Diamond Mines in Africa. Her real name is Hazel Alice Shively-Sheldon and she doesn't think it suits her."

"When did she decide to stay in one place long enough for you to get to know her?"

Gram loved the road so she didn't settle down until I was born. She had some great adventures. She's always been my idol because she has lived her life, really lived it, exactly as she's wished."

"That's an important point, Sunny. You should be thinking about what you want to do with your life. Forget your husband for once, put your children's needs aside for the time being too, and really think about what would make you, and only you, happy. Now, back to your story; how did Gram get away from the gangster?" Dr. Carroll's face was flushed and he looked like a kid at the movies.

It was my turn to laugh. "I've made you curious," I teased, "Well, she was able to return to Chicago within the year when word reached her in Florida; the mobster had been gunned down in the street."

"Who was it? Would I recognize his name?" Dr. Carroll leaned forward elbows on his desk.

"I don't know. Honestly I don't. Gram has yet to breathe his name aloud to anyone in our family in spite of the fact that by now his friends are either dead or a hundred and three!"

"So…it was at the height of the depression when Gram returned to Iowa to check in with my mother, and she found her three brothers, as well as her father, all laid off by the railroad. Not surprisingly, she was the only one out of twelve adults who could figure out how to make a living during those hard times."

"It was obvious my mother was better off, for the time being, in a stable environment, with the family, so Gram headed back to Chicago to work this time as a human tape recorder."

"What on earth is that?"

"It was really a great job. All she had to do was hide in a fake fireplace in the office of a private detective and using her short hand, record everything that was said in the office."

"Amazing. It makes sense, though. I never thought about what people did before tape recorders in situations like that."

I nodded. "From this job she moved up to one in a travel agency, quickly becoming engaged to the elderly, though wealthy, owner. The wedding date got postponed, though, indefinitely, when Gram made the huge mistake of taking my mother along with them on a cruise to Bermuda. My mother was such a little bitch that before the ship reached home, she had successfully planted serious doubts in the old guy's mind as to the wisdom of becoming her step-father."

"Gram was the one who actually called the wedding off, though. She was visited nightly for a period of at least a month by a frail, little white-haired spirit who kept shaking her head at Gram and whispering, "Don't do it, Hazel. Don't do it.""

"Did you say, spirit, as in ghost?" Dr. Carroll's eyes appeared larger than normal through the windows of his glasses.

"Yeah. Gram was always comfortable around spirits, having accepted her psychic ability early in life, and she enjoys helping them out when she can, but this spirit had her confused. She kept asking the little spirit what it was she wasn't supposed to do, but the woman acted as if she couldn't hear Gram. And she continued to come each night and deliver her ominous message, despite Gram's requests for more information."

"So what happened?"

"Well, Gram became obsessed with trying to find out who this spirit had been in life. After making a sketch of the woman and showing it to her landlord, she was assured this woman had never lived in the building. At a loss as to what to do next, Gram brought the sketch with her to work and happened to leave it out on her desk as she went about her business."

"One day the owner's adult daughter stopped in at the office. She and Gram had become friendly and as they chatted together, the girl caught sight of the sketch on Gram's desk. "Hazel, why did you draw a picture of my mother?" she asked."

"Gram thought, Bingo! Now we're getting somewhere. Gram had some questions about her mother's death and this was the perfect time to ask, so she did."

"I thought you knew," the daughter said, "My mother died in a horrible accident. She fell down the stairs and broke her neck. My poor father was at home at the time and it took years for him to get over finding her like that, and I think he still wonders if there was something he might have done to prevent the accident."

"That night Gram questioned her fiance about his wife's untimely death and he couldn't look her in the eye as he answered her questions evasively. Gram knew the wife had been the one with the money and that he had inherited it all when she died. So she decided to give the ring back and call off the engagement. She quit the job too, and moved to another part of town and the mysterious spirit never appeared to her again."

"I'd love to meet Gram. She sounds so fascinating."

"She is, Doctor, and she's really funny too. She had a dyed skunk coat as a souvenir of her relationship with that rich man and I recently had the remains of it made into a big, fluffy stole. Gram took one look at it and said, "Thank God that thing can't talk.""

"Mah said, "Mother!" In this shocked voice because that's the way she thinks she should react to things like that, I guess. It's ridiculous since she's known Gram all of her life."

"So what did Gram do for a job when she left her fiancé's business?"

"Next she became a store detective at Marshall Field's Department Store, where she chased many a shoplifter down the street before tackling them around the knees and dragging them back to justice. Gram has always been a big woman at five eleven and she's always been able to defend herself."

"For as long as I've known her she's walked the streets at all hours with an opened can of cayenne pepper in her hand. Not that Gram has often been bothered. She always expects the best from humanity and that's what she usually gets."

"So it was soon after you were born that Gram decided to settle down?"

"Not settle down, exactly, because that hasn't happened yet, but she did decide to move to Newark to be near us. She got her own apartment and a steady regular-person-job with the government as a clerk/typist at Picatinny Arsenal. Knowing it would be difficult, if not impossible, to completely give up her adventures, Gram charmed her bosses into allowing her to take two months off every year so she could travel. She even found temporary replacements to do her job for her until she returned. Money wasn't a problem for her because after a few weeks of traveling to exotic places like Capistrano to watch the swallows return, she would head for Reno and there she had her seasonal job as a shill."

"Gram loves the horses too and I would imagine she's visited every major racetrack in the country. She's the only gambler I've ever known who wins nearly all of the time. I think it's because she never got greedy and only bets small amounts and she always knows when to quit. I also think she's been allowed to win because she always shares whatever she has with those in need."

"What do you mean by allowed?"

"I mean, God lets her win. In addition to sending regular donations to a school for Indian children, she's always the secret 'angel of mercy' in any neighborhood in which she lives. She'll find out which families around her are having hard times and then she'll leave anonymous gifts outside their doors."

"My little brother and I used to have the best time helping Gram buy toys and warm clothing and the fixings for a Christmas dinner for the poor families she'd picked out to help. And I don't think she ever went into the corner drug store on a hot summer afternoon without buying at least three or four raggedy little kids ice cream cones."

"Let me get this straight, now. Gram believes in a combination of Astrology, Graphology, Foot Reflexology, Spiritualism, and God. Do I have that straight?" Dr. Carroll asked, rubbing his head as if a headache was starting."

"Almost. Gram puts God first. She was raised Presbyterian, just like we all were but she was a student of religion, and she told me she found similar blueprints for leading a good life among the teachings of all of the world's great religions. She took Joe-Joe and me to visit different churches each Saturday during the days when churches were left open so anyone could be trusted to come inside and say a prayer. She called these various churches different rooms in God's house."

"Spiritually, she's always been ahead of her time. Gram has always trusted, beyond a doubt, that whatever she really needed in life would be provided for her. Of course she was more than willing to work, which helped a lot, and often during the depression she would send so much of her pay check home to her family in Iowa, that before the end of the week, she'd be forced to ransom her library books for coffee and a doughnut."

"Once after being sick and missing a few days of work, Gram mailed her entire check off to Iowa and then cried, not because she wouldn't have money to live on, but because she so desperately wanted to visit my mother and she couldn't afford the train fare."

"Gram doesn't believe in feeling sorry for yourself so she stepped outside into the windy city and said a prayer to thank God for all the blessings she did have and to her amazement, a gust of wind carried a fifty dollar bill right down to rest at her feet. Gratefully, Gram snatched it up, sent up a big thank you, and then jumped on the next train to spend the weekend with her little girl."

My eyes met Dr. Carroll's and I wanted so much for him to believe in Gram's story. I didn't think I'd be able to face it if he told me it couldn't be true. I didn't want to hear that sometimes desperate people did desperate things and I didn't want to even think Gram might have gotten into some kind of mischief to earn that money. "What do you think?" I asked in a small voice.

"I think it's more likely her horse placed first that day and she didn't want the rest of the family to know it. But it's evident you got your talent for telling a great story from Gram. And I think you got a lot of other wonderful things from her as well."

I sighed with relief. "We all did. My brother and I both lived for our Saturdays with Gram. We loved do go exploring, wearing our sneakers and packing our lunches in bandannas which we carried on sticks over our shoulders, hobo style. We'd walk to the first street corner and then Gram would let Joe-Joe and I take turns choosing whether we'd turn left or right. We never knew where we were or where we were headed. It was the perfect game for two kids with strict, perfectionist parents. When it started to get dark, Gram would knock on a door, or go into a store, ask where we were, then borrow a phone to call a cab to come and get us."

"Some Saturdays we'd just jump on a bus and let it take us wherever it was going. It was so much fun. After Gram bought a car, an old Ford named Napoleon, we often brought our artist's paper and paints with us to the country. There we would sit in the grass, have a picnic, make up plays using the fluffy cloud shapes as characters, and paint the landscape."

"Toward the end of a Saturday, we'd ask Gram to tell us some of her true stories. Not only did Gram know the best true ghost stories, but her ancestors were very interesting too."

"She told us all about Kitty Savage, our great-great grandmother who had come over from Ireland during the potato famine. She married someone from the Hamilton Watch Company family and settled in Ohio. At one time she owned all of the land that Lancaster, Pennsylvania, now stands on."

"One of her daughters, Gram's Granny, had twelve children and when her third husband, Kirby Jobes hung himself in the barn (we never had to ask why with twelve children), she gave up on men and relied on herself."

"She and her daughters opened a half-way house way out in the middle of the wild west where they had to make friends with the Indians, and insist that all of the cowboys and drifters who stopped there for the night, check their guns at the door before they could come in to eat supper."

"They were all a little afraid of Granny Jobes because she was the type of woman who knew how to command respect and the cowboys always called her 'mother' and there was never a fight in her house."

"By the time Gram knew Granny Jobes, she was old and mellow and she always had a fat, gray cat draped around her shoulders, and once when a hungry wild cat tried to get into her cabin, she single-handedly fought it off with a fiery torch. Her sister was as spunky as she was and when her husband ran off, she decided to mine for diamonds in The Dakotas. If a rattlesnake slithered down into the dark mine where she was working, she'd just split it in two with a hoe. That was her specialty as rattlesnakes were a chronic problem."

"You come from a long line of strong women, Sunny."

"I do. But it's pretty obvious that none of the women on that side of the family, with the exception of my mother, had much luck in their choice of a mate. The men in Gram's family either died young, hung themselves, ran off, or were such weasels they had to be divorced."

Dr. Carroll laughed. "I'm surprised Gram never married again. She sounds like an appealing woman."

"She is…and it isn't as if Gram doesn't like men because she always has a boyfriend. One especially nice old gentleman dropped dead at his ninety fifth birthday party when all of his friends from the Senior Citizen's Club and most of his large family jumped out of hiding places and yelled, "Surprise!"

"You're making that up."

"I swear I'm not. Gram told me. She says it's getting harder every year to find men to whom she can appear to be a sweet young thing since she's now past eighty. And do you know that in all the years since her last divorce in the late twenties, she has never lived with a man. She says the best advice she can offer me about men is to be sure I send them home to wash their own dirty socks."

"That's good advice for a woman who doesn't want to get married again."

"Again?" The tears began to well up and overflow. How would I ever get over Bull?

How could I go through with something as final an ending to our story as a divorce?

Dr. Carroll sat up straight and pulled his chair closer to the desk. All business again, he cleaned his glasses then replaced them on his prominent nose. "Sunny," he began, "You mentioned earlier that your mother has never remarried either."

"That's right. My mother is a strong independent woman even though she had a sad childhood. She never saw her father after her parents' last divorce, and Gram made her go to a boarding school in Chicago."

"Made her go? How could Gram afford it during the depression?"

"Well, when Gram was a child she said she had delusions of grandeur and hated the peaceful life on the farm. She couldn't wait to grow up and move to the exciting city. More than anything in the world she longed to go to boarding school in glamorous Chicago, and that is why, when my mother turned seven in 1928, Gram saved and sacrificed to send her to the fanciest French boarding school she could find."

"And of course my mother hated it. She spent years of miserable, lonely nights there, crying herself to sleep, and living for the weekends when her larger than life mother would come and rescue her after her week of work had ended, and for two days she would revel in Gram's unconditional love and complete indulgence."

"According to Mah, the only good things that came of that school, is that she learned impeccable and in my opinion, irritating overly lady-like manners, how to order from a French menu, and how to play Bach, Mozart, and Beethoven on the piano with the skill of a virtuoso."

"She found solace in her music and spent hours each day practicing until they had to drag her off the stool and make her go to bed at night. She grew so proficient she was selected to perform a piece of classical music she had composed herself at The Chicago Conservatory of Music before the actual concert began, as an opening act. She was praised in the newspapers as a child prodigy and Gram was certain she had done the right thing in forcing my mother to attend that school."

"But my mother continued to hate school, even though it meant she and Gram were at least living in the same town and had all of their weekends together. As a small child I would cry for her suffering when she would tell me about those years, and I was confused to learn the best person I knew on earth, my gram, could have damaged my mother so deeply, and scarred her emotionally for all time in the name of misguided love. Now I know we all scar our kids in some way…No one gets out of childhood completely unscathed."

"How old was Gram when you were born?"

"Gram was fifty. I love to look at the pictures we have of her holding me as if I were her own baby. I look so happy nestled against her large breasts, gazing up into her soft, sexy hazel eyes; watching her fine, wavy hair move gently in the breeze, loving the sound of the best wild laugh I will ever hear."

"Back in those days, Gram was always in such a hurry to get going, she usually had her make-up on a little crooked. Maybe she'd have too much rouge on one cheek, or a section of her mouth would be pale, where the lipstick missed making contact, but she always took the time to manicure her stubby typist's nails and to apply Real Real Red nail polish by Revlon."

"I loved to sit on her lap and poke at her big bosom and catch whiffs of either Evening In Paris or Temptation perfume. "What's in there, Gram?" I'd ask, peering down the front of her dress at the quivering cleavage, tamed and trapped by the huge construction of lace brassiere. (No mere bra for my gram.)"

"That's my lunch, Sweetheart," she'd say. For years I wondered why Gram would want to carry her lunch around stuffed in both cups of her brassiere especially when she carried a purse as big as a small suitcase. But despite her open, honest ways, Gram was also a woman of mystery and we liked not knowing all of the answers."

"If Joe-Joe and I asked her to draw with us as we sat at the kitchen table, eating the gooey doughnuts Gram always brought for us and waiting for her to finish up her boring talk with Mah so we could get on with the fun, she always drew pictures of graceful birds in flight."

"You and Joe-Joe were lucky growing up with a gram like that, Sunny."

"I've often thought she saved my life."

"In a way she still can save your life," the doctor said, nodding. "Think of her when you feel especially vulnerable. Remember how Gram has made her own way in life and how she lives each day to the fullest.

There's nothing you can't do, Sunny, if you just make up your mind to do it. And that includes getting over Bull and moving on."

I nodded, but only half believed it. I still couldn't imagine life without my husband without feeling a crushing pain in the center of my being.

"Now tomorrow I want you to be prepared to get down to work. I want to finish up the stories about your childhood and then get into Bull and your life together. Also, I want you to prepare yourself for a session with Bull. He called me back and is scheduled to come in next Tuesday at 11 A.M."

CHAPTER 8

I felt better after my long session with Dr. Carroll. For the rest of the afternoon whenever I was on the verge of tears at the thought of Bull, I would instantly replace him with Gram's face, smiling at me and saying, "Men are wonderful…as long as you send them home to wash their own smelly socks." And it worked.

Joe-Joe was bringing Mah and Gram for a visit on Sunday and although I missed them, I dreaded seeing them because I was ashamed of breaking down. But lately I'd decided to believe my doctors when they said thinking like that only made things worse and if I was to get better I was going to have to learn to reach out for help, not only to the doctors, but to my family and friends as well.

Helen was out of her room and back with the rest of us, but she was very different now. I'd never seen anyone this deeply depressed. It was as if the Helen we'd known was hiding and every now and then she'd let just enough of herself come out, to hold her place, until she was ready to give a meaningful amount of her energy to the task of living again. She never even laughed anymore at the stories I told in group and I didn't know what to do to help her.

Most of the people who had been here on the day I was admitted had either gone home or on to be committed to various mental hospitals and treatment centers. Despite that, Alexander had calmed down a bit on the subject of my revealing too much to Dr. Carroll. He wasn't as concerned I'd 'talk too much' to Dr. Fazio since he was a behavioral psychologist and wasn't at all interested in hearing about my childhood. Mostly, Dr. Fazio's goal was to get me 'back on my feet and functioning in society,' as he was fond of saying.

"We'd better talk about your drinking," he'd said to me that very afternoon.

"What about it?" I'd asked, walking over to the window and enjoying the view of the East Stroudsburg University campus which stretched below us and continued into the distance. The mountains rose up to meet the sky as far away as my eye could discern shapes. It was a perfect spring day and I longed to be outside and feel the air and sunlight on my skin.

"Have you ever had an episode of uncontrolled anger or deep depression or suicidal behavior when you were stone-cold sober?"

I thought for a moment before answering, "No...I acted out in anger, but I wasn't uncontrollable."

He grinned and nodded. "So doesn't it follow that if you stop drinking, you will stop acting crazy?"

"You tell me. But I guess it's certainly worth a shot."

He leaned back in his swivel chair and put his hands behind his head. "It certainly is."

Dr. Fazio worked in his shirt sleeves rolled up to his elbows and I liked his informal style. Sometimes, though, I thought he was looking for easy answers to solve the most confusing and complex issues of my life.

I felt my cheeks burn with resentment and my first instinct was to turn away, say something smart, and cover up my feelings. Instead I took a deep breath and spoke my mind.

"Dr. Fazio, you know I've been under an extreme amount of stress for a very long time. I hid my anger and my pain from my husband and children, the best that I could, and I don't think it's at all surprising I finally erupted in a fit of 'uncontrolled anger.' I think I may have been justified in expressing that anger and I resent the way you have of looking for easy answers to my problems. Yes, I drank wine nearly every day, but I'm not convinced my anger or my so-called craziness was necessarily caused by drinking. I was self -medicating, and without the tranquillizing effects of the wine I might have killed someone."

He sat up in his chair and leaned forward. "By 'someone' I assume you mean your husband or maybe his girlfriend"

"Oh, I don't want to kill anybody," I said, dropping into the chair opposite his desk as if I were dead weight.

"Not even yourself?"

I just shook my head and wished I were someplace else. "I'm not the type of person who does things half-assed. If I wanted to be dead, I would be dead right now. End of discussion."

If only I'd handled things better I would have been able to spend this lovely day with my kids. We might have taken a long walk in the woods, stopped to have a picnic on the banks of the wild rushing creek behind our farmhouse. Now that I had some distance from Bull, I was

beginning to think I had allowed him to become so much more important to me than he ever deserved to be.

Doctor Fazio crossed his arms over his broad chest then cleared his
throat before speaking, as if he knew I wasn't going to like what he had
to say. "You know, Sunny, you've appeared to be much more stable than
we first suspected since about a day after you got here. In fact some of
the staff doubts you have a serious problem and have gone so far as to
suggest you're faking it. Like maybe you thought you needed a vacation
from your life, or wanted to punish your husband by scaring him."

I fought tears, and to hide my confusion, I rose and went back to
stand before the window. How could they not recognize my suffering? I
forced a laugh. "Doctor," I said, "The next time I go someplace where it
costs me $5000.00 a week, it's going to be where they have palm trees,
turquoise water and no doctors who ask annoying questions. And that
nut-job, Mrs. Hollander, is definitely not coming on my next vacation."

He laughed. "She is something with that table, isn't she? But she is
good at analyzing art."

"Since analyze means to study critically, I believe it. You know,
Doctor Fazio, I came here because I felt like dying, but a much stronger
part of me wanted to live for my kids and I had high hopes you people
could help me. I felt better the second day I was here because it was
such a relief to be out of the stress and tension of my marriage. It hurts a
lot that the fact that I'm feeling better bugs the hell out of the very people I thought truly wanted to see me get better. I'm confused. I would
think you all should be hoping I'll make a full recovery and become a
reasonably happy, well-adjusted citizen."

Dr. Fazio looked uncomfortable. "Of course that's the eventual goal,
Sunny, but it just can't happen overnight. And in your case it appears as
if you want to believe it can, and has."

"Ha!" I said, "I'm still dying inside. You'll be relieved to know I'm
still a very unhappy woman. I don't know what the hell I'm going to
do when I get out of here. I still can't even deal with the idea of a
separation." I gulped, my throat aching with unshed tears, "And I can
barely even say the word divorce. I've never felt so alone. The kids will
have a million questions and they'll expect me to have answers for
them, because I always did before…and they'll expect me to be there
for them…to be strong." I was fidgeting with the drapery chord and I

noticed my hands were trembling. I crossed my arms and faced him, glaring. "Is that fucked up enough for you?"

"Now Sunny," he said, "don't get upset. The only point I'm trying to make is you don't have to pretend here. You can relax. We want you to be honest about your feelings, with yourself, as well as with us. It's the only way we'll ever be able to sort it all out. And everyone on the staff here wants to help you. I hope you believe that."

I was trembling all over from holding the tears back and so I let them fall. All of my life I had prided myself on being able to act well enough to hide my pain and most of my true thoughts from everyone around me. Maybe it was a talent I shouldn't have taken so much pride in.

"If you say so," I said, "And I'll think about my drinking. I'll probably stop, at least until I get back on my feet. It doesn't really help, and it definitely doesn't change anything."

"You've got that right."

I faced him squarely. "You sound as if you speak from experience."

He stared at me for a few beats then said, "I do."

*   *   *

Early in the evening, the weather turned colder. "Chilly for late June," the nurse said when she came in with the dinner cart. A violent storm bent the trees nearly in half. I could see them far below the long glass wall of windows. Bright spring leaves flew through electrically charged air while brand new flowers were beaten down into the mud by sharp needles of rain.

Inside the community room, various groups of people sat playing board games, card games, sketching pictures, or just reading quietly by themselves.

Alexander was so anxious to escape back into the world of my novel that he suggested we help serve the dinner trays to hurry the whole thing along. We ate quickly that night, barely tasting the broiled chicken, broccoli and mashed potatoes, with warm cheesecake for dessert.

"I believe this is a true story, Sunny," Alexander said, as we settled into our special corner and I opened the manuscript to the page where we had stopped the night before. "Sometimes when you're reading to me; I feel as if you're articulating my own memories." He shook his head and scratched his nose. Then he settled into his customary position when listening to me, head back against the sofa, hands resting on his knees.

With one finger I traced the rough map his prominent veins made on the back of his hands. He smiled at me and didn't move.

He definitely reminded me of Reverend Putnam, not in looks, but in his manner, and as I read on into the evening I recognized more similarities.

*   *   *

Adelaide Sullivan dressed with special care each Sunday in anticipation of Charles Putnam's sermon. She used every opportunity that came her way to speak to the reverend and I wondered if it was as obvious to the others as it was to me.

She peered myopically into her silver hand mirror and adjusted the lace collar she had added to soften the effect of her simple dark-blue taffeta dress.

Her hair was parted in the middle, plaited, and arranged in a large coil at the nape of her neck. The fringe I had just helped her to cut was frizzled in a frame about her face in an attempt to soften her looks. Still, her unremarkable face, with nearly invisible eyelashes, stared unchanged from the mirror and she frowned slightly.

Adelaide was nearing her twenty-ninth birthday and she had never had a serious beau, according to the rumors. I hoped teaching was a joy to her, for she appeared to have so little else in her life.

She sighed and turned toward me. I sat on a trunk in the rear corner of the wagon, waiting for her. We had gotten into the habit of sitting together each Sunday while the reverend preached. "You look pretty today, Miss Sullivan," I said.

"Thank you, Dear." She smiled gratefully and for that brief moment she did look pretty.

The flap at the rear of the wagon lifted and Madeleine Sullivan stuck her white-haired head inside and said, "Hurry Girls, the reverend is about to begin. I've spread a blanket for us near the front, but we should hurry or we'll have to walk past everyone with the reverend speaking. Oh, dear! Perhaps I should have chosen a place for us toward the rear of the crowd."

I patted Mrs. Sullivan on her fragile, bowed shoulder. "Don't fret. I'm sure we'll make it in plenty of time. He never begins before eight."

As we walked toward the grassy hill beside which we had made our camp, Mrs. Sullivan clutched at Adelaide's arm and whispered constantly into her ear. I was walking on Adelaide's other side and although I couldn't make out her exact words, I could plainly hear Adelaide's sullen replies. "Yes, Mother. I am sure you're right, Mother. I shall be careful. As you well know, Mother, I am prone to be cautious."

Papa stood at the rear of the crowd with several men and he called out to us as we hurried past, "Hello, there, Miss Sullivan. Mrs. Sullivan. A fine morning, don't you agree? And Little Mite you look fetching today."

Mrs. Sullivan flinched at his boisterous greeting, but I gave him a smile and waved. Although Papa had ruined my life, he was still my Papa...and all I had left in my world.

As we settled ourselves on the blanket, I ran my fingers through the tall, sweet-smelling Pennsylvania grass all around us. The sun was already warm on my back despite the early hour and I was glad I had chosen to wear a light, green-sprigged frock of voile. My hair was caught up by a ribbon and I was glad of that, too. The reverend had been known to preach until the sun was a fireball high in the August sky.

The crowd grew suddenly quiet and I looked up to find Charles Putnam had stepped forward and was standing tall, commanding our attention by the natural force of his presence among us.

He was a man of contradictions. Very shy on first meeting and hard to get to know, but when he functioned as a minister, when he stepped in front of a crowd, he was transformed.

His rich, deep voice carried easily on the summer air. "Friends, as another week begins, I ask you to bow your heads and join me in giving thanks to The Lord God our Savior for the safe passage he has granted us through this wild country."

We all bowed our heads over clasped hands. "Dear lord, as we draw ever closer to our destination in the great Ohio Territory, we thank you for your blessings."

I opened my eyes and sneaked a look around at the others. Adelaide was flushed with excitement as she leaned over her tightly clasped hands and trembled slightly. Papa had moved forward and was sitting on a blanket with Bruin. They both looked nearly angelic as they prayed with as much enthusiasm as they gave to any task they set their minds to.

Cassie Taylor was edging toward Bruin, slowly inching her way through the grass, so very much like a poisonous snake, as she targeted Bruin, moving from her parent's blanket toward the one Bruin and Papa shared. Her head was bowed and her eyes were downcast as if she were still praying. What a bold witch! I felt the pull of other eyes coming from the left. I turned slightly and found myself staring straight into the tiny, piggy-eyes of the great hulking Margaret Taylor, mother of Cassie.

Mrs. Taylor stared back at me as if I was some sort of insect and I shivered and looked quickly away. I could certainly see where Cassie got her meanness.

I pulled my attention back to the reverend. He never looked happier than when he was preaching a sermon, reading from the scriptures, or leading his flock in prayer.

Finally the prayer was over and people began to raise their heads rubbing their eyes at the sudden blinding effects of the brilliant sunlight. The reverend launched directly into what I prayed would be a blessedly brief sermon and I took this opportunity to study him as he spoke on…and on.

I knew little about him personally, but in the weeks since we had been on the road, I'd come to rely on his strength and integrity, as had all of the others in our number. The reverend was a man who took his role as spiritual leader very seriously, and I often wondered if he cared as much for anything else, or if he ever could.

It was certainly odd he had never married. I glanced over at Adelaide and was amazed by the look of naked adoration on her face. She stared up at Reverend Putnam as if he was God himself, and I pitied her and was a bit frightened for her all at the same time. What if the reverend failed to return her feelings? Could she survive such a crushing disappointment?

The reverend gave a heartfelt benediction and then we were free of our religious obligations for the day. I stood gratefully on stiff legs and stretched my back. Adelaide helped her mother to her feet and then scanned the crowd until her eyes finally rested upon Reverend Putnam.

She turned to me and placed two long white fingers against my sleeve, "He is a superb speaker. Don't you agree, Jessamyn?" she asked. Her light-hazel eyes were soft and rather pretty as she turned her head again to follow his progress from couple to couple.

Sunday morning was hand shaking time for the reverend and he appeared to thrive on it. He smiled at Amanda Masters and tickled her grandson, James, under the chin before moving on to pat ailing old Mrs. Atherton on her stooped back and to give words of encouragement to her son and daughter-in-law.

"I think he was born to the calling," I said to Adelaide, but she didn't appear to hear me. She was coaxing her mother along and moving as inconspicuously as possible toward Reverend Putnam.

"Feeling better today, Jessamyn?" Bruin asked from directly behind me.

I spun around to face him. "Better than what?"

He laughed at me and I gave him a mean look. I held Bruin partially responsible or Papa's folly in dragging me half-way to hell on this god-forsaken wagon train. But if truth be told I was glad that if I had to be here, at least I had Bruin's company as a diversion. Of course I had no intention of letting him know that, at least not until he was properly punished for his part in all of this.

He tapped my chin with his finger and raised his left eyebrow at me. "What I meant to say is you look as if you feel a good bit better than you did the last time I saw you."

I stuck my tongue out at him and he scratched his head and looked down at the ground. "Jessamyn, I…I'm really sorry you hate going west. I won't lie and say I'm not glad you and your papa are with us, but it saddens me to see you suffer. And I don't know why your papa didn't let you bring your easel and painting equipment. If I had been told, I would have found room in my wagon. I think it was wrong of your papa to do that, but I won't give you permission to tell him that." His smile was so disarming I had to fight to hold onto my bad mood.

"Wrong doesn't even begin to address it, Bruin," I snapped, "It's criminal. But it's an old fight between Papa and me and I don't think we'll ever get it resolved. Papa just hates my painting. If you ask him about it he'll tell you it's a terrible waste of time and effort and I know in my heart that is the real reason he couldn't find room in the wagon for the only thing that matters to me."

Bruin flinched. He looked as wounded by my words as I was by Papa's thoughtless actions. "Listen, Jessamyn," he said, "If your papa doesn't replace your art supplies when we get to Marietta, I'll see to it you get them."

Bruin's eyes were kind. I gifted him with a weak smile. "That is very sweet of you, but I'm sure it won't be necessary since I shall torture Papa until he replaces them at the first opportunity. I can't imagine he will be able to hold out for very long under the attack I have planned for him."

Bruin and I laughed together until Cassie Taylor crept up behind us and insinuated herself herself into the thick of our conversation.

"Share the joke with me, Bruin," she said in her snaky little voice.

Honestly, I couldn't see what any man would possibly see in her. Her long auburn hair did move somewhat appealingly about her shoulders on a windy day, but her green eyes flashed with a cold light I can only describe as unnatural, and truly, she was far too skinny for the current fashion. In my opinion, her face held the lean, hungry look of a she-wolf.

But Bruin, ever the gentleman, spoke with her for a few moments while I looked about for someone else to gossip with. I had no stomach for Cassie and her nonsense. Bruin would have to take care of himself.

I turned gratefully to watch the reverend and Adelaide saunter up to us and instantly I felt my eyes drawn to his. He always stared at me so beseechingly, as if unanswered questions plagued him; questions to which only I had the answer. He was a strange man, but one who tried his best to live a life above reproach.

"G-Good Morning, Miss Jessamyn," he said, "Is your father well? I noticed he appeared unusually weary last evening."

"My father is famously as strong as an ox, Reverend," I said, thinking the question a bit odd. "In truth he is thriving on this trip, though for the life of me, I can't imagine why."

The reverend shifted his gaze to Cassie. "And how are you this fine morning, Miss Cassandra?" he inquired, "And you, Bruin?"

"Couldn't be better on so fine a day," Bruin shook his offered hand and complimented him on his sermon while Cassie bobbed down in a ridiculous, affected curtsy as if she were three years old.

"I am absolutely wonderful, Sir. Thank you so much for asking." The foolish girl was actually flirting with the reverend. Cassie Taylor was and always would be, shameless.

A touch of color sprang into Reverend Putnam's cheeks. Adelaide stood silent at his side, her eyes fixed upon him, that look of slavish devotion once again visiting her plain face.

The reverend turned toward Adelaide and his cheeks grew even pinker as he shied away from her gaze. "Adelaide and I were just t-talking about our mutual admiration for the sonnets of William Shakespeare." He looked somewhere over my head and off into the dense brush.

Adelaide shifted her weight from side to side as if dreading what might come next. Her hands fluttered up to play with the lace collar in a gesture so like one I'd seen her mother use on many occasions.

"M-Miss J-Jessamyn…Miss Cassandra…Bruin…I-I was wondering if perhaps the three of you would like to join us at my campfire this evening after supper for a reading of Mr. Shakespeare's work?"

Adelaide appeared to be in danger of fainting and I took her cold, limp hand in mine. "Are you ill, Miss Sullivan?"

She snatched her hand away and I felt resentment in her glance. But I couldn't see what I might have done to offend her. Then a possible explanation occurred to me. Perhaps she, too, had noticed the way the reverend looked at me and stuttered slightly whenever he came too near.

"Don't be a foolish child, Jessamyn," Adelaide said through tight lips, "I am perfectly fine. And please call me Adelaide. I told you we aren't in a classroom any longer."

Bruin was grinning like a cat and I wanted to give him a little kick in the shin, but of course I had to control myself in front of the group, so I merely frowned at him.

"Charles!" he said in an amused voice. "You surprise me. I had no idea there was a romantic side to you."

The poor reverend flushed crimson and I felt so sorry for him, I spoke to divert the attention away from his embarrassment. "Well, I for one, think it's a charming idea to have a reading of Shakespeare's sonnets around a campfire. In fact, I think it is past due the time we had some culture around here. I don't know about the rest of you, but I am bored beyond bearing by this monotonous dust-laden countryside."

The reverend smiled weakly at me. "You can thank Miss Sullivan. It was actually her idea."

"And it's a very good one. Why it'll be almost as if we're back in Boston," I continued, "Thank you for asking me, Reverend. Adelaide. I will certainly come."

Adelaide stood as silent as a sphinx. Bruin, then Cassie, each accepted his invitation. Only then did I realize what I had done. I had ruined Adelaide's evening.

*   *   *

After supper Papa declined my suggestion that he join us, begging off in order to join several of the older men in what I suspected would be a lively game of cards. I kissed the top of his head and reminded him not to gamble for money since the reverend would surely frown upon it should he find out and it was the quickest way to ruin a friendship, or to incite violence, especially if they planned to mix in a bit of the jug I knew Papa, and most of the other men, had hidden under the wagon seat.

Then I was off to the reverend's campsite, and for the first time since leaving home, my step was light and I felt almost festive. I wasn't tired this evening either since we rested on the Sabbath and never traveled at all. This one day of respite from the hellacious jostling of a wagon that leaked when it rained and admitted no fresh air when it didn't, permitted me to recover sufficiently to face another week of torture by mud or dust on this endless journey westward.

I had resisted the impulse to dress up for this 'little party' since I didn't want to risk stealing any more of Adelaide's thunder. It made me sad to think she might grow to dislike me just because a man I had no interest in, and who was far too old for me, seemed to fancy me. Especially since I had no control over whether or not he would choose to court Adelaide.

I secretly hoped he would court her since in my mind they already appeared to resemble each other, and they both had quiet, shy natures unless they were functioning in their respective professional capacities.

The evening had brought a chill to the air and I gathered my dark-red shawl more tightly about me. The wagons' were arranged in our customary semi-circle, and since the reverend's wagon was ten wagons around to the left of ours, I hurried along in that direction.

I was passing the Master's wagon and couldn't help overhearing the squeals of their three small children who protested an early bedtime. "Silence!" roared Mr. Masters from outside the wagon. He splashed a bucket of dirty washing-up water on the fire. Sizzle and wood smoke rose up to blend in a great cloud of steam. We smiled at each other as the children settled quietly down to bed inside. "Evening, Jessamyn," he said, as sweet as you please.

"Evening, Mr. Masters."

Amanda Master's strong soprano voice rang out into the night as she sang a sweet lullaby to her little ones and I hurried on, sidestepping a small boy who darted by in his nightshirt.

"Catch that devil!" his mother shouted from the next wagon and I snatched him up, a bundle of flailing arms and giggles. His brown eyes laughed at me and I rubbed his chubby cheek against mine before turning him over to his mama.

She held him around the middle, belly-side-down like a suitcase, and sighed, rubbing her protruding abdomen with the other hand and looking pitifully exhausted. Her name was Veronica Sue Larner and she was obviously pregnant and due shortly, but of course I couldn't dare ask when her day was to come. "I'll carry him inside for you," I offered, reaching out to take him back, but she shook her head and half smiled. "No bother. I'm used to it."

They waved to me as they went inside the wagon and as I moved along I whispered a prayer for her, hoping she wouldn't give birth until after our arrival in Marietta.

Cal Witherspoon sat on a rock near the edge of the brush a bit beyond the circle of wagons. He strummed a banjo and hummed along. "Nice night for a walk, Miss Jessamyn," he said in that mellow voice of his. "But don't go off beyond the last wagon. We haven't seen any Injuns yet, still that doesn't mean they aren't out there."

"I'll be careful. Papa already warned me. Play a ballad next, Cal, will you?"

He nodded and played. 'Roses never open to the moonlight,' one of his best songs. Cal made it up himself.

"I have a feeling you could get that song published in New York City if you sent it in to one of those music-sheet companies," I suggested.

He laughed at the notion and went back to the song. I hummed along with him as I made my way past the other three wagons that stood between me and the reverend's wagon. As I hurried past the Kelly's, the honeymooners in our group, I heard a giggle and muffled murmur, and I swear the wagon swayed back and forth a few times before settling back down. I clapped my hands over my ears and stared down at the ground. What a place for a honeymoon! And on the sabbath! Some people had strange ideas indeed.

I could smell the coffee two wagons away. The reverend had obviously made a fresh pot of coffee for our poetry meeting. He sat alone on a wooden crate in front of his fire and thumbed through a worn copy of what I assumed was Shakespeare's sonnets.

Adelaide approached from the other side of the clearing since she and her mother were two wagons further to the left. She carried a covered dish and I wished I'd thought to bring something too.

Adelaide had uncoiled her hair and it fell in waves nearly to her waist. She had added a ribbon tied in a bow on the top of her head, and I almost giggled. I was certain her mother had talked her into wearing it. She still wore her good blue taffeta dress and I hoped she would have a good time tonight. She was a dear soul and deserved some happiness in life.

The reverend stood to greet us. "I'm so glad you ladies could join me this evening," he said, gesturing to the other crates he'd placed around the fire.

Adelaide thrust the tin of muffins at him. "I hope you like blackberry," she said, wringing her hands. "I picked them fresh this afternoon. Mother made the muffins, though."

"How nice of both of you," I said, lifting a corner of the linen towel she had covered them with and taking a breath of the fragrant golden treats.

"I don't know how your mother can bake so perfectly over a campfire," I said, "I try, but nothing comes out half as well as it did in the oven back home."

"It requires patience to bake well, Jessamyn," she said with a teacher-like look. "Mother sets her footed Dutch oven on a firm base of flat stones and she has the knack of regulating the size and therefore the temperature of her fire."

"Perhaps I could watch her the next time she bakes and maybe I'll pick up the knack," I said. It was obvious to me I was upsetting Adelaide just by being there.

"Don't start without me," Bruin called from the back of his wagon. He was camped next to the reverend, and all he had to do was jump down and amble over, which he did sporting a big friendly grin.

"Would you like some coffee, Bruin? Ladies?" the reverend asked.

"Sure would," Bruin answered, "Hot and black."

Adelaide insisted on pouring for everyone and acting as hostess for the reverend's little party, bustling about serving us each steaming mugs of coffee that would keep us up all night, and warm, delicious, blackberry muffins.

Bruin and I sat down on the crates across the fire from Adelaide and the reverend, and this seemed to improve Adelaide's mood somewhat.

"Mother is very excited about moving to Beaver Valley, Reverend," she said, beaming at him.

"Isn't that nice," he said, scratching his head and shifting on his crate.

"I can't wait to get there," Bruin added with a chuckle. "How about you, Jessamyn? Aren't you itching to get your first look at Beaver Valley?"

I frowned at Bruin. "Itching at the thought of it."

The firelight cast shadows on Adelaide's features and in this dim light the ribbon in her hair made her appear younger. Her hair had always been her best feature, and it looked especially nice flowing down in light burnished-copper ringlets.

"You look especially lovely tonight, Miss Adelaide," Bruin said, as if reading my thoughts.

Her hands flew to her face. "Why...thank you, Bruin. I...appreciate your kind compliment. She glanced at the reverend and then straightened her already straight spine.

She smiled; then blushed.

The crickets chirped in the tall grass and the slight chill in the air caused us all to move closer to the fire. A long shadow fell across our gathering and we all were drawn to look toward the intruder.

Cassie stood tapping her foot angrily, her arms crossed over the low-cut bodice of her tart-like frock. "I thought you were coming to escort me, Bruin. Did you forget our conversation earlier?"

Bruin stood and extended his hand. "I'm sorry, Cassie, I guess I did forget. But no harm done, you're here now."

She smirked at him and pulled the crate around to Bruin's other side. As she bent over the crate and scooted it along the ground, her cleavage grew more pronounced and threatened to overflow the tenuous boundaries of her bodice; yet she remained in this position far longer than necessary and spoke boldly to Bruin.

"I didn't realize, Bruin, that you had such a strong passion for poetry you would forget all else in your haste to get here. Yet I must admit nothing I learn about you seems to surprise me."

Bruin laughed. "Now, Cassie, I didn't have that far to go." He gestured toward his wagon.

"Why don't we all sit down now so the reverend can begin reading," I suggested, "If your voice grows tired, Reverend, we can take turns."

The reverend smiled warmly at me. "Do you have a personal favorite, M-Miss Jessamyn?"

I shrugged. "Not really. I like them all. You pick."

Adelaide fidgeted upon her crate, uncomfortable whenever the reverend's attention strayed to me, and Bruin appeared mindlessly mesmerized by the brevity of Cassie's attire. I wanted to kick his crate out from under him, but I restrained myself.

The reverend took one last sip of coffee and began in his deep soft voice:

> "When I have seen by time's fell hand defaced
> The rich proud cost of outworn buried age;
> When sometimes lofty towers I see down-razed
> And brass eternal slave to mortal rage;
> When I have seen the hungry ocean gain
> Advantage on the kingdom of the shore,
> And the firm soil win of the watery main,"

That shameless hussy Cassie Taylor was actually running the toe of her slipper up the underside of Bruin's outstretched leg. She probably thought she could get away with it in the darkness, but as he began to shake with suppressed laughter, I glanced down and caught her at it. I hoped a spark from the blazing fire would shoot up and burn a hole in her stocking. She deserved more than that to my way of thinking!

> "When I have seen such interchange of state,
> Or state itself confound decay;
> Ruin hath taught me thus to ruminate,"

I glanced across at Adelaide and wondered how she could keep her face set in such a look of mindless worship. It would wear me out to do so…and if I were a man, I would grow quite bored with such adoration. Unfortunately for Adelaide, and perhaps for me as well, the reverend had ceased to read from the text and was reciting by heart, all the time staring into my own eyes with such a rapt gaze I couldn't look away. He held my eyes with the power of his own and recited on…

> "That time will come and take my love away.
> This thought is as a death, which it fears to lose."

Although it was warm enough by the fire, I shivered and then pulled my gaze from his. Adelaide cleared her throat and spoke first. "That was lovely, Reverend. I've never heard it recited with so much feeling."

I shivered again and Bruin asked if I needed another shawl. I assured him I would be fine as I was but Cassie interrupted, nearly shouting, "She must be very cold-blooded if she needs two shawls in August."

Her loud, cruel laughter rang out into the night as the reverend fixed her with a stern look. "That remark was uncalled for, Miss Taylor. This is a friendly gathering and I insist you act accordingly if you wish to remain in our company."

Cassie sprang to her feet, and hands on hips, she glared at the reverend. "I am insulted, Reverend Putnam. And I shall tell my father what you have said to me this evening."

"You do that, Miss Taylor. In fact, you might want to go do that right now," the reverend said in his quiet voice.

Bruin and I exchanged a look and we both had to fight the desire to laugh out loud. As large and repulsive and imposing as Cassie's mother, Margaret Taylor was, Cassie's father, Henry Taylor, was as womanish as a man could get and still retain the label. He fairly quaked in fear of his unpleasant wife and as far as anyone knew stood up to no man for any reason and most likely never would. Margaret Taylor fought all the battles in that family and he was wise to stay out of her way.

Cassie saw our exchange and grew angrier. She stamped her foot in the dirt. "I'm leaving Bruin; are you coming with me?"

Bruin nearly choked on his muffin. "No, Cassie," he said, "I'm enjoying the sonnets. You know your way back to your wagon."

Cassie flounced off in a snit and it took the rest of us a moment to regain our composure.

Adelaide looked the most uncomfortable of us all and I expected her to be the next one to bid us all goodnight.

The reverend appeared strangely unconcerned by the drama Cassie Taylor always left in her wake. He turned several pages in his book and cleared his throat as if to begin reading again.

"May I have a turn at reading, Charles?" Bruin asked suddenly. "I have a particular favorite I'd like to share with all of you if you don't mind."

The reverend stared at Bruin for a brief moment as if not certain what he might have in mind, but, reluctantly, he did finally hand the book over to Bruin.

Bruin searched about for only a short time before he located the sonnet he was after. He turned to me and smiled. "Listen carefully to this one, Jessamyn. It was written for you even if Shakespeare was unaware of it at the time."

The reverend stood abruptly and excused himself, stating that the fire needed another log. Adelaide chose this moment to re-fill our coffee cups and I was left to wonder which sonnet Bruin felt would bring me to mind.

Soon we all had settled down once again, and so Bruin began in a deep, strong voice:

> "Who will believe my verse in time to come,
> If it were fill'd with your most high desserts?
> Though yet, heaven knows, it is but as a tomb
> Which hides your life and shows not half your parts.
> If in fresh numbers all your graces,
> The age to come would say 'That poet lies;
> Such heavenly touches ne'er touch'd earthly faces.'
> So should my papers yellow'd with their age
> Be scorn'd like old men of less truth than tongue,

> And your true rights be term'd a poet's rage
> And stretched meter of an antique song:
> But were some child of yours alive that time,
> You should live twice; in it and in my rhyme."

Everyone was staring at me and my cheeks burned with embarrassment. I didn't know what to think. It was a lovely sonnet and it had been kind of Bruin to say it was written for me; especially since he had spent most of the evening staring down the front of Cassie Taylor's dress. But he was still a dear friend to me. I glanced at him and then looked away. I was uncomfortable making a comment in front of the others.

"Shall I compare you to a summer's day?"

It was Adelaide reciting now. She sat still, her eyes shut as she continued, reciting by heart.

> "Thou art more lovely and temperate,
> Rough winds do shake the darling buds of May,
> And summer's lease hath all too short a date:"

I was taken by surprise at the depth of feeling and passion in her voice. The reverend appeared shocked too.

> "Sometimes too hot the eye of Heaven shines,
> And often is his gold complexion dimm'd:
> And every fair from fair sometimes declines,
> By chance or nature's changing course untrimm'd;
> But thy eternal summer shall fade.
> Nor lose possession of that fair thou owest;
> Nor shall Death brag thou wander'st in his shade,
> When in eternal lines to time thou growest."

I gazed up at the full moon as if drawn by its' ancient allure, its' mysterious hold over us all. Perhaps the full moon was to blame for the strong emotions stirring within Adelaide Sullivan.

The reverend reached out to her and touched the long fingers of her white hand.

Bruin and I hid grins behind our good manners.

Adelaide's eyes flew open at the first touch of the reverend's hand upon hers; then she leaned toward him, taking his hand in both of hers as if she were a drowning woman, and he, a sturdy raft on a stormy night. Together they recited the last two lines of the sonnet.

"So long as men can breathe or eyes can see,
So long lives this and this gives life to thee."

They sat motionless, clutching hands and staring into each other's eyes as if they'd both just been granted the gift of sight.

Bruin stood over me, then bent down and whispered in my ear, "I'll walk you back to your wagon."

I nodded. We rose and left quietly. Neither the reverend nor Adelaide seemed to take notice.

*   *   *

I closed the manuscript and Alexander and I sat holding hands. Neither one of us wanted to ruin the moment.

Finally Alexander spoke. "Do you know the rest of the story, Sunny?"

"I know what happens next and I have a pretty good idea of the ending."

"Don't tell me. I think I know, too."

CHAPTER 9

Since that terrible day when I'd shot the bedroom ceiling with Bull's gun, I'd spoken to the kids several times on the phone but I hadn't seen them yet. Bull had warned me he'd tell them I tried to kill myself and I had no doubt he'd done just that. Even though Ben and Gillian never asked me about it during our too short conversations, I knew Bull Harris would do anything to get back at me for hurting him, and in his mind I'd hurt him by leaving him. It didn't matter what he may have done, or that I was in a hospital; in his opinion I'd committed the ultimate sin of abandoning him.

Today my opportunity had finally come to set the record straight. Both Ben and Gillian were waiting for me in Dr. Carroll's office. I clutched at Alexander's hand and asked him what I should say to them.

"Trust your instincts, Sunny, and you'll know better than anyone else exactly what to say to your own children. Now take a few deep breaths," he added, smiling at me in his encouraging way.

The nurse stood over us. "It's time now, Sunny. Dr. Carroll is waiting."

Alexander gave me a quick hug. "You'll do just fine, Sunny. Enjoy your visit."

I nodded and followed the nurse out the door and down the hallway. She opened the door to the office and gestured for me to enter.

Dr. Carroll sat behind his desk. He was smiling at Ben and Gillian. They sat on the edges of two chairs that faced him.

"Hi, Guys," I said, and before I was all the way into the room, they'd rushed at me and so we stood in a wonderful, healing, three-way hug. For the first time since coming here, I felt more full than hollow.

We all had tears in our eyes and Dr. Carroll came forward, offering Kleenex. We each took one and laughed together as we wiped our tears away.

Dr. Carroll suggested we sit down and we chose to sit together on the leather sofa to the right of his desk. I clutched Gillian's hand in my right one, and Ben's hand in my left.

They looked a bit thinner, but healthy, with bright eyes and shining hair and I marveled at how well they were doing without me. "Is Gramma still staying with you?" I asked, even though I knew Bull's mother had been taking care of them since the day before I came to the hospital.

Ben nodded. "She made stuffed-shells yesterday and froze a tray for when you get…" He paused, gave me a solemn look and swallowed hard, "when you come home."

My eyes flew to Dr. Carroll's as I wondered if I should dare to bring up the possibility that I wouldn't be coming home. That 'home' for us all might very well be in an entirely different place.

Dr. Carroll shook his head slightly and so I turned to Gillian. Her beautiful, green eyes were round and scared. I brushed the honey-colored bangs away from her forehead and she put her head on my shoulder.

"I miss you, Mom."

Oh, Sweetie, I miss you both so much! But I am getting better here and it won't be too much longer before I can…leave here."

Ben noticed the hesitation in my voice and he questioned me with his warm, dark eyes. When I looked into Ben's eyes it was like looking into a mirror. His dark, curly hair, so like his father's was growing over the back of his collar. I grinned at him as I pulled it gently.

"Ask Dad for a haircut," I said, "Or have you decided to join a commune?"

He flashed his movie-star grin at me and then ducked his head in a typical thirteen year old gesture. "Mom, cut it out."

Gillian snorted with laughter. She was only ten and adored her brother, but found him hopelessly conservative. Gillian was the 'wild child' of the two, and Ben was our more quiet and serious child.

Our child, our children; how could I unlearn the language of marriage? The reality of so many years shared with one man, one lover my entire life, weighed on my heart like dead dreams will.

"So, Guys," I began, "I guess your Dad's waiting downstairs. How is he?"

They both stared at me as if they didn't know how to answer.

Of course they would want to be careful of me. I had to learn to control the reflex that just naturally drove me to wonder about Bull.

Ben stared down at his too-large-for-his-body feet and shrugged.

"He's the same. He works all the time." I saw resentment flash in his expressive eyes, "We don't really see that much of him. But Gramma's neat. She does stuff with us, makes sure we do our homework and take baths and all that. He glanced over at Dr. Carroll and then gave me a questioning look. Ben was always shy and cautious around new people and here we were having a very private and intimate meeting in front of a man who was a complete stranger to him.

"Dr. Carroll has to be here," I said, smiling at him to soften my words.

"Well this is his office, isn't it?" Gillian piped in, looking around with her usual out-going curiosity.

"Yes, it is," Dr. Carroll said. He was smiling more than I'd ever seen him smile before. It was probably his way of putting the kids at ease.

"Gillian," he said, "your mother has been very anxious to know what your dad may have told you about the day she found it necessary to come here and ask for our help. Would you like to tell her what your dad said to you?"

The doctor went up several notches in my estimation of him. He'd picked the right kid. Gillian couldn't keep quiet about anything.

"Well," she said, looking sad, "I wouldn't really like to tell her, but if she really wants to know…" She searched my face for an answer.

I drew a deep breath and nodded.

"O.K. then," she said, "Well, Ben and I were still at the lake." She glanced at Dr. Carroll. "At Gramma's. And Dad came up on Sunday morning and said he had something to tell us. I got really scared because I knew Mom and Dad weren't getting along so good and when you weren't with Dad…"

She turned toward me. "I kind of knew it wasn't going to be good news."

"Just tell her," Ben said wearily, "Just get it over with and tell her." His lower lip trembled slightly as he set his jaw.

Gillian's little face crumpled and tears poured down her cheeks. I handed her another Kleenex and said, "I know this is hard for you, Honey, but please tell me."

Her voice hitched. "Dad said you tried to kill yourself and you're crazy"

She threw herself into my arms and I held her while she sobbed.

Ben shook his head and leaned forward, his elbows rested on his knees, his hands were clasped tightly in front of him. That was the way my father used to sit when he was very troubled.

If Bull had been in the room, I would have slapped his face. I looked to Dr. Carroll for guidance. What could I possibly say or do to explain the worst day of my life to these children?"

"I am so sorry you had to hear that." I said, knowing my words were painfully inadequate; knowing no words could erase the impact that day would always have on all of our lives.

"Your mother isn't crazy," Dr. Carroll said, coming to the rescue. I'm certain of that and you must both believe it. Your mother has been under a tremendous amount of stress brought on by events and conditions in her marriage to your father. These problems have nothing whatsoever to do with either of you. Both of your parents love you. They do the best they can to provide a good and happy life for you. It's unfortunate your father told you she tried to kill herself because the truth is that your mother chose life with you when she came here for help. That was a very brave and sensible move on her part and you should be proud of her. I believe if your mother wanted to die she would have. By coming here she has proven herself to be a survivor, and she'll need your love and support to work through this difficult time and return to you."

I didn't want to cry, but the tears flowed anyway. I mopped at them with a limp Kleenex and then blew my nose. Ben grinned at me and got up to get a fresh supply of Kleenex. "Throw that thing away, Mom, it's gross," he said.

Gillian sat up and blew her nose too. "So you really didn't try to kill yourself, Mom? You do love us?"

I put an arm around each child. "Of course I love you. I love you both more than anything. I did get very depressed and I drank too much wine, which was dumb. And I did get your Dad's gun out of the case…and I sat on the bed and for maybe a minute I thought you kids might be better off without me. Dad said he wanted a divorce. I'd promised you both there would never be a divorce and I didn't know how I was going to tell you I'd failed you."

"I'm ashamed to tell you I shot the gun into the ceiling in anger and that's the truth. Then I came here for help so I can be the mother you both deserve."

"I figured it was something like that," Ben said. "You know, Mom, in health class we were studying teen suicide and Mr. Osborne showed us a picture of a kid who blew his head off with a gun. He used a 357 magnum and you should have seen what it did to him. He didn't have much head left. You should have seen the pictures, Mom."

I faced Ben and once again he looked exactly like my father did whenever I'd disappointed him as a child. And in that moment I felt as stupid and guilty as the child I had once been when I'd had to face my father and answer for foolish behavior.

"You're right, Ben, I should have seen the pictures. I haven't been any kind of a role model for you in some time. I promise you both I'll never do anything like this again. And I don't want you to worry about your father and me. He's coming in Tuesday for a session with Dr. Carroll and with his help we'll work things out one way or another. You know I love your father but we did marry very young and we've both made mistakes. I'm willing to try to work through this, but I think this time he wants out of the marriage. We may all have to accept that and find a way to live with it."

My daughter's lip curled, "I don't think he knows what he wants. This is all Teri's fault. I hate her," Gillian said, spitting the words out like sour milk, "She's such a bitch. And she thinks she can tell us what to do. "

"You're not my mother," I tell her, "You have nothing to say to me."

Ben shot a warning look at her and then threw his hands up in the air, "You have a big mouth, Gil," he said.

My heart was leaping around in my chest like a trout on a fishing line, and I felt as dizzy and nauseous as if I'd eaten something rotten. How could Bull have brought that woman into our home while I was sick in the hospital? They had no decency, no pity.

Gillian's eyes begged Ben for permission to speak again.

"Go ahead. Finish it, it's too late to stop now," he said, his head in his hands.

"Gramma cooks for us and then goes home at night. That Teri comes home with Dad for dinner. One time she tried to bake a cake and it was so yuk we couldn't even eat it."

Gillian stared up at the painting of the sheep that hung over Dr. Carroll's desk. "She even sleeps in your bed, Mom. They think we don't know because she makes up the couch, but we hear her sneak up the stairs after she thinks we're asleep. They're both disgusting."

Dr. Carroll watched me carefully to see how I would react. I met his eyes and gave him a weak smile. I was hurt, but this time I wouldn't have to face the pain alone and that would make all the difference.

*   *   *

As I walked back to the community room, I began to feel numb. Exhaustion was spreading through me like sluggish blood through tired veins and I didn't think I'd be able to read to Alexander.

It had been great to see my kids and to finally hug them, but now all I could feel was the shock of Bull's latest betrayal. Bull Harris was a cruel man. This was my punishment for not checking out of the hospital and coming home with him on that first night. This was the price I was made to pay for not accepting the phone calls he made to me several times a day.

The nurse held the door open for me and I went back inside. I heard the click of the lock as the door closed behind me. I felt a twinge of panic whenever I heard that sound, as if the air in the room had grown suddenly stale and thin.

Alexander gestured to me to join him on our favorite sofa. I sank down against the faded blue cushions and sighed deeply.

"Was it rough?" he asked.

"The kids were wonderful. I just hope they believe I'm going to do everything I can to make this up to them. Bull isn't helping any, though. The bastard has moved his girlfriend into the house. Do you believe it?"

Alexander put his arm around my shoulders and rubbed my arm. "I do, actually. From what you've told me about him and the way he loves to blame you and punish you, it sounds exactly like what he would do to try to hurt you. He only thinks of himself, and from his point of view, he didn't leave you, you left him and that hurt him a lot. And don't forget, he's pretty much capable of anything."

Alexander was right. "It still doesn't make it hurt any less."

"I wish you could get over him, Sunny. He does not deserve your love. I want to see you when we leave here. Since he's living with Teri, I don't see why he would object to your dating me."

I shook my head. "Bull's crazier than both of us put together. I'm his virgin wife, his possession. He's insanely jealous even on a good day, and he won't want anyone else to have me no matter how many girlfriends he might have. And logic has nothing to do with it."

"But Sunny, how long are you going to let this guy rule your life?"

I ran a finger along his high cheekbone and then down his strong jaw line. "You're so sweet to me. It's easy to imagine loving you, but I don't want to put you in any danger."

His blue eyes went hard for a second. "Don't worry about me. I'm a big boy."

Alexander's warmth and caring were working to heal me in much the same way as the various therapies were. I felt as grateful to him as I did to my doctors. "Would you like me to read tonight? Or are you too tired?"

"I thought I was, but I'm feeling a lot better now. You seem to have that effect on me."

"Still grinning, Alexander leaned forward and drew my manuscript out from under the sofa where he'd had it hidden. "I was hoping you'd ask."

*   *   *

We had passed the last way station many miles back and I was mourning my lost opportunity for a proper bath. We had to be careful of our water supply and I found it alarming to think I wouldn't be able to bathe until we reached the next creek, lake, or river. And the thought of bathing with the other women was upsetting as well. I hoped we would find a water source with a thick enough cover of brush to provide some measure of privacy. Such were the inconveniences and irritations of travel upon the open road.

The day was extremely beautiful, the perfect mixture of breeze and sunlight. I decided to put aside my resentments for this one lovely day and so I sat up front with Papa on the wagon seat.

Despite the perfect weather, I felt strangely nervous and apprehensive as if something unusual or tragic was about to happen, and I wasn't at all surprised to see the man, Booth Wade, who was acting as the scout, come riding back toward us from over the hills, racing at a wild pace. He headed straight to the wagon master and I watched them speak in loud voices, with frantic gestures, but I couldn't make out their words.

It looked like trouble to me and when I turned to question Papa, I froze in my seat at the stormy look quickly transforming his face.

"Get into the back of the wagon, Jessamyn. Now!" he shouted as if he were angry at me.

"Why, Papa? What's happening?"

"Don't argue. Just do as I say. And stay down low."

I did as Papa said, at first, but then my curiosity got the better of me and I bobbed back up to peer out at the horizon and was shocked speechless at the sight looming ahead. The hill in the distance was black with feathered Indians astride crazed horses. My breath caught in the back of my throat and my body grew numb with terror. What in God's name would become of us so far from any hope of help?

"They're all fancied up for war!" Papa shouted to Mr. Taylor in the next wagon, and before he had a chance to answer, Booth Wade streaked past, shouting orders to all the men, "Pull up! Pull the wagons in a circle! Wagons in a circle! Prepare to return fire!"

I thought of Bruin and wished he was here with us. I couldn't imagine an Indian getting the better of him. I whispered a prayer for all of us.

"Why are they doing this, Papa? We haven't done anything to them." I gasped, quickly lining Papa's guns in a row to check them and to be certain each was loaded and ready to fire.

"Probably a treaty violation; or some liquored up white-trash raided one of their villages while the men were out hunting. It doesn't matter why now, Little Mite. We're thrust into the thick of it, and we'll have to defend ourselves. Load that last rifle and hand it to me."

My hands were trembling as I did what Papa asked of me, and when I heard the shrieks of the savages coming nearer I felt the unearthly sounds echo inside my own body. I had never known such terror.

"Heavenly Father; watch over the little children among us. Protect us all."

A child's cry rent the air, a horrific wail that ended in a frantic call, "Maaa! Maaa!"

I think I could smell the Indians before I actually saw them. Their fondness for bear grease as a grooming tool was legendary and they reeked of a feral, sickening stench.

We forced the wagons around into a wide, unruly circle to the shouts of men and the crack of every whip. The wagon lurched under me and I was thrown to the side against my trunk. I put my hands and arms over my head and then clutched at the trunk for stability.

"Sweet Jesus," I whispered, "Be with us now."

When our wagon came to an abrupt halt, the team reared up and screeched back at the Indians who sped past on bare back, so at one with the animals they rode they could balance perfectly while taking dead aim with a bow and arrow or a flaming spear. Some even had guns, though not very many, and I was glad of that.

Papa spun around on the seat and shot a young buck. He raced past; a blur of paint, feathers, and fierce war-cries, then he fell from the horse and was trampled by those who rode behind him. His twisted body rolled and flopped crazily to a stop against a tree.

"Got you; you red-skinned son of a dog!" Papa yelled. He looked younger and more excited than I'd ever seen him as he re-loaded his rifle and asked me, "Did you see that one fall, Jessamyn? At least he won't be around to father any more red devils."

I felt sick to my stomach and although I was aware of my duty to help Papa load his guns, I was gripped with an overwhelming desire to get out of the wagon, to get away from Papa...from this Papa I didn't know.

"I've got to get out of here, Papa," I called back over my shoulder as I leaped from the back of the wagon and crouching low, darted behind the wheel of the wagon directly behind us.

"Jessamyn!" Papa roared between the crack of his gunshots, "Come back here!"

I covered my ears and gulped great breaths of fresh air. I looked back at our wagon, feeling guilty. Then I saw Bruin run along the ground and hop into the back of our wagon. I knew he would be an even better helper for Papa and so, at least for a while, I was free.

Chaos everywhere; if I turned to my right, I could see the clash of hooves and dust as the Indians thundered past in full attack against us. If I turned to my left, I could see the scurrying feet of women and children as they ran in panic and confusion. Several of the wagons burst into flames while those families ran from the insanity of the attack in search of new shelter.

I popped out into the relative safety to be found in the center of the ring of wagons and looked about to see where I might do the most good. If Papa had Bruin's help, perhaps I could be of assistance to some of the mothers, or to help the single men re-load their rifles.

"Help me! Save me! Mother-of-God!" I heard a terrified, feminine voice shriek insanely.

My eyes darted from wagon to wagon until I identified the screamer as that twit Cassie Taylor. She huddled under the family wagon clinging to the wheel, and kicking away at her fat mother, Margaret, who tried her best to dislodge her.

"You foolish ass!" Margaret bellowed, red in the face. She was down on all fours now, huffing and gasping for each breath as she grabbed onto one of Cassie's legs and tried to twist her loose and then out from under the wagon.

Cassie let out a squeal to wake the dead, and kicked back with her other leg. The blow was forceful enough to send her mother sprawling backward, her calico dress whipping up into her livid face.

"Go away!" Cassie wailed. "I can't let them have my beautiful hair!! They love red hair! You know they love red hair!"

Her eyes were glassy and I had never seen her so undone. She was clearly terrified at the thought of losing her glory of a mane to an Indian's sharp blade.

"You are a coward, Cassandra Sue Taylor!" Margaret raged, "Just like your useless father. Get out from under that wagon or I'll see you disowned. You are making a spectacle of yourself! And I'll be damned if you are going to embarrass me!" Her squinty eyes glared with something close to hatred.

I shuddered, grateful once again to have been blessed with loving parents. "I'll try to get her out from under there for you, Mrs. Taylor," I offered, reaching out to Cassie.

The huge woman slapped my hand away. "We don't want your help, Jessamyn Miles!" she spat at me with the same contempt I'd often heard in her daughter's voice. "You'd like nothing more than to be able to tell everyone how brave you are. How you saved Cassandra from the savages!"

"Go away! Go away!" Cassie whined, just as her eyes rolled back in her head and she fainted dead away.

"Thank God!" Margaret snarled, "She's better off this way."

Margaret yanked Cassie out from under the wagon and lifting her as if she were a basket of wet laundry, she heaved her into the rear of the wagon. An arrow sped past Margaret's head and stuck in the frame of the wagon. She let out a low growl, snatched up a rifled from inside the wagon and started shooting in the direction from which the attack had come.

What a strange family. And the father was no better. As round and awful as his wife, he leered at all the girls, but rarely ever spoke, even when addressed directly. Margaret Taylor did most of the talking in that family. Even brassy Cassie rarely crossed her.

I crouched low in the tall grass once more as arrows sped overhead. A man fell from the seat of his wagon and sank down out of sight under the hooves of his team of oxen. The canvas of his wagon burst into flames and his horses reared off only to be stopped by their tethers. His wife appeared and beat the fire out with a blanket; then she and their six children scrambled out of the wagon and ran to drag him free of the oxen.

Reverend Putnam appeared next to the man's wife and gathered the children around him. On all fours, I crawled to the reverend, hugging the youngest boy, no more than three. He buried his face in my dress and sobbed against me, trembling.

"It will be all right," I lied, even as his mother threw herself upon the dead body of his father.

"Joshua is a big, brave boy, Miss Jessamyn," the reverend said in a steady, confident voice. "Come now, Children, I know the perfect place for a game of hide and seek. Only you must promise to hide very quietly until I come back for you. If you expect to win the game you must be as quiet as little mice."

He led us to a thicket of tall grass surrounded by thick berry bushes and showed the children how to crouch down low out of sight. "Not even a squeak, now, promise. Trust in the Lord Jesus Christ. He is here with you. He is always with you."

The bright-eyed girl of at least six beamed up at him and wrapped her arms around her little brother. She nodded vigorously. "We know Jesus is always with us, and we promise to wait here for you."

As the reverend walked away, I followed him, but he spun around toward me and grabbing my arm with an air of authority he had never dared use with me before, said, "Miss Jessamyn, you must stay with the children. You will all be safe here." His eyes flashed at me as if to challenge me to talk back; and talk back I did.

"I am not one of the children, Reverend," I said with as much dignity as I could muster under the circumstances. "I'll be getting back to my father now. He may need my help."

I pulled my arm from his grasp and avoiding his eyes; I turned and started in the direction of our wagon. I walked cautiously along, wondering how one can find the strength to cope with the most unspeakably intolerable situations, when I heard Adelaide Sullivan's voice pleading, "Please! Let me go!"

The Sullivan wagon was dead ahead of me so I ran the last few feet and just as I was climbing through the back opening, a fierce Indian burst forth and plowed into me with great force. I few back through the air and landed on my backside in the dirt. The Indian loomed large as I struggled to regain the breath he had knocked from my lungs. My ribs hurt, too, and I wheezed as I choked on dust and fear.

Adelaide struggled to break the Indian's one-armed iron grip about her waist. Her light-red hair a tangle that fell across her face while her dress told the whole story; smudged with dirt and tattered as if she had just waged a mortal struggle for her life.

She stared down at me with crazed-eyes. "Mother," she gasped, "Help Mother, Jessamyn! Please! She's in the wagon."

The Indian, muscles taut, his power invincible, grunted and shook her as if to quiet her, then made a lunge for me with his free arm. I rolled as quickly as I could out of his path and sprang to a crouching position.

The Indian and I faced each other, his face fierce with paint, and Adelaide began to shriek once again, "Help us! Someone please help us!"

It was then I noticed the bloody scalp hanging from his side. It was long and white. Poor Mrs. Sullivan!

A slow smile spread across the face of the savage as he started for me again. Adelaide's skinny legs flailed the air as he dragged her along with him. He meant to take us both!

I didn't even have time to scream as I lifted my muddy skirt and darted off, running as fast as I could go. The Indian was close at my heels and so I raced across the circle of wagons. Would he dare expose himself in the open? I glanced over my shoulder and to my relief, the

Indian dropped back to untie the Sullivan's mare from where she was tethered by the wagon.

Then the unthinkable happened. He flung Adelaide over the horse's back and leaping behind her, he whipped the horse and sped off. The hopeless hysteria of Adelaide's screams would haunt my dreams for years to come, even though I knew there was nothing I could have done to help her.

When I reached the other side of the circle, I leaped up into the first wagon I came to, praying I wouldn't be shot for a savage, and that I would find help for Adelaide. I didn't know these people very well, but I recognized the woman who lay still at my feet. She was Emmaline Boothe, apparently alone in the wagon and I kneeled checking to see if her heart was still beating.

It was, so I called her name and shook her gently in an attempt to revive her. She stirred once and then one of the Indians shot a flaming arrow, and then another, into the canvas frame of the wagon. The sun-bleached cloth burned quickly and without wasting another second, I attempted to drag Emmaline to the opening in the rear of the wagon. As I pulled and tugged at her limp body, I wondered where her husband and child could possibly be.

The smoke was suffocating me and I held my breath as I inched my burden the last few steps to the opening. When we were both safely on the ground I shouted for help once again, and Will Montgomery, a young boy of twelve, answered my call. His eyes were round with the shock of the day's horrors, with all he had had to endure. "Miss Jessamyn, Mrs. Boothe here, has a little girl; little Emma. The Indians wounded her husband and he's over with the Master's getting first aide, but I haven't seen little Emma all day. Do you think she's still in the wagon?"

We both stared up at a wagon filled with billowing black smoke, and, without thinking it through; I leaped back inside. I stayed down low and still I could barely see. The smoke stung my eyes and robbed me of my breath. I crawled toward the front of the wagon knowing a little child would hide from the Indians, as well as the fire.

"Miss Jessamyn! Did you find her yet?" Will called from the opening.

"Stay out there!" I warned, "I don't want to have to come back in here to look for you, too."

I hunted under the seat of the wagon and just when I thought I'd faint and die in the fire, I felt the child's soft arm. I snatched the little girl to my breast and with my last strength I struggled toward the opening, half fell to the ground, and made it over to the next wagon just as the canvas covering caved in. Flaming cinders stung my back, but my first concern was for the child. Her face was pale, but she coughed as she fought for breath and her eyes opened and closed while she struggled to gain consciousness.

"I think Mrs. Boothe is going to live, Miss Jessamyn. She must have only fainted, cause she's still breathing. How's Emma?" Will asked.

"She's alive, Will."

We sat under the wagon, comforting the little girl as she coughed and spit and finally cried for her mother. It was at this point I noticed the worst of the battle had passed and the whoops of the Indians and the pounding hoof-beats were fading mercifully away into the distance. Will and I hugged each other and cried together in relief. It was finally over.

My knees were weak, but I found the strength to crawl back out from under the wagon and to revive Emmaline and return little Emma to her. Her husband was weak from the arrows he'd taken in his arm and shoulder, but if it was to be God's will he had a good chance of recovery.

Both Bruin and Reverend Putnam were rushing about from wagon to wagon calling my name and I imagined they had been set on my trail by Papa.

When Bruin saw me he raced to my side and swept me into the air in a hug that nearly crushed the life from me. Bruin was a powerful man and luckily he heard my muffled cries against the broad muscles of his chest and set me back down before I met my maker.

"Your Papa is fine. He made it through safely," he said, "We were so worried about you."

Reverend Putnam stood behind him and I had never seen such a huge grin on his face before. He looked very human and much more like a man than a minister for the first time since I'd met him.

Seeing him reminded me suddenly of Adelaide. "Oh, Reverend, I have something terrible to tell you," I said as gently as I could. The smile slowly faded from his face as I began, "It's Adelaide and her mother."

He swallowed hard. I watched his Adam's apple move up and then quiver on the way down. "Are they dead?"

"An Indian kidnapped Adelaide, and he tried to take me too, but I got away. He had a long, white scalp tied to his side, and Reverend, I think it belonged to Mrs. Sullivan."

Bruin put his arm around my shoulders and pulled me closer to him. "How did you get away? Where was I? Where did all of this happen?"

I pointed across the circle and for the first time I noticed the Sullivan wagon was a charred, smoking wreck. I felt sick to my stomach and as I realized how dizzy and nauseous I was becoming, it occurred to me that an unfamiliar sickeningly sweet odor of what must be burning flesh was pervading the air around us.

The horror of all we had suffered on this cataclysmic day overcame me and I ran off into the brush to retch. Tears clouded my vision, and I sank down under a tree; the branches of the oak spread strong and tall above me. It was such a beautiful day. How could these hellacious things have happened on such a perfect day? I leaned back and watched the sunlight filter down through brilliant leaves that danced in the light, cooling breeze, while all around me the others wept for their lost loved ones and shattered lives. My tears dried upon my cheeks and still I hadn't the strength to stand.

*   *   *

I closed the manuscript and glanced at Alexander. Tears were running down his face and he made no move to wipe them away. "Oh, Alexander," I said, reaching for his hand. "I've upset you. This had been a rough day all the way around. I'm really sorry. I shouldn't have read tonight."

"It isn't your fault, Sunny, it's just that I've dreamed that part of the book. This is like deja vue; only different somehow. It's hard for me to explain. It's strange for me."

"You don't have to explain strange to me, Alexander," I said, hoping for a smile. He gave me one and I returned it. "Let's go check out the moon before we go to our rooms," I suggested.

We started to hold hands as we walked together, but one glance at the nurse's station reminded us we'd better not. So we walked separate, but together, down the long hall to the west window.

The moon was high and so round and bright it reminded me of that white ball on the billiard table, the one you have to poke with the cue and send careening into the other more colorful balls to make your point.

"Full moon" Alexander said.

"I wonder if they'll chain us to our beds tonight?" I asked and grinned at him.

"That's not so far from the truth."

"You're kidding. I was only joking."

"I didn't mean us, but we're going to be in for a crazy night. You know the origin of the word, 'lunatic.'"

"I'd forgotten about that."

Alexander slid his arm around my shoulders and drew me toward him. His blue eyes were dark in the dim light. I glanced over his shoulder and checked to see if anyone was coming. "Be careful," I whispered, "We don't want to get caught."

"You're pretty when you're scared," he said, as his lips came down on mine and he pressed my body tightly against him. I worked my arms up around his neck and tangled my fingers in his thick, dark hair. It felt like Bull's hair and as the realization hit me, I felt a stabbing pain in my chest as if my heart was rebelling against this special moment. My shattered, stubborn heart insisted on loving only one man; one very unworthy man.

I fought to deny the sob growing in the back of my throat, but Alexander was too sensitive not to know I was suffering. He reared back and gently asked, "What did I do wrong?"

"You can't do anything wrong as far as I'm concerned," I whispered, grateful for the warmth of Alexander's arm around me as he took my hand and gently kissed my palm.

He sighed sadly. "That son of a bitch just isn't worth it, Sunny. But you have to figure that out for yourself."

CHAPTER 10

Alexander was right about the full moon. We got three new patients that night; two women and one man. I was jolted awake several times during the night by shrieking, swearing, and sobbing that raged on until dawn. I felt like a child who lies wide awake and rigid in the darkness while the angry voices of her parents cut cruelly into all her vulnerable places.

The nurse stuck her head in my room several times to apologize, but I assured her I realized it was nothing she could control. I was just glad she hadn't put one of the women in my room. I still didn't have a roommate and since I was writing at night, I was hoping it would stay that way.

We were all sluggish as we dragged through our morning routines. As I dusted the community room I couldn't help chuckling over the racket this place had going for them. We were paying at least $5,000.00 a week to be here and we were being made to clean as a form of therapy. It was amazing how they could get away with it.

Later, in group, Vince complained we weren't any fun. "Come on, People," he urged, "Wake up and tell me something scary. Curl that hair on the back of my neck!"

Alexander and I were the only ones who laughed. Helen stared sullenly at her feet and sighed very now and then.

"Do you want to talk?" I asked Alexander.

He shook his head. "I'm beat, Sunny. I don't think I slept an hour all night. You go ahead."

I raised my hand and Vince called on me. "Way to go, Sun," he said, "Lay a good one on us."

"I could tell you about when my little brother was born. That was pretty traumatic…not very original, though."

"We can all relate…sounds good to me." Vince said.

I took a sip from the cup of water I held and began: "Poor little Joe-Joe. It wasn't his fault that I resented him so much when he first came home from the hospital and through my front door, held in my father's arms, the center of attention for all of my old fans; all the friends and relatives who had given me the impression the world revolved around me and was lucky to do so. In those first few seconds he took my place as the baby and I was very upset."

"I was sad and offended and very mixed up for a good twenty-four hours. I had thought I loved babies. I loved the babies the other mothers brought to the park, and I loved my baby cousins, but I definitely did not love my little brother on the first day I met him."

Helen raised her head. "I hear ya, Sunny," she said, "I hate my brother too."

Vince smiled. This was the first time Helen had said anything in group in a week.

"We have a terrible picture of me sitting on the sofa with poor Joe-Joe sort of leaning sideways against my lap," I continued, "my hands clamped to the sofa cushions, my angry face staring into the camera."

"I'm not proud of it now, but I began to plot his disappearance. I reasoned since we put the garbage down the dumb waiter out in the hall each evening and it never came back to bother us, little Joe should go down the dumb waiter too. I had no thoughts of harming him; I just wanted him to disappear like yesterday's garbage. Luckily I changed my mind about him before I got the chance to do it."

"The next morning, after my father had gone back to work where he belonged instead of hovering over his wonderful new son, and all of my grandparents and Ba, and the other relatives had also returned to wherever it was they went every day, Joe-Joe began to look more interesting to me."

As my eyes scanned the faces of the others in the circle, I was taken with the smile of one of the new women, Charlotte. She was elderly with carefully set gray hair and I couldn't imagine how her hairdo had survived the drama of the night before. She caught my eye and spoke to me.

"Do you have children, Sunny?" she asked in a dreamy, little voice that didn't fit her age or her look.

"Yes, Charlotte, two; Ben is thirteen and Gillian is ten. Do you have kids?"

Her chin began to tremble and her eyes grew fierce, and startlingly blue. "Kids," she whispered, "I thought I had some kids."

Vince took over before it got any worse. "Charlotte has devoted her life to the care of foster children. Her husband recently passed away and her health has suffered from the shock.

As a result the state has decided not to assign any more children to her care for the time being. At least until after she has been here with us for a while and the doctors can assess her condition. You'll most likely be able to work in a group home with the children when you leave here. You'd like that, wouldn't you, Charlotte?"

Charlotte drew a shaky breath and nodded.

Suddenly little Jessie jumped out of her chair and we all stared at her. "Why couldn't they have placed me with Charlotte? I could have helped her. We could have been there for each other!" Tears were streaming down her cheeks.

Charlotte stood and opened her arms. "Child!" she whispered.

Jessie ran across the circle and into Charlotte's arms. Bob stood and rearranged the chairs so the two of them could sit together. The two sat down gratefully, still holding hands.

"Finish your story, Sunny," Bob urged, "I can already see listening to you is going to be the high point of the day." His eyes darted around the group. Mostly everyone glared back at him. He threw his hands in the air. "No offense to anyone else, but I'm just sayin' that's pretty sad."

I laughed and nodded. Bob was a recovering alcoholic, restless to leave here and head for the local tavern. He said that's where all his friends would be waiting for him.

"Let's see," I said, "I was at the part where I realized Joe-Joe was going to be some sort of company for me. My mother rolled his crib into my room and told me he was my baby, too. And in that instant, little Joe-Joe became my first best friend."

"I don't buy it," Helen muttered, "My lousy little brother has been rotten to me from the first day of his life."

"That's sad, Helen," I said, "Because my experience has been different. I saw my brother as the helpless, needy, little guy he was, and I soon realized I had a lot to offer him. I figured he needed me because he was a funny-looking little thing at first who looked more like an anorexic monkey-on-speed than a baby."

Helen let out a long manic laugh. "Now you're talkin'."

"The constant care he needed soon made him less of a celebrity around our house and I liked helping my mother by fetching his diapers, bottles, and clean T-shirts."

"And Joe-Joe was grateful when I put my stool by the side of his crib and, whenever he cried, day or night, I would stand on the stool and rub his wiry little back. At first his wild, dark eyes would search the room until he found my face, then he would begin to relax, knowing he wasn't alone in the world. I would sing to him and he would quiet down and listen."

"And as soon as he could smile, he smiled at me. Later when he learned to talk he called me, Shishy, until his slushy S cleared up and then he called me Sissy, for years. He was a crazy little guy who could think up more mischief than anyone I've ever known."

"Once when my mother was on the phone he started jumping on our parent's bed until he bounced up so high he flew off and through the air like a little comet, until he eventually came down on the hard wood floor and broke his collar bone. I had tried to stop him, but he was too excited to stop."

"Now you might think this would have slowed him down for a few days, but not Joe-Joe. The very next day, arm and shoulder swathed in this great mass of tape and bandage, he dragged his tricycle up to the outside third floor landing of the house."

"My mother and I were concentrating on trying to make sunflowers grow in the one bright corner of our gray, dirt yard when we heard him call out to us, "Mommy! Shishy! Look at me!""

"We turned as one and watched helplessly as a grinning Joe-Joe came barreling down the stairs on the tricycle, steering with his one good arm. "Look at me! Look at me!" he shouted as he clattered down to the second floor, shot across the landing and then, picking up speed, fairly flew over the remaining stairs as if transported by angels, and ripped across the dirt yard to stop directly in front of the both of us. My mother and I sank down to our knees in the dirt and hugged him. We couldn't believe he had survived without a scratch."

"He became famous in the neighborhood after that, and Mah decided to keep a harness on him in public, despite the sometimes openly hostile stares of strangers. She really had no choice after that cold October day when we took him for a walk across the street to

Branch Brook Park, and he spotted the ducks gathering to fly south. I guess Joe-Joe wanted to go too because he took off with a whoop, flying through the air, faster than either my mother or I could run, arms and legs pumping like a wheel, as he landed with a splash right in the middle of the duck pond."

Everyone in the group began to laugh and Alexander said he couldn't wait to meet Joe-Joe this coming Sunday.

Charlotte grinned at me and said, "I love sunflowers. Did yours grow?"

I assured her they had and then she and Jessie smiled at each other. I could imagine they were planning a garden together when they each got better and could find a way to become foster mother and child.

Then Helen asked, "Is Joe-Joe cute? He doesn't still look like a monkey anymore, does he?"

I laughed and Vince leaned forward and said, "Finish the story, Sunny. So how did Joe-Joe survive childhood?

"He came out O.K. Now, having a crazy little brother was fine with me because he provided some excitement to life in Newark, New Jersey, especially before we got our first T.V., but I was concerned he might not survive, so I came up with a plan to slow him down a little."

"Our new game kept us quiet for hours on end, so much so that my mother got plenty of writing done and she never thought to investigate. I talked Joe-Joe into playing 'Suzy'.

"I'd always wanted a little sister and I thought I could help Joe-Joe to be quieter and less of a threat to himself, if I could teach him to be a girl."

"Holy shit!" Bob said and snorted with laughter.

"I dressed him up in an old rose-colored velvet coat and a blue velvet bonnet of mine. It even had a matching muff and Joe-Joe made an adorable little girl. By this time his hair had turned golden, and he was a good looking kid. I told him he was now my little sister, Suzy, and he had to act very quiet and lady-like now. I would then load him into my doll carriage and wheel him around the apartment. In those days toys were built like actual sturdy miniatures of their counterparts and it could easily take his weight.

"And then Dad found out about our game. Joe-Joe appeared in the living room one night dressed in the velvet hat and coat, his wide, boyish hands stuffed into the muff. "Shishy," he said, "Let's play Suzy."

"My father nearly had a stroke. "What the hell do you think you're doing to my son? My only son! You…are never, ever to put a *dress* on my only son as long as you live in this house! And after you leave home you can't do it either. You can't ever, *ever* do it again! Do you understand me?"

"He was staring at me as if I'd turned into the devil. He actually looked a little bit afraid of me. I watched him make a big effort to calm down."

"Sunny," he began again, more gently in the face of my guilty tears, "this is really serious. You must not try to change Joe-Joe into a girl. You're going to get him confused."

"My mother came hurrying into the room to see what all the yelling was about and he turned on her for not paying enough attention to our games. I remember feeling sad at first because we wouldn't be able to play Suzy anymore. It had become our favorite game and Joe-Joe made a great little sister. Then I kind of felt important. I'd never thought of the games we played as being of much consequence, but my father certainly seemed to think the Suzy game could have some sort of lasting effect; that it mattered."

"For a few weeks after that, Joe-Joe continued to ask if we could play Suzy and I hated telling him we could never play it again. A few times he asked in front of Dad, and I'll never forget how Dad would flinch and then sit quietly for a few minutes with his head in his hands, shaking it slowly from side to side and shuddering every so often."

"Well, Joe-Joe grew up to be as wild a man as he was a boy. At least until he hit twenty one. For years he played guitar in a series of rock and blues bands and not less than three times the jaws of life had to rescue him from the crumpled remains of three rather expensive cars in the dawn hours when Joe-Joe had been playing tag with the trees on his way home from a gig."

"But he always popped out of each wreck, smiling Joe, with only a cut over one eye or a bruised arm. We were all relieved when he announced he was going to settle down. He waited until one of our Sunday dinners to make the announcement."

"Dad," he began, "I've decided to stop this carefree, happy living. I'm going to go back to school and study for a regular-person job."

"AAAH!" Dad enthused, as we all toasted him with Chianti. "And what sort of job are you planning to study for? Lawyer? Teacher? Second story man?"

"I've decided to use my artistic talents in a practical way and become a hairdresser."

"Dad's head whipped around so fast in my direction, I thought he was doing an impression of that kid in *The Exorcist*. "See, Sunny!" he bellowed, "See what you've done?"

"Years have passed since then and I'm glad to be able to tell you I didn't 'confuse' Joe-Joe at all. He turned out to be a talented hairdresser and he owns his own shop now. But I don't think Dad really relaxed until Joe-Joe married his beautiful little Italian High School sweetheart, Maria…and became a father. They have an adorable little girl named…Suzy."

Everyone laughed at the story, but I think Vince laughed the longest, being Italian. Helen said she was disappointed Joe-Joe was happily married, but my story made her begin to consider trying to get along with her brother. And Alexander suggested I try writing a story about my family after I've finished Jessamyn's story; and I think I just might do that.

* * *

After lunch I had another session with Dr. Carroll. I felt more like taking a nap than slugging back through the muck of childhood like a female Holmes with Dr. Carroll as my Watson. But I showed up and curled into the old, brown, leather chair anyway. It was still warm from the rumps of the endless crazies Dr. Carroll had to endure during the course of his work day, and I resented being one of them. It was easy to understand why psychiatrists had the highest suicide rate of any other profession.

"I don't feel like talking today." I said, gazing over his head at my favorite painting, wishing I could escape into the impossible tranquility of the painted meadow. Dart around the sheep, roll down the hill, then streak off among the trees on the perfect fantasy get-away.

"Sometimes I don't feel like listening, but I don't get a vote," Dr. Carroll said.

I grinned at him. "I can see how being perfectly sane and well-adjusted could often be a terrible burden to bear."

He laughed harder than I thought he should.

"The other day you said you wanted me to finish up the stories about my childhood," I said, "So I guess I'd better just plunge ahead and get it over with. Then we can start working through the marriage before next Tuesday when Bull comes..."

"Try to restrain your enthusiasm, Sunny," he said, leaning forward and cupping his chin in his hand.

I yawned and stretched. "This place was nuts last night. Nobody got any sleep. Did you hear about it?"

He nodded and shrugged. "Full moon."

"I feel so lousy today, I might as well tell you about Chloe."

"Chloe? That's an unusual name."

"I come from an unusual family, remember? Chloe was my cat. My best friend, after Joe-Joe, and I loved her as much as a person; probably more than most people. I love animals. They don't lie or cheat. Sometimes they steal, especially cats, but nobody's perfect."

Dr. Carroll began to clap. "That's progress: A statement grounded in reality."

"Do you think I have a problem with reality?"

"Don't you? How long did it take you to see the truth about Bull?"

"About fifteen years...or more, if you count the five years we dated in school. I guess you have a point."

"So," Dr. Carroll said, "Why are we talking about this cat?"

"This is a Dad story too. Dad was passing the local bar on his way home from work one night and although he wasn't in the habit of stopping in, or so the story goes, he was lured in this evening by the rowdy laughter of the men inside. It was here he discovered a tiny kitten, gray-striped and drunk. It was nearly starved and thirsty, so it eagerly lapped up the beer these guys were feeding it, then it attempted to walk down the bar and fell over on its' back, which is why the men were laughing."

"Dad rescued the kitten and brought it home to me. The men didn't put up much of a fight because they all knew me as that cute kid down the block who always smiled and said hi to everyone who passed by the house."

"God, I loved that kitten with all the passion and obsession of a lonely child growing up in a big, rough city. And best of all, Dad had thought of me, and my pleasure in the gift was multiplied many times over by the fact that it was a totally unexpected gift. It wasn't Christmas or my birthday so there wasn't any 'have to give' in this gift at all."

"My father named the kitten Chloe so he could stand on the back porch and sing the old Chloe song whenever he called her home. He got a big kick out of that. And to me, Chloe was all the more precious because she represented how much my father loved me. You see, he didn't really like cats but he knew I did. My father was a difficult man, but to me he was a romantic figure. He was artistic and well-read, clearly the smartest man I would ever know."

"He became a photographer after giving up his music career, didn't he?" Dr. Carroll asked.

I nodded. "He worked in downtown Newark and sometimes in New York City. He took photos of a lot of famous people. The governor of the state and quite a few movie and T.V. stars."

"In 1950 downtown Newark was a mysterious, exotic place. Don't laugh…it was very different then. I always loved it best at night, after Bambergers had closed and we would take our shopping bags with us out into the bright, night lights and then, into the nearest Chock Full O' Nuts Restaurant for a root beer and one of those amazing shiny red hot-dogs with bright yellow mustard. This was haute cuisine for me."

"My mother was a salt and pepper cook at best. Canned veggies, leather liver even Chloe passed on, and dry, rubbery roasts were her usual offerings while I was cursed with a taste for prime rib, medium rare, and anything Italian and spicy."

"I discovered my mother couldn't cook early in life whenever I had the treat of eating out in a nice restaurant." "What do you call this wonderful food?" I once asked a startled waiter, dodging the daggers in my mother's flashing-green eyes. It was actually a perfectly ordinary meal to the average person. I, of course, had been born into a dramatic and unusual family."

"With the culinary situation being what it was at home, you can understand why Chock Full O' Nuts was one of my favorite places to go. As an added attraction, all of the employees were Negro, as African-Americans were called then, which made it even more exotic and these dark-eyed velvety-skinned strangers, who never looked me directly in the eye, were the first black people I had ever come in contact with. I was never taught to be prejudiced, but I sensed a distance between myself and these 'Negroes' who served us our hot dogs. They projected an aura of sadness and lowered expectations."

"Later on, when Gram told me something of their history; about slavery and the civil rights struggles going on in the south, I understood what it was I had sensed at the restaurant."

"I used to wonder what it would have been like to be born black, to have to sit in the back of a bus, drink from a separate water fountain, and never be able to look a white female directly in the eye for fear of offending someone and causing a violent, sometimes murderous scene. I remember being glad I was born white and then feeling guilty for thinking it. I walked around grinning at every black person I passed on the street, trying singlehandedly to make up for what had been done to them by my race."

"My father identified with them and he had many African-American musician friends, so he always told me to remember everyone bleeds the same color blood. We might look different, but we were all the same inside."

"Sometimes he would tell us incidents in his life when he had been looked down on for being of Italian descent on both sides of his family. He'd laugh and say, "Italians aren't considered all that white, you know…Sicily is pretty close to Africa.""

"You Kids were born American, "he'd say, making it sound like a privilege instead of an accident of birth. This is why he wouldn't teach us to speak Italian and insisted when we were questioned about our nationality because our last name ended in a vowel, we were to say, "We are American. We were born here and not in Italy.""

"Dad may have been the first generation of his family to be born in this country, but with his black, wavy hair, olive complexion, and straight Roman nose, he sure did look Italian, just as Joe-Joe and I did. In fact Dad looked so much like Perry Como, I secretly wondered if we might be related to the singer in some way."

"Since Perry's show came on well past my bed-time, I always had to sneak up to watch it from behind the green, velvet chair just inside the archway to the living room. My mother sat in that chair, tall and lovely, crocheting doilies and laughing out loud at all the jokes in a hearty way you wouldn't expect from so delicate a beauty."

"On the nights when Perry was on, Chloe would always spread herself luxuriously about in true Egyptian-cat-queen-style right in front of the blonde mahogany console television. I've always thought she assumed we were watching her. I would hold my breath and pray to be ignored whenever Chloe glanced my way, but we were great friends who shared perfect understanding and Chloe always sensed when I was attempting to become invisible. Not once did my wonderful friend give me away. My parents were both as strict as only former hell- raisers can be, and I almost never dared to defy them, but Perry Como's music was too seductive a lure. It was worth the risk."

"My father would sit watching the show on the sofa and depending on who Perry's guests were, he would tell my mother an exciting story about when he was on the same bill with Red Skelton and a woman who danced with huge snakes, and several times with Frank Sinatra when he was still with The Hoboken Four. I loved those stories and I loved the part of my father that still loved show business and always would."

"Many times during the day I missed my father so much I didn't think I'd be able to make it until the evening when he came home from work. My mother was a dreamy sort of a woman who would play with me for a while and read to me for an hour or so each day, but she, too, was driven by a desire to create, and I grew up thinking all mothers sat at the kitchen table and typed out stories, books, poems, and plays for children."

"How I loved to sit under the table on my mother's feet, hypnotized by the comforting click-clack of her old Royal manual typewriter. And every day when the mail came I shared her anxiety and frustration when for months on end all we found were big, manila envelopes, stuffed with rejected stories and regretful notes. But then, one wonderful morning the mail brought her first check for a sale. We both made it into print that day in a Golden Book entitled, Sunny And The Witch."

"Get out!" Dr. Carroll said, "That's pretty neat."

"It really was," I agreed. "I loved that story and was so excited I did a tap dance on the red and gray Formica and chrome kitchen table, and my mother actually forgot to make me 'get down from there this very instant.'"

"Is that when you first decided you wanted to be a writer, Sunny?"

"Actually, I think I was born with a desire to write books. I would spend hours copying the printed words out of my story-books onto the blank pages of my tablet assuming I was actually writing a book. Then The Wizard of Oz was re-released and my parents took me to see it. That film changed my life. I discovered I had been born a star even if no one else knew it yet. Judy Garland and I were like secret twins and now I knew what I would do with the rest of my life. I became an actress in search of a good role before the closing credits had rolled."

"I studied old movies on T. V., learning bits of dialog and dressing like the actresses I admired in Mah and Gram's old cast-off cloche hats, limp fox-tails and aging high heels that were ridiculously big on me since Mah's feet were a size nine and Gram's were an eleven."

"I watched 'I love Lucy', and 'Uncle Miltie,' every week and honed my comic timing. I drank in Perry's show from behind the green chair, paying attention to every song and trying to learn the lyrics. Television became my teacher. I could study all day if I wanted to, providing I watched my step. Once after studying the soap, 'Search for Tomorrow,' I informed my mother in a loud dramatic voice, "I'm not going to stand for your interference in my life a moment longer!"

Dr. Carroll stifled a laugh.

"She wasn't amused and that episode cost me a few days of freedom while I was forced to play in my room, away from the bad influence of daytime television."

"I longed to grow older and taller. I told Chloe to be patient. One day soon I would be grown and then we would escape the drab, gray and brown existence of our dirt yard. Together we would race over the back fence to a wonderful, techni-color world of free choice with no strict parents to tell us what to do and when to do it."

"Every night Chloe and I sat on the low window sill and watched the sunset cast a rosy glow of hope across the shades of gray crushed into the dirty city landscape outside of my window. I knew one day I would own my life and it would be up to me to create it like a great painting; to live all of my dreams like in a movie."

"Umhmmm…" Dr. Carroll said, scribbling on his pad.

"What?" I asked, "What did you mean by that, Doctor?" By that snotty little Umhmmm?"

He smiled. "I'm just beginning to understand you; to see how you were formed, psychologically speaking. You experienced an awful lot of fantasy in your childhood; too much perhaps."

"Perhaps," I agreed, shrugging. "But aren't most creative people formed in this way?"

He nodded. "That's certainly true. So when did you actually begin to perform?"

"Well, my mother recognized my talent and tried to help me to develop it. She would turn on the radio to the 'Make Believe Ballroom,' and then call out different themes for me to dance."

"Sunny," she'd say, "dance a waterfall," and for her I would bend and twist and sparkle around the room, totally absorbed in our fantasy."

Dr. Carroll stopped making notes and met my eyes. He raised his eyebrows and so I raised mine too. "Well, that's the way it was. You want the truth, don't you?"

He nodded. "Go on."

"I can be practical, too, you know," I said, "I do have a practical side. For months, when I was little, I longed for pink satin toe slippers with long, pink ribbons to twist up my legs. I would have wanted a pink tutu, as well, but I knew I would never in a million years get that. It was much too impractical a purchase for two Capricorn parents living on a budget and saving for a house in the country."

"Your parents were both Capricorn? I'm a Capricorn, too."

"Umhummm," I said, grinning at him. "Anyway, it was on my fourth birthday when I really did myself in and caused my father to forbid me to ever have dancing lessons."

"My cousins and the other school-age kids in the neighborhood came to my party. I made the mistake when I insisted they all had to wait to have cake and ice cream until after I had performed my veil dance for them. I'd learned it from some old movie on T.V. I draped myself with Mah's silk scarves, and to the bored stares of my captive audience, I stood on the coffee table and began to wriggle and undulate like a belly dancer. I'll never forget the look of horror on my fathers' face when he walked into the room and saw his worst nightmare happening right before his eyes."

"Skinny, get in here!" he shouted at my confused mother, busy in the kitchen, "This dancing business has got to stop. I've never yet known a dancer who didn't end up stripping in Hoboken." Then he dragged me off the table in front of all my guests and off to my room to change into something 'decent.'"

"Later, when I opened my presents, I was deeply disappointed, though not surprised, when there wasn't a toe shoe among them. I decided this was important enough to me to take my life into my hands and confront my father."

"No!" he shouted, "Absolutely not! You will not become a dancer!"

"But I promise I'll never go to Hoboken!" I shouted back. "I don't even know where it is!"

"Then I started to think like the enemy and the answer came to me. For once I was grateful for the military training my father had insisted on giving both Joe-Joe and me. I told him I would forget the dancing lessons if I could just have the pink satin toe-shoes. And I would work around the house and earn every single penny of the money to pay for them myself."

"My father and I stared into our identical dark eyes with equal determination. This time I won a small battle. Actually the work-ethic won it for me. He said, yes, but only if I earned all the money myself. The catch? I was never to ask for the lessons again. I was to face the rest of my childhood without dancing lessons."

"I shrugged that off as a minor wrinkle in my plan. At four you just know you can do anything. I was convinced the minute I put the slippers on my feet, I would miraculously know how to dance. Just like the dancers in a movie musical, who, when the music starts, leap up and somehow suddenly dance the same perfectly executed steps."

"Every afternoon I dusted the tops of all the furniture in the apartment for a nickel a day. I usually helped my mother for free anyway, but my father didn't know that. My mother was about as enthusiastic about housekeeping as she was about cooking."

"I, at least, shared her distain for cleaning and helped her out of pity. But my father was a bit of a pain in the ass about housework. He'd never gotten over his officer's training and since he was also a perfectionist, he generally drove the rest of the family crazy."

"He'd write, "Help! Please dust me!" on the tops of dusty furniture if he was in a good mood. If he was in a bad mood, he'd scream and yell and brow-beat everyone around him. Although he'd been a Second

Lieutenant during the War, in our house he was the General, and the rest of us were all buck-privates with no hope of promotion."

"You couldn't even argue with the man because he was so meticulous about his own personal habits, always setting a perfect example for us mere mortals. If he ate a snack at night, as soon as he was finished eating, he'd get up and wash, dry, and return the plate to its' proper place. When he undressed for bed, his shoes went onto shoe stands, his pants were hung on a special hanger, and his shirt and underwear went directly into the hamper. A person like that could help you to understand the motivation for *The Caine Mutiny*."

Dr. Carroll chuckled. "Since you were so close to your father I'm surprised you didn't mimic his perfectionism."

"Oh, I did, for a while, after I was first married. I was one of those super-women for a couple of years. My house was immaculate, my children squeaky clean; orderly, and miserable. I didn't even let Bull get past the front door without surrendering his shoes."

"How did you change that compulsive behavior? Most people have trouble recovering from that kind of a curse."

"It just started to depress me. I felt like my life was based on fighting a war I had no hope of winning. Dirt was the enemy and it was all around me. So I decided to de-fuse the battle. I decided not to care so much anymore and to find a level of cleanliness and order we could all live with comfortably. I set up a schedule for cleaning, baking, cooking, etc. based on how much time we were each willing to give to these chores and I never deviated from it; even if we were having company."

"The other members of the family shared some of my chores, and we each had a night to create the dinner of our choice, and we even picked the household tasks we least minded doing. Now I have time for a real life, too. It's worked out great."

"It sounds great. It's a creative, intelligent solution to what could become a major problem. You should be proud of how you handled that one, Sunny."

"Thanks, Doctor," I said, "I just wish I could handle my marital problems with the same finesse."

"Don't beat yourself up, Sunny. Marital problems are not to be handled alone, but to be shared by the two people in a marriage. And if people never needed any help in doing that, I'd be out of a job."

"Ha!" I said, "And a better world it would be…no offense."

He made a face at me. "How about your mother? How did she handle your father's perfectionism?"

"My mother and I were both clean, but naturally messy. We usually did as we pleased during the days, reading, writing, dancing, watching old movies on T.V., visiting the park, having lunch with Ba, then at 3:30 we raced around the apartment like maniacs, dusting, running the carpet-sweeper, making the beds, doing the dishes, peeling the potatoes for dinner."

"Sounds like fun," Dr. Carroll said.

"Not really. It was kind of nervous. I still get a tense feeling in the pit of my stomach every day around 3:30, until I reason my way past the feeling. I tell myself I'm not a child anymore and my chores for the day were done early in the morning, and Daddy isn't coming home to 'judge' my mother and give the family either his approval or his bad temper. That's one of the great things about being grown-up."

"I would imagine you'd project those feelings onto Bull. Didn't you ever get nervous, not because Dad was coming home, but because your husband was coming home?"

"At the beginning of the marriage I did, but it fizzled out right away. Bull is a lot of different things, some almost evil, but on the surface, at least for the most part, he acts like a pussy-cat at home. He didn't put any expectations on me. In some ways that was a little weird. He was very passive and guarded at home, so much so that I'm not even sure I really know him even after all these years of marriage."

Dr. Carroll sat forward in his chair. "But didn't Bull try to control your actions, most aspects of your life, with passive aggression?"

I thought about that for a while. "Yeah…I guess he did. You mean like when I'd be excited about my writing, or I'd be asked to act in a local play and then he'd have an affair and spoil it for me. Put me in my place. I see what you mean."

"Sometimes he was violent, wasn't he?"

I nodded again. "Not often though…usually it was my fault because I didn't know when to shut-up. I'd start in on his latest girlfriend, and believe me, I can really start in, and he'd just go kind of crazy."

"Sunny," Dr. Carroll cut in, "You have got to stop taking responsibility for what everyone else does around you. Bull had freedom of choice. When he didn't have the words, or the courage to answer your accusations truthfully, he was absolutely wrong to use violence against you. And he sometimes beat the children too, didn't he? Do you have a way of justifying that too?"

The tears started to roll down my cheeks, and the pain in my chest was so real I was sure I'd die of it. "No, Doctor, I have no excuse for his beating our children. It's so confusing. He can be so sweet, and then, you just don't know what will set him off and he's dangerous." I stared down at my trembling hands and made them into fists.

"Sunny," Dr. Carroll said gently, "we'll talk about Bull tomorrow. Finish the story about the toe-shoes, and Chloe. You wanted to tell me about Chloe."

I mopped at my tears with soggy Kleenex. "Yes. I'll finish the story. Well, it took me a couple of months to earn the money and I will never forget my feeling of pride and accomplishment as I put those toe slippers on for the first time and twisted those pink satin ribbons up and around my legs. It was my first feel of real satin and as I stood and posed like the ballerina who lived only in my mind, I felt like living proof that all things are possible if you only dare to believe and work toward your goals."

"Like Dorothy in The Wizard of Oz, like Peter Pan and Wendy, I had no doubt I could now fly across the room, dancing as gracefully as Tinker Bell flew. I pointed my toe and leaped into the air, came down on top of that toe, twisted my ankle, and fell flat on my face."

"My toe throbbed but it didn't hurt half as much as my bruised heart. Reality had collided with my expectations and I had learned a sad, but necessary lesson. Slightly daunted, I decided to try walking around in the slippers before I tried dancing and leaping again. For the next few days I stood on my toes and hobbled around the living room in great and terrible pain. My beloved toe shoes had turned into instruments of torture. I couldn't believe how much I had longed for those slippers. Like a disappointed lover, I marveled at how I could have been so naïve."

"My mother showed me how to stuff the toes with lamb's wool, but it didn't help much. My toes grew angry red and blistered and still I wouldn't give up. My mother was worried about me. She argued with my father to please allow me to have the dancing lessons before

I seriously injured my feet and ankles. I didn't get them; and nothing changed. After all, a deal was a deal in my father's house."

"I continued to practice daily and I did eventually teach myself to dance on them: a little. It wasn't until I was approaching my twelfth birthday and, being a tomboy, had developed a bouncing, masculine, walk like my father's that he suddenly came up with the idea that I should take *ballet lessons!*"

"But only for one year until I had learned to carry myself with the proper feminine grace. In that year I learned as much as I could and practiced so hard for the spring recital that I was featured in a long, modern jazz solo. Outfitted like an old M.G.M. movie queen in a beautiful pale green and lavender costume trimmed with sequins, I danced for my audience."

"For one night I was a real dancer. I was hoping hard that if I was very good, my father would let me continue with the lessons, but everyone praised my performance so enthusiastically my plan back-fired and he made me quit."

"I cried and begged and came out of that confrontation with a promise of singing lessons. I was a pretty good singer, a lyric soprano with some coloratura notes, and at least my father believed I was good enough so I would never be tempted to earn a living by taking my clothes off in a place like Hoboken, New Jersey."

"Despite the conflicts I had with my father I practically worshipped him. In the lonely years before I started school, I would kneel on the emerald-green velvet sofa and watch the cars race past our front window. I always watched for my father to come down our walk so I could slip out into the front hall and be the first one to greet him. Then we could have a private moment together before he started talking to my mother. He was always so glad to see me. "Hi, there, Cockroach," he would say before picking me up and giving me a big hug. I would bury my face against his shoulder and breathe in the special Dad smell, and I don't think I ever smiled back into my father's face without thinking how handsome he was. I especially loved his inky- black hair with the streak of silver in the wave above his left eye."

"After giving me my hug, Dad would do his magic trick and I always gave him a big reaction. He would say some magic words, "Hocus pocus, dominocus!" and then pull a dime out of my ear."

"I would clap my hands and jump up and down and beg him to tell me how to get the dimes to come out of my ears on a regular basis. I tried digging them out myself, but never once did I come up with a dime. He loved me the most when I loved his magic trick and he always gave me the softest caress on the cheek and the saddest, most tender smile. I think he wanted me to always be four and to always adore him."

"I made it one of my responsibilities to try to chase the sadness out of his eyes. I didn't know why it was there, but I recognized how sadness lay on him like a layer of old dust. I would try to learn a song, or a comic line or two to thrill him with each evening."

"Despite his fears that I was destined for a life of debauchery in show business, he was proud of my talent and if I was especially adorable he would take me upstairs to perform for my Aunt Angelina and Uncle Lou on the second floor and then up to his parents on the third floor. I always tried to be very good for Aunt Angelina because she was outgoing and friendly and the one most likely to reward me with some of her incredible pasta."

"One night I was so good that not only did she give me pasta, but she arranged to have me appear on a local children's television show. The other kids and I sat around the host, a man named Uncle Herbie, who only seemed to like kids when the camera was on him. I had a show business instinct early on because I figured out how to beat out all the other cute kids and was picked to do the commercial."

"The director poured some evil tasting brown vitamin tonic in a paper cup for each of us to sample. Then he walked down the line and asked each child to take a sip and tell him how it tasted. They each made faces, each child making a worse face than the one before him, as if this were a nasty-face-contest instead of a commercial audition, and some of them even went so far as to say, "Yuck, this stuff stinks!""

"So I must have been the only preschooler in the bunch with hopes of becoming a star, because when my turn came, I took the cup, drained it, looked the director in the eye, smiled sweetly, and said, "This tastes great!""

"The director and I grinned at each other for some time. I was four and he was forty, but in that instant we recognized each other as kindred spirits."

"I ended up doing all the commercials, sometimes singing them, and I often got to sit on Uncle Herbie's knee during the segment when he would talk to the audience between cartoons and pretend he liked little kids. He seemed to like me, though, and sometimes he even smiled at me when the camera light was off. "You're O.K., Kid," he'd say. But I knew not to trust him. He was unpredictable and childish, and I knew he only liked me because I was smart enough to smile on cue, speak my lines at the right time, and get off his lap fast at the end of the show."

"So," Dr. Carroll said, "like most little girls who grew up in the fifties, you learned at an early age how to manipulate men to get what you wanted. And you were good at it. Now tell me about the cat."

I laughed. "You summed that up very well. Let's see, now, the cat was very important to me because my mother was afraid of our 'rough city neighborhood' and I wasn't allowed to play in the street with the other kids. My short show business career, which lasted until I started Kindergarten, helped me to fill the days, but mostly I missed my father."

"He was really my favorite playmate and I could actually wish him into being. I would close my eyes and concentrate so hard that when I opened them, I would see my father sitting next to me on the green velvet sofa. The 'thought form' Daddy would smile at me, but whenever I tried to climb up on its' lap it would fade away to nothing and I would realize this daddy hadn't been real at all. I had a very powerful imagination and I spent much of my time living in a world of my own creation."

Dr. Carroll cleared his throat and I watched him as he removed his glasses and rubbed his eyes. "Sunny, it sounds like you were hallucinating. Can you recall any trauma that may have triggered these episodes?"

I thought about it for a few seconds. "Honestly, no," I said, "Sorry, but hallucinations in children aren't as serious as they are in adults, are they?"

He watched me thoughtfully for a while; then shook his head. "Not usually. I'm curious as to why you're avoiding finishing the cat story. When did the hallucinations start? Was it around the time you had this cat?"

"Maybe…it must have been. You know Chloe was the best thing I can remember about my childhood, apart from Joe-Joe, and she was also the worst thing, so maybe a trauma did trigger the 'thought form daddy."

"I wonder why the worst things seem to happen on the most gorgeous days. It was in the spring and Chloe had just come back from her walk in the yard, when she lay down on the back porch and wouldn't move again. I could hear her moan and I begged my mother to call a doctor for her. I thought she had a bad case of indigestion since she had been putting on weight lately. It seemed she'd gotten into the habit of over-eating."

"My mother was worried, too, since we didn't have a car and she wouldn't have been able to drive it if we had it anyway. She did make a bunch of frantic phone calls. My dad couldn't leave work to help us, and, at his suggestion, she tried to find a Vet who would make a house call. No one would come to help us, but she was given some instructions over the phone. As Chloe's shrieks and moans increased in volume, I began to cry too."

"Mah called Ba and she came right over on the bus to take Joe-Joe and me to the park across the street to play on the swings. I loved Ba, but I didn't want to leave Chloe. Mah insisted."

"When we got to the park, I asked Ba to tell us the truth about what was wrong with Chloe. I knew she was sick and I didn't believe my mother when she said it wasn't serious. I knew I could count on Ba for the hard facts and she looked me in the eye and told me Chloe was pregnant. She explained this meant she was going to soon have a family of kittens, but she was also sick and might not get better."

"I cried and so did Joe-Joe, but we were both glad Ba had told us the truth. We were still sad, but our stomachs calmed down a little because we felt more secure in knowing what was really happening."

"By the time we got home, we were feeling a bit more cheerful. We hoped Chloe had been visited by her kittens and was feeling better. I ran through the apartment and tried to get out onto the porch, but my mother had locked the door and used the chain that was up too high for me to reach. She wouldn't let me go out there. It was much too quiet on the porch now and I was very frightened."

"I cried and begged Mah to let me be with Chloe and to see the kittens, but she sent me to my room and told me I'd have to wait until Dad got home. Then she turned on Ba for telling us about the kittens, and after Ba hung her head and apologized; she left in a hurry."

"Joe-Joe kept visiting me in our room and telling me what was happening on Howdy Doody, but I could see he was upset too."

"It seemed like hours until Dad got home. Right away, he took us on his lap and told us that Chloe had had to leave us. Her husband and five little gray-striped kittens had come to take her with them to Cat-Land. Cat-Land was a wonderful place with lollipop trees and soda pop falls, just like in a Raggedy Ann book, and we should be happy for her. We shouldn't be selfish and cry for ourselves. Chloe wouldn't want that."

"Joe-Joe slipped his little hand into mine and we looked into each other's eyes. We were confused. Should we cry or not? I know I felt empty inside and betrayed.

"But Daddy," I said, speaking for the two of us, "Chloe really loves us. She would never leave us, and I know she would never go on a trip without at least saying goodbye."

"My father's eyes filled with tears, but he tried to smile. "But Sunny, Chloe wanted to get married and make a family with her husband and kittens. When a little cat-girl, or any girl gets married, she has to go off and live with her husband."

"No!" I shouted, jumping down from his lap and heading toward the room I shared with Joe-Joe. "Chloe really loves us and she would never leave us. Not for a husband and five little kittens, or Perry Como, or anyone. I know Chloe. I know her better than you do! She'll be back to see us. I know it."

"I mourned for Chloe for months that may have turned into years... I'm not sure. My parents wouldn't let us have another kitten. They didn't want us to be hurt when it eventually went off to 'Cat-Land.'"

"For a long time my father tried to make me feel better by coming home with presents from Chloe; little cat books, cat jewelry, and once a gray-striped cat puppet, which lies yellowing in the bottom drawer of my dresser to this very day. I take it out whenever I want to remind myself how much my father loved me and how misguided a parent's love can so often be..."

"I pretended to be delighted by these gifts because I could see how important it was to my father to lessen my grief, and I grew very good at acting to please others. Yet, secretly, I would shudder when every few weeks Dad would come through the door and say, "Guess who I ran into downtown this afternoon?"

"It was always Chloe. He'd met her while she was shopping for ribbons or blankets for the kittens and she and Dad had had lunch together, of course, and she had sent her love along with another present for us."

"I always beamed at Dad and hung on his every word, but deep down inside, I was hurt and angry. I had loved that damn cat with my whole heart and it was becoming increasingly obvious that she hadn't loved me at all. She didn't even care enough about me to see me herself, or to call me on the phone, or to invite me to have lunch with her and Dad at Chock Full O' Nuts. I vowed to never trust love again."

"The next completely happy day I remember is the day I finally found out Chloe had died on the back porch the day she'd given birth to five dead kittens. Then I knew she really had loved me. She hadn't left us because she wanted to leave; she'd just gone on to Heaven to wait for me there. It's a shame I found out a little too late."

"God, Sunny you can really tell a story," Dr. Carroll said, "I'm exhausted. How about you?" And before I could answer, he leaned forward and put his head down on his desk.

CHAPTER 11

I'd worn poor Dr. Carroll out. He had the same glazed look I'd noticed Bull would sometimes get after spending too much time with me. All the evidence seemed to point to the conclusion that I was a bit hard to take; at least for men. I got that impression when I spent too much time out of either the kitchen or the bedroom...I seemed to be popular in those two venues. At least with Bull I was...

My women friends were a lot more resilient, or maybe just less affected by me. It was a mystery, but maybe not so much. I'd always known I was different.

Alexander was glad to see me come back to the community room. There were so few people he could connect with in any meaningful way. I was glad to see him too, because he was my gentle giant, the first tall man I'd ever felt close to, mostly because Dad had convinced me tall men were deformed.

Dad was only five six and a half and he would always point out the tall men in any group and say, "Big guys don't look right in a suit. Little guys are cuter. Our clothes fit us so well and we don't take up as much space."

So it was a big step for me to be involved with a man over six feet tall; even Bull was on the short side. But mostly I loved Alexander for his accepting spirit. He never judged anyone, and he was so smart and open to different ideas. And the fact that he was a decent male of the species who was attracted to me at a time when my self-esteem was nearly non-existent, didn't hurt either. I needed the reinforcement of his admiration and attention. I hoped I was giving something positive back to him as well.

*　*　*

Dinner that night was a dull affair. Hospital Italian is doomed by definition. "One of these days I'll cook some great pasta for you," I whispered to Alexander as I wrapped the limp linguine around my fork. He grinned and looked as debonair as a man can look in a mental health ward.

"I'm a pretty good cook myself," he whispered back, "but if you really want to please me you'll read me another chapter of that mystical book to me."

My heart swelled with what felt like true love. My mystical book; I loved how he loved my writing. I really, really loved it, and I would read to him until he begged me to stop. But it didn't look as if he'd ever get tired of it. And that was truly scary; but scary good.

"Read to me, Sunny," he said, as we settled into our favorite spot after dinner. "I can't wait to see what happens to Jessamyn and the rest of the gang."

"It's so easy to love you, Alexander," I said, "I wish we'd met years ago when we were practically living next door to one another."

"Don't question fate, Sunny. All things happen in their own good time. We met when we were supposed to meet."

"I love your wisdom, Alexander."

"Read."

                              *   *   *

For several days after the attack, we were all in shock. We buried four men, three women, and one child. We didn't have to bury Madeleine Sullivan since her body had burned with her wagon. We grieved mightily and in our grief we suffered all the more since we didn't know whether or not to include Adelaide among our count of the dead. The great savage who had stolen her away, left not a clue or a trace of evidence as to where he might have taken her.

The reverend had been tense, and obviously struggling to keep under tight control when he asked for volunteers to go off in search of Adelaide. Bruin had been the first to step forward. Then Papa followed his lead; and only after Bruin spoke for fifteen minutes or more, to persuade Papa he was sorely needed by the other members of our train to help with the many repairs to the wagons, did he relent and agree to stay behind.

Papa was pale and his hands shook often as we worked together to help our friends. Papa ignored his weakened state and I did, too, knowing how angry he became if he thought anyone fussed over him, or worst of all, pitied him.

Since each family had started the journey supplied with 150 pounds of flour, 100 pounds of bacon, twenty pounds of coffee, 10 pounds of salt, as well as large amounts of chipped beef and rice, tea, dried beans, dried fruit, baking soda, vinegar, pickles, mustard, and tallow, we hadn't worried thus far about running short of provisions. But now five families had either lost their wagons and all of their possessions, or at least half of their provisions, to the Indian's fire.

Those of us who had survived the raid unscathed, shared with those of us in need.

Papa's spirits improved as the day wore on for he was much in demand for his fine skills. I was proud of Papa as I watched him root through the charred ruins of the various wagons for parts that could be re-used. Again, we all pitched in to loan our friends the extra wheels, the odd axle, the extra bolts, most everyone had tied up under the bottom of their wagons before we had begun our journey.

I was a wreck of nerves the entire time the men were gone. Adelaide rested heavily upon my mind as I relived that horrendous day when she had been taken…and I had escaped and been spared.

Perhaps it was guilt that made me think she was at peace in her new surroundings. Perhaps it was frustration at feeling so powerless to help her…to never know the truth about what might have happened to her.

Still, I met her in my dreams at night and she was happier than I could ever have hoped. She wore a loose, beaded garment and gazed with what looked like love into the face of a wild and handsome savage. In one dream she was surrounded by Indian children. They sat together in the shade of a giant tree. The sun set in the distance looming over rolling green hills; the bold slashes of tangerine blended to deep fuchsia, then into the purple haze of night.

Adelaide taught the children words of English. She laughed in musical tones I'd never before heard in her voice at their awkward attempts to copy her speech and then they laughed together as she tried to speak their language.

I wanted to believe Adelaide was alive and had found her great adventure. I wanted to believe her true destiny lay in this wild country as the wife of an Indian man. From what I knew of her, she would enjoy being a cultural bridge between these two worlds. I could see her riding bareback into the wind, her hair a flowing red and golden river scorched to glory by the summer sun. I wanted to believe my dreams of her were true; but most of all I longed for some proof that the secret wild, passionate heart of this timid woman had found her true home.

On the second day of searching, riding long and hard into the early evening, the men found her dress. Her calico dress, torn, but not bloodied, had been hammered to an oak tree. It was said it was the way the Indians taunted us by letting us know she was still alive but lost to us forever. For me it provided comfort that she hadn't been harmed.

That night we sat around the campfire and prayed. The reverend slumped forward over his clasped hands and drew shaky breaths as he prayed for Adelaide's safety. The hard, masculine planes of his face were drawn and streaked with dirt. His long, light hair had come undone from his queue and hung limp and damp around his haunted clear-gray eyes.

I looked to Bruin for possible answers. "What can we do to help? The reverend appears to be on the verge of collapse. Is there anything we can do to help him?"

Bruin looked weary as well; but not half as undone as the poor reverend did. I was grateful when Bruin smiled at me; a small, special smile that made everything better.

He brushed the stray curls back from his forehead and sighed. "There isn't much sense in searching any longer, Jessie. We're no match for them. We're like a band of Indians trying to sneak unnoticed around downtown Boston. We're out of our depth here. The best thing we can do for the reverend is try to help him to accept the futility of going on with it. He needs to acknowledge there is a great element of potential danger here. The Indians just might decide to attack us again if we don't move out of their territory."

Bruin's voice conveyed all the emotions he didn't have the words to express. "I know it sounds harsh, but I hope you understand. We can't risk the entire group on the outside chance we might find one woman. And believe me there is as good as no chance at all."

I turned away to cry alone. He put his arm around my shoulders. "I know," he said, "one woman…one friend…one priceless human life. I'm so sorry, Jessie."

I nodded, glad for once I was not a man and responsible for such terrible, hard decisions.

Papa sat down beside us. The white, pinched look of his face was alarming.

"Please rest, Mr. Miles," Bruin coaxed, placing a wide hand on Papa's broad shoulder. "You've done a fine day's work by anyone's standards."

Papa shrugged Bruin's kind words away. "It was little enough to do, Son. I don't know what to say when I write to Madeleine's Sullivan's son. How can I tell the young man both his mother and Adelaide are gone from our midst…just like that?"

"I'll help you, Papa," I cut in, "I'd like to add something to the letter." I hoped to tell Adelaide's brother of my dreams and I hoped he would find comfort in them, as well as in the fact they had nailed her dress to a tree, and it appeared as if she was, indeed, still alive.

The reverend stood at this moment and towered over us. "We'll search for Adelaide one more day," he said with a finality that invited no opposition. "Delay all letter writing until then. I'm hoping within twenty-four hours we'll have better news to send back to Boston."

*   *   *

The men rose before dawn. I opened my eyes to the dark as I heard their hoof-beats thunder off.

All day I prayed for Adelaide's safe return, but once again we were all devastated when the men returned to camp without her.

"We searched for miles around the tree where we discovered her dress; miles in each direction," Bruin told me that night as we sat by the cozy warmth of our campfire. The firelight threw long shadows up over his face, giving it a stark, defeated look.

He poked the wood with a stick and the log broke apart, crackling a blue and orange spit of renewed flame, and fragrant wood smoke. "We must have traveled a five or six mile radius around that tree and not one sign did we find. Not one indication that a band of Indians had even traveled through that area. We're just not going to find her, Jessamyn. It's got to become obvious, even to the reverend. Adelaide is gone… gone with the Indians to God only knows where."

I dreamed about Adelaide once more; just two days after we resumed our journey. It was the dream I decided to include in my addition to Papa's letter to Adelaide's brother. Even though we knew we couldn't

post the letter until we reached Marietta, Papa and I worked on our
solitary contributions as we sat together following our evening meal.

Dear Mr. Sullivan, (I began.)

I grew close to your beloved sister, Adelaide, as we traveled together
upon this journey. Before our departure from Boston I knew her as the
fine teacher who had inspired me to develop a love of literature, and
most especially, poetry.

One of my fondest memories of your sister is of the evening we
gathered together at Reverend Putnam's campfire and read the sonnets of William Shakespeare aloud to one another. Your graceful, lovely
sister read with a deep understanding of each profound word and I am
honored to remember her as a cherished friend.

Since Adelaide's abduction I have had several dreams about her.
Since I am given to have prophetic dreams, I wish to share my latest
dream with you out of the sincere wish it will help to alleviate in some
small way the enormity of your terrible loss.

Last night I saw Adelaide once again as I have seen her in several dreams during these past difficult days. She was dressed in a loose,
flowing garment trimmed with beads and feathers. She stood tall and
confident at the top of a grassy hill. She held the hand of a small Indian
boy and other children followed closely behind them.

She smiled at me in greeting. "Jessamyn!" she said, "please tell
everyone I have found my greatest adventure. It is more than I could
have imagined!"

"But Adelaide," I said, feeling a mixture of emotions. I was happy
for her joyful, high spirits, but I was confused as well. "We miss you so
much, Adelaide. You are sorely missed by all of your friends. Won't you
return to us?"

"No, Jessamyn. I won't be coming back," she said. "I've found a place
among these amazing people. They are very spiritual, you know...no
one ever mentions that. They honor our sacred earth and God, whom
they call The Great Spirit. We could take some lessons from them. We
could learn a lot from these so called, 'savages.'"

"But Adelaide," I entreated, "The burned wagons...all the death.
How can you forgive them?"

She smiled at me as if I were a foolish child. "Even the law recognizes a man's right to defend his land as well as his possessions. If we had more respect for the wealth of nature around us we might be able to live peacefully with these Indians."

"Oh, Adelaide," I said, "I shall miss you terribly. We all will. Please be safe and happy."

And then I awoke and still I can feel the chills whenever I think of Adelaide's powerful presence in that dream; her tremendous 'joie de vivre.' And I must believe this is a message of some kind. I must believe Adelaide has found her place and her heart's desire.

I hope I have done the correct thing in sharing this dream with you. I hope you will forgive my presumption since we don't know each other very well and I have no idea how you will view my revelations. I pray they will comfort you as they have comforted me.

With Heartfelt Condolences,
Miss Jessamyn Miles

*   *   *

I worried about Papa as we continued upon our journey to Marietta, Ohio. We were nearly all the way through Pennsylvania when far upon the horizon appeared the beginning of the foothills of the great Allegheny Mountains. Papa's natural high spirits had been dulled by the Indian raid and the deaths…and of course by the tragic abduction of Adelaide. He spoke of Adelaide nearly every day and it was apparent he had never considered he might be putting me in serious danger when he agreed to join this caravan. He looked almost sheepish at times when he spoke to me, and my reference to our old life in Boston, brought a confused, tearful look to his eyes.

I pitied Papa and decided to stop berating him for stealing me away from my former happy life; my art lessons. I turned nearly every day to my drawing tablets and charcoal. I was proud of a sketch I had done in memory of Adelaide, but when I showed it to Papa, to Bruin, and finally to the reverend, I was disappointed by their comments.

"You've flattered her a bit, Little Mite," Papa said, "And I'm sure that is a good thing. She was a good, decent woman, but she really wasn't much to look at."

It seemed a sorry comment to make about an intelligent, caring woman who had given so much of herself to other peoples' children and then faded from our lives before we had the chance to thank her properly, or to fully get to know her.

Bruin had stared at the sketch for the longest time. I found it impossible to read the expression on his face, and so I waited eagerly for him to speak.

"Too bad she died before she ever truly became a woman," he said, and turned away from me and my drawing, shaking his head sadly.

'But we don't know if she is dead, Bruin. We can't be certain of that at all. You know yourself it is quite common for the Indians to abduct a woman and bring her into the tribe; most especially women with lighter colored hair. There are many tales of white women living out their days as the wives of Indian braves…as the mothers of their children.

Bruin's firm grasp closed around my wrist. "You sound as if you approve of such abominations."

"And you sound as if you consider a woman a woman only if she's been taken to wife and to bed by a man…a white man!" His hand went limp on my arm and I pulled away from him.

Bruin scratched his head and grinned at me. "You've got an unusual way of looking at things, Jessie, and I'll be needing some time to think about what you just said…before we discuss this again."

"Ha!" I shot back, "Don't think too hard on it or you'll have to take to your bed with an aching head."

At least Bruin had the good nature to laugh with me. "There is more truth to that than I'd like to admit," he said, "But at least I'm willing to think on it."

"I'll give you that, Bruin Mahoney," I returned, "But you failed to give me your opinion of my drawing."

Bruin's smile was slow and sly. "I'm shocked to hear you care at all for my opinion on any subject."

I smiled back at him. "If you need time to come up with one; meaning an opinion on this subject as well, I'll give you another minute or two, but really, Bruin, I have other things to accomplish today," I snapped, enjoying the way he squirmed in his heavy boots as he kicked a line through the dirt.

"I think you made her look livelier than I remember her being either here on the trail or back in Boston," he said, as if pulling the words out of the air. "If that's a compliment then I give it to you freely, but I don't know enough about art to have my opinion count for much."

"That one will do for now, Bruin," I said, "And I know why she appears more alive in my sketch. It's because I have sketched Adelaide as she has appeared in my dreams. And that Adelaide is happier and more vivacious than the one we've known here on the trail. She told me so and I half believe my dreams are true."

Bruin looked as shocked as if I stood before him in my birthday suit. "You'd better not tell anyone else about these strange feelings and dreams of yours, Jessamyn, or they'll be gossiping among the wagons that George Miles' daughter has lost the good sense God gave her.

"I don't care what's said about me, Bruin," I said, laughing, "That is one legacy from Mama I prize more highly than the rings and necklaces she left to me in her will. I'll think whatever I please…and not even you can tell me if I'm right or wrong."

I left Bruin to sneeze in my dust as I hurried off to show the reverend my drawing and to find out what an educated man had to say on the subject. It was rumored among the women that Charles Putnam had graduated from the seminary at Princeton at the top of his class. I had found him to be both the smartest man I had ever known as well as the most socially awkward.

The reverend was stirring the contents of a smoking iron pot. It stood over the fire on three high legs. I sniffed the air, or I should say, choked in the clouds of smoke and guessed correctly he was making some kind of a stew; either rabbit or squirrel.

"Well," he said doubtfully when I asked him about it, "it is a stew. Rabbit and dandelion greens…I'll serve it over rice. W-would you care to join me for dinner, Miss Jessamyn? Of course your father is included in the invitation."

He looked almost frightened I might accept and find out he wasn't much of a cook, so I put him at ease by assuring him Papa and I had already eaten our evening meal.

"I do have a purpose in coming to see you, though, Reverend," I said, thrusting the tablet under his nose. "I would like your opinion of my drawing of Adelaide, since I am considering including it in the letter Papa and I have composed for Mr. Sullivan."

"It is quite lovely, Miss J-Jessamyn," he said, swallowing visibly, and then handing the drawing back to me hastily. He turned away from me to gather up his tin plate and utensils as if eager to dismiss both me and the memory of Adelaide and what might have been from his fireside.

I was puzzled by this lack of emotion from a man who had probably been the only suitor Adelaide had ever had. If suitor was even the correct word, for in truth they had been friends. It was really the rest of us who had hoped it might develop into something more.

"I'll draw one for you next, Reverend," I said cautiously, not certain how he would take that bit of information.

He stared past me into the forest beyond the boundaries of our campsite and raised his eyebrows. "May I speak frankly to you, Miss Jessamyn?"

I nodded.

"You are obviously an artist of some talent, but I can't say I recognize Miss Sullivan from your sketch. I don't mean to offend you, but the Adelaide Sullivan I knew was a much plainer woman than the one you have depicted here. She had a shy, demure personality and there was no trace of the…" He paused, searching for the right words. He tugged at his stiff clerical collar. "Adelaide Sullivan simply did not have any trace of the wild spirit you have clearly indicated in your artistic vision of her."

His lower lip trembled slightly and it was plain he found it difficult to be so candid with me.

"I appreciate your comments, Reverend," I said, hoping my cheeks wouldn't flush with the embarrassment I was hoping to conceal. "You are correct in describing my sketch as my artistic vision of Adelaide, for I believe her to be alive and living what she feels to be her great adventure with the Indians. I have seen her in my dreams…she has actually spoken to me and told me this very thing." I paused and drew my cotton shawl more closely around me despite the relative warmth of the evening.

I watched the reverend as he studied me with as much interest, and none of the shock Bruin had shown.

"Are you saying, Miss J-Jessamyn, you have experienced divine prophesy? Do you look upon your dreams as a sign from God that Adelaide is alive and adjusting to life among the Indians?" His intelligent piercing gaze held mine.

I could only nod.

"I hope you are correct," he said, and then smiled and he looked most impressive as he stood, towering over me, a man suddenly at ease as we discussed a subject he was completely comfortable with. "I had dreams of my mother when she passed on," he said, taking one step nearer. "They were a great comfort and I was profoundly grateful to our Lord for them. We'll never know for certain how real such visitations are…but why question when the dreams have such a positive effect upon those lucky enough to be graced by them."

I reached out to grasp the reverend's hand, and as I squeezed it, I thanked him for all his kind words. He turned suddenly scarlet from the roots of his pale hair to the top of his clerical collar.

As I started back to our wagon, he spoke one last time. "You should include the sketch of Adelaide with the letter to her brother. Your vision of his sister is very lovely and will be a comfort to him."

*　　*　　*

I was glad when it was decided we should have a celebration to commemorate our survival of the hardest part of the journey. We made camp at the foot of The Allegheny Mountains in Pennsylvania and morale was high as the women soaked beans and baked wild berry pies while the hunters brought back fifteen of the plentiful wild turkeys who populated the region. The air was fragrant as they roasted for hours upon spits in preparation for our feast.

As I mixed up a huge vat of corn bread, I chattered away at Papa and was glad to see a spark of his old self once again shining from his Irish-blue eyes.

"Throw in an extra handful of sugar, Little Mite," he coaxed, "We're almost there and we can be a bit less careful with provisions. We have only to travel through the mountains and then it's an easy float down the river to Marietta."

"Will we have to make rafts, Papa? And will we have to remove the wheels from the wagons?'

Papa shook his head. "There are flatboats for hire, but we will probably have to remove the wheels unless we can brace and tie them securely. Don't fret; it's easy enough after all we've been through already."

I gave Papa a hug and a kiss on his leathery cheek; then laughed when I saw the flour I'd left there. "I must be a sight!" I said glad of the clear, cool creek we'd stopped beside.

The luxury of daily baths was probably the real impetus for the decision to remain here by the banks of this glorious creek for these few days more. I had to admit it had been a major factor in my prompting Papa to cast his vote in favor of the celebration.

Later, after I'd finished my baking, I ran down to the creek for a long soak. There were three other women bathing there and several others were doing laundry on the large rocks farther down toward the bend in the creek.

Several large weeping willows grew close to our side of the shore and I ducked under their leafy cover to remove my shoes, stockings, apron, petticoat, and plain brown dress. I snatched up my soap, left my thin cotton shift on for the sake of modesty, and then stepped lightly into the muddy bed of the rushing water.

The cold water was a pleasant shock and I caught my breath and breathed the fresh water fragrance. The earth squished up from between my toes, but I continued on, pushing all thoughts of eels and snapping turtles from my mind.

Amanda Masters and her daughter, Elisha, were a few yards upstream floating in the deeper water. I called to them and they urged me to join them.

"You can swim, too, Jessamyn, can't you?" Elisha called, dipping her head back into the water and then bouncing up, water dripping from her mass of dark-blonde curls. "Did you bring your soap? We have plenty if you forgot," she called, then squealed and splashed Cassie Taylor who surfaced like the water snake I knew her to be.

I braced myself for potential trouble and waded toward the others. "I can swim and I've got soap," I answered, "But thanks anyway."

Cassie twisted her thin lips into a sneer that passed for a smile and kicked water into my face as she floated backward, treading water. "Sorry," she said in a mock-sweet voice.

"I'd like to make you sorry," I muttered under my breath and fake smiled back at her.

A breeze swooped past, showering us with the first leaves of early autumn. Leaves barely touched with color, mostly deep viridian, others decorated with spots of flame, ocher, and amber. A few waved past my face in a gleam of snapdragon.

I spoke the colors aloud, gathering the leaves up from the surface of the water, hoping to fashion some decorations for the party.

Cassie swam toward me, her arms and legs making frog-like motions. "You artistic ones do tend to overstate things," she said, laughing as if she'd made a witty remark.

"I like the way Jessamyn describes things like leaves and sunsets… and people," Elisha said, "I don't know anyone else who reads as much into life as Jessamyn. I find her company to be a welcome change from most of the boring people I know."

I thanked her for the compliment while Cassie swam off with powerful, manly strokes, then floated on her back, and shouted back to us. "I'll grant you the fact that Jessamyn has always been different…but I certainly wouldn't say that difference has always been welcome."

"Now girls," Amanda said, making her way toward the bank of the creek. "Be friends. I know you are bored with the monotony of this journey, but just you wait until this evening!"

She paused to wring her wet shift out and then stepped gingerly among the sharper rocks. She reached the grassy bank and turned to grin at us all. "I hear the reverend has agreed to allow dancing!" With swaying hips, Amanda raised her arms to an invisible partner and danced about in a wide circle. "You girls had better dance your meanness away tonight and quit your bickering!" She called, before ducking under the swaying willow fronds to dress.

"I can't wait to dance again," Cassie murmured, moving her arms through the water like a scandalous dancer from Paris, France.

I knew she was thinking about dancing with Bruin. We would just have to wait to see which one of us he preferred dancing with.

"I hear Booth Wade is an accomplished fiddler and caller, and he has agreed to lead the festivities. Of course Cal Witherspoon will join in with his banjo," Elisha said, beaming shyly as she turned toward the deeper water once again.

I swam to her. "You like him, don't you?" I asked.

She dove under the water and then burst back up through the calm surface next to me. Her light-blue eyes shimmered with the reflection of the sky on creek water. "I do, Jessamyn…I really do! He's so handsome and gentle, yet manly in the nicest way!"

I brought Cal's image to mind and although his physical charms failed to register with me, I had to admit he was a decent, likeable, young man.

"He's certainly very talented," I said, "Does he know you fancy him?"

Elisha looked about to faint. "Oh, I hope not!"

Cassie laughed at her. "How old are you, Elisha?"

"I turned fourteen this past June."

"That's old enough to know what's what. You should learn to be bold about what you want."

Amanda poked her head out from among the willows. The tree bobbed up and down and rustled like the wind had swept back through. "And perhaps you should learn to keep your progressive opinions to yourself, Miss Cassie Taylor! Elisha is doing just fine without your advice. Should Cal Witherspoon have the good sense to choose to court my sweet, young, daughter it will be without any help or interference from you! And I will see to that, make no mistake!"

I loved it. Amanda Masters was a woman to be reckoned with, and Cassie Taylor had just been put in her place.

Cassie sniffed with distain like the little snot I remembered from school, and, lifting the skirt of her shift, she swept around like a very wet queen then struggled up the slippery bank of the creek. She tottered a bit at the top; then paused long enough to snatch up her dry clothing, and without another word to anyone, she stamped off toward the campsite.

I glanced at Elisha and we burst into laughter, falling back into the water. "Mrs. Masters," I gasped, "Hooray for you! I only wish more women had been here to see you give that obnoxious witch a tongue-lashing!"

Amanda waved away my praise and busied herself folding wet towels. "Witch? Don't flatter her. She's no more irritating than a fly on the end of my nose. And my Elisha has more good sense than to listen to Cassie Taylor, of all people!"

Elisha tugged at my shift. I looked down at her and marveled that blue eyes could look so fawn-like. "Do you think Cassie is right, Jessamyn?" she whispered. "Should I act more forward with Cal, or wait to see if he comes to me?"

I tapped the tip of her pert nose. "Wait and see. A smart and pretty girl like you won't have to wait and wonder for long. You'll see."

"I hope he takes an intermission from playing the banjo tonight so he can ask me to dance," she said, soaping her arms and then rinsing them off in the rushing water.

I lathered my mass of thick, annoying curls and massaged my hot scalp with cool, soapy water. It felt glorious. "I'll suggest it to him, if he doesn't think of it, himself," I promised.

"Thank you, Jessamyn, thank you! Can I help you with the reverend?"

"The reverend?" I was shocked. "What do you mean?"

"He fancies you a great deal," she said smugly, "Everyone has noticed it. Surely you have, too?"

I shook my head. "We like each other well enough…and there was a time when I thought he might…but Elisha, surely you and everyone else was aware of his interest in Adelaide Sullivan. I-I thought they might marry one day."

Elisha shook her head with conviction. "No. He was only being kind to Miss Sullivan. Everyone knows he is fascinated with you. The man can't take his eyes off of you, Jessamyn. Surely you must be aware of it."

The idea the reverend might have serious intentions toward me was so new and in some ways so disturbing, I could only think to change the subject, "Mrs. Masters," I called out, "Doesn't it surprise you a little that the reverend agreed to allow dancing at the celebration? I know it isn't completely unheard of, but usually not under a clergyman's nose. Do you think he'll join the celebration? I've never heard of a preacher attending a dancing party, have you?"

"I have; but on rare occasions; usually wedding parties but never Baptist or Methodist preachers, though." She adjusted her petticoats, and settling primly upon a large boulder, she dangled her toes in the fast moving creek water.

"It seems out of character for a Presbyterian preacher as well. And especially one as shy as the reverend," I mused.

Mrs. Masters watched me bob about in the water, rinsing my hair, and then running the piece of soap through all ten of my toes. She leaned forward and brushed her chestnut hair, taking long, slow stokes with her brush. "You know, Jessamyn, she said, "I wouldn't be surprised to learn one day that the reverend agreed to the dancing in order to create an opportunity to dance with you."

*   *   *

"Oooh, Bruin!" Cassie simpered, "You are so strong! I just bet you could split all that wood by yourself. You don't even need any help from those other boys."

Bruin ignored her. The muscles of his massive arms stood out, as he swung the axe over his head and brought it down with stunning force, again and again; faster than any of the others. Faster even than Papa, who looked strange and much too tired to be competing, as he paused to mop his brow with a bandanna. He rubbed his left arm and shoulder and I hurried to his side to see if he had sprained it.

"Are you hurt, Papa?" I asked, shocked to see how soaked with perspiration he was upon closer inspection. His shirt stuck to his back and his gray hair was damp across his forehead. I tried to smooth it for him, and suggested he tie it back so it wouldn't fall forward into his face.

He looked embarrassed by my attentions. "Let me be, Little Mite. Have fun and don't trouble yourself with me. I intend to dance like a tornado tonight and to more than eat my fill, so you go along and find your own good time."

"Just sit down and rest a moment, Papa," I said, "It won't hurt to rest. You won't miss anything. This contest will go on a while longer."

He scowled at me and agreed to sit with his old friend, Ben Masters, who had dropped out of the contest himself ten minutes earlier. Within two more minutes I heard Papa laugh too long and too loud and I knew someone had opened another jug of the spirits the men had hidden in their various wagons.

I scanned the crowd of those watching the log splitting competition, trying to locate the reverend, anxious to see if he was near enough to notice Papa and the other men drinking together.

I wondered why it hadn't been enough for them when the reverend endorsed the dancing. To my way of thinking it was disrespectful of them to push their luck by adding alcohol to the party as well.

When my eyes found those of the reverend, he was staring straight at me. I was glad to see he was on the opposite side of the crowd, and I waved at him and then ducked back to speak to Papa. "What if the reverend finds out you've been drinking with your buddies?" I asked.

Papa smirked at me and answered in a brogue made thicker by the spirits. "I am not a selfish man, Little Mite, I shall offer him a long swallow as any gentleman would."

The other men roared with laughter and I couldn't help joining them. Papa was and always would be a rascal; an exasperating, dear and funny man. I kissed his cheek. "Have fun," I said, "But not too much fun."

He grabbed me up and hugged me hard. "You know I love you, don't you? You're my favorite little girl," he said, grinning with pride, "But why do you care so much for the opinion of that minister?"

"I don't really." I answered, shrugging.

"You could do worse," he said in a voice so low I had to lean close to him to hear his next words. "If you could stand the man and manage to avoid dying of boredom, you would make a fine wife for that minister, My Girl! And it wouldn't be a bad life for you. You could make your pictures all day and live like a fine lady."

My shock must have shown plainly on my face, for Papa began to roar again with laughter, this time at my expense. He wheezed and sputtered as he fought to regain his breath. "You should see the look on your face." He gasped; then settled down to a chuckle. "God, Child, I miss your mama"

Tears sprang into his eyes and he quickly brushed them away and took a long swallow from his mug. He cleared his throat with a growl. "She was taken too soon. It wasn't fair…to her…to any of us." He stared at me and his eyes were fierce. "I will never love another woman."

I nodded and rubbed his back. "I know, Papa."

"Your mama would approve of the minister too, you know," he continued, "She would want you to have an easy life; a genteel life."

It was my turn to laugh. "She would tell me the same thing she always told me. Follow your heart." She did and I am glad she did.

Papa drained his mug. "So am I, Little Mite, so am I," he said, standing and ambling over to the next wagon for a refill.

The crowd began to shout and call out to their favorite ax-wielders, urging them on to victory. I wandered back to where Bruin stood splitting log after log, his shirt sticking to his back in places now and still he went on swinging the ax. His face was a study in concentration and a deep grunt issued from his parted lips as he drove the iron deep into the wood.

I drew as near to Bruin as I could safely go and studied this powerful, lunging beast of a man. I had only known him as a boy, and then a businessman...and a cultured friend who shared my love of theater, art, and music. This Bruin was new to me and my heart hammered hard within my chest and still I moved a step nearer. I caught his scent as he swung his ax in a deadly arc and my heart beat all the more frantically. Bruin Mahoney was a very attractive man, more complex and interesting than I had given him credit for.

I felt lightheaded as I watched his every movement like a cobra under the spell of the weaving flute; the movements and the song blending in a seductive dance.

I heard Booth Wade's voice as if from a great distance despite the fact I stood not more than ten feet from him. "One minute more, Men!" he shouted, eyes fixed upon the minute hand of his pocket watch as it swept relentlessly around to mark the final moment of the big contest.

And then the roar of a shout went up from the crowd and I was pushed nearly off my feet by Cassie Taylor who lunged at Bruin, flinging her arms around his strong neck as he was declared the winner by ten logs.

Bruin swung Cassie in a circle, and then he swung her around two more times. She sneered at me over his shoulder, her green eyes flashing jade fire at me in the fading sunlight. Then she leaned back to gaze up into his face and they laughed together.

I turned away, walking into the dying light of day, away from the loud voices. I moved beyond the clearing, out of the circle of wagons to stand on the high ground above the wide rushing river below.

The sky above was ablaze in shades of damson, indigo, and...blinding gold where the hot ball of sun was gliding slowly down...down to rest. I drew a breath that hurt my dry throat and I wished I was as bold and wild and wanton as Cassie, with eyes capable of throwing green flames to drive away anyone who threatened what I had decided to claim as my own. Bold since birth, it was only my pride and a fear of rejection that held me back now.

The pride of my ancestors was deep in my blood. Bruin would just have to make his own best choice. I would never allow myself to chase after a man who fancied that shameless witch. And in truth, I wanted a man with enough good sense to choose a suitable companion for himself. If Bruin Mahoney could so easily be led by a tart like Cassie Taylor, I didn't want him. It was just that simple.

I drew another deep breath and the fragrance of the freshly baked pies and the roasting turkeys traveled toward me on the evening breeze. I heard the strum of Cal's banjo and the lively high-pitched whine of Booth Wade's fiddle and I knew it was time to go back.

As I passed by the reverend's wagon, he stepped out from the darkest shadow and spoke to me, "You must not wander away from camp in the dark, Miss J-Jessamyn," he cautioned, "I came to look for you."

"But I thought we were safe now, Reverend," I said, "I thought the Indians were friendly in this part of the country."

"In theory; but we cannot take any foolish chances. Please, Miss Jessamyn, I-I could not...I would not...want anything to happen to you. You must be careful."

We re-joined the others and the reverend insisted on getting heaping plates of food for the both of us, even though I protested I could easily fetch my own supper.

I caught sight of Papa, still carousing with his old friends, but I was relieved to see him eating from a great platter of turkey, gravy, biscuits, beans and I even saw a huge wedge of berry pie teetering precariously on the edge of his plate. Amanda Master hovered over the group of men and I knew she would see to it they sobered up on the good, hot home-cooked feast all the women had worked to make for them.

I sat on the blanket I had spread near our wagon and while I waited for the reverend to return, I watched Bruin dance with that hateful Cassie Taylor. He caught my eye as they spun past and as he twirled Cassie around and around, he waved to me and gestured as if trying to tell me something in pantomime.

It served him right to be stuck out there dancing with Cassie. If he wished to speak to me he would just have to come to me like a gentleman.

The reverend handed me a plate and I offered to take his as well while he slowly lowered his large, angular frame down onto the blanket beside me. His knee joints creaked and I spoke to cover any embarrassment he might be suffering. The reverend was at least thirty years old and not an agile man at that.

"Oh, look!" I said, "Look at Veronica Sue Larner dancing with her little son, Natty. See how he keeps up with her steps. How adorable!"

The reverend looked up, then blushed, and I realized he was truly shy and very embarrassed by Veronica Sue's advancing state of pregnancy.

I waved to Veronica and Natty, then took a bite of turkey and gravy. "This is absolutely delicious," I said. "After all these weeks of rabbit stew and beef jerky, I'd forgotten how good food can taste when we have the time to prepare it properly."

"Hello there, Jessamyn. Reverend!" Elisha called to us as she glided past, radiant in the arms of Cal Witherspoon, who looked as if he'd discovered the finest treasure on earth.

We waved back; then sat in silence until the reverend took a bite of my corn bread and declared it was the best he'd ever eaten and it was my turn to blush since I'd burned the bottom, and then trimmed it away with Papa's big, sharp hunting knife.

Bruin joined us as the heat in my cheeks began to subside. He groaned as he sank down on my other side. "I am sore," he complained, rubbing his muscles and flexing his arm.

"Serves you right for showing off," I teased, just as Cassie came hurrying up and plopped down right next to Bruin looking ever so much like the spider that landed beside the unfortunate fly.

"However did you manage to burn the corn bread, Jessamyn?" Cassie inquired in a thin, mean voice.

"It's just my luck," I said, trying to look mysterious. "What did you contribute to the dinner, Cassie, so I can look out for it?" I asked, suspecting she wasn't going to be any better at cooking over a campfire than I had turned out to be.

She blinked once and said, "Mama and I made the pie."

"Which pie, Cassie?" I asked grinning as she squirmed.

"One of those berry kind of wild pies," she said, her eyes warning me to drop the subject.

Bruin's shoulder's shook with laughter. "One of the lattice-topped pies, or one of the ones with the three holes poked into the top crust?"

Cassie stood haughtily and went back for second helpings. "Who cares? I picked some kind of berries I found on a bush, and Mama did the baking. Who can bake over a campfire?" she said in her usual nasty way, then dodged around some enthusiastic dancers and headed for one of the turkeys that turned golden and fragrant upon it's spit.

The reverend had been very quiet as he ate his food, but suddenly he cleared his throat and said, "Congratulations on winning the log-splitting contest, Bruin. You were very impressive."

Bruin shrugged off the praise and made a joke about not having much competition from the others. "Most of the men who participated have quite a few years on me. It was nothing, really."

I glanced at the reverend and saw what might have been regret in his eyes. Perhaps he wished he were more of a he-man than an intellectual. I put my plate aside and Bruin immediately asked if I would dance with him.

The reverend looked up quickly from the pie he had been eating and held Bruin's eyes for a moment.

I wondered what was passing between them, but at the moment I just wanted to dance and so I stood and shook the crumbs of dinner from my sensible yellow, calico dress with the tiny blue flowers. "Sure, Bruin," I said, "we might as well not let all this good music go to waste." I re-tied the yellow ribbon I'd used to pull the hair back from my face, and then Bruin took my hand and drew me into a close embrace.

I hoped he wouldn't feel the thumping of my heart against his chest. I thought I could actually hear it echoing up into the base of my throat. I felt my pulse throb there as we spun under the leaves and the star-shine, dancing through shadows, twirling in and out of flickering pools of light thrown by the cooking fires and the lanterns that hung from the trees.

I felt so at home in Bruin's arms, I threw my head back and closed my eyes, giving myself up completely to the dance, trusting Bruin's touch to guide me as we moved and swayed together, and when I finally opened my eyes the moon was bright above us and Bruin was watching me intensely in the shadowy light.

I sighed and his arm drew me closer and closer still, and then the reverend tapped Bruin's shoulder and in another few seconds my hand was in the cool grasp of the reverend's damp palm and Cassie was laughing up into Bruin's face and whispering something into his ear that made him laugh even harder.

The reverend's steps were slow and labored. He smiled nervously at me and I told him he was a fine dancer...for a minister. We both laughed then and I was beginning to relax and forget my fears that he would crush one of my feet with a huge misplaced boot, when I heard Papa's voice across the crowd of swirling dancers.

"Play a lively one, Cal!" he shouted, slurring his words. "This group needs a lesson in how to have fun!"

I shuddered and sneaked a look at the reverend's stern face. He frowned at Papa and then asked, "Would you like to sit down and rest for a while, Miss Jessamyn?"

"Yes," I said, "maybe that would be best."

We started toward my blanket, but I hung back, deciding to stay and watch for a bit, and it was then I heard Papa let out a loud whoop. I turned and stood on the fringes of the crowd watching my papa spin and leap and kick his heels. He danced like a man possessed with a passion for music, for life. He was the papa I had always loved, and missed these past few weeks. But I had to remind myself, he was so much older now since Mama had died, and he seemed to grow more tired and less himself with each passing day.

"Hey, Jessamyn!" he cried, "Look at your papa dance! Are you having fun? I am!" He waved to me and grinned, then spun off, darting among the dancers.

The reverend appeared at my side. "Would you like me to persuade you father to stop dancing now and go to bed? I fear this dancing will prove to be too much for a man of his advanced years."

"Yes," I said, suddenly going cold all over with a dreadful feeling that it might already be too late to avoid a terrible disaster.

When I heard a woman scream I knew it had something to do with Papa. I screamed too, even before I knew for certain he was in trouble. I rushed forward, the reverend close behind me.

"Papa!" I screamed, pushing people out of the way and then flinging myself down beside my stricken papa. He was clutching his chest and gasping for breath. My tears fell upon his pale cheeks and I watched in horror as his eyes glowed with an unearthly light and a smile lit his face.

"It's you!" he whispered reaching past me at something the rest of us would never see. The crowd parted, murmuring as they searched the tree branches for whatever it was Papa had seen…for whatever it was that had given him such happiness in his last moments on earth.

At the moment my papa died and left me completely alone in the world, he never looked happier.

"No!" I shrieked, as the shock settled upon me like an avalanche of ice and snow. "You can't die, Papa! You can't leave me!"

I flung myself upon my father's corpse and cried until I ran out of strength. It was then the reverend lifted me up and carried me like a child off into the darkness.

I searched the faces of those around us and finally located Bruin's sad, dark eyes. He reached out for my hand and as I lifted mine to meet his outstretched fingers, Cassie stepped in front of him and held his hand up to her cheek.

Her hateful voice echoed to the depths of my soul as I heard her say, "Let the reverend tend to her, Bruin. She will need the comfort of his spiritual counseling tonight. You can go to her in the morning."

Bruin had loved my papa, and although I wanted the comfort of his presence for myself, and at that moment I truly hated Cassie for keeping him away from me, I was certain he would tend lovingly to my papa's body and see he was kept safe until the light of day.

"Take care of Papa, Bruin!" I called to him, and his tear-filled eyes met mine as he nodded and lifted Papa into his arms.

We brushed past Amanda Masters who offered to spend the night with me. I was too weak to answer, or to care, and I was glad when the reverend decided for me. "You have a family to take care of, Amanda, and Jessamyn is completely exhausted," he said, "I'll watch over her tonight. She may need me…she may need me to pray with her. This has been so sudden I fear she'll go into shock."

Amanda murmured her agreement, and someone held the canvas cover open for us, as the reverend stepped up into our wagon with little effort. I thought I had run out of tears, but when the reverend set me down upon my pallet, and I opened my eyes, the familiar sight of Papa's things, his pallet, his clothing, his tools which hung all about the frame of the wagon, broke my heart into yet smaller pieces, and I sobbed harder. I clutched my pillow and shuddered with grief.

After a while I grew quiet again and then I heard Ben Master's voice outside the wagon, "Cal," he called, "Bruin needs two pennies. Do you have any pennies in your pocket?'

Pennies for Papa's eyes! I groaned and stuffed my fist into my mouth and bit down hard. I never knew a person could feel such pain, sustain such an unexpected mortal wound to the heart, and go on living.

The reverend sat back against the wagon seat and gently drew me into his arms. I snuggled against his black vest and sobbed upon the musty-smelling linen. "Papa, my papa," I whispered like a prayer.

"There now, Jessamyn," he whispered back, "Rest now…and know your father is in heaven with all of his loved ones. He is safe within God's arms."

As I continued to sob, he rocked me gently from side to side. "Reverend," I choked out after some time had passed. "There is something we must do." I raised my face to his and was surprised to find tears on the planes of his angular features.

He wiped them quickly away. "What is it, Jessamyn?"

"I noticed Papa had a tear in his hose when he was dancing. Mama would want him to look as fine as…as much like himself as possible when we bury him. So we must go and take him a pair of clean hose."

With great tenderness, the reverend smoothed the hair back from my wet cheeks. "Sleep now, Child. We'll see to it in the morning."

I set my cheek against his vest again, and felt strangely comforted by the sight of his hand upon my arm. His fingers were long and smooth, not wide and gnarled with calluses like Papa's had been, but the rough blue rivers of veins that traversed the back of his hands spoke of age and experience, as did the deep lines and crevices that told a story of their own. The reverend was a good, strong man. I could feel it in his touch, in the way his hand trembled when he stroked my hair and in his voice as he spoke aloud the sacred words of *The Twenty-third Psalm*.

"The Lord is my shepherd. I shall not want."

*   *   *

"The coyotes!" I screamed, struggling back to wakefulness. "The coyotes!"

The reverend held me more tightly against him. "Don't fear, Child. We'll build a fence around the grave, and we'll mark it with his name… I promise."

"We can use the wood from the log splitting contest. Your father would like that. And don't fret about the coyotes ever again. We will pile a mountain of rocks upon the grave. There are plenty in the creek. Sleep now," he crooned in a deep, low pitched voice that soothed my soul like salve on a bad burn. "Sleep now…Sweet Jessamyn; you are not alone."

CHAPTER 12

Alexander wasn't feeling well. I heard the aides whispering among themselves that he was experiencing anxiety at the prospect of being released within another week or two.

I missed him terribly at art therapy. His artistic creations were such complex and colorful designs that I loved to watch Mrs. Hollander's face as she studied them and had no clue as to what to make of them.

I felt very alone that afternoon as I sat sketching butterflies and coloring them in ice cream colors. And then Mrs. Hollander stopped in front of me and tapped the desk with her pinkly manicured finger. I delayed looking up from my drawing.

"Really, Sunny, you've done butterflies to death," she complained, "Close your eyes right now and draw the first image that comes to mind."

I sighed, but did as she told me, and immediately, I saw the butterflies circling over a black pit in the ground. The rest of the ground surrounding the pit was covered with the pure white of new snow. The old witch would love this.

For the first time since coming to the sixth floor I reached for the black pastel and plunged into representing the exact scene I had visualized. Mr. Hollander cooed encouragingly, now at my elbow, all in a sick frenzy to finally be able to judge one of my drawings suitably disturbed. As I swirled the black color into a spiral, a twister of despair, I began to grow angry. I had felt every human emotion magnified off the charts since coming here, but the one thing I hadn't felt much of, was anger.

I drifted my white snow in mounds around the pit, then stood and flung the drawing onto Mrs. Hollander's desk. Her eyes were huge behind her plastic frames. I studied her short, stubby body, unfriendly mouth, and helmet of champagne-colored, over-processed hair, and then I turned and headed for the door.

"Where're you going, Sunny?" Bob asked.

"I'm going to check on Alexander," I said.

"Not until the hour is up, Missy," Mrs. Hollander challenged, though half-heartedly.

"The hour is up for me, Mrs. Hollander," I said, facing her with crossed arms. "Someone else will have to feed your neurotic desire for a spotless, artless, art table. You will all have to manage without me for the remainder of the hour."

"Right on, Girl!" Bob shouted, howling at an imaginary moon and shifting Mrs. Hollander's disapproval over to himself. The others sat obediently silent, moving the pastels around the surface of the paper as if they weighed many pounds each. Barbara picked her nose and then wiped the result across the front of her drawing and waved it gaily at me as I backed through the door and let it slam behind me.

I felt as if I'd had a big old glass of wine. I almost raised my arms for balance as I made my way shakily down the corridor to Alexander's room. I had never in my life told an authority figure off on my own behalf, and it felt pretty good. At least until I got as far as the community room and doubt began to set in. What would Dr. Carroll think of my rude behavior? I'd never dared to speak back to my teachers, or my doctors. I'd always been a very good, little girl…and then an even better little woman. But now I was thirty-three years old and it was more than time for me to grow up and to learn to express my anger, or at least to speak up assertively.

I walked boldly past the nurse's station and avoided eye contact with the R.N. who was complaining to an L.P.N. and an aide, and then, I scooted the last few feet to Alexander's room, slipping inside of his opened door.

He was dressed and resting on top of the bedspread, but turned toward the windows. I started toward him to check to see if he was asleep, but he startled and reared around to face me.

"I'm sorry, Alexander," I said, "I hope I didn't wake you, but I missed you in art therapy and I had to see for myself if you were O.K."

He was breathing fast as if I had frightened him and his eyes were alarmingly wide and blank.

I sank down beside him on the bed, not caring if a nurse walked past and caught us together like this. I grabbed up his cool hand and pressed it against my warm cheek. His fingers were long and well-formed and his nails were uniformly oval and still trimmed to the same length. "You have such nice hands, Alexander," I said, searching his face for expression. "Did something happen to upset you?"

He rubbed his eyes hard and shook his head slowly from side to side as if clearing it of the effects of deep sleep, "I'm just a little down, that's all. I…I have to fill out all of the necessary forms for financial aid to the graduate program at Harvard…And I have to obtain the records of my most recent test scores."

"I'll help you fill out the forms," I said.

He stared at me for nearly thirty seconds before it appeared as if he recognized me. "Sunny," he whispered, "thanks, but I can do it. I've done it before, you know." Then he smiled and I watched as the warmth returned to his eyes.

"Oh, Alexander," I said, fighting tears, "You were going away again. You can't leave me here all alone. Please don't."

He rewarded me with a broad, healthy grin. "You're right, Sunny. I can't slip away until I hear the rest of your book."

"Did they change your medication? Is that what's wrong with you?"

He laughed. "It's actually the opposite. I'm trying to get used to not being on my meds. I haven't had anything for at least a week."

I grinned back at him. "Maybe that's it. I feel a lot better on this Centrax pill they give me."

He touched my cheek. "I just bet you do, but I'd advise giving those things up as soon as possible. You're better off not becoming dependent on that sort of thing for your mood elevation. I'd hate to find out someday our whole relationship has been based on the heady effects of Centrax."

"I guess you're right," I agreed. "That would be pretty awful; and not too good for the ego."

"We'd better get out of here, before I get in trouble for entertaining a beautiful woman in my bedroom," he said, standing and shuffling into his slippers.

"Beautiful? Thank you, Alexander. That's nice to hear even if it isn't all that true."

"You don't ever have to thank me for stating the obvious. You are definitely beautiful, multi-talented, intelligent, and as an added bonus… psychic! Sunny, I've been meaning to ask you how long you've known you were psychic. I remember trying to explain it to my parents and having them tell me I was losing my mind. I think I just got tired of hearing it and decided to oblige them."

"You don't seem crazy to me, Alexander. You're just a little troubled, like the rest of the world. How old were you when you had your first premonition?"

"In the womb; I predicted the day of my birth. Of course I had some help from my best friend, the psychedelic baby. We discussed it, as we do most things, and settled on the correct day as being August 10th."

"That's such a charming story, Alexander," I laughed, "It reminds me of the fairies who used to visit me when I was a child. It's wonderful to have such a rich, creative mind."

He stared ahead for a moment and looked sad. "I guess it is, sometimes. Tell me about your first psychic experiences; but don't talk too loud. We don't want the nurses to make notes on those hateful charts."

We settled into our favorite seats on the sofa by the T.V. A soap opera came on and the nurse strode across the carpet to switch it off, disappointing poor old Mr. Markowitz, who shuffled away, engrossed in a heated three-way conversation with himself. The nurse walked off, too, muttering under her breath, "You people have enough problems without dwelling on fictitious ones."

"Let's see," I said, curling my feet up under me. "You know about my out-of-body experience."

He nodded.

"And you know about my first flash-back to Jessamyn's life?"

He nodded again.

"Well, I guess the first time I predicted an event out loud, and then it happened in front of a witness was when I was about five."

"We'd just moved to the country in Summit, New Jersey and my mother and I had an evening appointment at the hairdresser's. My mother had recently learned to drive and we proudly drove ourselves to town after Dad got home from work and could stay with Joe-Joe."

"We were a one-car family then, as most families were, and Mah didn't have that many chances to practice driving so she crept along so slowly, that we were running late when we finally maneuvered the car into a space in the municipal lot, and started to walk through a well-lit alley heading to Main Street where our hairdresser had his shop."

"We had just entered the alley when I stopped suddenly and sat down on the pavement. I was filled with a terrible fear. I was so filled with terror I absolutely could not move."

"Mommy!" I said, "We have to go around the block instead. Something awful is going to happen here."

"I remember grabbing a handful of her cotton circle skirt. The black and white paisley design swirled before my eyes as I held it against my cheek, took a deep breath of her perfume, and begged her to listen to me. "Please, Mommy, please!"

"We're living in the country now, Sunny," she said, all practical business and losing patience by the second. "This isn't Newark. See that bright light up there," she pointed, "We can plainly see there is no-one around here but us…And we'll be in the shop in a matter of seconds. We're already late and it'll take too long to go all the way around the block. Now stop your nonsense and stand up right this minute!"

"She yanked me to my feet, but I went limp in her hands. 'I'm sorry, Mommy,' I said, "You'll have to kill me. I'm not going down that alley. And neither should you."

"I was apologetically, politely defiant. "We have to go around the long way. Something terrible is going to happen here."

"My mother was very angry as she dragged me around the block, taking long strides with her showgirl legs. She muttered under her breath, and I found myself praying that if something terrible was going to happen, it had better happen within the next few seconds or I was dead meat."

"So did anything happen?" Alexander was on the edge of his seat.

"Well, as we rounded the corner to Main Street, we heard police sirens and then screaming people were running toward us. My mother ducked into the doorway of an office building and shielded me with her body, but I peered out from around her skirt."

Two men had just robbed the liquor store, backed into the alley with drawn guns, and had fired shots before the police could persuade them to give up. That same alley I had refused to go down."

"As the odor of gun powder drifted our way, my mother stared down at me with wide, frightened eyes and a new respect. "I'll always listen to you, Sunny," she lied, "It's in the family, you know. Gram has it too; the gift of knowing things before they happen. Her Gran had it, and so do you."

"Everybody has it," Alexander said.

"I know that now. But it doesn't do them any good if they get scared and block it. It's in the *Bible*, you know. Jesus predicted everything that was going to happen to him and he never said it was a 'bad gift,' but he did warn us about false prophets. Gram says those are the ones who charge more than twenty dollars for a psychic reading."

Alexander laughed. "I don't believe in charging."

"I guess that's O.K. if it's the only skill you think you have and you're hungry and have to pay the rent."

"Did you like having the knowing?" Alexander asked.

I shrugged. "It was like having brown eyes and a big butt. It wasn't something I figured I had any choice about."

"You're butt actually isn't big, Sunny," Alexander said, frowning like a scientist would when puzzling over a difficult experiment."

I laughed. "That's right, I keep forgetting how thin I am now! But I probably won't stay this small."

"I don't care what you weigh, Sunny, as long as you're healthy."

"You're such a doll, Alexander. Promise me you won't get depressed anymore. I need you in my life."

"I promise to try."

I squeezed his hand. "Wanna hear about a dream I had when I was about seven?

The sun was spotlighting Alexander and shining directly into his eyes. He squinted and looked away, then moved in his slow, deliberate manner to the drapes and closed them part-way. "Sure, I want to hear your dream," he said, settling back into the dark, blue cushions and resting his hands on his knees.

I checked around for eavesdroppers. Barbara and Charlotte were playing gin. Mr. Markowitz was bothering the nurses, and Bob was leafing through a magazine and twitching in anticipation of the next cigarette break. Alexander and I didn't smoke, but most everyone else did."

Most everyone smoked so much that their fingers were stained a permanent yellow. Here they had to wait to smoke until the clock hit every hour on the hour. That was when Alexander and I usually took a walk down to the end of the long hall just so we could keep on breathing.

I checked the clock over the nurse's station and noted we had another half hour to go before our next walk. "I don't know how long I'd been asleep that night," I began, "before the man in the flowing white robe came to get me. I thought he was Jesus and he laughed when I called him that but he said I could call him any name that made me feel comfortable. He had long, curling, blond hair and eyes as blue as a summer sky, but he still seemed like Jesus to me."

"I've heard theories that Jesus was a blue-eyed blond," Alexander stated.

"Really? That's interesting. But whatever his name may have been, I knew he was the most purely good individual either living or dead that I had ever come in contact with. At first I thought he was my one of my guardian angels, but now I think he was an archangel."

"You have more than one guide?" Alexander looked surprised.

I nodded. "Three that I know of…Hey, sometimes it takes a village…I never said I was easy to influence…Anyway, his robe had long, billowing sleeves and his feet were bare, and so finely formed they looked as if they had never touched the rough roads of the real world. I could feel warm vibrations of love through the fingers of the hand he offered to me, and I had no fear as I grasped his hand and he literally pulled my soul out of my body, out of my bed, and into what I can only describe as another realm of existence."

"Cool!" Alexander whispered.

"The colors of this sky and grass were more intensely beautiful than any colors I'd ever experienced. We seemed to be on the top of a very high hill because I couldn't see anything but rich, grass and cool, breezy turquoise sky. At the very top of the hill stood a glorious tree with twisting branches and flowers in varying hues of pink. I was intoxicated with the vibrant colors. Everything here vibrated with life force."

"The man led me to the tree and there were many other children waiting in the clover. Some were my age and some were younger; a few were older. They were all dressed in white robes and when I looked down I was surprised to find I, too, wore a similar robe. It was obvious we came from many different countries; our skin tones confirmed it, and yet I sensed I wouldn't need words to be understood here."

"We were all smiling as we moved naturally together and joined hands in a circle around the tree. The wingless angel-man stood in the center, under the tree, moving around it as he spoke so we could all hear what he had to say."

"I glanced to my right and a taller boy with golden skin and gently slanting eyes squeezed my hand and nodded at me. To my left stood a very dark brown girl, smaller than I was, with a head full of tiny braids and chocolate eyes that sparkled like candy stars. As we stood listening I noticed how the grass felt like velvet between my bare toes and I remember thinking I had never smelled anything as lovely as the perfume of that graceful, blossoming tree."

"You have each been selected for a special purpose in the new times that are coming," he said, "Each one of you has a job to do on earth and I am here to tell you what that shall be."

"Then he moved around the circle and spoke to each of us separately. When he got to me he took my face between his hands and gazed into my eyes with affection and tenderness."

"Sunny," he said, "You will help to unite all the world's religions. Always remember the golden rule and that God is love."

"I was shocked. "How am I supposed to do that?" I blurted out."

"He almost laughed, but smiled instead. "Don't worry about that now. I said you were to help, not do it all by yourself. You'll have plenty of help…trust me Sunny…you won't be the only one."

"I nodded at him and decided not to worry about it, as he had advised. I was only seven and it would be many years before I grew into an adult with any hope of being taken seriously. But his profound words settled into my memory, and although I didn't begin to understand how I'd actually go about this huge task, I knew I must remember this dream and I have always hoped that if it was a real message dream, when the time is right; I will be shown the way."

"The angel moved on to speak with the next child and as soon as the power of his incredible eyes left my face, I began to wonder if my desire to write might have something to do with my purpose on this earth. And I made a promise to myself to try to always act with love toward others."

"I'd already experienced the playground battles over religion…and this was only among elementary age school children."

Insults were thrown daily.

"You have to go to Catechism class while we all get to play; and you worship statues in your church!"

"Our church teaches us it's wrong to worship a graven image!"

"Your people killed Jesus Christ!"

"You Protestants and Jews won't be able to enter the Kingdom of Heaven if you aren't baptized in the one true religion: the holy Catholic church!"

"Every little kid had been programed to believe the religion their family practiced was the only way to get into God's house."

"I never participated in these fights. They seemed silly and sad to me. I would sometimes speak up and tell them all about Saturday afternoons with Joe-Joe and Gram when we would often visit the different churches; the different rooms in God's house, according to Gram."

"I quietly told them all how Gram was teaching us there was room for everyone in our loving God's Heavenly home. Like the archangel who had come for me that night Gram believed that God is love; always had been, and always would be."

"Sometimes the kids would quiet down and actually listen to me and in my small way I was making a difference, at least on the playground. Maybe the dream meant I should take those small opportunities we each get to help out, to make the world a little bit better."

"Before I awakened the morning after my visitation by the angel, I had a series of dreams; a collage of scenes from all seven years of my short life. In the first dream I was in Kindergarten and sitting next to Lynn, my blind friend who had lost her sight at age two when someone threw a firecracker in her face at the Fourth of July celebration at Memorial Field."

"Some of the kids felt uncomfortable around her, but I went out of my way to be her friend. I asked her what it was like to be blind and she tried to tell me. She seemed almost relieved to be able to talk about it."

"I was devastated for her, and sometimes at home, in an attempt to gain more understanding, I would blindfold myself and try to find the bathroom. I would skin my shins on the furniture, trip and fall over Joe-Joe's toy trucks, and knock into the doorways. Being blind was a huge challenge and my respect and admiration for Lynn grew."

"I wanted her to see so desperately, I spent most of the day describing our surroundings and our classmates to her and she told me I made the best pictures appear in the darkness inside her head. I was glad I was good at telling stories, and glad I could brighten her dark days."

"In the dream I remembered how proud she had been on the day she brought a Braille book to school and the teacher, Mrs. Ward, passed it around the room so we could feel the bumps on the paper. We were children who couldn't read yet in any language, but Lynn could."

"She stood in front of the class and as her fingers moved over the Braille, her voice grew stronger. Her face glowed with her special light as she read the morning psalm to us. Her favorite: "Yea, though I walk through the valley of the shadow of death…I shall fear no evil for Thou art with me." She read that psalm to us as if she were sharing her own story with us, and in many ways, she was doing just that."

"I cried the day Lynn's parents took her out of Washington Elementary so she could go on to a school for the blind, and although I knew in my heart that school was what she really needed, I selfishly cried for my own loss."

"After she left, one of the boys, Billy Nunzio, who liked to show-off, stumbled around the room with his eyes closed, doing a cruel imitation of Lynn, and my Italian rose up like a monster taking me along with it. I tackled him like a linebacker and gave him what may have been his first well deserved bloody nose. "

"Old, kindly, Mrs. Ward, stared at me like I'd sprouted devil horns on the top of my head and before she could find her voice, I said, "I know. I'm going to see the principal.""

And that's what I did. I marched in there and told Mr. J. Bindley Hoff, a heavyset man who looked exactly like the image his name conjures up, listened to my story, shook my hand, gave me a lollipop, then said, "Young lady, this is just between you and me, but that little twit deserved a bloody nose and probably a lot more. Just sit here for a while and finish the lollipop before you go back to class."

"I grinned at him and ripped the paper off my treat. "Thanks, Mr. Hoff, I'll tell everyone you were very scary.""

"He grinned back at me. "Thanks, Kiddo, I have a reputation to protect.""

"In the next dream I was back in first grade and the child beside me was my new friend,

Sally Wilson. Her skin was chocolate brown and her hair was all twisted in little braids all over her head in a style I'd never seen before, but she had the most beautiful, frightened, big brown eyes I had ever seen. She was frightened because her family had just moved into the neighborhood and she was the only African American child in our entire school."

"We sat together in the lunch room and there was no one else at our table. There never was anyone else at our table because no one else would sit with us. Mostly the other kids were bigger, much bigger than we were, and they spent the lunch hour taunting us and throwing food whenever the lunch monitor turned her head."

"At first I thought we could ignore them and they'd eventually get tired of messing with us, but instead it got steadily worse. Sally was terrified most of the time, but I was growing more defiant by the minute, and I refused to let them scare me. I remembered Dad's stories about being chased as a little boy and thrown into the Passaic River just for being Italian so I wasn't surprised when they started in on me, too."

"Hey, DeAngelo! Since Italians are almost as black as niggers, you might as well sit with one! Wilson, why don't you go back to Africa and take your nigger loving friend with you!"

"I watched Sally's hand tremble as she took a sip from her milk carton. Don't be scared, Sally," I said, we can always get a teacher or the janitor to help us if we have to. And your mother picks you up after school so they can't get after you then."

"But Sunny," she whispered, "You walk home alone. They might hurt you for being my friend."

"They might try to hurt me just for being an Italian, so don't feel bad. But remember, I'm a greasy guinea so I shouldn't have any trouble just slipping away." I smiled at her. "And if they do lay a hand on me, my crazy Italian father will teach them how to show respect for everyone… the hard way."

"Our conversation was interrupted by a shower of milk cartons, and some of them still had the milk in them. And that's when I got mad; Irish/Italian fighting mad. I stood up and faced our tormentors. I made fists of my trembling hands and said, "You can call me anything you want and it doesn't change a thing. Sally is my friend. She didn't ask for the color of her skin any more than you could ask for the color of yours. I'd say we're all the same, but I don't think we are. I wouldn't want to be friends with people like you."

"It was a brave speech, but it didn't help because now they were throwing half-eaten fruit. Sally burst into tears and ducked under the table. She wouldn't come out even though I tried to convince her we could go to Mr. Hoff's office and he would protect us. I'd told her about the lollipop incident and that Mr. Hoff was scary looking, but secretly very cool."

"I don't know what happened to the lunchroom monitor, because no one came to help us, so I crawled under the table with Sally and waited the last few minutes there until the bell rang and it was time to go back to class."

"I'm ashamed to be white," I said to her, wiping tears from the corner of my own eyes."

"Sally smiled at me for the first time in a long time. "You aren't all that white, Sunny." she said, and then we started to laugh. We couldn't stop laughing and that was when the crowd left us alone. They probably thought we were crazy."

"I'd like to tell you that I made a difference in that little town, and that I helped to change the hearts of those mean kids, but that's not what happened. When school closed for the summer that June, I lost another best friend. Sally's family moved to another town with more families like them. Considering the times, they made the right choice."

"We kept up by phone for a while, but our parents, the same ones who had taught us both that all people are created equal, discouraged our friendship away from school. Sally and I decided we would be different. We promised each other that our children would be allowed to play together."

"When I woke up the next morning after these dreams and the amazing trip with the angel, I couldn't wait to draw a picture of the tree, the children, and the wonderful angel-man who had taken me there. I knew I must have been dreaming, but I also knew it was more than a dream, because I had been as fully conscious as I was every morning when I woke up. I knew I must never forget this experience, and I'm grateful Mah took me seriously enough to save the awkward drawing I made. I still have it…"

I'd become so involved in telling the dreams, I'd forgotten Alexander was listening to me. I looked up to see him sitting like a statue in the same position, in his usual place, but tears were running in paths down his angular face and over his strong jaw and chin. I couldn't read the expression in his eyes, and he made no attempt to wipe the tears away.

"Oh, Alexander," I whispered, moving closer to him and wiping the thin streams away with some of the ever present tissues that populated every surface of this crazy house. "Did my dream make you sad?"

He shook his head, then accepted several of the tissues and blew his nose twice, "It's a beautiful dream, Sunny. I think I'm a little jealous of it. I wonder why the spiritual man didn't come for me too. I've always wanted to make the world a better place. I've spent a lot of my time trying to do just that. Wouldn't you think these people would want to give me some encouragement? I don't understand it. He really should have come for me too."

Uh-Oh...I had miscalculated Alexander's mental state. "But Alexander," I proceeded cautiously, "It might have all been just a regular dream; a fantastic creation of my imaginative mind. It doesn't matter whether it's real or not, because we all have free choice in this lifetime. Maybe it's just a manifestation of my personal dream and maybe believing I can make a difference is the only function it was supposed to serve in the first place. We each are what we are...and we each accomplish what we believe we can accomplish. I don't have to tell you that..."

He nodded. "I do know that. I'm sorry Sunny. I just wish I had a dream like that to call my own. It would re-set the course of my life and give it the meaning I've been searching for."

I looked deep into his expressive dark eyes and brushed his hair to the side of his forehead. "Then create a dream, Sweetie, and live it. Make it happen."

The light in the room had diminished. Alexander stood and walked slowly to the windows. As he opened the drapes he said, "We mustn't miss the sunset."

The clock hit five and Bob jumped out of his seat, "Cigarette break!" he yelled; then rushed up to the nurse's station to be first in line.

Alexander and I stood for a moment before the window. We watched miniature people, the size you see in doll houses, rushing through the rain to their cars, juggling packages and umbrellas, the only colorful additions to the gray landscape below.

"Alexander," I said gently, "Not only is it raining right now, but the sun doesn't set until nearly nine o'clock. What's wrong with the both of us?"

He smiled at me. "I guess we just got too deep into our own little world. That's easy to do in a place like this. When you can't feel the sun on your skin and the seasonable temperatures...they become less real. It seems like even the time blurs a bit."

The menace of smoke was moving toward us. We could smell it before we could see it gathering above our heads, permeating our environment, on little gray rat feet, dominating every corner of the room, of the little world we were presently trapped in. I put my hand on Alexander's arm. "Let's walk."

As soon as we passed the nurse's station, Alexander reached over and took my hand. I squeezed it hard and tried to match my steps to his longer stride.

"Sunny," he said, "Don't tell those dreams to Dr. Carroll, or to Dr. Fazio either. It's too risky."

"Risky?"

"They'll label you delusional. You don't need that on your record."

"Delusional, Alexander; do you mean like Einstein...or Michaelangelo...Emily Dickenson, Lincoln, Washington, Franklin, or maybe like Oprah Winfrey? Maybe you mean like those ghetto dwellers who plant gardens in city lots and paint murals over the graffiti... At least I'd be in good company. Oh, Alexander, the fine line between craziness and creativity is all a matter of degree and interpretation. Am I right?"

"Right. But don't forget judgment. You had better choose carefully to whom you grant the power of judgment over you and your future. You never know who you're going to piss off in a place like this. And if you're lucky it won't be the guy who holds the key to the front door."

I sighed, properly defeated by his logic. "O.K." I said, as we paused at the big window at the end of the hall. "I'll be careful'

*   *   *

Predictably Mah told two people off before she even made it to the nurse's station. Misplaced anger was her favorite defense mechanism. Right now it was protecting her from the severity of my sad situation.

Gram, decked out in a big, purple picture hat, was close at her heels, carrying her cane in her right hand, obviously at Mah's insistence; but moving along at a brisk pace just under a run.

Poor Joe-Joe, tall, thin, and handsome in an Italian sort of way, though visibly rattled by a long ride trapped in a car with two eccentric women, was inching along at the rear; eyes darting, looking scared to death someone would find him out and throw a net over him.

Alexander and I were waiting on our sofa in the corner and he saw them first. "That has got to be them," he said, grinning. "Thanks to your vivid descriptions I could have picked them out if they were hiding in the last row at Madison Square Garden."

"That parking lot is much too far away from the hospital for people with heart conditions," Mah complained to the head nurse who looked unimpressed by the news flash. "What on earth are you people thinking? Do you need new patients? Is that it? Is there some sort of patient quota you have to fill by the end of visiting day?"

I hurried up to my little family. "I'm so glad you're here!" I said, hugging Mah and then Joe-Joe; saving Gram for last.

We hugged hard and Gram said, "Well, you look normal enough to me."

"You can't go by looks, Gram," I said, "You should know that."

"Joe-Joe laughed. "Are you O.K., Sun? Bull told us a bunch of shit about you being totally nuts and trying to kill yourself. What's with him? He's always been a liar, but this is going too far."

I looked up into Joe-Joe's sensitive brown eyes. "You know what they say about a good rumor, Joe-Joe it has to have at least a kernel of truth to it." I took a big shaky breath. "I've been depressed and anxious lately…I found out Bull is still seeing Teri and the both of them are involved in some kind of illegal business with the Mafia. He's been keeping me away from you guys and all my friends and so…I actually did kind of lose it. The short version is I took a gun from his collection, stared down the barrel, and then fired it into the bedroom ceiling."

"So what's the big panic about? That's a pretty typical day in this family," Joe-Joe said, and we took off in shouts of laughter; using humor to smooth over the sharp and dangerous edges of our crazy lives. I was so glad and grateful to see him, I gave him another hug.

Joe-Joe took a seat in the nearest chair at one of the visiting tables, and ran his fingers through his wavy, black hair. "I mean, what does he really have to complain about? It's not as if you shot his balls off, which might have been an even better idea."

"Now you two stop it this instant!" Mah said, hands on tailored hips, lips in a prune, her strawberry blonde coif quivering. "I won't listen to language of this sort."

"Oh, get human, Jeannine," Gram said, sitting down next to Joe-Joe and adjusting her hat to a jauntier angle. "Sometimes you act like you think your shit don't stink."

"Mother! You're too loud. Everyone will hear you." Mah whispered and shook her head, "Well, I think this whole mess is a shame, a dirty, rotten shame. And I can't for the life of me imagine what you two can find to laugh about in all of this."

I stared down at my shoes and tried to use my acting training to conjure up a suitably somber demeanor, but I heard Joe-Joe snort with suppressed laughter and I was gone again.

"Now quit it! Just quit it!" Mah said, stamping her Naturalizer pump and causing a conference to occur at the nurse's station between Big Jake and Kathy the L.P.N. They kept peering over at Mah and then whispering to each other as if debating whether or not to start filling out the paperwork to check her in.

"What's with Lurch? Is he your bodyguard?" Joe-Joe asked, gesturing toward Alexander who stood forgotten behind me, politely waiting to be introduced.

"Alexander!" I said, jumping up and pulling him forward. "This is my new best friend, Alexander Grandy."

Joe-Joe stood and stuck his hand out, "Nice to meet you, Alex. What are you in for?"

"I was found naked in the men's room of The Plaza Hotel in Manhattan on the night of the full moon meditation meeting in Central Park."

"Sounds good to me," Joe-Joe said, and sat back down.

"Sounds pretty good to me, too," Gram said, "Tell us more, Alexander."

"Mother!" Mah scolded as if after having been raised by this woman she could possibly be shocked by anything she might say, much less do." She eyed Alexander warily and moved to the other side of the table before choosing the chair next to Joe-Joe. She settled in and folded her arms protectively across her chest.

Everyone was watching Alexander expectantly. "Well," he began, "It's kind of a long involved story. Perhaps you'd rather visit with Sunny. You've come a long way to see her."

"You can say that again," Mah muttered, glaring at the nurses again. "That parking lot is in France, the hospital is in Switzerland…and I'm more than ready for a hot shower and a nap."

"And I'm feeling a little bit better these days since my whole life went to hell in a hand basket," I said, "How nice of you to be so concerned about how I'm doing."

Mah glared at me, but ignored my sarcasm. "What's wrong with that husband of yours? His directions were horrible; just totally wrong. It took us nearly three hours to get here. Can you imagine that? You just wait until I can give him a piece of my mind."

"Knock yourself out, Mah. He's not exactly at the top of my Christmas list at the moment.

"Having any trouble at home, Joe-Joe?" Helen asked hopefully, appearing suddenly at Joe-Joe's side.

Joe-Joe checked around him. "Are you talking to me, Miss?" he asked, his eyes growing wider as he took in the full effect of Helen's bizarre costume. She was dressed in what looked like an old pink tulle prom dress from the late fifties and she'd teased her limp hair into an enormous beehive. In the area of her mouth she'd drawn on a pair of Lucy Ricardo hot-pink lips and upon each cheek her rouge was applied in twin, symmetrically round dots. Her false eyelashes, brushed the top of her bangs whenever she batted her eyes at Joe-Joe and her eye shadow was purple, and so far out it was caked into her hairline.

It crossed my mind that no one in their right mind would pack their old prom dress to take to the nut ward…but then again, no one in their right mind needed to check into the nut ward.

"Hello, Honey," Gram said, "What's your name?"

"I'm Sunny's friend, Helen," she said grabbing hold of Joe-Joe's left hand and checking out his wedding band. "Oh," she sighed, "You're still wearing your wedding ring."

"I'm a married man, Helen," Joe-Joe said, "My wife, Maria, had to stay home today with our little daughter, Suzy, or she'd be here with me right now. I mean, we're a very close couple. A happy, close couple… and we're married."

Helen covered her mossy smile with make-up streaked hands and giggled, "Suzy!" she said in a delighted little voice then giggled again.

"Sunny!" Joe-Joe wailed, as he caught on, "You didn't tell about Suzy!"

"I'm sorry, Joe-Joe" I said, "But they make us talk all the time in here and I guess I just ran out of things to say…"

"Is Suzy here yet?" Bob asked on his way to the front desk for his cigarette fix.

"Jesus Christ, Sunny! Everybody knows! Who the hell is that guy, anyway?" Joe-Joe shook his head from side to side in a perfect imitation of Dad on the night he found out about the Suzy game. "Is nothing sacred with you, Woman?"

"I'll never do it again," I lied, "I'll never tell anyone else about Suzy."

"Don't make such a fuss, Joe-Joe," Gram said, "You turned out just fine. You're a handsome man and a good person…And we can all thank God you did turn out so well in spite of the Suzy game. But as I recall, you weren't a bad looking little girl either and there aren't many men who can make that claim."

*   *   *

I was worn out from my family's visit. It had been great to see them, and entertaining in its' own way, but I felt drained emotionally. Alexander thought my family was an interesting bunch of characters, almost as interesting as Jessamyn and her gang of characters.

That night during out dinner of roast beef, mashed potatoes, salad, steamed carrots and vanilla pudding, Helen didn't stop rhapsodizing over Joe-Joe. "You be sure and call me the second one of them files for divorce!" she said, laughing to punctuate her every sentence. It was obvious Helen was in the manic phase of her bi-polar disorder, and I liked her better this way. It was scary when she was so down she couldn't even speak.

"Are you too tired to read to me tonight, Sunny?" Alexander asked with anxious eyes.

I was so grateful we'd averted his threatened bout with depression I would have walked across the room on my hands to entertain him. "Not at all," I said, "I'll be happy to read to my favorite fan."

Alexander handed me my manuscript and soon we were traveling together back to the late seventeen hundreds.

My hands grew raw with open sores from the ruined blisters that came from driving the horses every day. Amanda Masters made me soak my hands in warm water and soothing herbs every night and then she and Elisha salved the wounds with a mix of sage, borax, and alum before wrapping my hands again in clean rags. I was wearing Papa's old leather gloves every day when I drove the team, and although I didn't want to give them up, as they made me feel closer to Papa, Amanda insisted I use a smaller pair that belonged to her youngest son, Jared.

They didn't chafe my hands as much because they fit me better, but they weren't my Papa's.

I had plenty of time to myself each day as we threaded our way through the Allegheny Mountains and during the long hours of the journey, I thought back over the years I had lived as the daughter of George and Marie Miles. Happy, peaceful years that hadn't in any way prepared me for the pain and shock of finding myself completely alone in the world. I was a young woman totally unprotected, with not one living relative on either side of the family.

For the first week following Papa's death I was alternately engulfed in the most consuming pain and suffering a person can imagine and then gratefully redeemed by a spate of time during which I was as numb as a severed limb.

Mr. and Mrs. Masters had invited me to consider myself a daughter of their family, but I felt too proud to accept such charity. I was old enough to earn my own living and although the prospect of a life lived as a wash woman, a seamstress, a cook, a housekeeper, or a governess didn't fill me with any hope of happiness or contentment. I was determined to make my own way.

As I rested upon my pallet each night and cried in my wretchedness, I would examine my tattered hands and yearn for the feel of a slim, sable brush: pray that one day soon I would lose my sad self in the scent and texture of oil paints and in the sanctuary of artistic expression.

I left Mama's portrait uncovered each night now. I promised us both as soon as I had settled myself in Marietta, for that was the biggest town around and the one where I would have the best chance of finding passage on a wagon train bound back for Boston; I would begin a twin portrait of Papa.

One day they would hang side by side in whatever rooms I found myself living in. Perhaps in Boston I could earn a living as a hat maker and also teach art to the children of the wealthy. Papa had left enough money to keep me going for at least a few months at best.

The days of hard, dusty work, holding the wagon onto treacherous winding roads began to run together for me and there were days when my arms ached like rotten teeth must and I was in such a deep despair I cared not whether I lived or died.

Our caravan had been lucky to avoid the curses of cholera and typhoid, and we hadn't had to contend with an illness any more damaging than a few mild cases of dysentery, yet, God forgive me, I prayed I would fall victim to something unnamed, yet strong enough to kill me and re-unite me with my parents.

I rarely had to eat my evening meal alone, for Elisha constantly cajoled me to join her family for supper. And of course Bruin often insisted I join him instead. Although he was only an adequate cook, he was good company and not shy about reminiscing with me. He had loved Papa too, and admired Mama a great deal. Somehow, our conversations helped to reduce the pain I bore. It brought them closer and made my loss more manageable.

Reverend Putnam usually joined with us on these evenings and we took turns reading from our favorite volumes. I read from the plays of Shakespeare, Bruin favored Dickens, and the reverend was a lover of poetry...so much so that any poet would do, and often did, since he had bought quite an impressive library in the book stores of Boston to ease the monotony of the road.

The reverend and I settled into an easy companionable friendship and I was often annoyed when Amanda Masters and Elisha would tease me about him, hinting that 'something more' might come of our platonic alliance.

I preferred to think of Bruin in that way…and it bothered me when no one ever suggested he might grow to fancy me and perhaps court me…after a decent period of mourning had passed.

So it was with great surprise and confusion I at first absorbed my second great shock of the journey. We were finally through the green Alleghenies and we could actually look down upon the impressive body of the Ohio River, when we made camp that fateful night.

For the first time in weeks, I took my evening meal alone and then walked toward the end of the line of wagons to where Bruin and the reverend were camped. I was hoping they would be sitting together in front of the campfire and would be glad of my company. That was the worst part about being alone in the world…the end of the day. There was no cheerful papa beside my solitary fire to laugh with, to share with.

On this particular evening Bruin wasn't there, but the reverend sat before the bright flames of his fire reading from one of his many books. I approached with mixed emotions, for he looked content, sitting alone, reading to himself.

The look on his face when he first saw me quieted my doubts in coming. "Miss Jessamyn," he said, standing, "sit with me…perhaps you'd grace this quiet evening with a reading. I've grown quite tired of the silence."

Restless, I hesitated to accept the seat he offered me. "I'd actually rather walk for a bit.

Would you join me?"

Together we walked along the road, ahead of the wagons, westward into the dim beginnings of another night. The sky was cloudy up ahead and the brilliant apricot and mandarin-orange sky peeked through the dark design of smoky storm clouds.

"I love a sky like this," I said, "I'd like to capture it on canvas."

"Painting is a hobby of yours, is it, Miss J-Jessamyn?"

"It is far from a hobby, it is my life."

"It won't be easy to find the time to paint if you must occupy so much of your time earning a living in Marietta," he said.

I shivered in a sudden chill and sense of dread at the very thought. I nodded.

"Where is Bruin?" I asked.

"Miss Cassie Taylor came by to speak to him just as we were finishing our supper, and I believe they went for a walk as well."

Cassie Taylor! Was Bruin such a fool as to be flattered by her attention? Any male would do for the likes of Cassie Taylor! He'd learn that soon enough.

"Come Reverend," I coaxed, reaching for his hand, "Let's be adventurous and leave the road. I want to see what the river looks like in this light."

The reverend's smile was unselfconscious and very pleasant. His wispy hair rose in the breeze and fell across his broad forehead as I practically dragged him through the tall grass toward the stand of pines that lined the long steep slope down to the river.

We stood side by side. I leaned back against the wide, gnarled trunk of an ancient pine and drank in the impact of the scene below us. The river was blue-green with flashes of gold glinting off in the slanting light. We could smell the fresh water, even from this height and the massive mounds of land that snaked along beside the water were rich in shades of green and brown.

It was an exhilarating sight, but my light heart was soon weighed heavily with deep sadness. This was the day my papa had longed to see. He had counted on it for his brave new start; his desperate dream of a transformed life in a new land.

"Papa," I whispered, as tears sprang to the surface, and mortified, I turned away from the reverend to the comfort of the thick, sturdy tree trunk, and sobbed.

"M-Miss Jessamyn," he said in a startled voice, "You mustn't trouble yourself…" He reached out for me and pulled me into his arms.

I clutched at him like a child and sobbed until I could cry no more.

"Your tears break my heart, Child," he said, his voice a soft breath that tickled the top of my head. "Please don't be afraid of the future. I promise to take care of you."

I pulled away from his embrace and stared up into his lucid, intelligent gray eyes, gone soft and darker with feeling. "You must not concern yourself with me, Reverend, I come from strong stock and I shall survive."

His voice changed as anguish filled his eyes along with a few tears. "I can't stand by and watch you bear your pain alone," he said, rubbing my arms with his smooth, long fingered hands. "You need not suffer...and you shall not suffer since it is within my power to save you. Marry me sweet Jessamyn...let me be your strength and your family. Let me give you a life rich with all the comforts you deserve. My home is large...two stories with spacious rooms...Mrs. Less, my housekeeper, would see to most of the daily tasks."

He stepped closer to me and I gasped, clutching my throat, startled at the drum beat of my own pulse. The weight of his words lay like a fallen pine across my chest and I felt in danger of smothering.

His eyes bore into mine, asking for an answer. "You would be free to paint, Jessamyn; to paint all day, every day. I would ask very l-little of you..." He paused, blushing as he gazed down at his hands, as if realizing for the first time that he held me fast in a caressing grasp that frightened me even more than his confusing tumble of unbidden words.

"Forgive me," he said, a sob in his whisper, as he dropped his hands and turned toward the view below. "I know I have shocked you, Child. Forgive me; I spoke impulsively...but from my heart."

The sound of the birds circling among the tall trees overhead was nearly deafening to me as all of my senses were intensified and the forest echoed with excesses of sound, color, and most of all, emotion. I felt weak, as if I'd fall to my knees if I were not careful to lean back against the comforting bulk of the tree.

"I don't know how to answer you, Reverend," I said, searching the confusion of my mind for the words I needed. "I am shocked to learn of your feelings for me. I thought we were the best of friends."

He was smiling when he turned back to face me, and I'd never seen him look happier. "Of course we are friends, Child; wonderful friends, with many common interests. We both appreciate Shakespeare, and I, too, have an interest in art. I found your drawings of Miss Sullivan to be quite beautiful.

He paused and I studied him, noting his smile, marveling over how he could speak her name with no sign of the feelings I had seen upon his face when he watched her read that night beside his campfire. Was the heart of this man of God so fickle? Was his head so easily turned?

I felt empty inside. Then a hard lump rose up into the back of my throat, and I felt very weary. "Does Bruin know you were going to propose to me?" I asked, my heart thumping even harder in anticipation of his answer.

"No," he said, studying me in the quickly dimming light. "Would you rather I discussed my proposal with him? I'm aware your families have been close for years. Would you like me to speak to Bruin since there is no other male relative for me to stand before?"

"Yes. Please. I think that's a good idea, Reverend," I said, feeling hopeful. "Bruin is the closest friend of my family and he should be told. I will be very interested in hearing what he has to say."

*   *   *

That night I waited desperately for Bruin to come to me. I prayed for guidance. I had never been so confused in my life. My head ached terribly and I cried into my quilt when I wasn't pacing the wagon, cursing my feminine state. If I were a man, I would face my beloved directly. I would state my feelings and my intentions as the reverend had done with me.

I peered through the opening in the back of the wagon, parting the cloth covering and letting the chilly night air sneak inside. There was no moon tonight; no stars and no Bruin waiting there for me.

Perhaps he didn't care for me as I secretly did for him. Perhaps he preferred the wanton wildness of Cassie Taylor to my more controlled nature. Little did he know what lay beneath the façade of my everyday demeanor. There was a passion in me to rival the posings and prat- tlings of that vicious, mean-minded vixen. With the right man, I knew I would blossom like a sunflower rising toward the sun.

Like a great, hot flower I would totally command the interest of my chosen man. I would surprise him with the profound love I've been saving for him alone. I would delight him in all the ways a woman can delight a man, and inflame him with the deepest everlasting desire.

If Bruin was so shallow a man as to be fascinated by the likes of Cassie Taylor, I didn't want him. Surely if he cared at all whether or not I married another man he would come to me.

And perhaps if he did care, yet hadn't the gumption to come to me…then I was better off without him and it would serve him right if I did marry the reverend.

I heard the rain pound the top of the canvas and I moaned. The canvas leaked in a driving rain, as it did upon all of the wagons and I was in for a difficult night. I hurried to cover everything inside with extra canvas tarpaulins. I was especially worried about Mama's grandfather clock and my painting of her also, so I placed two covers upon these few treasures.

I was considering sleeping under the wagon, when I heard a suspicious rustling of bushes outside and I tore back the covering and strained my eyes to see into the darkness. I watched the bushes move off in the direction of the trees beyond my campsite, wondering if it was a deer, a bear, or a man…and then there was nothing but the clatter of the punishing rain and the pounding of my troubled heart

CHAPTER 13

"I called Bull this morning to confirm our appointment for tomorrow afternoon at one o'clock," Dr. Carroll said, making a steeple with his pointer fingers.

"So is he going to show?"

"So he says."

"Where are those kid students you used to have in here?" I asked, scooting down around in the leather chair, feeling sweaty and sticky.

He shrugged. "They've moved on...back to class...I guess. Why?"

"I kind of miss them now that they're gone."

"Aren't I enough of an audience for you anymore, Sunny?"

I made a face at him. "I was just wondering if they passed whatever they were being tested on; if they're going to be psychiatric nurses. I'm just a curious person."

"Perhaps; and perhaps you're trying to avoid thinking about Bull's visit tomorrow. Or talking about Bull today?"

"Perhaps...maybe...probably...so o.k., where do you want me to start in the Sunny and Bull saga?"

"I don't even know when you first met Bull. Start there." He leaned back in his chair, pulled his lower desk drawer out, and propped his feet on it.

"Don't get too comfortable Doctor," I said, "or you're liable to fall asleep."

"Not a chance."

"My family moved from Summit to the next town of New Providence when I was in the seventh grade. I remember noticing Bull that first year, but we didn't have any classes together. He seemed to be watching me, but he never spoke to me. And of course I noticed he was dark and good looking, and not very approachable, so I didn't speak to him."

"That summer I met him again at the community pool. He started talking to me and then he put his towel down close to mine on the grass, and once when we were both swimming underwater, he pulled me down to the bottom with him and he kissed me hard and long. It was very romantic and from then on I had a secret crush on him."

"When did he finally ask you out on a date?"

I laughed. "In eighth-grade English. He sat two rows ahead of me and he kept staring at me. In fact one day he refused to turn around and face the board and was sent to the office. I was embarrassed, but in a way I admired his nerve. I would never have dared to defy a teacher or to have broken the rules."

"So Bull was a rule breaker even then."

"But not in a big way. He never got into any serious trouble, but he definitely did things his way. He was admirable in several ways. He studied Judo and was excellent at it, and even gave up his Saturday mornings to teach a class of little kids. He took me there to watch him teach and he was so cute with the kids, I think I started to fall for him then."

"I guess you could say Bull seemed more like a man than any other guy at school. He had a really nice voice and when he called me on the phone for the first time, I actually thought he was Dad. He had a great sense of humor and he played along with me for a few minutes until I caught on. I'd forgotten that, how his voiced reminded me of Dad's at first."

"That's a little creepy for me," Dr. Carroll said and I ignored him.

"Anyway, he was cute even then. He looked like a very young Burt Reynolds, only prettier because he had these long, curly, black eyelashes. And he had black hair. Now he has the beard I suggested he grow to hide his somewhat weak chin, and he also has hair on his chest."

"He invited me to go to the Friday night basketball game and I don't remember even glancing at the court because our attraction was strong from the first time he held my hand. He was known as a quiet boy-but with me, he talked-not a great deal, but just enough so I felt special to see a side of him he hid from most everyone else."

"And that first night I learned a great deal about him. His parents had married as teenagers, and although his Dad was in his early thirties, he was seriously ill. He had a diseased heart and was a candidate for the first heart transplant."

"Bull would go to school all day, then hurry home to do his father's work for him. He was superintendent of a large apartment complex in town, and Bull did all the repairs, landscaped the property, and painted the apartments, too. Several nights a week he also worked at the local

A&P stocking shelves, and saving the money for college. In those days he thought he wanted to be a veterinarian."

"I never saw Bull bring a book home from school and he was mostly a B student, so I knew he had brains, even though his speech didn't always reflect it since he came from a blue-collar family and had never been exposed to any culture. The first time he took me to a restaurant with menus he broke out in a sweat and had a mild anxiety attack."

"It doesn't sound as if you two had very much in common."

I laughed. "Well, let's see. We had our mutual attraction, a love of animals, nature, and Italian food. That's about it. But I admired the character he showed by helping his family."

"Why did you keep on dating him? You could have been his friend. Surely there were other boys in high school who attracted you and shared more of your interests?"

"Yes; one in particular, Jeff Connor. He was gorgeous, student council president, captain of the football team, and my co-star in all of the plays."

"Did he like you?"

"He did, but I didn't realize how much. He called me nearly every night on the phone. And whenever Bull and I would break up, Jeff and I would sneak off to a movie, or a play in another town; then go for a hamburger and share a long talk."

"Was it ever a romance?"

I shook my head. "He was scared shitless of Bull, and Bull could be pretty scary. He still is, sometimes. He has a violent, dangerous side. Jeff was shy with girls. I know because he confided in me about who he liked and he was honest about his insecurities. I used to fantasize that one day I would walk up to him in the hall and say, "Jeff, I think we'd make the perfect couple. Why don't we date and see what happens?"

"Ha! You should have taken a chance and done it!"

"In the early sixties?" I shook my head again. "Back then girls didn't know we had the right to choose."

"Do you realize it now?"

"Now it's too late."

"Sunny, has Bull been abusive to you?"

I stared down at the gold carpeting and swallowed hard. I didn't want to remember. "Not often. Don't you want to hear about high school?"

He nodded.

"New Providence was the kind of a town where your standing in the D.A.R really counted. I don't know if that's true now, but it was then. You know, the people wear clothes with little alligators on them and all the women style their hair like identical hats."

"My eccentric, artistic family didn't even try to fit in. The neighbors actually went to court to stop my father from having one small, tasteful sign outside of our home. He only wanted his name on it to landmark his photography business on the bottom two floors of our split level home."

"Dad's request was denied at first, even though the zoning board had previously granted variances for signs to two doctors, a realtor, and a dentist, all on our same street. But of course they didn't have Italian last names like we did."

"Dad offered to compromise by dropping the issue of having 'photographer' on the sign, but he needed to have his name out there so his customers could find him. We eventually won the right to have our less than acceptable Italian name on the sign outside, but I never forgot we weren't really welcome in that town."

"How can you be certain you weren't welcome because your family is Italian? Maybe the neighbors didn't like signs."

"I know because the next-door-neighbor's daughter was as close to a hippie as New Providence would ever see and she hated the snobs who dominated the town and told me the terrible things she heard her parents and the rest of the neighbors saying about 'the situation with the wops' next door. She couldn't stand her parents either and actually ran away the day after graduation and I don't think she's come back yet."

"Did what she told you hurt?"

"Not really hurt, but it did amaze me my father had been right about the attitudes we might encounter just for being Italian. I mean, I knew Frank Sinatra and Dean Martin, and countless other Italian-American entertainers had become famous and popular with the American public, and just about everyone loved Sophia Loren, so I knew it was possible to become a success with an Italian last name. But it was the first time I had personally encountered prejudice based solely on my heritage. And to answer your original question, I'd say it made me more mad than sad, and it made me determined to win them all over. I would kill these shallow bastards with kindness and dazzle them with my talents."

"Actually Joe-Joe, who was a gifted lead guitar player, and I both decided to excel in spite of the vowels at the end of our last name. We both became acclaimed local celebrities."

"But in spite of all that, I knew I didn't look like everyone else. Beige, navy, and gray were definitely not my best colors, and my parents were too frugal to buy me the over-priced designer clone outfits most every other teenager wore anyway, so I chose from the current youthful mainstream fashion. And I guess I looked more like a secretary in a movie, in my bright sweaters, straight skirts and black flats. I think I styled myself after Jill St. John, or Debbie Reynolds playing a part in a Frank Sinatra romantic comedy film."

"I'm curious, Sunny," Dr. Carroll cut in, peering at me over his glasses. "Why would you mention your high school wardrobe now? Did it bother you to be different? That kind of confuses me since you seem to define yourself by your individuality."

I shrugged. "I do now. Back then it kind of bothered me, but not enough to wear penny loafers and knee socks. I also think I wanted to look older because I felt older and more mature than most of the others, and I was secretly in love with my Speech and English teacher."

Dr. Carroll sat up in his chair. He leaned forward on his elbows. This bit of information apparently got his full attention. I noticed his hair was sticking up a little bit in back, but I didn't mention it because he looked so human and kind of cute. "Tell me," he said.

"His name is Dylan Callahan, he's fifteen years older than me, and he was, and probably still is, gorgeous. He's a Gregory Peck look-a-like with a deep, sexy voice to match. I was convinced Dylan Callahan was the perfect man."

"He always smelled of Aramis. He was talented, intelligent, sensitive, quietly masculine; a real Renaissance man of the sixties. He could quote Shakespeare to the girls, and discuss the latest football scores with the boys. Even though I had a soft spot for Bull, a big portion of my heart belonged to Mr. Callahan. But it was an innocent love."

Dr. Carroll raised an eyebrow at me.

"Seriously. He was married to a charming, friendly cute woman and they had three kids, and I would never cause problems in someone's marriage. I respected marriage as well as feared it."

"Feared it?"

"As a dead end. My father was the boss in our house…as was the style at the time, and I accepted it because he was my father. I just couldn't imagine growing up and giving a husband that kind of power over me and my life."

"Was your mother happy with the balance of power in the house?"

"Hardly. She accepted it most of the time when we were little. I don't think my parents fought more than other parents did. But by the time my brother and I were teenagers, and she began to go through menopause, she completely rebelled. I remember my father raving about how the books she was reading were responsible for her 'crazy behavior,' and I once watched him confiscate her copy of *The Feminine Mystique*, by Betty Friedan. I don't remember if he burned it or took it out with the trash."

"How did your mother deal with all of this?"

"She locked him out of the bedroom and spent most of her time sleeping."

"Why didn't she get a job?"

"She had built a modest business she loved, teaching piano to little kids. But since Dad's photography studio was in the house, he claimed the noise from the student's bothered his customers and he insisted she give it up. She did, and then she withdrew from him, and got increasingly more depressed."

"How did you feel about this?"

"I wasn't very understanding. It was obvious Dad hadn't changed… she had. So I felt as if she was the one trying to back out of her original commitment. I remember yelling at her, "Why are you complaining about him? You married him and had kids. He's the same guy you married. You're the one who's changing."

"Dad and I got very close during this time. He hadn't paid much attention to me during my awkward kid years, but now I was his darling again. And so I took his side…and he relied on me as a friend. It was difficult because I wasn't really equipped to handle his confidences. I was flattered and I 'acted' as if I was mature enough to hear the details of his intimate life, but I wasn't."

"So I imagine your relationship with your mother was strained during this time?"

"That's the weird part. Sometimes we were enemies just because I was a teenager…and yet, I could tell her things I couldn't tell Dad; especially about sneaking around to see Bull. My dad hated him and hated anyone I ever dated. Mah understood this and was good about listening to me. I rarely did any of the typical teenage mischief, but the few times I did do something, I'd tell Mah about it and she seemed to enjoy the stories. That's probably because she had been so much more adventurous and brave than I was at that age."

"You mean like when she ran away from the farm in Iowa at sixteen, quit school, and became a model in Chicago all on her own?"

I laughed. "Yeah."

"So what kind of mischief did you get up to back then?"

"Well, the biggest adventure was in junior year of high school. I'd just gotten my license and was allowed to use one of the family cars. It was a little red V.W. bug. One of the girls in our 'group' had an aunt who was a Broadway star married to a rich man and she had given her niece permission to bring a few friends to New York to stay overnight in her Park Avenue penthouse apartment."

"Cool!"

"Super cool! The aunt was vacationing in Europe, and we were going to have the place to ourselves. I was elected to drive us there. We crammed eight girls into that little car, luggage and all, and by the grace of God, we made it to the city. I had told my parents I was staying overnight at this girl's house, and they didn't think to check out my story since I had always been so trustworthy."

"So I was a guilty, nervous wreck the entire time, but it was all worth it. A doorman let us into the apartment and it was like stepping into a movie: marble foyer as big as most apartments, fifteen-foot ceilings, sunken tubs, canopy beds, satin sheets, a marble fireplace in every room, and a wall of glass in the living room with a spectacular view of the city lights."

"We all took bubble baths in the sunken tubs, did each other's hair and nails, then dressed in our most grown-up outfits and headed for the

Village. We ended up being chased through the streets by the drunken sailors we'd danced and flirted with…but it was all worth it and a great adventure. Mah thought so too when I told her about it the next day."

"Why did you tell her? You just said they never checked up on you."

I grinned at Dr. Carroll. "A little self-revelation in that statement, Doctor? I'm just not comfortable with lies and I never have been. I can't handle the guilt. I guess I'd rather take my chances and tell the truth."

"Weren't you punished for the original lie?"

"No. She actually understood. We're all characters in this family, and she's never predictable, so she said she would have done the same thing if she had been me, and very possibly worse."

"Did this improve your relationship?"

"For a while; I talked her into letting me do a make-over on her. We dyed her hair red and her green eyes zoomed in and out at you, then we went shopping for some shorter outfits to show off her great legs. I tried to talk to her about Dad, and they started 'dating' and for a while things improved between them."

"Sunny, you got sidetracked from the story about Mr. Callahan. Did your mother know about him, too?"

"Mah actually knew Mr. Callahan. She was having her writing published regularly and he was starting to write and so they exchanged information and supported each other's efforts for a while."

"Did this make you jealous?"

I laughed. "No. Mr. Callahan was very professional. He always called her Mrs. DeAngelo and he was a bit in awe of her publishing record, but he was a real friend to me. We spent a lot of time together and we had a great deal in common. It was a magical time for me."

"In what way?"

"Well, Mr. Callahan insisted his students give him oral book reports once a month…and you could do several books for extra credit if you wanted to, so I had it made since I read constantly. I devoured the works of Daphne DuMaurier."

"Who?"

"She wrote Rebecca, they made it into a movie…an old movie…"

"Gotcha."

"I also read all of Ernest Hemingway, F. Scott Fitzgerald, the Brontes…as well as all the trashy bestsellers of the day. Mr. Callahan

loved my book reports because I would get up and move around the
room acting out all of the parts for him. He had been an actor before
he became a teacher and he insisted I try out for the school play. I got
a big part my first time out and since he was the director, we grew
even closer."

"Soon the other kids got tired of waiting around for me to finish
my marathon book reports and they unanimously insisted I go last. I
didn't mind this a bit since it gave me more time with Mr. Callahan. We
discussed everything that was important to me, the latest programs on
P.B.S., our favorite authors, the plays we admired most."

"Before long Mr. Callahan began reading to me from his 'works
in progress.' They were very adult and sometimes things went over my
head, but I always nodded wisely and it was easy to praise his obvious talent."

"What did Bull think about this relationship?"

"He hated it. He despised Mr. Callahan. They had several confron-
tations that I was afraid would become physical. And Mr. Callahan
referred to Bull as that 'stupid gorilla who carries your books around for
you.' But I wouldn't give either one of them up."

"At one point Bull broke up with me because at Mr. Callahan's generous suggestion, we were spending every Thursday afternoon together
in his classroom while he gave me free speech lessons. Bull would scowl
at us through the glass window in the door."

"Once Mr. Callahan got up and taped a big piece of construction
paper over the glass, right over Bull's angry face. We recorded these
meetings on tape and I would recite poetry as we worked on eliminat-
ing my Jersey accent. It was only a slight one, but Mr. Callahan said I
should get rid of it for the sake of my future acting career. At that time
he and I were the only ones who believed I could make it. Or perhaps
a better way to put it is that he was supporting my desire for a career in
show business."

"Dad was totally against it. He once came to school and insisted Mr.
Callahan discourage me from acting, but Mr. Callahan refused. I think
Dad may have threatened him, because I was shocked when he asked
me if my father was in the Mafia. Of course you get used to that sort of
comment when you have a last name like DeAngelo, but it hurt hearing
it from Mr. Callahan."

"Did that end your inappropriate friendship with Mr. Callahan?"

"I thought shrinks weren't supposed to judge."

Dr. Carroll shrugged. "So did it?"

"Not at all. He wrote a play for our drama club and gave me the lead. I didn't even have to audition. Then he entered us in a play contest at Fairleigh Dickenson University and we were given permission to take the day off from school to travel there and perform."

"I was assigned to ride in Mr. Callahan's car."

Dr. Carroll snorted and I glared at him. "Jeff Connors was playing the male lead and he sat beside me on the back seat. We all talked and laughed and had a great time, but I remember being drawn to look in the rearview mirror up front, and each time I did, Mr. Callahan was staring at me with those wonderful blue eyes of his. It was so exciting and very different from being with him at school."

"At lunch he and I naturally had a million things to say to each other since we were such great friends. As we settled into one of our 'heads-together-chats' trading family news, gossip about Broadway stars, and discussing the latest draft of his next play, the other kids looked shocked and the rumors about 'us' got worse that day."

"So did you win the contest?"

"Let me tell you the whole story. It was fantastic! They had the most charming little theater on campus. It had these ancient dressing rooms, and the make-up mirrors had those round lights all around them like you see in old movies."

"It was spring time and as we dressed and made-up, we kept the windows open and I remember looking down at these beautiful lilac bushes, the scent of lilac everywhere, but I could still smell the old grease paint in the dressing room, I felt like a real actress; like I was a part of the theater."

"I knew this contest meant a lot to Mr. Callahan because the winner was to have his or her play published. I was especially nervous because of this and I wanted to win for Mr. Callahan. more than for myself and just before the curtain rose and the lights came up, he came out of the darkness and he took my hand, squeezed it and said, "Break a leg, Sunny, and don't be nervous. Remember you're my star, Sunshine."

"I floated around on that stage, acting for Mr. Callahan, winning for Mr. Callahan; helping Mr. Callahan reach for his dream. And we won!

We took several curtain calls, and in the blinding lights, I strained to find Mr. Callahan in the crowd out front. The curtain went down and we left the stage, and still I couldn't find him."

"I wandered out into the hallway to look for him and there he was in a phone booth at the end of the hall. I walked toward him and I could hear his words over the click of my heels on the tile floor. I can still hear those heels clicking. It was a very lonely sound."

"I stood outside of the booth and grinned in at him. He was talking to his wife. "Honey, we won! I can't believe it!" he said, "They're going to publish my play! Finally!"

"When I caught his eye, he returned a victory sign, smiled and said, "Sunny was wonderful in the part," then shook the trophy in my direction. "We couldn't have won without her! Do you think so? You're just prejudiced."

"I walked a few feet away to give him privacy, and to join my friends. Jeff and I hugged and congratulated each other on our performances. We were all hugging now, and chattering away, but I kept one ear tuned to the conversation going on in that phone booth."

"I love you, too, Honey. I can't wait to get home. We're leaving in just a few minutes; as soon as I can round up the kids."

"I felt as if I were going to cry so I tried to turn away from the others. Then Jeff asked, "Sunny, are you O.K.?"

"Of course I am," I said, "I'm just so happy we won. And Mr. Callahan is going to have his play published. I'm just so happy for him…"

"Call a sitter and put on that black dress I love so much," Mr. Callahan said, then whispered something I couldn't catch and laughed. "Tonight we are going to celebrate!"

"But Sunny, you knew he was married," Dr. Carroll interrupted, "You even said you respected his marriage. What did you think was going to happen between the two of you when you won that contest for him?"

"I don't know…maybe I thought his wife would die suddenly… although I never actually wished for such a terrible thing to happen. I didn't think much in those days, I guess. I was so young…"

"I think you thought too much then…and now…and most of your thoughts are based on fantasy and the way you wish things could be instead of how they really are."

I stared at him as the truth of his words sank into my stubborn psyche.

Dr. Carroll took off his glasses and rubbed his eyes. "So…did anything ever actually happen between the two of you?"

I stood and walked to the window. A delivery truck was parked down there on the asphalt and several men in white were carrying bulky bags and big boxes toward the building.

To the left of the truck were two big dumpsters overflowing with garbage. "This is some view you've got here, Doctor," I said. "Do they pay you extra to occupy this office?"

He laughed; then continued to study me in silence over his clasped hands. He was clearly going to wait me out.

"The last play of my senior year was the spring musical. The class picked *Bye Bye, Birdie* and the only part my soprano voice was suited for was Kim, the blonde, all-American teenage girl who develops a crush on Conrad Birdie. Jeff was perfect for Conrad and he got the part, but there wasn't much in this play for me."

"I wanted to play the part of Rosie, the more mature, exotic secretary played by Chita Rivera on Broadway, but the part called for a contralto voice. So I studied for the part of Kim and tried to become more of a teenager. I was born an old soul and I thought most teenagers were silly."

"I gave a decent acting audition, but when I'd finished my song, I realized there wasn't a chance I'd get the part. The guys in the auditorium were whistling and cheering, and leering at me and I realized I'd been too sexy. Even the musical director was looking at me with new interest. My singing style, learned from old movies and Dad's jazz records, was way too mature for a teenage girl."

"I begged Mr. Callahan to let me try out for the part of Albert's Jewish mother. He shrugged and let me try, but I didn't know why he wasn't more enthusiastic. I knew I could act the part. And I got the biggest laughs from the audience watching the audition."

"But it turned out I was given the part of Kim's mother, and I was deeply disappointed. I did have some songs to sing in my soprano key, and some funny lines, but I had wanted to finish my high school career with a starring role."

"I found a way to shine, though. I talked the choreographer into letting me come up with a dance for my husband and I to do while we sang our big 'Kids' number and we stopped the show every night with our comic Charleston. The reviews raved about us and I learned how effective a small part can be if you give it all you've got."

"The night after our last performance, the cast and crew came back to school to clean up the theater. We'd had a pretty great cast party the night before, and as we all worked together, I felt Mr. Callahan's eyes on me. He was unusually quiet and thoughtful and I was too, because this was a very sad night for me: my last play on that stage."

"As the others started drifting off, I went outside to bring the V.W. Bug around to the front of the school so Joe-Joe could load his guitar, mikes and amps in the backseat. I was proud of Joe-Joe, because he had played all of the guitar solos for Conrad Birdie from off-stage while Jeff faked it. Joe-Joe was mega-talented even then. He started his first band when he was in the seventh grade."

"Well, I was really sad about graduating and leaving Mr. Callahan behind and I planned to go back inside to say goodbye to him when the car door opened suddenly and he slid into the front passenger seat."

"No!"

I nodded gravely. "Swear to God. I was so surprised to have him appear like that from out of the darkness. So big and handsome...so much a grown man right there in my car, after years of hopeless school-girl fantasies. It was dark and we were alone together in a parked car and I thought I would die on the spot."

"I'm going to miss my star when you graduate," he said; his kind, blue eyes so serious and intense.

"My throat was so dry I was surprised when my voice didn't come out in a squeak. "I'm going to miss you, too, Mr. Callahan." My hand rested on the gear shift knob right where it had been when he'd entered the car. It was trembling and I hoped he wouldn't notice."

"Sunny," he said, "I know you were disappointed when you didn't get a bigger part in this show, but you were great...as always. I can't believe what you did with that part." He shook his head and grinned at me."

"I grinned back and took a deep breath and all I could smell was his cologne. "Thanks," I said, "But...Mr. Callahan, can you tell me why I didn't get to play the Jewish mother? Everyone laughed so hard at my audition. I thought I did a good job."

"The car was suddenly too hot. I could actually feel the temperature rise. "You're too pretty, Sunny. You gave the best reading for all of the characters, but you are nobody's old mother. It's just not conceivable. And as for the part of Kim…you're just not believable as a teenager either. Sometimes I think you're the oldest person I know."

"It was very quiet now and so hot my face felt scorched by a hot sun. I stared down at my hand and jiggled the gear shift knob nervously, and then I watched as Mr. Callahan's hand came down on top of mine. My eyes flew to his and we sat frozen in a precious moment I'll hold in my heart forever."

"Remember the movie of *The Diary of Anne Frank*?"

Dr. Carroll nodded.

"One of the last scenes in the movie reminds me of the way it was that night between us. You know when Anne and Peter are up in the attic and they hear that terrible siren coming toward them and they know their time is up. In a matter of a few seconds the Nazis are going to come crashing through the bookcase. They stare into each other's eyes, and in those few seconds their wildest dreams, their greatest hope and chance for happiness are just within reach. And then it's all over. The moment passes and it will never come again."

"We didn't even hear Joe-Joe walk toward the car, but when he pulled the door open, Mr. Callahan snatched his hand away from mine and whatever might have been between us was over. In the glare of the overhead light I ignored Joe-Joe's curious look."

"So Mr. Callahan never made his move. No stolen kiss before graduation? If I remember correctly, Anne and Peter kissed just before the Nazi's came through that bookcase."

I nodded. "That they did. You sound a little disappointed in the way this story ends, Doctor," I teased. "But no, he was a better man than that. He was probably the finest man I've ever known. I will always be disappointed he didn't kiss me, but I don't think I could have handled the greater disappointment if he had."

Dr. Carroll sighed. "Why would getting exactly what you wanted cause you great disappointment?"

"Well, for one thing it wouldn't have been exactly what I wanted. He still would have been a married man, and most importantly, Bull would have been proven right about him."

"How so?"

"Bull always said, "Don't flatter yourself, Sunny, Callahan is only trying to get in your pants. You're nuts if you think he admires your talent.""

"I can see by your expression just how angry that made you."

"You bet. He always made me feel the only thing I had going for me was my sexuality."

"Why do you think his opinion matters to you so much? You know you have more going for you than that."

I stared at the sheep on the hill grazing eternally in that painting over his desk. I shook my head. "We've been together for so long. It's like we're pups from the same litter. No matter how horrendous our battles have been, we always sleep all tangled together, tangled up in so many complicated ways."

"Marriages between very young people are often like that. You become dependent on the relationship whether it's a healthy one or not. Making the break can be devastating."

"I think I've figured out why we got together in the first place, even though we didn't have much in common. He flattered me by making me so important to him. He put me on a pedestal and eventually I grew to love him for it. That was long before I realized how lonely it is up on a pedestal."

"You know my instinct warned me not to go steady with Bull, but he was so charming and he refused to give up. It wasn't until years later I learned he had terrorized and discouraged the assorted football players and visiting college boys who had shown an interest in asking me out. I had always assumed I was too ethnic to be popular in a town of blonde cheerleader types, with their bouncy bangs, Peter Pan collars, and circle pins."

"So you ended up dating Bull exclusively because he was the only one you thought wanted to ask you out?"

"You've got it. Crazy how well it worked for him."

"But didn't you get away from him when you went to college, Sunny?"

"Yes, I went to Montclair State Teacher's College in Upper Montclair, New Jersey. By the end of senior year at high school I had won the area award for excellence in the performing arts and that helped me to get into college along with a great recommendation from Mr. Callahan who had been in *Who's Who In American Colleges,* and was a big star at Montclair State. I also did extremely well on my acting audition."

"Didn't your grades help you to be accepted?"

"I had good grades in everything but math. I passed geometry by making up a song-and-dance-act and performing for the teacher. Of course it had a mathematical theme."

"You're making that up."

"Sadly, Sir, I am not. But my best accomplishment was landing a summer job as an apprentice at a professional regional theater. It was The Paper Mill Playhouse in Millburn, New Jersey, and one week after graduation I had a speaking role on stage. Most of the kids from school came to see me, and so did Mr. Callahan, but Bull was furious. He wanted me to give up the acting 'bullshit' and agree to marry him. He didn't even want me to go to college."

"Did Bull go to college?"

"Now that's a sad story. Bull had been saving for a career as a veterinarian for many years. He'd had his first paper route at ten…but when his father got so sick, he gave all of his college money to his parents. It made me love him all the more…or maybe that's what made me love him in the first place."

I pushed away from the window sill where I had been perched and crossed the room back to my big comfy chair where I settled in again, feet tucked up under me. "And then Mr. Harris died. He was such a sweet man, noble and courageous. If my son, Ben favors anyone, it's him, even though he never got to meet him. He was only thirty-seven when he passed away. I loved that man. He wanted me to marry Bull, and many times I went back to our relationship knowing it would please and comfort Mr. Harris. I hated how sick he was and that there was nothing the doctors could do to save him…at least not back then."

Dr. Carroll shifted in his seat. "So you're telling me you might have broken up with Bull if his father hadn't died so young and so tragically.

"Maybe. Actually we almost did break up for good when Bull found out I'd be acting on a professional stage the summer after graduation. It was the last day of classes and I was cleaning out my locker when Bull appeared next to me. "I've had it with you, Sunny," he snarled. "You didn't tell me being an apprentice meant you'd be up there acting on the stage. I was hoping you'd finally grown out of all that crap."

"Bull's rages made me feel dizzy and a little nauseous, but I stood my ground and faced him. "I knew you'd flip out if I told you. I didn't actually lie I just didn't tell you the whole thing."

"You call prancing around on a stage like you think you're hot stuff a job?"

"I'll be getting paid for it, Bull," I said, "And that defines a job. And what's more important, I'll love every second of it. Can't you be happy for me? The whole school is happy for me, and half the town, too!"

"He looked as if I'd squeezed his heart with both of my hands. Bull had the sweetest, sad eyes. His mother had told me that when he was in Kindergarten, the other kids called him Elsie the Cow because of his thick, black lashes."

"I love you, too, Bull," I added quickly. "Acting isn't the only thing I care about. You're the guy for me and you never have to worry I'd cheat on you or anything like that."

"Well, that's too bad, Sunny, because that isn't enough for me. I want a girl who only wants me. I want a wife who is happy just to be my wife and to have my children."

"I've always been like this, Bull, and you know that. Why did you pick me, then? I really wanted to know why. "You know Bull," I said, "I bet you'd be bored if you got what you think you want. I can't see you with a dull little wimp who just hangs on your arm and tells you how wonderful you are all the time. I think you find me interesting because I do have other interests."

"He was all red in the face now and looking dangerous. He grabbed my arm and shoved me hard against the lockers. I stared him down like I would any Doberman crouched for attack. I knew never to show fear, even back then."

"His hands pinned me like a towel on the line. I couldn't move and I hated him for it. Whenever I said something he didn't like, or he couldn't come up with a fast enough come-back, he always had to remind me he was stronger."

"Classic abuser, "Dr. Carroll said, and I glanced over at him. "I'm just saying," he added.

I nodded. "I remember we stood there for some time just staring at each other, and I remember breathing hard, determined not to give in to his demands. And then I watched him as his face changed. His anger was turning to passion and I fought against my own response to his excitement."

He pulled his eyes from mine and fell forward against me, his breath hot against my ear. His grip on my arms hurt, but his lips were soft as they slid up and down the side of my throat and around my ear. "I've changed for you, Sunny," he whispered, "But you won't even try to change for me."

"I pushed against his broad chest but he didn't move."

"He tried to kiss my lips and I turned away. I wanted to be indifferent to him, but already my heart was thundering and little thrills were shooting through me."

"If you really cared about me you wouldn't want to change me. I've never asked you to change Bull. People in love shouldn't try to change each other."

"But I've given up other girls for you, and I don't hang out with my friends anymore after I drop you off on a Saturday night. I'd give up a lot more for you, too, if I had to…"

"But Bull," I said, "When you find the one you love, you naturally give up seeing other people. That's just what happens…But I've never asked you to sell that money-pit of a car you have, or to give up your Judo. And I never would ask you to give up something you love as much as I love acting."

"Love!" he spit the word at me.

"I would hope you gave up the other girls for both of us," I said, "Honestly, Bull, if you don't want to go steady with me you should just come out and say so."

"And the truth was, Dr. Carroll, I couldn't be certain, even back then, that Bull had given up other girls for me. I'd heard the rumors about him and one of the 'greaser' girls who lived near him. But since we weren't going all the way yet, I figured I couldn't say much if he sneaked out sometimes with one of the 'bad' girls. That's the way it was in those days…"

Dr. Carroll nodded. "I remember. So why didn't you just let him go, then, Sunny? I think you knew even then you weren't right for each other."

It was my turn to nod. "There was something about Bull that grabbed at my heart and wouldn't let go…still hasn't. He had this soft voice that went right through me, and there was always a sadness to his voice whenever he told me he loved me…as if loving me was a hopeless cause."

"So what happened that day in front of your locker? How did he get you back?"

"He drew me into a long, slow kiss and we both nearly fell into the locker. I didn't care anymore if he hated my acting; I barely cared if he hated me as long as he kept on kissing me like that. It was tragic. It was dramatic. I thought it was my destiny."

"We practically flew out of the parking spot. We couldn't keep our hands off of each other and we took turns shifting gears and watching for the cops as we streaked up into the Watchung Hills near New Providence."

"We threw ourselves together and fell into the back seat. It was electric…it was forbidden…it was fabulous. Fumbling pseudo-sex was the thing we did best."

"You both had orgasms from fumbling around fully clothed? That's incredible,"

Dr. Carroll said.

"It was. You see, I was a nice girl and in 1966 nice girls didn't actually 'do it.' Just about everything else was acceptable, but you had to make the boy wait for years to reach each new step. Then if he gave you an engagement ring, and it had to be real diamond, even if you couldn't see it with the naked eye, because then it was alright to 'go all the way.' Isn't that how it was when you were a teenager?"

He snorted. "It was worse than that. I'm ten years older than you are, Sunny."

"Oh, well at first I let Bull unhook my bra and touch me, but only if I kept my blouse on. The third year, only one of us could have our underpants off at any given time. By the time I went away to college we were going at it like a Singapore whore and a sailor, doing anything and everything we could come up with, stopping short of the complete act of normal intercourse."

"Groovy," Dr. Carroll said and we both laughed.

"My parents got a divorce the summer I graduated from high school. Dad got the house because that's where his business was, and I stayed with him since I was going away to college in the fall and I hadn't asked to be divorced from our family home. At least that's what I thought. Since Joe-Joe was still in high school, Mah had custody of him and they moved to a little house across town that she bought with her settlement money. It was a strange and rotten summer; confusing and sad."

"Dad was very depressed. He started drinking every evening and sometimes he'd want to go out and play drums with some of the bands that played within driving distance. It I was off from The Paper Mill Playhouse, I went with him so I could drive him home."

"He liked to have me get up and sing a few songs with the band and although I was nervous at first, I got better at it and I realized I could probably make a living as a singer if I had to. And Dad was proud of me, and we would dance together. It was fun, but Bull hated it. He was always jealous of my father. He was jealous of everyone in my life including all of my girlfriends. Most of the time our relationship was more of a burden to me than a joy."

"Except for the sex, or the pseudo-sex, I should say," Dr. Carroll said. "That's right."

"Sunny, don't you realize Bull didn't invent sex? Other men can do the same things for you. Would be very happy to; you don't necessarily need Bull for sex."

I stared at Dr. Carroll. "I don't know about that, Doctor," I said, "I've never been with anyone else. It's a scary thought."

Dr. Carroll sighed and shook his head. "We'll leave that alone for now. So what happened to your father? Did he become an alcoholic?"

"No. He met a girl, a younger woman only four years older than me. Her name was Cynthia and he called her Cyndy. She was actually the one who chased after him. He met her through a mutual friend…a friend of Dad's who was a friend of her father."

"Cyndy was like a friendly, eager puppy. She was short and plump and very out-going and warm and giving. I couldn't help liking her. She treated me like the little sister she'd never had, being an only child, and surprisingly, my mother liked her too. They actually became friends."

"Cyndy adored Dad and put up with all of his old fashioned ideas about relationships. She often went to Mah for advice and whenever she and Dad went out of town overnight, Mah would babysit her toy apricot poodle, a terror named Horatio."

"You didn't resent Cyndy at all?" Dr. Carroll asked.

"Not really. She went out of her way to be nice to me. She was kind and we got along really well. Sometimes I thought she liked me more than Mah did. Mah always seemed to be jealous of me and Dad."

"Did you feel disloyal to your mother?"

I shrugged. "I probably should have, but like I said, Dad was always an issue between us, and I knew Mah hadn't understood when I stayed behind with him. But in my mind, Mah had chosen to end the marriage, and I felt overwhelmed at the prospect of trying to handle Dad's sadness, along with my own, and the pressure of adjusting to college and my first time away from home."

"I remember the first night I had to walk into the house after Mah and Joe-Joe had moved across town. I had been at work that afternoon for the matinee, working as a dresser for the actors in that particular play for that week."

"I stepped inside of the kitchen and was immediately shocked to find Dad had given all of the furniture to Mah along with most of the kitchen equipment. My room was untouched and Dad still had his entire photography studio intact, along with a fold-out sofa in the waiting room, but it was a terrible shock to find we didn't have a chair to sit on or a kitchen table. We did have one big color T.V., and the sterio left in the empty family room, though. That's where I found Dad. He was sitting on the floor with his head against the sterio speaker. He was listening to his old jazz recordings, as if it was the end of an important chapter in his life. He looked pitiful, sipping Chivas Regal on the rocks, and keeping the beat better than anyone else I've ever known on his old practice pad, his sticks moving like lightening."

"He was glad to see me. I always recognized the mournful child in dad, and that night he was a sensitive boy hiding behind a brave grin."

"It's just you and me now, Kid," he said, lifting his glass in a toast, and then draining it without flinching. I could smell his breath from where I stood in the doorway."

"We'll be O.K., Dad," I said, and smiled back at him. "But what should we do about dinner?"

"He shrugged his shoulders and we laughed together. Neither one of us had considered that now we were the ones responsible for coming up with a dinner each night…as well as clean clothes…and God forbid, a clean house. I thought of our big empty house. There really wasn't much left to clean, and I was reasonably confident I could fit cleaning in and still have time for my job at the Playhouse and some fun."

"Dad stood and faced me. "Let's go out tonight. We'll eat at Mama Gina's and then hit all the clubs and look up some of my old band buddies. I can play a little and you can sing for me; how 'bout it?"

"Only if I can drive."

"Dad looked disappointed in me. "I can drive, Cockroach," he said as if he really believed it. "But I don't mind if you want to get some practice in since you're so new at it."

"I agreed and ran up the stairs to change. I avoided looking into the empty master bedroom and then I found myself staring into Joe-Joe's bare room as tears welled up in my eyes. Why did Mah suddenly change the rules? Why did she decide to just give up on him? It was so hard to believe my little brother was really gone."

"His room looked so much smaller and so empty without his model airplanes and his guitar and James Brown and Joe Cocker records all over the floor. His usual mess of stale sandwich crusts and dirty clothes was gone too, along with his loyal, gentle, funny self. "Hey, Sunny," he used to say as I passed down the hall. "Got a minute? Listen to this."

"And then he'd play a wild lick on his guitar and dance like Chuck Berry, and I would laugh and tell him how good he was and how talented. We needed each other. We always had in this crazy family; especially whenever we couldn't sleep because of angry voices cutting through the peace of our night. Everything was different now and I would miss him for the rest of my life. Our lives as we had known them would never be the same again."

"Then I stopped feeling sorry for myself because the reality of the situation was that Joe-Joe and Mah weren't gone, they were just a minute and a half away by red V.W. Bug. I would stop in to help them un-pack in the morning, but tonight, Dad was a mess and he needed me."

"Neither one of us had an appetite for dinner, but we soaked up the music at Mama Gina's and let it begin to heal us. I didn't have any more appetite for singing than I did for pasta, but I sang for Dad, just like I had when I was a little girl and I tried to chase the sadness out of his eyes. I sang a Mel Torme number; Bluesette…light and jazzy. I closed my eyes and settled into the fake, happy emotion of the song, and when the room exploded with applause, I felt better, stronger."

"Then, while Dad was deep into a drum solo at our third stop of the night, Cyndy appeared and sat down beside me. I knew who she was from Dad's description of her. And I knew she was going to be important in our lives by the way she worshipped Dad with her big, green, almond-shaped eyes. She was quite beautiful, and all the more appealing because of her full figure."

"Hi," I said, when she glanced at me. "You must be Cyndy. Dad told me about you."

"Hi, Sunny!" she beamed, obviously pleased Dad had spoken of her, "I knew you from your pictures. Your father adores you, you know, and Joe-Joe too. I'm sorry it didn't work out with your parents."

"To her credit she did, indeed, look sorry, despite the love I could see lurking in her gaze every time she glanced at Dad."

"Suddenly Dad appeared. "What are you doing here, Cyndy?, he asked, drumsticks still in hand.

"Don't be mad, Joe," she said, her full lips curving appealingly. "I knew this was going to be a sad day for you and I thought I'd come looking to see if I could find you. I'm glad you aren't alone. And it's great to finally meet Sunny. She's even prettier than you said she is."

"Dad's face softened. He sat beside me. "This is Cyndy," he said, "As you can see, she's much too young for me, and strangely enough, I met her and her father at the same time. Still, for some unknown reason she thinks she wants to date me now that your mom has left me and filed for divorce. So, what do you think about that? Would it bother you?'

"I looked from one face to the other and shrugged. "You should do what you want, Dad," I said. "It wouldn't bother me if you guys dated. I'm going away to school in about a month and you'll be all by yourself then. At least I won't have to worry about you being so lonely now."

"He grinned at me as if I'd given him an early birthday gift. "Really?"

"I nodded and Cyndy beamed at me and squirmed on her chair as if she'd just been informed Christmas was coming twice this year. "See, Joe, I told you it was silly to worry about the difference in our ages. Age doesn't mean a thing."

"They got up to dance and as I watched them I could feel the muscles in the back of my neck twist into knots. My emotions were confused. I liked Cyndy; no one could help but like her, and I was glad Dad had a new friend. It was a good thing he would have a new playmate to take my place; a playmate who could take both my place and Mah's place. Now I could leave for college with a clear conscience. I knew Cyndy would take care of Dad for me."

"Cyndy waved at me over Dad's shoulder and let loose with an incredibly expensive smile. I would learn she came from a very wealthy family which was why she had such pearly straight teeth; a triumph of orthodontic skill over reality. She caressed Dad's shoulder and snuggled her head against the hollow of his neck, her blonde hair a contrast to Dad's black, wavy hair. I thought about Bull and considered calling him as I tried to pretend, even to myself, that I didn't mind this was the tenth time in two minutes Cyndy had found some excuse to touch my father. They turned gracefully in their dance and Dad's face was toward me, but he didn't see me. He was running his hand up and down her back intimately and his eyes were closed."

Dr. Carroll leaned forward and handed me a wad of Kleenex. I hadn't even noticed the tears that were running down my face.

"Freud would love this one," he said.

CHAPTER 14

"I'm really nervous about tomorrow, Alexander," I said, pulling the cord that closed the drapes in the Community Room.

"Come over here and sit down, Sunny," he said, patting my place with slow, deliberate thumps.

I sat like a good girl and faced him, clasping my hands together to hide the trembling. My stomach twisted and gurgled with a mean reaction to the sour cream from our fake- Stroganoff-over-noodles dinner.

"I can't believe it, but I'm looking forward to getting back to cooking...soon." I moaned, leaning back and rubbing my belly. "After so many years of housekeeping, cooking, and laundry I never thought I'd miss it. It's bizarre."

"Not really. It's more a question of survival," Alexander whispered, as the nurse walked by and we both smiled at her.

"I don't see the logic in feeding people with mental issues, sour cream. It's like a symbolic slap in the face."

Alexander chuckled, a slow, delighted rumble. "Stop stalling. Now what bothers you the most about seeing Bull tomorrow?"

I sighed and rolled my eyes. "Probably the fact that I'll have to be in the same room with him."

"No smart answers."

"Oh, please, Alexander, don't be mean. Where would I be without my smart answers?"

"Probably a lot farther along in therapy."

"O.K., I'll go a little deeper. The thing that bothers me the most about seeing Bull tomorrow is my uncertainty about how to react to him. He can hurt me so easily. I don't feel strong enough to face him." I stood and wandered back to the window. "It's like I've found the 'old Sunny' again. I'm more myself here, with you and the doctors, than I've been in so many years at home. I'm just me here and I kind of like it. It's a relief not having to deal with being Bull's wife, even if it's just for a few weeks."

"Good. Very Good! Tell this to Dr. Carroll and don't forget. And I'm glad you'll be seeing Bull under his direction. Think how much worse it would be if you had to deal with Bull out there, without Dr. Carroll to supervise at least the first confrontation."

"That is truly scary."

"So try to become focused on your goals for the meeting. A little nervousness is normal and healthy. Just think through exactly what you want to say to him, make notes if you have to, and don't have any expectations about what you can accomplish with a first visit."

I drew a deep shaky breath. "You are so wise, Alexander," I said, stroking his long fingers, with one of mine. "Thank you for being my friend."

It was his turn to sigh. "You don't ever have to thank me for loving you, Sunny. Accept it as your due. Do you resent being a friend to others?"

"Of course not! Oh…I see what you mean…I'll work on that; just one more thing to work on."

He smiled at me. "Good. Now be a great good friend to me and read another chapter of the book."

*   *   *

The sounds of camp beginning to stir, and the smell of morning coffee pulled me back from a deep, troubled sleep. I poked my head out from my tent of quilts and canvas and was glad to feel the sun on my cheeks as it shone through a slit in the front opening in the canvas. At least the day would be dry and bright.

I washed quickly and dressed in a plain brown plaid frock of heavy cotton with matching bonnet suitable for a day of traveling down muddy mountain passes. Then I took thick cloth rags and soaked up the rain water from the floor of the wagon. After removing tarpaulins, I wiped everything else down too.

I hung the damp rags on the back of the wagon and ate some dried apples and a cold biscuit from the night before, but I hadn't much appetite and could barely wash it all down with the welcome cup of steaming tea Elisha brought to me so I wouldn't have to bother with a fire, as I had slept overly long.

I almost told Elisha of the reverend's proposal, but since I wasn't sure how I felt about it myself, I wasn't ready for another opinion unless it came from Bruin. I very much needed to hear what Bruin thought.

Elisha want back to help her mother dress the younger children and I interrupted the horses where they grazed upon wild grasses. I quickly watered them, led them to the wagon, and then struggled to harness them securely. The horses were thin from the rigors of our journey, but in decent shape, and they whinnied softly to me as I ran my hands along their thick coats, wiping them down, and preparing them for another day of challenge on the open road.

Daisy, Thomas, Amelia, Howard, Michelangelo, Pierre, G.W. for our beloved President George Washington, and Mr. Jefferson with the wild red mane and tail were fine beasts, and I had come to enjoy their company. I had named them for the fun of it and now understood how eccentric old women could live so happily among the society of many cats. Animals gave of their love and trust effortlessly and without guile…Blessed with speechlessness they never hurt those they loved with thoughtless words…or lies.

I turned my back from my task and faced Bruin who stood watching me from the other side of the wagon. Motionless, caught up in the moment, we gazed at each other. I was suddenly as speechless as my gentle team of horses. We each waited for the other to break the silence that lay in our path like a great crack in the earth. Which of us would make the first move and risk the fall? Who had the greater courage?

"The reverend is a fine, admirable man, Jessie," Bruin said, his eyes dark and unreadable.

I cleared my throat. "So my papa said the night he died. He said I could do worse. What do you think, Bruin, could I do worse? Could I do better?" I challenged him with my eyes.

"Your opinion is the only one that matters on this subject." Bruin spoke in a strong voice.

"Perhaps," I said, fighting to control my trembling, hoping it wouldn't creep into the tone of my voice and betray me.

"Charles is very anxious to hear your reply to his proposal, as is every unmarried man in our party. Why don't you go to him and give him your answer? It is only fitting you speak to him first."

"Have you no advice for me, then, Bruin?" I asked, stepping toward him even as he turned away from me. "No suggestion…"

He shook his head and kept his face down from my sight. "Give your answer to the man who had the courage to ask the question," he said, and strode away from me, his boots crushing the tall grass, crushing my foolish, desperate hopes, as he left me to cry alone.

*   *   *

The reverend found me in the stand of pines. There in the same place where he had given me his proposal, we stood and faced one another. The expression in his clear light-gray eyes was very different from the hardness I had met in Bruin's dark gaze.

The reverend looked upon me with affection and unmistakable devotion. Alone in the world, I responded to his warmth and kindness as any orphan would and I decided to take my papa's advice for once and 'do no worse' in my quest for a new life as a woman fully grown.

"I accept your kind proposal, Reverend," I said, feeling a bit of the happiness that surged forth in his exuberant cry.

"Thank you! Thank you, Sweet Jessamyn!" He fell to his knees and kissed the hem of my ordinary frock. "Thank you, God," he whispered, taking both of my hands in his long, slender, surprisingly strong ones, as he stood once again, and spun me around in an awkward dance.

He was almost handsome in his euphoria. He threw his tall, black Beaver hat into the trees and then laughed when it tumbled back down in a shower of early autumn leaves. I laughed with him when he grabbed up handfuls of the bits of color, and pressed them into my hands.

"I wish they were roses, My Dear," he whispered, and I saw the tears shining in his luminous eyes as he dropped his head and, bowing over my leafy bouquet, he pressed long, gentle kisses over the rough backs of my weathered hands. I fought not to react to his touch.

"When we settle into our home in Beaver Valley," he said, caressing my hands with warm, quick gestures. "I will rub scented oil into these precious hands...the hands of an artist. And you will paint again. We will be so happy, Jessamyn, I promise you that on the truth of my life."

I could only smile in answer. I felt a numbness creeping through me, as if I were listening to his voice from beneath the surface of a pond. And I prayed I was doing the right thing.

*   *   *

Many days later I got my first view of Marietta from the log flatboat upon which I was traveling with my wagon. We were all being borne swiftly along by the powerful current of the Ohio River. I pulled my heavy woolen shawl closer about me, enjoying the robin's egg blue sky and the exhilaration of a windy, fall day.

Amanda Masters and Elisha called out from the boat behind me, "Isn't it the most beautiful city you've ever seen?"

"We're almost there! It won't be long now before you're a bride, Jessamyn," Elisha yelled, doing a few waltz turns around the flat-boat her family was traveling on and waving at me until I raised my own hand, pretending to share her enthusiasm for my fate.

I strained to see Bruin, riding on a boat further back, but I couldn't see quite that far. He had been avoiding me since the day I gave the reverend my answer to his proposal. I didn't know what to make of that. If Bruin wanted me, wouldn't he have declared his feelings? I had worn myself out puzzling over it. But I guess it didn't matter now.

The reverend was transformed with happiness at the prospect of our wedding. His jubilance was contagious and we had been a merry group these past few weeks. I concentrated on looking forward to our future. But if truth be told, I was suffering secretly. Only my pillow knew the magnitude and bitterness of my nightly tears.

Then in the morning, the reverend would come to my wagon and in his face would be such an abundance of high spirits and gentle admiration, I couldn't help but treat him with kindness, if less enthusiasm than he deserved.

There was suddenly a confusion of shouting and hurried activity as our boats drew up to dock in Marietta. My boat master bumped our craft into position, tethering it fast to one of the massive logs that poked up from the harbor for that purpose.

A massive fort stood upon the highest hill of the town and dominated the landscape. To me, the survivor of an Indian raid, the fort was a beacon of security and safety.

I was glad to see the reverend well occupied with directing the unloading of the horses and wagons, and soon after I had disembarked from my flat-boat, I took the opportunity to slip away from the others. I needed time alone with my thoughts; time to adjust to the chilling prospect of my wedding, surely to take place within another day or two.

The town of Marietta was reminiscent of Boston since it had been founded by settlers from home. The place was much smaller, but it did have a land office, a doctor, an attorney, two churches, an entire street of shops and small service businesses, as well as a large hotel and saloon. I hurried down Main Street, enjoying the act of moving forward on my own two feet after so many hours of inactivity on the flat-boat.

The town square contained neat gardens of asters and marigolds, enclosed by tiny white picket fences. It was quite charming and I sank down upon a bench near a wishing well, to catch my breath and prepare myself for the events to come.

"There you are, Jessamyn," Elisha called out, hurrying toward me, a flurry of yellow calico, petticoats, and floppy bonnet. "The reverend is frantic to find you, and Mama is too!

Even Bruin has taken up the search and of course Cassie Taylor is hanging on his arm, pretending to be worried about you. The poor thing!"

"Ha!" I said, and Elisha giggled, sinking down beside me. She sat very straight as if her back would be burned if she allowed it to touch the bench.

"Why is everyone looking for me? I can't be that indispensable."

When Elisha grinned, her eyes disappeared to impish half-moons. "You are to the reverend! And Mama needs you to finalize the wedding preparations. I also think you are expected to meet with the reverend's friend, the minister who will be marrying you both…Reverend Thomas, I think he said."

"You will be my maid of honor, won't you, Elisha. It would mean so much to me."

Heads turned all around the square as she shrieked and hugged me. "Yes, yes! I was afraid you would not think to ask me," she breathed, leaping to her feet and dragging me after her. "I will wear my good pink frock with the eyelet lace. Mama has satin slippers that should fit me well enough, and perhaps we can make a hat suitable for the occasion!"

We hurried past the tall oak and maple trees as the leaves turned in the gentle wind, rustling crimson, blush, and sunlight. We approached a wagon bursting with vegetables and fruit, heaped high with squash, pumpkin, apples, corn, and beans. We stopped and bought all we could carry from the ancient farmer who sat on a stump and appeared annoyed when we interrupted his conversation with a plump old woman, as if taking our money was too much trouble to bear.

* * *

On my wedding day I awoke before dawn and prayed all would work out for the best. Was it fair to marry the reverend when I did not love him? I had not lied to him and surely he knew…but I worried no good could come of a union lacking the bond of true love.

"You are just nervous, Dear," Amanda Masters insisted later as she helped me to dress in Mama's wedding gown of burnished satin and French lace. "I thought I would surely die of nervousness on my own wedding day," she remembered, laughing and smoothing her dark hair back and pinning her lace cap over the cluster of curls she wore on the top of her head.

"You, Mrs. Masters?" I asked, "But you and Mr. Masters are a perfect love-match. Why were you nervous?"

She caressed my cheek and her hazel eyes were tender, "Every bride is nervous, Jessamyn. You cannot be a proper bride unless you are nervous. That's the way it's supposed to be."

We both laughed, and then Elisha peeked into the wagon, and asked permission to enter.

We gave it to her and she bounced up inside and I declared it should be the lovely Elisha, glowing pinkly in her finery who should be playing the part of the bride today.

She hugged me and whispered, "I would gladly take the next turn, Jessamyn. And you will be my matron of honor."

"Have you accepted a proposal from Cal?" I whispered, hugging her harder.

"We have an understanding, but we have not made our announcement yet. Don't tell," she whispered, swaying back and forth in front of the mirror, arranging the fragrant pink roses she had tucked among her abundant honey-blonde curls. She smoothed the taffeta skirt and arranged her eyelet lace mantle around her shoulders.

"I'm so happy for you," I whispered back.

"What are you two whispering about?" Amanda asked from where she stood in the corner of the wagon, folding clean laundry.

"Secrets," I said, sitting upon a crate while Elisha brushed my hair and we decided how I should wear my thick, unruly mop for the ceremony.

I raised my hands to hold my curls in place while Elisha pinned them, and my hands began to tremble enough so she noticed it.

"Look, Mother," Elisha called to Amanda, "Jessamyn is so frightened, her hands are flapping like a flag in a windstorm."

Amanda dropped the petticoat she was folding and came over to us. She took one of my hands and rubbed it as if I were bitten by the cold.

"Poor Child," Amanda crooned, "You are in a bad way...I didn't have any idea you were so distressed."

She dropped my hand and I fell forward, sobbing and shaking all over as I hid my face in both my hands.

"Jessamyn!" Elisha cried, throwing her arms around me. "What is wrong with her, Mother? Why is she sobbing?"

"It's just nerves," Amanda said, but with less confidence now.

"I...I don't know if I am doing the right thing," I squeaked, nearly choking on my tears, "I don't know if I will be a good wife to him. I...I am confused. He asked me to marry him when I was so sad...Papa had just passed on...Oh, Mrs. Masters, what should I do?"

There were tears in both Amanda's and Elisha's blue eyes. "Do you love him?" Amanda asked in a quiet voice.

I sniffed and wiped at my tears. "I admire him. I respect him. And Papa said I could do worse. It was one of the last things he ever said to me. Papa would be glad to see me married to a fine man like the reverend. He told me so the very night he died."

Amanda stroked my hot flushed cheek and Elisha rubbed my back. "The reverend loves you very much...and often that can be enough for a woman. But if you don't want to marry him, I will explain it to him for you. You will always be welcome as a daughter in our home, Jessamyn. Both Ben and I loved your parents and we will always love you and be there for you. Do not do this because you feel you have no other choice."

Elisha tried to speak, but a sob caught the words in her throat and she kneeled and hugged me once again. "It is so tragic," she barely managed to speak between her fits of weeping. "A wedding day should be a happy day...the happiest day of all. I thought you were in love, Jessamyn. It never once occurred to me to imagine you were not as happy as I was at the very thought of your wedding day."

Amanda and I looked at each other and then smiled. "Don't cry, Elisha," I coaxed, "It's not as bad as it sounds. I do care for the reverend...and I am certain we will have a good life together. He treats me with as much care as Mama gave to her finest crystal, and I might look a lifetime and never find a man half as fine as Charles Putnam. Please don't cry. We will both look a wreck at the ceremony if we don't gain control of ourselves."

Elisha raised her head and wiped at her tears, sniffed, and then blew her nose into a pink lace hanky. "Cold water," she gasped, "We will have to bathe our eyes in cold water to take the swelling down.

Amanda bustled about applying cool, wet cloths to our eyes and arranging Mama's veil, as light as mountain mist, upon my crown of curls and then added fresh white rosebuds and baby's breath in a wreath, securing the whole with my ivory hairpins.

The perfume of the rosebuds filled the room and I thought of Mama's rose garden and wished with all my heart that both she and Papa could have been here with me on my wedding day. Yet if they were still with me there would be no need of a wedding.

Amanda took a shaky breath, "What a lovely bride you are Jessamyn. You will have the happy life you deserve. Your guardian angels will see to that. I just know your parents are sending love and blessings to you from heaven above."

"I wish they could see me in Mama's gown," I whispered, gazing upon my reflection in Amanda's long mirror. I had been grateful when she had insisted her biggest boy, Clay Michael, carry it into the wagon for me.

I did look nice. Mama and I were the same size and I, and the gown, had been spared the bother of alterations. The cut of the neckline was daring for the current fashion, but I had the fullness of figure to do it justice and Mrs. Masters had added a bit of lace for the sake of modesty. The puffed sleeves and long, lace gloves were a quaint and flattering style for me, and the yards of skirt and expanse of train, stitched in many places with tiny pearls, was most impressive.

"You are gorgeous," Elisha breathed as she fussed with the tiny pearl buttons down the back, her face as reverent as a child in church. "The reverend will be breathless at the sight of you; breathless and speechless. You will see. I doubt he'll find his tongue to say, 'I do.'"

*   *   *

I was glad Mama's gown was made of a rich, satin as there was a nip in the crisp, fresh autumn air. Elisha and I stood at the start of the tree-lined main street. The Presbyterian Church of Marietta waited for us at the end of this long road. The sun reflected in a blinding glint off of the glass window in the tall steeple, and I took the flash of brilliance as a sign that all would be well: that I was indeed heading toward my true destiny, and that Papa had known in some mystical way what was best for me.

Elisha walked with me, but a bit behind, as she lifted my train up from the dusty brick road. We passed the saloon and a ruddy-faced stranger called out to me, "Have a good life, Miss." He saluted me with a mug of ale, even though it was early morning, and I thanked him with a smile, willing my legs to remain steady enough to continue to carry me forward.

Sunlight and fresh air embraced us as we passed a long row of shops and then the town square, where I had hidden the day before, and I felt like an oddity, a carnival attraction, as I listened to the whispered compliments and more boldly shouted good wishes of the townspeople who had come to wish us well, and to watch me make my way toward my new life.

We were nearly half-way up the begonia lined path leading to the heavy oaken door of the church when the door sprang open and there, framed in the candlelight from within, stood Bruin, my Bruin.

My head grew light at the sight of him and I forced myself to smile as I approached him, although I had never seen him look so grim.

"What is wrong with him?" Elisha whispered from behind me. I shook my head and had no reply.

"I will be giving you away," he said in a voice that shook slightly from what I imagined to be nervousness. Bruin was no more accustomed to parading about in front of a crowd than I was...

"Thank you, Dear Friend," I said, and wondered why he appeared to wince at my words.

When I heard the opening strains of the organ music, I felt a weakness in my knees and I grabbed for Bruin's arm and clung there as if he were a log in a churning river.

"Jessamyn," he whispered, with a depth of feeling that surprised me. "Will you be happy?"

We stood together by the door, Elisha clearing her throat behind us, and fidgeting about in her pink satin slippers.

I touched Bruin's bearded cheek, and his eyes grew softer and darker than my deepest fears. "I hope so, Bruin…He is a good man. Everyone says it is so. Papa told me so, too, just before he died. I can't feel much joy yet, Bruin; not since Papa left me."

Bruin nodded. "Charles is an exceptional man," he said, staring past my face. "And there is something else you don't know, Jessamyn. Charles saved my life during the raid. That man of God shot and killed the Indian who stood behind me with a spear raised to attack."

Bruin's eyes bore into mine as he shook his head, "He made me give him my word that I would not speak of it to anyone. But I think you need to know I owe him. I owe him my life."

The room spun briefly for me. "I had no idea," I whispered, as the organ music grew more intense and as I wondered how much Bruin felt he did, indeed, owe the reverend, Elisha spoke, "Now! We are to start down the aisle now!"

We all moved forward. I walked in a daze, my ears dulled as if an unearthly cloud had descended about me and I felt numbed, yet drawn toward the alter; pulled by a force far stronger than I was in my grief-stricken state. I hoped Papa and Mama were proud.

From the corner of my eye I caught sight of Amanda and Ben Masters, filling an entire pew with their big family of bright-eyed children, all clean at the same time, and sporting damp hair tamed for church.

Cal Witherspoon never once glanced my way, his eyes were only for Elisha and I wished she was indeed the one to be married in a few minutes.

Booth Wade sat with the wagon master, a Mr. Califon, normally rather dour and uninvolved with the rest of us, but today, the journey and all of his responsibilities behind him, he was smiling at me. I nearly laughed to see his hair parted in the middle and slicked fast to the sides of his large head. Then Booth Wade caught my eye and winked.

I was beginning to feel lighter at heart when I unexpectedly found myself staring straight into the wily eyes of Cassie Taylor. She raised her brows at me and smirked, mocking me. As if she knew I didn't really love the reverend, and that this ceremony would be one big lie from start to finish. I smiled radiantly at her…and hated her smugness. More than anything, I wished to prove her wrong.

Her parents, fat and stupid, were equally offensive to me, and I avoided any eye contact with either one of them, as Bruin and I sailed by, and I clutched ever tighter to the cloth of the arm of his best black suit.

The reverend waited for me at the end of this endless aisle. He was taller than I had remembered, or maybe he just looked taller here in this relatively small church. And for that moment I thought I might have been better off had I taken a job as a maid or a governess.

Soon we reached the reverend's side and Bruin spoke some words I didn't catch. And then, as I placed my hand in the reverend's strong, yet gentle grasp, my eyes locked with his and I was carried along for the rest of the ceremony by the sheer force of his feelings for me. It was evident he loved me…and love, we all know, is the most powerful force on this earth.

*   *   *

I had really gone and done it this time. I was now the wife of a stranger. A nice enough, kind and unthreatening type of a stranger, but a stranger nonetheless. My liar's heart was racketing about somewhere between my chest and my throat as I paced up and down over the bleached pine boards of the reverend's bedroom.

I was a liar all right, plain and simple. And a liar of the worst sort, for I'd lied not to the reverend, who knew right from the start I did not love him, but I had lied to myself thinking I could carry off this sham of a marriage day to the conclusion of a wedding night.

I strode to the mirror and gazed upon the stricken reflection of my grown orphan's face. Tears threatened to erupt again and I squeezed my eyes shut and vowed not to mourn and whimper any longer. I had had wonderful parents and in that I was luckier than most. They had passed the example of their strength down to me, and if I chose to be weak, I was doing their memory a disservice.

I was in every bone and sinew the young woman they had made me. I was indeed Jessamyn Bouchard Miles…Putnam and I would face the life I had chosen for myself in a moment of weakness and despair and make the very best of it. I would not forget my ancestors who had left their marks upon me, from the strength of my determination when I believed I was right, to the color of my hair- dark as my French mothers- yet with the reddish glint it had in the sunlight bestowed upon me by my father's Irish mother's famous red mane.

And what was right and just was that the reverend was blameless in this situation. He was a very good man who deserved a willing wife. I turned back to the mirror and decided to practice smiling again. I hadn't smiled and meant it in weeks and my husband deserved to be greeted with a genuine smile on his wedding night.

Good God! I looked like a citizen of Bedlam with my wild curls gone to frizz and my black, demon-eyes as expressive and gentle as lumps of coal. My mouth was bent in a silly simper and no matter how hard I tried I couldn't will a trace of a smile to rise up into my eyes. So at least my eyes had trouble accepting lies.

I snatched up my hairbrush and tore into my mop of Medusa snarls as if I needed to feel the pain to remind myself I was still alive. Then I twisted my hair into a long, braided rope to hang over my right shoulder and tied a slightly limp satin ribbon around the end in a white bow.

My trunk stood open in the corner of the room and I rummaged about in it for my last clean nightdress. It was as virginal as all of my others; white cotton, high necked with sleeves puffed and trimmed with lace. I opened the door of the reverend's chifforobe and stood behind it as I quickly scrambled out of my dusty traveling dress, then washed as fast as I could manage in the chilly water I found left for me in the pitcher and bowl on its' wooden stand.

I didn't like standing naked in the reverend's house so I fairly leaped into my nightdress, struggling to quickly button the tiny, mother-of-pearl buttons running inconveniently from my neck to my navel. I wished someone would invent a better method of closing a garment than these fashionably annoying little buttons.

As I went to close the door of the reverend's chifforobe I couldn't help noticing he owned only a few garments smelling faintly of musty cedar and a touch of perspiration, and I pushed them to the side, making room for at least a few of my own things. I considered unpacking now, but decided instead to go to bed with a book and try to calm myself until the reverend finished tending to our teams of exhausted horses and came up to bed.

Again, I rummaged through the trunk, in search of my copy of Shakespeare's plays. I thought Romeo and Juliet would be a fitting choice for a wedding night and I hoped to gain some insight into the mechanics of romance. If I was to be a wife, I fully intended to throw myself into the job with my usual attention to detail.

My book pressed against my breast like a shield, I faced the reverend's masculine oaken bed. As hard to face as an unanswered question of great consequence it loomed to taunt me. That faded, limp, patchwork quilt would simply have to be replaced as would the thin, colorless lace curtains that hung from the windows. I didn't at all mind the rough-hewn sills of soft bleached pine and I hoped the reverend would give me my head in matters of re-decoration.

The blank, stucco walls of this bachelor's house cried out to me to be adorned with my bright paintings and I hoped the reverend wouldn't mind taking a day from his work to cart me into Marietta for paints, an easel, and canvases. How strange it was to have to consider a husband as I made my plans for the week.

I climbed up onto the high bed and on hands and knees, crept toward the side where he had placed the oil lamp for me. I imagined that had been his way of designating which side I was to occupy. I set my rather flattened pillow up against the sturdy backboard of the bed and settled myself beneath the covers, grateful for the fresh, crisp smell of clean sheets. It appeared the reverend's housekeeper, Mrs. Less, was indeed as competent as I'd been told and I would be sure to tell her how grateful I was for the water she had left for me in the pitcher, as well as the blessed clean bed, as soon as I had the opportunity.

Not knowing how much longer the reverend would remain occupied with the care of our horses, I quickly leafed through my Shakespeare in search of the part of the play I wanted to review again, to check against my own ideas of what a girl waiting for her 'love', for her first chance at discovering the mysteries of physical love, should be thinking.

And as I relaxed a bit against the pillow and prepared to read, I found myself sliding toward the center of the mattress, drifting into a cavernous hole. It was obvious my husband had indeed lived alone for all of his thirty years and this mattress had learned his shape far too well for my taste. I made a mental note to add the mattress to my list of items to replace.

I found I could achieve some measure of comfort if I scooted far toward the edge of the bed and hooked my toe over the bed frame. Balanced thusly, I began to read:

> 'Give me my Romeo, and, when he shall die,
> Take him and cut him out in little stars,
> And he will make the face of Heaven so fine
> That all the world will be in love with night
> And pay no worship to the garish sun.
> O' I have bought a mansion of a love,
> But not possess'd it, and, though I am sold,
> Not yet enjoyed: so tedious is this day
> As is the night before some festival
> To an impatient child that hath new robes
> And may not wear them...'

I closed the book and sat weeping. The reverend would never, could never, be my Romeo.

As if summoned by my emotion, the reverend knocked upon the door. "Just one moment, please!" I called out, my voice as stuffy as if I were coming down with a case of the sniffles. Quickly, I dried my tears and wiped my nose on the corner of the quilt. I wasn't about to rummage around in the trunk again for a hanky.

I blew out the lamp, throwing the room into concealing shadow then gave my new husband permission to enter his bedroom. My heart was galloping around like a young colt and I hoped the bed wouldn't shake with my trembling.

The reverend's heavy, black boots thumped across the floor boards toward me, and I shrank down under the covers and peered up at him over his unattractive and unsuitable quilt.

"Are you tired, Child?" he asked in his soft, yet deep voice. His earnest gray eyes shone strangely with a light all their own, and for a moment, I was frightened of him; truly frightened.

"I...I am tired, Reverend...from our long journey."

He turned his face away from me and I studied his profile. His hawkish nose and fly away, yellowish hair, as well as his thin-lipped mouth, were suddenly as new to me as if I'd only just met him. I did admire his strong, square jaw and was secretly glad I had at least married a man with a decent chin.

He walked back to the dresser and blew out the remaining lamp, and the darkness I had come to dread rolled over me like a suffocating wave of black water. This was finally it. I was about to become a woman…a wife.

The rich tones of his voice found me shivering in apprehension. "Excuse me, Child," he said, nodding toward the chifforobe, "while I prepare for bed."

"Of course, Reverend," I blurted out in too loud a voice, gathering his meaning and blushing, as I turned toward the other side of the room.

I had never seen an unclothed male and while I was indeed as curious as anyone would have been in my circumstances, I fought the urge to peek back over my shoulder. I supposed I would be confronted with the reality of his body next to mine under these very sheets before another few turns of the minute hand upon the clock I watched. It was mahogany and foreign, either Swiss or perhaps German, and old enough to show it's age in the concave shape of its' yellowed face. In my nervousness, the ticking of this clock upon my night stand grew louder and more distracting by the second.

I fought to control myself, for I shook as if beset by a punishing chill, and as if I hadn't enough to worry me, the face of Bruin Mahoney kept leaping into my mind.

My mind race with tortured thoughts and I wished he were standing before me and that I could speak my true mind for once. 'You devil, Bruin,' I would say, 'if only you had asked me to marry you instead. Was it your pride or your honor that paralyzed your tongue; or am I deluding myself? Did I stir your blood and cause your breath to catch in your throat, with the same confused excitement you produced in me. You might have been my Romeo. I could so easily have fallen all the way into love with you.'

The corner of the covers lifted and I felt a chill breeze as the reverend slid into the bed. I prayed silently for the self-control it would take to keep from leaping up and running screaming back toward Boston. My breath was coming in fits and starts as if I'd already run half-way there, and I thought I would surely faint and die when the reverend suddenly reared up on his elbow and stared me full in the face.

"Do not fear me, Child," he said, "I will not demand your love. I understand you are confused and still suffering the sudden loss of your father." He reached out hesitantly and finally stroked my cheek and I jerked in reaction as if his hand were made of ice.

He smiled down at me and there was kindness and wisdom mixed with a deep sadness in the depths of his eyes. I tried to look pleasant and friendly. If I could not love this fine man who had suddenly become my husband, I could at the very least be friendly to him.

"You may kiss me goodnight," I said, in the trembling voice of the silly child I was, then shutting my eyes tightly, I pursed my lips together and waited…and waited.

It seemed forever before I felt his hot breath against my cheek and when he pressed his lips against it, I felt the full force of his controlled passion, the same passion I had heard in his voice when he preached each Sunday morning.

Finally he drew back and I opened my eyes. He was staring down at me with a fire in his eyes that nearly overwhelmed me with its' force, its' power. I'd only seen my husband look like this when he spoke of God.

"I will wait for you to grow to love me. I am a patient man," he said, his smile as shy as a gentle caress. "But please call me by my given name. It will make my time in waiting a bit easier to bear."

I smiled back at him with the first genuine smile I had been able to conjure up in weeks. "I shall be glad to call you…Charles," I said, my heart pounding, not with fear now, but with excitement.

And then he said goodnight to me and turned away to sleep and I found to my great surprise I was disappointed. Strangely enough, it appeared somewhere within me, I had been looking forward to my first experience with romantic love, and now I found I felt quite let down.

As I lay awake watching the stars outside the reverend's window, mock me with their cheerful little lights winking. I remembered Juliet's words and began to plot a way to seduce my new husband.

And as I finally drifted into sleep, I realized at least Charles had made me feel, 'As is the night before some festival. To an impatient child that hath new robes and may not wear them.' And that, I decided, was far better than feeling nothing at all.

I had so much to think about I found myself fighting the idea of sleep but my exhausted body finally won that battle, and I eventually passed over the invisible line and into the chasm of deep sleep.

I know logically I must have been dreaming, but the events of my incredible dream were very real and so totally unfamiliar to my experience I doubt this particular dream could have been created within the dream territory of my mind alone. I truly felt at some point in the night my soul actually lifted itself up and away from my body. Then, as if borne along on borrowed wings, I found myself floating out of the bedroom, down the staircase and through the front door!

When I found I had survived the trip through the door, a new, exhilarated feeling coursed through me and I decided I quite enjoyed this new sensation of dream-flying.

I had to keep reminding myself I was probably only dreaming and I was perfectly safe outside the rev...I mean, Charles' house, in the middle of the night only a few weeks away from All Hallows' Eve. And as I began to feel more comfortable with my bodiless state, I decided to soar up into the air and visit the top-most branches of the tremendous oak tree I was pleased to discover in Charles' front yard.

This was, of course, the first time I had ever come face to face with a crimson autumn leaf that had yet to fall to the ground. To say the leaves were beautiful doesn't nearly do them justice, but I will say they were so exquisite I forgot for several moments to turn my head and enjoy the spectacular view from this great height. It was much different from looking out of a window because here I felt as one with the night breeze, with the leaves in my hand. Like one of Juliet's stars, I glowed back at the rolling hills of fallow farmland. The crops were all taken in by now and the land lay resting in the star-light.

Then, from within the branches of the tree, I heard an eerie hoot and I froze. An owl was a mysterious creature I'd rather not come upon nose to nose at a first meeting. Then I remembered I was invisible since I was only dreaming and not really there at all.

So I took advantage of my opportunity and carefully parting the branches with a minimum of rustle, I peered inside and met the startling, golden stare of a very large, very menacing, brown and white spotted barn-owl. They say the owl is intelligent and he did seem to sense my presence, but nothing prepared me for the quick movement he made in my direction as he shot up on powerful wings and sped past me, actually passing through a portion of my shadowy, left arm as he screeched once, then headed toward Marietta.

I decided that since I was following all of my reckless impulses on this starry night, I might as well follow the bird to Marietta and see how Bruin was doing. I wondered as we sped together through the rushing wind, if Bruin was celebrating the fact that he had escaped marrying me or mourning his lost opportunity. I just had to find out, and as I flew over the dusty, rutted road, I realized I hoped to find Bruin in a most miserable state. I was actually counting on it.

Dream-flying felt so marvelous and free, I decided it was the only way to travel. From now on, I would envy the birds with new insight. And if I ever again found myself flying in a dream, I would head directly for some exotic island with turquoise water.

I threw back my head and lifted my face to the moon. It glared imperiously at me like the monacle of a nobleman and then I understood perfectly why I had had such trouble falling asleep. The full moon had always called out to me, demanding I lie sleepless, while it, like an uninvited suitor, held me to the spot, a bored, captive audience, until the first light of morning.

Soon the lights of Marietta came into view and I coasted down Main Street, noting how all evidence of our wedding celebration had been cleared away from the church lawn.

I skimmed over to the store window to my right and as I passed slowly along, a good twelve inches off the ground, I gazed into each window I encountered and made note of what was offered for sale inside. The milliner's shop had lovely bonnets and straw hats trimmed with ribbons and lace, and the dressmaker's headless form modeled a style of gown popular in Boston since early last year.

Then I came to Ned Taylor's Emporium and I couldn't help crying out with delight. Ned Taylor's actually had books in the window, and there, in the third row, to the left of the front door, was an entire display of oil paints, brushes, and canvases; who knew, so far from civilization as I knew it, I had found an unlikely supplier of art supplies, my very life-line. And to think it was a Taylor who had saved my life.

I leaned back as I was accustomed to when falling into a deep creek on a hot day, and then bounced upon a springy mattress of air and I found by waving my arms like oars I could whiz back out into the middle of the road. It was then the swinging doors of The Painted Pony Saloon sprang open, letting loose with a burst of stale, smoky, liquor-scented air, and my dear friend, Bruin Mahoney stumbled outside and half sprawled, half lay upon the front porch, clutching at the thick newel post as if it were his own mother and he, a naughty boy playing hide and seek behind her skirts.

He was most definitely intoxicated. I had seen Papa after he'd had a few too many drafts of ale, but he never looked as silly as Bruin did lying there in the darkness. But then, again, Papa had always claimed to have hollow boots and he was able to consume great quantities of spirits before he showed any ill-effects at all. Mama always explained this was a special talent born into every Irishman, although I never knew exactly why. Whenever I asked Papa about it he explained it was a special gift from God. God always made sure each nationality had something they could excel at; which made Bruin's drunken state even more curious for he was Irish too.

I drew closer to him and the stench of his breath told me he had been drinking strong liquor and from the looks of him he'd been at it steadily since Charles and I left town for Beaver Valley. I'd never known Bruin to drink before so I could safely assume he was reacting in some way to my wedding.

I was pleased. It certainly served him right if he suffered. I wished there was some way I could find out why Bruin had not come to me first and asked me to marry him. When he told me today that the reverend had saved his life during the Indian raid, I understood why he had not interfered when the reverend proposed...but I would never understand why he had not stepped forward to ask me first. Perhaps he thought he had all the time in the world.

I inched closer to him and then sat down on the step next to him. He was indeed a handsome man with bold features, a strong body, and gentle, dark eyes. I was beginning to like being invisible and I trailed a finger lightly along the line of his great, dark beard when he whispered my name suddenly and peered into the darkness behind me.

"Jessamyn," he whispered, "Is it really you?" And as I watched him, the truth of his feelings for me was revealed in every expression, every muscle and line upon his face. He was transformed before my eyes into a man in love!

He was far too drunk to lie and my own heart wrung with despair as I realized what a terrible mistake I had made in marrying the reverend, or Charles, as I was expected to call him. But what had stopped Bruin from telling me how he felt? What was it that had kept us apart?

"There you are, Bruin."

I turned quickly and found out just what Bruin had been gazing at with such rapt attention. And I could have slapped him for thinking it was me! That obnoxious witch, Cassie Taylor, stood posing like a dance hall girl in the middle of the road.

"Is it you?" he breathed, "Is it really you?"

"No! Fool!" I shouted, "She isn't me. Have you gone blind?" Then I remembered I was invisible, and dreaming, and not really there at all… so he couldn't possible hear, or see me.

Cassie swung her skinny haunches seductively as she stalked Bruin and the long, thin fingers of her grasping hands reached out for him.

"Don't do it, Bruin," I screamed, "You will surely regret it later. She isn't at all like me!"

Bruin took her hand anyway. Laughing, Cassie swung her great mane of fiery, auburn hair back out of her way and over her shoulder while she yanked him up to totter on unsteady feet. "Lean on me, Love," she coaxed, sliding her snaky arm around his waist. And then pulling his head down and engaging his lips in a sinuous kiss that went on forever, and took my breath away. I could only imagine the effect it must have been having on Bruin.

There was nothing I could do to save him. I was frustrated and angry. Cassie was obviously so much more acquainted with the ways of the world than I was. I had never paid much attention to the rumors I had heard about her, but now I could plainly see there was more than a little bit of truth to them. Not only was Cassie Taylor, a skinny mean witch, but she was also a vixen, a wanton woman, and a public menace.

I pounded my fists against the wooden steps and roared, wretched in my silence, as Bruin began to laugh along with Cassie as they lurched together down the street and then back through an alley.

I hated myself for doing it, but I couldn't help following them. I had to know what went on next. I had to know if Bruin would give his love to another woman when he clearly loved me.

I found them behind the saloon in a wooded area and I didn't know whether to be grateful for the moonlight or to curse if, for I saw much more than I wanted to see. I saw Cassie Taylor throw her witch's cloak upon the ground and I watched her tempt Bruin with tricks I had to admit were quite effective.

She faced him in the moon's bright light and slowly unbuttoned the bodice of her dress.

Bruin was as shocked by this as I was and I gave out with a cheer when I heard him say, "You had better run back to your parent's wagon while you still have the chance, Cassie. It is not my practice to ruin young virgins."

"But I'm not a virgin, Bruin."

Not a virgin! Cassie had never been married. How could this be? Oh, I was scandalized. Cassie Taylor was a secret courtesan. Would she dare ask him for money next?

Well, there was no talk of money, and I am sorry to have to admit Bruin appeared to have forgotten all about me and the love I had seen in his eyes must certainly only have been a trick of the light because what went on between them next was so shocking I could not bear to watch so I hid behind a tree and listened...being too curious to leave altogether.

This was not at all the thing I had imagined Romeo and Juliet had intended to do had they gotten the chance. I'm afraid my romantic imaginings were pitifully innocent.

And as Cassie's wanton screams pierced my ears, I began to feel a terrible jealousy roiling away in my guts. Here it was my wedding night and Cassie was acting the part of Bruin's bride while my body lay sleeping coldly beside the reverend, a man I would surely never shriek for in the night.

I would never have known I was capable of such a strong jealousy, but it was there nonetheless and before I had given myself time to think my actions through, I found myself flying straight back to the horse's trough in front of the saloon. I found a wooden bucket on the ground, and Lord knows what may have been in it previously, but I now filled it with the slimy water and flew quickly back to the sick little drama being enacted beside the woods.

I swooped toward my prey like a great bat, and as I drew nearer to the heaving, twisting figures upon the dark ground, I heard Bruin cry out and the son of a dog spoke my name!

"Oh, shut up!" I shouted, slinging the contents onto the both of them.

Cassie screamed like the simpering sissy she always has been and I thoroughly enjoyed watching her bare, skinny rump disappear into the woods. Bruin at least had the sense to pull his trousers up before he took off after her, carrying her dress and cloak along with him.

I watched him look back in my direction and I laughed all the harder. They would never be able to figure out where that water had come from.

In high spirits I flew home and slid back under the sheets. It appeared to me as if Charles had barely stirred. The next morning at breakfast, though, he told me I had been laughing in my sleep and he had grown concerned when he had tried to awaken me and could not…but I guess that is what sometimes happens when you are totally exhausted and fall into a deep, deep sleep. You do have the strangest dreams.

*   *   *

I put my manuscript aside and sank back against the sofa cushions. I was exhausted and troubled by the emotions this part of the story had stirred up in me.

"Wow!" Alexander breathed, "You were astral traveling…even back then before it became fashionable."

"But Alexander," I said, touching his hand, "we don't know for sure it was me."

Alexander's eyes were wise and kind and in their depths I detected a deep sadness as he caressed my cheek and sighed. "Who else could it be?"

CHAPTER 15

"Sunny," Dr. Fazio said, sitting on a corner of his messy desk. "Are you planning on crying for the rest of our session? Because if you are, you might as well go back to the Community Room and I'll go grab a cup of coffee."

Bull wasn't coming this afternoon. I turned completely around in the old, green, corduroy armchair and sobbed harder against the over-stuffed back. "I…I didn't realize how much I wanted to see him," I sniffled into one of the endless tissues Dr. Fazio kept handing me. "Wouldn't you think he'd want to see me after all this time? I just don't know what to do."

The old chair smelled of many occupants and musty secrets and I turned away to face the doctor. He was staring up at the ceiling patiently, his beefy arms crossed, his foot tapping against the metal leg of his desk. "There's not too much you can do, Sunshine. It shouldn't be news to you at this point that Bull is a shithead. The guy specializes in torturing you, one way or another, and about the only way he can get to you in here is to play games with your head by making and breaking appointments. It's probably his way of getting you to talk to him on the phone. That way he doesn't have to deal with any doctors, and he can make you as crazy as he wants to."

I looked up at him through red, swollen eyes and blew my nose again. "You're probably right. I think I will talk to him on the phone. I can't wait to hear his excuse for breaking the appointment."

Dr. Fazio sighed and threw his hands in the air. "Sunny, when are you going to stop giving this bastard exactly what he wants?"

"The day I get my kids back."

* * *

"Well, well," Bull said, "how come I rate with my wife all of a sudden? When I call over there they tell me you're unavailable, so how come you're available today? Is this a holiday? I know it's not my birthday."

"Don't, Bull," I said, drawing a shaky breath. "I just want to know why you aren't coming this afternoon."

His laugh was cruel. "I have better things to do…like working to try to pay for that lunatic-hotel you've moved into. Damn it, Sunny! When are you coming home? I'm getting sick of running this whole show by myself."

It was my turn to laugh and there wasn't any joy in it either. "Since when are you running things on your own? Did your little, blonde playmate get tired of living my life?"

His silence was louder than the angry shout that followed. "I'm going to hang up if you insist on talking crazy!" He finally said.

I decided to drop the subject since I wasn't sure what he'd do to the kids if he knew they'd told me Teri was living at the house, sleeping in my bed, cooking on my stove, petting my Bear-dog, tucking my children in at night under the quilts I'd made for them, and then making love to my husband; the only lover I'd ever known.

Tears filled my eyes, and I leaned forward, resting my hot forehead against the cool metal of the pay phone. "Please call Dr. Carroll and make another appointment, Bull. It's the least you can do for all of us. It isn't too much to ask of you to come in here for one or two therapy sessions. Doesn't our family mean even that much to you?"

"You're the nut job, Sunny!" he exploded. "There isn't anything wrong with me except that I'm sick of your craziness! Which soap opera are we living this week?"

"Please, Bull," I said, trying to hold myself steady, trying not to shake so much I wouldn't be able to form sentences. "Please care enough to come in here and speak to Dr. Carroll. He's helped me a lot and he's made me believe I can get better so we can decide what to do about our marriage."

"What does that mean," he snapped, "'decide what to do about our marriage?' You're coming home with me where you belong so that wonderful helpful doctor of yours had better learn to live without you because he doesn't get to vote for or against our marriage!' Do you hear me?"

"Live without me?" I gasped, growing short of breath and wishing I had an asthma pill. "Bull, don't be silly. Dr. Carroll is saving my life. When I first came here I was a complete mess."

His hard-edged laugh made me wince. "That's just great, Sunny. You were a compete mess from living with me. That's how much you want to be my wife. That's how much you love your kids and our god-damned home that happens to look like a fucking bomb went off in it. And you expect me to come all the way down there to try to save our marriage. What fuckin' marriage?"

I was sobbing now and Alexander came over and took my hand. "Hang up, Sunny," he whispered. "You don't have to take this from him."

"Who the fuck is that?" Bull's voice cut into my ear like a gunshot. "Is that your boyfriend? Is that the wonderful doctor who saved your miserable life? Put him on the phone. Now!"

"No, Bull," I whispered, wheezing hard. "I have to go now. I need an asthma pill. Just please call Dr. Carroll. Do it for the kids if you can't do it for me. And please believe me, I never meant to hurt the kids. I don't know why I'm so messed up, but I have to go now. Just call Dr. Carroll."

"Oh, I will, Bitch, I have a lot to say to him!" I heard him laughing at me as I hung the phone on the cradle and allowed Alexander to lead me to the nurse's station.

"Alexander," I said, growing lightheaded as I swallowed my pill, "I have to get strong as fast as I can. I may be crazy, but Bull isn't any better. I have to get the kids back and make a stable life for them."

"First things first," he said, rubbing my back soothingly. "Let's get you breathing again. Then you can work on standing strong on your own two feet."

*   *   *

"How do you feel about Bull canceling the appointment today?" Dr. Carroll asked, with his analyst's stare locking into my more tentative one.

The pleasant, subtle scent of his expensive cologne wafted over the desk and made me think of Bull. I loved that scent on Bull. My glance slid over to the window, and then I stared at the ceiling. "I'm very sad."

He slapped his hand down on the desk and I jumped. "What about mad, Sunny? Don't you feel anger toward Bull? Hell, I feel angry for you!"

I thought about it for a moment. "I just can't get angry at him... maybe I think I deserve what I'm getting now. I've been such a mess... it can't have been easy for Bull to live with me like this. A part of me doesn't really blame him, Doctor. Anyway, I very rarely get mad at Bull, I usually just get hurt. I don't know why."

"I do; low self-esteem."

I drew a deep breath wishing the session was over. "I've never thought of myself like that."

"Then maybe you should give it more thought, Sunny. You're an intelligent woman. When a person is abused, psychologically, verbally, and physically…anger is the most appropriate response."

I stared down at the carpet and nodded as the tears began again. "My relationship with Bull is complicated. It isn't reasonable to think everything that's gone wrong with our marriage has been his fault. Let me tell you more."

Dr. Carroll smiled at me and nodded, "Good idea."

"Where did we stop last time?"

"Dad introduced you to Cyndy."

"Right. Well, Dad started dating Cyndy and I felt kind of relieved."

"Relieved? How so?"

"I knew how lonely and sad Dad was when Mah left, and Cyndy made him smile. So I felt free to throw myself into my job at The Paper Mill Playhouse. It was great sleeping late in the morning and then taking a swim at the community pool down the street, or puttering around the house while I did my chores and tried out different recipes to please Dad. Bull usually called me on his lunch hour. He was still working at the A. & P. and he kept me posted on the progress of his job hunting."

"He'd been offered a position as head of the produce department, but he just couldn't see himself knee-deep in limp lettuce for the rest of his life, and neither could I. It was just too big a departure from his original dream of becoming a veterinarian."

Dr. Carroll leaned back in his swivel chair and tapped his fingers on the arms. "Why didn't he try for a loan, or a scholarship? You said he has a high I.Q.?"

"Bull has always been insecure about stepping outside of what his family perceives as their world. His parents were good people, but I noticed they set limits on themselves and their children and had low expectations about what they could achieve."

"That's a shame. You, on the other hand, seem to believe you can do just about anything. Maybe that's one of the reasons Bull was drawn to you in high school."

"Maybe, but I didn't know how to get Bull to believe in himself more. He wasn't a very happy young man and I felt guilty about feeling so good about my job at the Playhouse, and I was also beginning to look forward to the start of college in September. I was actually half hoping Bull and I would eventually drift apart."

Dr. Carroll raised his eyebrows at me.

"I don't mean I was going to abandon him during the most difficult time of his life. His dad died that summer. I really loved Mr. Harris and I ached for the whole family. Bull continued to show good character by working even harder and helping his family financially. I thought it was huge when he gave them his college fund."

"I felt so helpless at that time. I couldn't do much of anything for Bull's family, or for my own, and the best part of my day was when I could escape from all of the conflicts of my real life and into the world of professional theater. The education I was getting there couldn't be had in a drama school."

"My new friend, the other apprentice at the Playhouse, a little Marlo Thomas, 'That Girl' look-alike named Lillith Summers, was trying to teach me some street smarts. She'd changed her name from something like Elsie Schwartz and I thought she'd picked a wonderful romantic name for herself. I toyed with the idea of changing my name to Gina Valente, but Lillith only laughed when I told her."

"'Sunny, at least change it to something American!'" she said, then cracked her gum and lit a long, thin cigarette. Lillith looked about twelve, but chain-smoked and told me not to tell anyone she was actually twenty-four because she would only admit to eighteen."

"'That way,' she said, 'by the time I make it at thirty I'll only be twenty-four.' She had the most radiant smile with these impressive rows of perfect caps."

"Her cigarette looked much too big for her tiny hand, but she puffed like an expert, when she wasn't applying a fifth coat of mascara. She always dressed in 'mod style' with white patent leather cap and boots, and the shortest skirts I'd ever seen. She had the most enormous, dark eyes and she always wore full stage-makeup as if she expected David

Merrick to pop up from behind a bush and beg her to go on that night as star of his latest Broadway hit."

Dr. Carroll chuckled. "Lillith made quite an impression on you."

I nodded. "I was lucky she wanted to be my friend, because I was disgustingly naïve and might have gotten into big trouble without her guidance."

"I could easily have been dazzled by the attention of the dancing boys in the chorus who would parade around nearly naked. The guys who didn't pinch each other's naked butts, would come on to me hard with great lines I'd never heard before. Not that I'd heard much of anything yet."

"And as if that weren't confusing enough, an occasional chorus girl would invite me into her dressing room and want to make friends with me, and I was lucky Lillith was there to spell things out for me, before I found myself in a difficult position."

"Several times she saved me from total disaster. The plays ran a week at a time here, and quite a few actors and actresses on the verge of making it big would come to act in the productions."

"Late one night, just as I was leaving, an older actor who later won a starring role in a hit T.V. series, called me into his dressing room, pretending to need my help with his costumes. I entered the room and he locked the door behind us and then chased me around the room. He threw his terry cloth robe into a corner and there he stood, naked and strange and truly more annoying than frightening."

"'Let's have a midnight snack,' he leered, wiggling his tongue at me and lunging for me. I screamed and dodged him, pushed the makeup chair into his erection and then fumbled at the lock…a padlock!"

"Fortunately, Lillith hadn't left yet, and she had my back. She had one of the dancing boys yell through the door that unless he let me out, they'd call both the local police and my dad."

"Wasn't that traumatic for you, Sunny? Didn't it frighten you?" Dr. Carroll asked.

"It wasn't pleasant, but I wasn't that scared. He was pretty old and it's not as if he was a stranger to me, and he was slightly drunk so I figured that explained his behavior. He apologized…and never tried anything again. I figured I could have knocked him on his ass if I absolutely had to, since growing up with Joe-Joe had taught me how to defend myself in a fight."

"One time, though, I was almost willingly seduced by a very handsome actor in his thirties with a deep voice and very broad shoulders. He offered to help me find an apartment in New York if I decided to skip college and go for a career."

"'Date a real man, Sunny,' he said as he backed me into a very hot corner of my dressing room, and caressed my cheek. 'Give up on little boys. They can't do anything for you. Fall off the deep end a few times with a guy like me and I guarantee your singing voice will improve a hundred percent. You'll know what you've been singing about then, and I bet you'll be on Broadway in less than a year.'"

Dr. Carroll snorted with laughter.

"I didn't dare tell Bull about any of these near disasters. And as the summer passed I could see for myself that most of the people I was meeting were just big insecure kids. They casually slept with each other and constantly created crises and dramas in their everyday lives. I quickly took on the roll of little-sister-confessor to these child-like adults with tremendous egos and a need for constant praise and reassurance. For the first time in my life I had serious doubts I would be happy living in this world."

"How do you feel about that now, Sunny? Do you regret not pursuing a career in show business?" Dr. Carroll asked, his hypnotic eyes wide with interest.

I laughed. "How do you know I didn't have a career in show business?"

"I guess I don't. Go on."

"All in all, the summer ended up better than it started. But then it was time to leave for college. Dad cried the day Mah drove me to school. I did too. We clung to each other and then laughed as we reminded each other I'd be home for the weekend in a matter of a few days."

"You came home every weekend?" Dr. Carroll asked, his eyebrows rising above the dark frames of his glasses.

"Yeah, pretty much. Dad expected it and so did Bull. And I had to keep an eye on Joe-Joe. He had a tough time adjusting to the divorce and got in with a fast crowd."

"Hmmm," Dr. Carroll said, rubbing his chin. "How did Bull take your decision to go off to college?"

"Not very well, but he seemed to accept it, and planned to visit me before the end of that first week. Mah and I arrived there on a Saturday, and as we drove up to my dorm, Hamilton Hall, I was amazed to find that the campus nearly perfectly fit into my fantasy of what a first fall day at college should look and feel like. The leaves were at their color peak and kids sat around on benches and joked with each other and some couples sat on blankets together under the trees."

"That first night I met the girls on my floor and made some new friends, but not one was a speech and drama major. The girls were nice enough, though, and as nervous and unsure as I was. At meals I sat with a table of freshmen and we all complained about the food and wondered what our first day of classes would be like on Monday morning."

"How was your first day?" Dr. Carroll asked.

"Pretty good. I slept a little too late, skipped breakfast and still I was nearly late for my eight o'clock gym class."

"Eight o'clock gym class? That's brutal," Dr. Carroll said, shuddering.

"Not too bad. Luckily the drama students weren't expected to take regular gym classes and I was in something called golf and fencing."

Dr. Carroll smothered another snort of laughter behind his hand, but his eyes laughed at me all the same.

"And I'm not making any of this up," I said. "But figuring the first day would be all orientation, I had dressed with little thought to gym-like activities."

"What does that mean? Don't tell me you wore your old prom dress?"

"Nooo...as I do remember...I wore a knit dress, black on top, with a boat neck, cap sleeves, and a short A-line black and white hounds-tooth skirt. My hair was cut in an asymmetrical Sassoon style, with the sides pulled back and held in a big black bow...and I wore black heels."

"What else would a drama major in the mid-sixties wear to the first day of golf and fencing...except maybe an old prom dress."

I smiled at him. "I was the last one inside the gym and I was embarrassed by the loud click-click of my heels on the shiny gym floor as I tried to slink in on tip-toes, and join the other girls standing in a line. Everyone was watching me and some of them giggled."

"One girl, short, dark-haired, and very pretty, laughed out loud in this great wild laugh that drew me to her end of the line."

"She grinned at me right away and said, 'Clearly you are lost and on a coffee break.'"

"'What do you mean?' I asked."

"'You look like Hollywood's idea of the perfect secretary,' she said, 'Or at the very least, a person with absolutely no idea of what you do in a gym class.'"

"We laughed together."

"'You're a paisan, right?' she asked."

"'I thought you were Italian, too! I'm Sunny DeAngelo.'"

"'Lillian Piccola…Just tell me one thing, Sunny DeAngelo, what in the name of God possessed you to wear those heels?'"

"I shrugged. 'I figured the first day would be all talk, you know.'"

"She nodded. 'Makes perfect sense to me: we're gonna talk about golf and fencing…you wear heels. Perfect sense. You are a crazy person. I love crazy people. We're gonna be friends.'"

"I asked her if she was a drama major too."

"She nodded at me and I knew I'd met a friend. Lillian was a cross between Gina Lollabrigida and Audrey Hepburn in looks, with a short, curvy body and the voice and comic timing of a young Barbra Streisand. I loved her nerve. While she made fun of my outfit, she stood there wearing a maroon suit in a heavy cotton twill fabric with huge epaulets and brass buttons all over it. It looked pretty strange with her thick bobby socks and Keds."

"'What do you call the outfit you have on?' I asked."

"'A fashion error. The sales lady told us this Eisenhower look was going to be a big thing this year.' She paused and glanced around the gym at the other girls. 'But to tell you the truth, I have yet to spot another General among us.'"

"I giggled and told her, 'With your figure, you'd look good in anything.'"

"'You lie!' she said, 'I have a huge ass!' her voice rose and she grabbed a handful just in case I wasn't sure what an ass was."

"I was amazed and apparently, so was the gym teacher…A short young guy who stared at Lillian through thick glasses and suddenly lost interest in writing in his attendance book."

"You've got some huge balls, too, Lillian," I whispered back.

"'I've also got a breast and a belly.'"

"The other girls were beginning to edge away from us, but Lillian didn't appear to notice, or to care. She walked around me and poked me in the belly. "You're pretty well-equipped yourself," she announced. "A woman should have a breast and a belly. The way people dress these days, it's one of the few ways we can tell the guys from the girls."

"'Do you always say exactly what pops into your head?'"

"'Always. Don't you?' she asked; then stared at me as if I were crazy."

"I hesitated for a moment. "'I'm going to start right now, I've decided I'm going to re-invent myself.'"

"We found our schedules were the same and we became instant best friends. We traded family stories and were our own best audience, spontaneously staging musicals in the outdoor amphitheater. Once we did the entire score of *Fiddler On The Roof*. Lillian had the lower voice so she sang all of the men's parts. Singing outside was a liberating experience. I'd never felt so free and alive and purely myself. With no responsibilities to anyone else, I sang and felt re-born."

"Do you still sing, Sunny?" Dr. Carroll interrupted.

I shook my head. "Not lately, anyway...Bull doesn't approve. But we'll get to that later. I was delighted to find out Lillian could play piano as if she'd worked in every piano-bar between Jersey and California, so together we worked out an act and whenever we felt tense, or bored, or pressured, we'd stop by the student lounge where they had an old grand piano and we'd run through our act."

"It was a great way to meet guys and we got asked to mixers at the frat houses where we were the free entertainment. We had a lot of fun, but we both stayed true to our boyfriends who waited for us back home."

"But I thought you said you went home every weekend?" Dr. Carroll said.

"We both did, but we had a nine A.M. English lit class on Saturday, so we couldn't go home until after that. Friday night was mixer night."

"Then things began to change between Bull and me. I met Francois. It started with heavy eye contact. We'd pass each other on campus and he'd give me his riveting sexy look. He had big, dark eyes and was stocky and muscular and he had beautiful black, curly hair. He was exotic and dangerous looking and definitely my worst type."

"Lillian warned me. 'He's probably a creep because if you're being honest you have to admit he looks like a creep, and you know what they say about ducks…'"

"'But he isn't quacking…'"

"'Maybe not yet…but that guy is nearly thirty years old and he goes out with that tall dance major with the hair that goes all the way down to her ass. You know, the bitchy-looking one with the skinny face who prances around here in leotards as if life is one big dance class…She wears those micro mini-skirts, which, actually, someone should point out to her do not in any way flatter a pair of walking stilts in ballet slippers. God, Sunny, why get mixed up with some older guy who's going to college on the G.I. Bill? You know 'Nam screws guys up big time.'"

"'You have information!' I pounced on her. '"Tell me everything you know.'"

"'I don't know that much. Let's see…He's a Jew, for Christ's sake, from France…go figure…Rumor has it he lived in a kibbutz in Israel. That's like a Yiddisha-commune. His name is Francois Trianon. He's a G.I. and- surprise- a French major which accounts for his 4.0 grade point average. And, most importantly of all, Miss Naples, he would be big trouble for you. Just because you have dark hair and your grandparents came over on the boat from Italy, doesn't mean you have to live a life of dramatic passion.'"

"I'd like to meet Lillian." Dr. Carroll said, "I wish she was a family member so she could come to visit you."

"She's the best. And she really tried to warn me, but I was stubborn, even then."

He leaned forward and rubbed his chin. "You were attracted to this older man, Sunny. What do you think attracted you?"

"I was young. Men are more interesting than boys and most of the guys I met were still boys."

"You've got a point," Dr. Carroll said thoughtfully.

"Anyway, I remember being curious enough about what she'd said to ask, 'What kind of trouble?'"

"'The kind that won't want to hold your hand past the third date.'"

"'Oh,' I said.'"

"'I assume you're still a technical-virgin like most of the rest of us.'"

"'Do you see an engagement ring anywhere on my person?' I shot back."

She nodded. "'I thought so. So stop giving this grown man the hairy eyeball or you'll be up shit's creek without a boat, never mind the paddle.'"

"I tried, Dr. Carroll, I really tried to stop giving the mysterious Francois, the hairy-eyeball, but I was just too curious to turn away. Dad always said, "'Sunny, you love to flirt with disaster.'"

"And flirt I did. A man like this was as unknown to me as algebra had been in high school. If I did A and B for one more week, would he do C? I simply had to know. I felt like a fisherwoman on the great river of life. I cast my line out in the form of friendly…okay…sexy looks and hoped to soon reel in the big one. Lord knew what I would do with him when, and if, I got him. I was definitely counting on Lillian to hold the net for me."

"One stormy October afternoon Lillian and I slogged along through the streets of Upper Montclair to the local Brownie meeting where we volunteered to satisfy a requirement for community service in psych. class. We had fun with the kids, and that day we made elaborate papier mache masks for Halloween, but on the way back to campus, we not only got drenched, but traumatized by the thunder and lightning which seemed to strike all around us as we ran screaming like banshees back to the college."

"We decided to dry off around the piano in the student lounge and we debated whether to pool our pennies and send out for pizza, or risk another soaking in the dash for the cafeteria. We delayed our decision and sang some torch songs which properly fit the mood of the day."

"Actually, I loved torch songs in any weather. We did "Tenderly," then slid into a forceful, "Can't Help Lovin' That Man of Mine." I was on the second verse, and slinking along the right side of the piano, egged on by the encouraging cat-calls of our quickly gathering audience when I looked up soulfully and directly into the eyes of the magnificent Francois."

"'You are quite wonderful,' he breathed in a slight accent, in that kind of a voice where you can actually hear the male hormones rolling around in the deepest tones."

I smiled shyly at him and then finished the song, leaning against the piano because my knees were actually getting weak.

"'What's the matter with you, Sunshine?' Lillian asked, 'You look like a demented calf.' Then she spotted Francois. 'Oh, I get it. Trouble beacons like the white whale. If it isn't Moby Dick…maybe not so much Moby…'"

"Lillian spun around on the piano bench to face the room and I sat down beside her. Francois pulled a chair around the wrong way and slowly lowered himself into it. His arms were muscular where they rested on the back of the chair."

"'So, Frenchman!' Lillian started, 'What's up with you…so to speak. Are you still seeing that Grande-Bitch-Donna broad with the long skinny legs and the relentless leotards?'"

"He smiled at her for a moment before answering. "'As a matter of fact Donna and I are no longer seeing each other.'"

"I tried to keep a benign expression on my face, but inside I was screaming, "Yes! Yes!" My cheeks were burning and I was certain my face was growing bright red."

"He looked amused as he watched me, then reached into the pocket of his jacket and pulled out a pipe and tobacco."

"Lillian's eyes spoke to me first. 'This is too much.'"

"He puffed on the pipe to get it going; then faced me again. 'You are Sunny DeAngelo, I think, and your friend, here, is Lillian Piccolilli…or something similar to that?'"

"I giggled and Lillian looked bored. 'Just call me Piccolilli Lil. But if you don't want my fist against your throat, call me Lillian Piccola.'"

"'Of course. I apologize.' He said, 'Are the both of you drama majors? I am with the French studies. I will receive a master's degree and then I will teach at a college. This is my goal.'"

"'Wonderful!' I enthused, hot and cold all at the same time, gushing, flustered, tortured and too excited to do anything about it. I couldn't shut up and I couldn't walk away. I was rooted to the spot."

Dr. Carroll burst out laughing. "Sorry," he wheezed…"You just really tell it so well, Sunny. I can imagine how wonderful your book must be…"

I smiled at him and thanked him, then continued. "So Francois ignored my childish behavior and asked me, 'And you, Sunny? What do you plan to do with your education?'"

"'I plan to stay here for two years to please my father,' I told him, 'And then I'm transferring to The American Academy of Dramatic Arts.'"

"He gave me a sullen stare. 'An actress?' he asked, looking as if the word stunk like day old shrimp."

"'Why yes,' I explained, 'I've already had some parts in summer stock and I've sung with a couple of bands, so I guess that makes me professional; at least a beginning professional.'"

"'I see you are afflicted with the same sickness as my Donna,' he sneered, 'You both think you want the excitement of a flashy career when the only true happiness for a woman is to be found beside the man she eventually comes to marry.'"

"What year was this?" Dr. Carroll interrupted.

"1966."

He smirked. "The good old days. Go on…"

"Well, Lillian and I stared at each other and she rolled her eyes first. We stood at the same time and started gathering up our books and struggling with our coats. There didn't seem to be much else to say after that. Was every man an asshole? Or did I just attract all of the self-centered assholes in my immediate vicinity?"

"'Where are you going, Sunny?' he asked in a tone that sounded strangely possessive even though we had yet to have a first date."

"'The cafeteria, Sunny?' Lillian asked, 'We might as well save our money.'"

"'We're going to dinner, Francois,' I said, 'Wanna come along?'"

"Lillian punched me in the back and I bobbed forward, then caught my balance."

"'I have a better idea,' Francois said, kicking his charm into high gear, 'Allow me to treat you two ladies to a pizza in town.'"

"Town! We hadn't been to town for real food in over a week. We both said yes without need of a consultation."

"Soon we were sitting in a red-vinyl booth at Luigi's pin-pointing Naples on the map of Italy pictured on the paper placemats. The smell of good pizza was everywhere, and as I watched Francois walk toward

us with the pizza and our soda's balanced on a big tray, I suddenly knew
he was the same sign as Bull."

"'You were born in the early part of May, weren't you, Francois?'
I asked."

"He nodded and Lillian snickered."

"'That would make your sign Taurus the Bull, right?'"

"'I was born on the fifteenth of May, so whatever that makes me,
that is what I am.'"

"'Lillian and I are both Sagittarius,' I volunteered."

"He stared at me and raised his black, unruly brows. 'So? Does this
have some meaning?' He reached for his soda and studied me over
the rim."

"I nodded, chewing quickly and swallowing a bit of pizza. 'Basically
it means you were born in May under an earth sign and Lillian and I,
having been born in December, are fire signs.'"

"Lillian crunched on her ice and laughed."

"'Which really means you are stubborn, love pastel shades of pink
and blue, notice a girl's perfume first, have a kind and loving heart which
tends to lead to falling in love a lot, and you think the ideal forms of
exercise are either sex or eating.' I stopped my recital and then felt my
cheeks go hot again, as I wished I'd left the sex part out."

"I glanced at Francois and was relieved to see an amused grin pulling at the corners of his sensuous mouth. I took a deep breath of pizza
air and sighed."

"'Smells like home, doesn't it, Sunny' Lillian asked."

"'Smells more like Nanna's or Aunt Angelina's to me...my mother's
Irish,' I explained to Francois."

"'You American's make me laugh,' Francois said, settling back against
the red-vinyl cushion. He cocked his head to one side and reached
inside his jacket for the pipe. 'You say, I am Irish, or I am Italian, when
it is perfectly clear you are all Americans!'"

"Lillian shrugged and looked bored."

"'I guess you do have a point,' I agreed, as I gazed into his hypnotic
French eyes."

"'Now... Francois continued, 'I am a Frenchman. I was born in a village near the coast, in the south of France. Both my Mama and my Papa
are Israelis. We owned a small restaurant there until I became twelve

years old. My family sold the restaurant, and along with an uncle and his family, we traveled to Israel, and there we lived in a kibbutz.'"

"'Like the hippies, but the hair is shorter and all the men are circumcised,' Lillian added."

"That Lillian is a little firecracker!" Dr. Carroll laughed. "Sorry…go ahead, Sunny, finish the story."

"Well, Francois didn't exactly appreciate Lillian's humor and he stared at her for a few beats and then continued, 'It was an interesting experience; not ideal, but interesting. The men and women lived separately from the children. I was lucky to be with my cousins. We all trained to serve in the army, the girls as well.'"

"'For combat?' I asked."

"'Yes,' he explained. 'Men and women fight side by side if necessary.'"

"'How long have you lived in this country?'"

"'Since before my seventeenth birthday; I became a citizen at eighteen and we all came here to live in Elizabeth, where another of my uncles had bought a restaurant. We have all invested in it, and we all work there. I am twenty-seven now and I use my G.I. bill to pay for the college. I want to teach French. I will not be waiting tables all of my life.' He stared into my eyes for what seemed a long time."

"Lillian began to get restless and nudge my foot under the table."

"'How old are you, Sunny?' he asked in a near whisper. I could feel his hot breath, from all the way across the table."

"'Watch out for that jailbait, Frenchie,' Lillian taunted. 'We wouldn't want to have a run-in with the gendarmes, now, would we?'"

"I shook my head slightly. 'I'm eighteen,' I whispered back and blushed as I watched for the smile in his eyes."

"As we walked back to his old V.W. bug, he took my hand and surprised me by tickling my palm with a light kiss. I shivered. My first kiss on the hand."

"He took charge when we got to the car. He opened the door on the passenger side and pushed the seat forward, then helped Lillian into the back seat. I shivered again and it wasn't from the rainy night. What a smooth way to get me to sit next to him. He was a man, a real grown man."

"Then he asked Lillian where she lived and drove there, stopped the car, got out and pulled the seat forward, extending his hand to her. She was renting a large room in a cozy Victorian house across the street from the college. Before she got out of the car, she bobbed forward and whispered in my ear, "Do you want to make an excuse and stay with me tonight?"

"My heart was pounding in my shoulder blades. 'No,' I better not. 'I still have some work to do for history class.'"

"I had to remind myself to breathe normally as the car pulled away from the curb. Without Lillian in the car, the mood had suddenly changed. Francois was quiet now as he took my hand. When he had to downshift to turn into the drive leading up to the dorm, he placed my hand on the gear knob, and with his hand firmly over mine, we shifted together, with his hand directing our movements. It was a kind of sexual experience in itself and totally unexpected."

"Dr. Carroll snorted, "Come on, Sunny! This guy was up to no good. Don't tell me you couldn't figure him out."

"I was only eighteen and it was a rainy night. The radio was playing elevator music, slow and syrupy with lots of strings and a predictable bounce beat. Francois pulled off the road and parked under a tree, freed my hand, and turned the car off."

"Of course he did," Dr. Carroll said.

"I waited to see what would happen next. I stared down at my knees, and waited."

"I felt the seat slide slowly backward, before I realized he was making it happen. I was afraid to turn my head when the seat finally clicked back and stopped."

"'Look at me, Sunny,' he breathed, reaching for me. Our eyes locked like a hunter and a doe frozen in silence before the big bang. Without breaking eye contact he managed to gently lift me out of my seat and turn me toward him. I gasped as he settled me down onto his lap."

"I wriggled around a bit trying to find a comfortable spot and his eyes grew hot and narrow. It was then I realized just what it was that was causing me so much discomfort. I was balanced precariously on the very tip of a most impressive male bulge. Francois moaned and I felt secretly proud to be responsible for such suffering."

"His eyes teased me and my breath came harder as I felt his hands work their way up over the tight muscles of my back. With a light caress, he brought his thumbs forward to lightly stroke my cheeks."

"'Soft,' he murmured, 'Beautiful.'"

"I closed my eyes as his fingers twisted around in my hair and he brought his lips toward mine. It was a dynamite kiss, the kind where you fuse together and you can't remember you're middle name, or the year you were born."

"I swear if my parents hadn't terrorized me so effectively throughout childhood, instilling me with the virgin ethic, that Frenchman would have had his way with me that very evening."

"Francois' hands worked on automatic pilot, no matter how earth-shattering the kiss his hands still came up with interesting things to do. I felt the clasp on the back of my bra give way before I had a clue he was up to anything, and by the time his hands snaked around under my sweater to capture my breasts, it was almost too late to stop him."

"'Stop...stop...oh, please,' I gasped, opening my eyes and staring into dreamy, dark eyes that mocked me."

"'Why should I stop?'"

"I pushed his hands away, but they came right back at me. "'I'm not...not that kind of...of a girl, Francois,' I said, 'I'm sorry if I gave you the wrong impression.'"

He laughed at me as if I had told an adorable joke. "'You gave me the right impression. The true one of you as a passionate girl. A girl about to become a woman.'"

"Are you kidding me with me with this crap?" Dr. Carroll interjected.

"Do you want me to talk about something else?" I asked.

"No! I mean, this is fine. I want you to speak about anything that's been bothering you."

"O.K. Well, I was pretty nervous to be in the midst of a seduction and I was actually trembling. "'I...I'm not ready for the kind of thing you want,' I said. 'I've only made out with my boyfriend, Bull. I've never, ever, done it before...or yet...I mean, I guess I'm still a virgin.'"

"He immediately removed his hands from my breasts and they felt strangely lonely. He shrugged regretfully, and moved me gently, but firmly back to my seat. 'I am the sorry one, Sunny. For weeks I have been watching you flash the eyes of a passionate woman in my direction. I thought your eyes were telling me the truth about you. I won't be bothering you again. Run along now'."

"'Run along! But…but!' I stammered, wanting suddenly to be the passionate woman he saw inside the foolish flirtatious girl I actually was. I wanted to see him again, to get to know him, to flirt with disaster, and to kiss him again, and again."

"'It is all right, really,' he assured me, reaching for his pipe. 'There are plenty of women of this campus who know what they want from a relationship with a man. I won't be alone for long.'"

"His eyes laughed as if he could read my thoughts."

"I decided to tell him the truth. 'Francois,' I began, sighing heavily, 'I'm fascinated with you. You're the most interesting man I've ever met, actually you're the only man I've ever met in a dating type of situation, but I feel terribly nervous around you. I don't know how to act. I'm used to Bull…to high school boys.' I squirmed on the hot plastic seat."

"'I don't know…' I continued, 'Maybe the rules change after high school. But I've been taught-and all my friends feel the same way- if you make love with a man before you're properly engaged with a ring, he will think you're a tramp.'"

"He ran his finger along my cheek bone. 'You are very young. I can only speak for myself, but Sunny, I never think badly of a woman who shares her affection, her lovely body with me. Perhaps I am more European in my attitudes but I don't really think that is it.'"

"He took my hand and traced the contours of each one of my nails. 'I would very much like to see you again, Sunny,' he said. 'If you need more time to feel comfortable with me you may take that time, but don't wait too long. I am a man with deep desires and I need a woman. I need to make love to a woman often and with total concentration.'"

"Holy crap!" Dr. Carroll interrupted again, "Tell me you didn't sleep with this asshole!"

I smiled at Dr. Carroll. "I'm sorry to have to tell you, Francois's words were getting me all excited again. 'I really should break up with Bull before we go out on a real date,' I told him, 'I don't believe in cheating, do you?'"

"'Cheating?' he asked, rubbing his chin thoughtfully, 'Like on an examination?'"

"I giggled. 'No. I mean like being unfaithful.'"

"He looked alarmed. 'Are you married to this boy?'"

"He rested his pipe in the ashtray and turned more fully toward me. He really did have incredible eyes…eyes that had seen so much more of the world than I had."

"'I believe in honesty,' he said, running his finger along my cheek again and down the side of my throat. 'I usually give all of my attention to one woman. If I spend time with anyone else, I will tell you. When I decide to marry, I will be faithful to my wife alone.'"

"He leaned forward and kissed my cheek, then nuzzled it. I could feel my pulse pumping hard in my throat."

"'I am ready to find my wife, Sunny,' he whispered against my ear. 'I will marry and start my family by the time I have reached thirty.'"

"Most girls couldn't wait to get married but I wasn't one of them. Why was it that every boy I met and now the first man I met wanted to get married? I decided to let his comment pass without adding one of my own. He was still three years away from thirty and a lot could happen in three years."

"Then Francois checked his watch again. 'Five minutes until they lock the door,' he announced, getting out of the car and coming around to open the car door for me.

"He took my hand as we walked toward the bright lights of the dorm, then he stopped and pulled me into the shadows where he kissed me long and deep and hard. My body vibrated with confusion, with a riot of conflicting desires. I nearly sank to my knees in the mud when he let me go and then strode to his car without once looking back."

"As I slipped inside the dorm and closed the door behind me, I heard his little car engine rev into action and I felt uneasy as if I'd never see him again. He hadn't asked for the number of my floor phone and he hadn't made another date with me. And I wondered had my inexperience lost me a chance at a great adventure?"

"But, Sunny," Dr. Carroll said, standing and stepping forward to sit on the edge of his desk. He scratched his ear. "This Francois sounds like a French version of Bull. You even made that connection when you figured out his astrological sign without being told. Why did you want two guys who were obviously wrong for you?"

"That's a good question, Doctor. I think at this point in my life I thought all men were like Bull and Francois and I was the odd one. I was the one who had strange ideas. On the one hand I was too sexy to turn away from men altogether, but it seemed as if being in a relation-ship meant giving up all my personal choices: my personal freedom to accomplish anything apart from becoming a man's wife and eventually a mother to his children. The saddest part of all is that I think I knew no man would want me if they knew who I was, what I really thought, what I actually wanted out of life."

"Sunny…think about what you've just said. In a healthy relationship you don't have to pretend to be someone you're not. And don't think all men are the same. There are intelligent men who want a woman with her own mind and her own interests. A good marriage is a partnership of like-minded individuals who treat each other with love, respect, and kindness. It's two people who want the best for each other, sharing life, creating a family and a future."

"That's beautiful, Dr. Carroll," I said. "But I didn't know that was possible for me back then. I hardly know it now. So, I moped through the rest of the week. And although I looked for Francois, I failed to run into him. Lillian was losing patience with me by the time he finally appeared in the cafeteria on Friday evening, just as we had chosen our seats and begun to eat."

"'There you are, Sunny,'he said from where he stood across the table."

"I looked up and nearly choked on a mouthful of fake-goulash that would have enraged any decent Hungarian."

"'Francois,' I beamed, wiping sauce from the corners of my mouth. 'Where have you been all week?'"

"'I was working in the restaurant. I take classes on Monday and Tuesday; then work as a waiter in the family restaurant on Wednesday and Thursday. I'm back here for a full day of classes on Friday, one more on Saturday morning,; then I go to work on Saturday night. Sunday is my day of rest and study.'"

"'Wow,' I said, 'I had no idea you were that busy'."

"'So, Monsieur,' Lillian interrupted, while she flipped the limper let-tuce out of her salad, 'How long will it take to get your masters?'"

"Francois and I were lost in ourselves and it took him a moment to pull his concentration away from me. He glared at Lillian and said, "I should be finished here in another year, maybe a year and a half."

"'Good for you,' she said, nodding and digging into her apple crisp, one of the few things they made decently in the cafeteria."

"He leaned across the table and reached for my hand. I quickly dropped my fork and offered my hand to him since I'd lost my appetite the minute I'd set eyes on him. 'Tonight, Cheri,' he declared, 'we will see a film.'"

"Was I a part of this 'we'?" I wondered."

"'Finish your dinner' he coaxed, 'the film begins at seven.'"

"So I was now half of a we with a sexy, neat Frenchman. Cool!"

"I watched Lillian stiffen in her seat. 'That isn't the way a man submits his request for a date in this country...or this century as a matter of fact,' she declared."

"I was torn between my loyalty to Lillian, who was obviously right, and my desire to 'play' with Francois. I pushed away the cold goulash and gulped down the rest of my warmish Tab instead."

"'Sunny and I are dating now, Lillian,' Francois stated coolly. 'She knew she would see me tonight.'"

"'Actually, Francois,' I said, 'I didn't know if I'd ever see you again. You didn't mention anything about a movie date for tonight when you dropped me off at the dorm on Tuesday night- I know you're busy, but- you might have called me'."

"'I haven't the time to sit about gabbing on the telephone, Sunny,' he snapped, rising to his feet. 'I will wait for you outside of the French Building until exactly 6:50. The film is Jules and Jim with Jeanne Moreau. It is an excellent film and as a drama student you should find it of interest.'"

"His eyes flashed a warning at me as he turned and strode out of the cafeteria."

"I felt queasy. Things weren't exactly going as planned. On the one hand I was flattered that Francois considered us a couple with a standing Friday night date. On the other hand, I suspected Lillian was right to be suspicious of him."

"'Give him a chance, Lillian,' I said."

"'Me? I don't have to give him the time of day. He's your problem, Sweetheart,' she returned, whistling through her teeth like Bogart. 'I would never date an Italian because they all think they're God's gift, and I wouldn't be caught dead with a Frenchman for the same reason. I won't end up the slave of some asshole with a huge ego. But if you want to, that's your business, Sun.'"

"'I don't intend to marry Francois,' I grinned. 'Just play with him a little'."

"'You are bad,' she scolded, 'Sunny DeAngelo, you are flirting with disaster.'"

"I choked on my Tab. 'You sound like Dad'."

"'A wise man…for an Italian; but it's true, Sunny. You do seem to enjoy fucking yourself up with these cavemen types. Why do you think that is?'"

"I shook my head. 'I wish I could change my type. I'll try. I'll really try, Lillian, but after tonight. I have to go on at least one real date with Francois. Why don't you go with us?'"

"'Leave me out of it. I refuse to be a witness to your destruction. And at least you took four years of high school French and can follow the dialog. Me, I took Spanish. Anyway, I'm going to study tonight and have the rest of the weekend free. See you tomorrow in English Lit. Don't forget to set your alarm.'"

"'I won't. I have to get up extra early to pack for the weekend. I'm supposed to see Bull tomorrow night. We'll probably break up, it's kind of inevitable.'"

"'I guess…like death, and sex, and chocolate,' she mumbled, heading for the door."

"'Just keep your wits about you, Sunshine.'"

"That was good advice, Sunny," Dr. Carroll said, all the time shaking his head, as if knowing the outcome.

"Well, I tried. I really did try to keep my wits somewhere about me, but Francois drove every sensible thought from my mind. He was virtually irresistible to me."

"We sat close together during the film, and in the concealing darkness, he stroked my thigh, working his hand slowly up under my dress. I stopped him just before he found his target, but not without a barely muffled squeal, so he switched to massaging the less volatile areas of my back and shoulders."

"During one of the sexiest scenes in this very sexy movie, he leaned over and nibbled on my ear, blowing hot breath, and then biting gently on my earlobe. I feared I'd faint or die. He was finding erogenous zones on my body that I never even suspected were there."

"After the film, we strolled along the leaf-strewn walkways of the campus. He put his arm around me and every now and then, he'd stop to sit on a stone wall or a deserted bench and pull me down on his lap. I was beginning to get used to kissing Francois, to being touched by him; and his constant caressing and massaging were lulling me into a trance."

"We were nearly all the way back to my dorm when he changed direction and pulled me along toward the parking lot where he'd left his car. 'Tonight you will learn all about the making of love between a man and a woman,' he whispered against my ear."

"I broke away from him and backed up a few steps. 'Hey, wait a minute,' I said, 'I have a nine o'clock English Lit class tomorrow morning'."

"He stepped toward me, smiling seductively, 'We can arrange to be finished by then, but it won't be easy to stop Sunny. Once we get together, I can tell it won't be easy to stop.'"

"'But I haven't packed yet for the weekend,' I explained, 'My father's girlfriend will be here by ten-fifteen to pick me up and drive me home.'"

"His eyes turned hard. He fumbled in his coat pocket for his pipe tobacco. He made a big production out of filling and lighting his pipe while I wondered what he'd finally say to me when, or if, he ever decided to speak to me again."

"He glared at me like an angry father; then said, 'I suppose you will be seeing the Buffalo, that infantile boyfriend of yours.'"

"I burst out laughing."

Dr. Carroll did as well. "That was perfect!" he said, "Hysterical!"

"I agree, but Francois was not amused. He continued to glare at me while I gasped, 'His name is Bull.'"

"'Whatever, it is of no great consequence,' he said dismissively, 'I knew it was a stupid name of a large, useless animal. Are you going to see him? Don't avoid my question.'"

"'I'm supposed to…but I really don't want to anymore…especially since I've met you.'"

"He relaxed a little and said, 'I want you to tell him you won't be seeing him again.'"

"'I'd planned to do that'."

"'Be sure you do, Sunny. And plan to spend next weekend with me.'"

"'But don't you have to work Saturday night?' I asked quickly."

"'I'm having the night off.'"

*   *   *

"**B**ull took the news badly. He said he would never give up on getting me back and that I wouldn't be rid of him until the day one of us died. Something about his tone of voice warned me I would most likely be the one to go first…and sooner than I'd ever expected."

Dr. Carroll cleared his throat and the sound brought me back to the moment. I'd almost forgotten he was in the room with me; I'd been so caught up in my story.

"Sunny," Dr. Carroll said, making a steeple with his index fingers and wrinkling his brow. "I'm curious about something. Didn't Bull's inability to let go of your relationship set off any internal alarms in you. Didn't it concern you?"

"Sure it did. I cried in my room for most of that Saturday. And then when Dad told me he'd be out late that night taking pictures at a wedding, I really got nervous."

"Did you think Bull would do something to you?"

"Not really…I was more afraid of myself. If I saw Bull I knew I'd be confused. He had, still has, a way of getting to me."

"So what happened?"

"Do we have time? Don't you have another appointment?"

He waved my question away. "I cleared three hours for you. We need to get all this out of the way before our meeting with Bull."

I grinned at him. "Well, Dad had to work, so I called all of my old high-school friends to see if anyone else was home for the weekend, but I was the only one. So I tried Mah and Joe-Joe. He was out with his squirrely friends at a James Brown concert in Newark, and Mah was going to a recital at Carnegie Hall with one of her friends. Gram had been my first choice as a companion for the evening, but she had committed to a big babysitting job."

"She insisted I come over for an early dinner, though, and so I settled securely into the dozens of pillows on Gram's big bed and flipped through the latest movie magazines while Gram burned the chicken in the way we liked it best and described the chocolate eclairs she'd bought for dessert."

"I thumped on my well-padded thighs." "Why don't I just smear the eclair directly on my body instead of going to all the bother of eating them," I suggested."

"Gram laughed. "You won't get fat from a little éclair, Honey," Gram assured me. "It's only dessert.""

"Gram logic. "Get fat? I'm not exactly thin.""

"Voluptuous, Sweetie. You are voluptuous, like the Venus DeMilo, but with arms.""

"Gram was amazing. She actually seemed to believe the bizarre things she said. So during dinner, Gram and I toasted each other with ginger ale, just like in the old days, and then we dug into the oven-barbequed chicken. "No-one can char a chicken indoors like you can, Gram," I said between bites. "What's your secret?""

"Never clean the oven, and when broiling the chicken, turn the control all the way to the right and hope for the best.""

"We grinned at each other. I loved being at Gram's and it wasn't due to her limited cooking and housekeeping skills. It was the Gram-glow that warmed her home with love."

"We lit the candles in her colorful, Italian Capodimonti candle-sticks and with the wind rattling the windows and the glow of the street-lights coming in through her windows, we both wished I could stay the night. But Gram was due to babysit in less than an hour, so we did the dishes together, reluctantly put on our coats, and then stepped outside into the chilly, late-fall evening."

"I'm following you home," Gram declared, marching toward her car before I could protest."

"When we got inside the house, I followed along behind her, as I had done for so many years, while she sneaked up on all of the closets and punched the shower curtains in all three of the bathrooms. Lastly, she checked under every bed and sofa with her little flashlight."

"By then my nerves were jangling with the anticipation of big trouble, but I knew Gram meant well so I didn't complain. After I kissed her goodbye, I stood at the front window and watched her stride confidently toward her car giving no apparent thought to the dangers she had expected to find lurking in every corner just moments before. As far as Gram was concerned, danger existed for everyone else but her."

"She roared up the long driveway in her ancient Bahama-blue V.W. bug; then honked three times, waved wildly, flashed a big lipstick grin at me, and rocketed off into the night."

"The house was huge and silent without Gram. As I turned toward the stairs, I caught a glimpse of a shape outside moving quickly past the glass door to the patio. I froze and my dog, Leonard, a big fluffy black and silver Keeshond, growled low in his throat. He darted over to the door and threw his body against the glass, barking and clawing as if he could see someone out there."

"My God, Sunny!" Dr. Carroll gasped, "What did you do?"

"I edged toward the phone, intending to call the police when I paused to consider what I might say. "Hello, Officer, come quick…I've seen a shadow outside and my dog is barking." I decided I needed more of a reason to call than that."

"I grabbed Leonard by the collar and pulled him away from the door. I figured we'd be better off locked upstairs in my bedroom. We were halfway up the stairs when both the front door and the back door-bells began to bong and bong in a dissonant nightmare, like in a horror movie. Leonard's expressive eyes were wild and he whimpered to me to let him go so he could investigate, but I was much too frightened to let him go. It was time to call the police so I ran to the phone in a burst of energy and found to my horror the line was dead. It was a windy night, but not that windy."

"I was really scared as I considered my options. I could hide in either the bathroom or my own room and lock myself in, but I knew the doors could easily be kicked open if whoever was torturing me, actually got inside of the house. I considered hiding in the basement but as I got closer to the door leading down there, I heard a faint banging on one of the basement windows. I bolted the lock on the basement door; then flew back up toward my room."

"Leonard tried to get away from me again, but I held fast. 'Please, Boy,' I panted, 'Stay with me!'"

"I locked the door of my room behind us, didn't turn on the light and sank down beside my dog, burying my face in his fluffy fur. I considered opening the window and screaming for help, but Joe-Joe and I had chased each other screaming around this house enough times when we were growing up to know our nearest neighbors were too far down the street to hear us."

"I considered screaming anyway, just to release the tension and fear that were growing by the minute. I felt as if my bones had turned to jelly. I was breathing fast, but my mind was slowing down like I imagined it does just before you freeze to death in an avalanche."

"The ringing of the bells began again, and so did Leonard's barking. I sprang to action, barricading the door with my dresser, and then my desk before crouching in front of the windows and peering outside."

"The outdoor lights cast large bright circles about our acre of lawn. I couldn't see anyone, and I was sure that if a friend was ringing the bell, they would have stepped back from the door and into the circle of porch light, so I could have identified them. Also, a friend wouldn't have another friend ringing the back door at the same time."

"You must have been terrified, Sunny," Dr. Carroll said; his eyes empathetic behind the heavy rims of his glasses."

"I was. I felt helpless and vulnerable. It was like a bad T.V. drama. After a short period of silence, the ringing began again and Leonard started up again. I begged him to stop, but he paid no attention to me. The constant taunting of the bells and Leonard's barking were driving me crazy."

"As it grew later, the ringing went on and on at fifteen-minute intervals. There were no cars parked outside on the street in either direction. I strained for a glimpse of my tormentor, too afraid to answer the door…too afraid to even open the door of my room when I couldn't be certain someone hadn't already entered the house and was using the doorbells to lure me out of my locked room. This felt like more than a prank since the phone was out and the line might well have been cut."

"I stared at the face of my bedside clock and watched the hands inch their way around the dial. And during all of the hours I waited for my father to return home I thought of Bull. Was he responsible for this night of terror? I knew he was capable of lashing out cruelly when he was hurt and he knew I was afraid to stay home alone."

"I lifted the hammer from where I had it hidden under my bed. I hugged it against me and found its' weight comforting. If there was a fight here tonight, I would be ready."

"I wondered if most victims experienced a level of terror when they were forced to face a survivor in the mirror and know themselves to be capable of killing in self-defense. I'd heard girls at school claim to be incapable of violence, even to save their own lives, and I'd always doubted they were telling the truth, or maybe they just weren't facing the truth."

"Abruptly, Leonard stopped pacing the room and dropped wearily down on the floor at my feet with a sigh. I'd noticed a change in the feel of the atmosphere just moments before the dog had relaxed and I was almost certain the prowlers had gone, and the danger had passed. But I wasn't about to bet my life on it, so I stayed safely locked in my room until my father turned down the driveway, and then I flew to meet him at the front door."

"Was it Bull?" Dr. Carroll asked, leaning forward on his desk.

"Do you mean was Bull my secret-tormentor?" I asked.

"Yeah."

"I never found out who it was, and it happened a few more times. Once, when we were all out, the house was actually broken into and nothing was taken, but my underwear was thrown all around the room and some of it was tampered with…and draped around on the lamps."

"Sunny, that's terrible."

"I felt violated. I couldn't sleep for months and I never felt safe in that house again."

"The police never came up with any leads?"

"They suspected Bull, too, but nothing was ever proven and Bull has always denied it."

"So how did you and Bull get back together? Did the frightening incidents at your house have anything to do with your getting back together?" He cocked his head to one side and leaned back in his swivel chair.

I thought about it for a moment. "In a way they did. I continued to date Francois throughout the winter and to avoid having sex with him…which wasn't easy."

"Why did you two finally break up?"

I stared at the painting over his desk and then shifted my gaze over to the window. "Do I have to tell you?"

"Maybe you should."

"In time it did become apparent to me that Bull and Francois were pretty much the same guy."

"Now we're getting somewhere," Dr. Carroll said, with enthusiasm. "But why didn't you get rid of both of them?"

I shook my head. "I wish I knew. I guess it was the unfortunate fact that I love Bull and probably always will."

Dr. Carroll stared down at his hands and shook his head slowly from side to side. "You don't have to love Bull anymore, Sunny. You can choose to live a normal life. I'm certain a decent, well-adjusted man will be there for you in time."

"Why would a decent, well-adjusted man want anything to do with me?"

Dr. Carroll just shook his head again and laughed. "Finish the story. We'll work out the answer to that question later."

"Well, Francois was putting a lot of pressure on me to spend the night with him and to learn 'all about making love and becoming a real woman.' I was tempted for a while, and then his domineering ways began to bother me. I figured that if I was going to be hassled by some guy, it might as well be Bull."

"That's terrible logic."

"Maybe so…but at the time I was certain there was no hope I'd ever be able to change my type. Remember the movie, 'The Hustler?'"

"The one with Paul Newman, Piper Laurie, and Jackie Gleason as Minnesota Fats…Great movie."

"It sure was, but you left out George C. Scott. Do you remember him in the movie?"

Dr. Carroll smiled at me and nodded slowly.

"He was the one I found most fascinating. I was mesmerized by that dangerous brand of sex-appeal he had. I couldn't get him out of my mind. And he wasn't even all that handsome, or young, for that matter."

"Maybe it was partly due to some of the things my father used to say when I was little. He always said, 'Nice guys finish last.' 'Stuff like that."

"Anyway, no matter what happened, Bull just wouldn't give up on me. And that was flattering. While Francois became more and more of a pain in the ass, Bull would drop by to see me at school and bring bags of food for me and my friends and after a while he stopped acting jealous of Francois and more and more like a real friend. And I think I panicked at the thought of losing his love."

"He asked me out on May 10th 1967. And I said yes."

"How come you have that date memorized?"

"Two reasons. It was Bull's nineteenth birthday, and the second reason will become clear to you in a minute."

"Bull took me out to eat at Mama Leone's in Manhattan, and we had a perfect romantic evening. After dinner we took a long walk around the city, holding hands, and enjoying the warm spring night. Then we drove slowly back to the college, kissing at all of the red lights. I felt warm and secure and very happy sitting next to Bull on the front seat of his new cranberry-colored Pontiac. It was like coming home."

"I remember the radio was playing love songs and we drove past my dorm and turned up the hill to the back of the campus where the kids often went to be alone, I swear the radio even played Bobbie Vinton singing, 'Blue Velvet.' That's our song."

"Our parking spot overlooked the twinkling fairy lights of Newark, New Jersey, and it was here he asked me to marry him."

"I must have looked like a dumb fish. 'Marry you?' I whispered in amazement. 'But why do you want to rush into this? There's plenty of time to think about marriage.'"

"Bull pulled a small, black box out of the glove compartment and he presented me with an engagement ring of considerable size and beauty. I was speechless. For a split second the thought flashed through my mind that the girls in the dorm would go crazy for a ring like that."

"He tried to slip it on my finger, but I panicked and pulled away from him. 'My father will never let me get engaged, Bull. He'll kill me. And what about college?'"

"Bull looked annoyed. 'Sunny, you're nineteen years old. When are you going to stop letting your father run your life? I know you two are close, but I'm getting sick of it. We love each other and we should be married. I've loved you since the seventh grade.'"

"I had never seen Bull look so stubborn and determined."

"'I do love you, Bull,' I told him, 'but I just can't marry you. I don't think being in love is the best reason to get married. I mean, I know it's important, but I think we should have more in common if we plan to spend a lifetime together'."

"There were tears on his cheeks. They made me sad, those tears, I hated to hurt him."

"'But Sunny,' he whispered, wiping his tears away, 'I don't want to live without you. You make me feel good.'"

"I put the ring back into the little, black box and put it in the glove compartment of his car. It was the last time I would see it. 'It's too expensive anyway, Bull,' I said, 'Take it back and use the money to help your mom out. We'll keep on seeing each other, and see where it leads, O.K.?'"

"His lip was trembling and his hands were shaking. I put my arms around him and hugged him tight. 'Please don't be sad,' I said, 'we do love each other. That should be enough for now. We're young and we have plenty of time to plan our future.'"

"And then he changed. He pushed me down on the seat and glared at me. 'I've waited for you for five years, Sunny, and since you don't want to marry me, you can't use the excuse of saving it for marriage any longer. Tonight is the night, Sunny. You belong to me.'"

"He pulled at my clothes. I tried to think fast. 'You have a point there, Bull,' I said, 'But let's plan this the right way,' I gasped, as I watched my lacy, pink panties disappear over my ankles and feet."

"'It's too late for that,' he said, holding them above his head like a trophy. 'It's my birthday, Sweetie, and the time has come.'"

"'O.K., Bull,' I gasped, trying to scramble away from him. 'We'll do it, but not here like this. We have to prepare. Get birth control pills, candles, pillows, a garter belt!'"

"'Now, Sunny! Now!' Bull didn't look at me as he pinned me down, struggled to free himself from his clothes and wriggled his way into my reluctant body."

"I talked all the way through it. It's a tribute to his powers of concentration that he didn't give up on the whole thing. I kept saying things like, 'I really think we should wait for birth control,' and, 'I've heard of girls getting pregnant the very first time,' and, 'I really don't think this is a good idea!'"

"When it was over, I remember wondering what all the fuss had been about. I hadn't felt much of anything and I didn't feel as if I'd been permanently changed in any significant way. I was still the same old Sunny."

"'Bull gave me a big kiss and I noticed a look of triumph in his eyes as he pulled slowly away from me. 'Now you're pregnant, Sunny, and you'll have to marry me,' he said.'"

"I stared up at him for a moment. 'Bull can you even tell me why you want to marry me so much?'"

"Suddenly shy, his eyes darted around the car before barely touching mine for an instant. 'Because…because I just love you and…You always make me laugh when I'm in a bad mood.'"

"I don't know. Maybe it was a better reason than most people had for wanting to get married. I just wish we both had felt the same way."

"It's a sad story, Sunny," Dr. Carroll said. "But at least you had Ben. He's a great kid."

I smiled at him. "He is the best thing that has ever happened to me. I never would have been happy if I'd jumped completely into show business. Some things are just meant to be."

CHAPTER 16

I was quiet at dinner. I nearly dozed off over my hamburger, macaroni and mixed veggie casserole. Alexander matched my mood, and we ate in silence, comfortable with each other to the point where we didn't need to talk.

Halfway through our cherry pie, something happened to wake us up in a big way. It started with Bob's laughter. We turned toward the sound in time to watch a young man named Stuart leap from his seat and lunge across the table, stabbing Bob in the back of the hand with his fork.

Big Jake was on duty, and in a matter of seconds, he was on top of Stuart, gently subduing him and crooning calmly into his ear. Stuart's face was twisted into a livid mask. His long, blonde, curly hair fell across his face. He shook his head violently and bucked back against Big Jake's powerful chest, spitting out obscenities like sour milk.

Some of the patients were screaming, and although my own hands shook, I hurried to comfort Helen, who had crawled under her end of the table, and was clutching the metal table leg and whimpering.

"What happened, Bob?" Alexander asked, holding his hand steady while the nurse poured peroxide into the fork wound.

"Jesus!" Bob yelped, squinting his eyes against the pain. "He's nuts! We were having a little exchange of words…You know, a little back and forth about his attitude being so poor. I was half kidding, I swear to God. but this crazy kid just snapped out on me. I knew it was a mistake to vote in favor of giving him a fork."

The nurse squirted a generous amount of antibiotic cream onto his bloody hand and then bandaged it with a long piece of gauze. I watched Big Jake wrestle Stuart into one of the rubber rooms. They'd probably have to put him in restraints.

"You can come out now, Helen," I coaxed, stroking her arm and then trying to gently pull her fingers away from the table leg. "It's safe now. Stuart's gone. He's in one of the locked rooms."

"I don't like it S-Sunny, when they act like that. I don't like it. My father was like that. We never knew when he'd…he'd hurt somebody."

I drew her out from her hiding place and brought her over to the R.N. on duty at the desk. I reported what Helen had said and then watched as the nurse led her down the hall to her room.

Next, Charlotte began to laugh and all attention shifted to her corner; she was taking the cherries out of her pie and smearing them across her forehead and then down both cheeks. "I'm bleeding too," she squealed between bursts of laughter. "I can bleed everywhere but the one place where it counts."

Two aides hurried to tend to Charlotte and I reached out to Alexander. He gave me a quick hug; then took my hand. Together we walked toward our sofa. "Bob should be thankful it was hamburger night and not steak, he said, "Then Stuart would have had a knife."

I shuddered. "Will they send him to Allentown?" I asked, referring to the state mental hospital.

"For sure."

"He was so quiet I didn't get the chance to get to know him very well, but he seemed so passive. He came across as almost gentle, at least not like someone capable of an attack like that."

"Maybe that's why they say, 'Watch out for the quiet ones.' Alexander said with a sad smile. "Sunny, I know you're tired, but do you feel like escaping to Beaver Valley tonight? I don't know about you, but I'd like to put some distance between all this craziness and the two of us."

"I'm too traumatized to sleep anyway," I said, "So I might as well read to my favorite fan."

*   *   *

I sat in Charles' front room waiting for him to emerge from his study so we could go to church. It would be my first formal introduction to the congregation and I was nervous and feeling ill-prepared.

My back felt as stiff as a ramrod, and my hands were given to shaking if I did not clutch them together in my lap. But most annoying of all was the strange intrusion of a muscle tic in my left cheek.

Mrs. Less, Charles' housekeeper, would be there this morning, so I would have one new friend to smooth my path. Mrs. Less was a warm and motherly soul with plump, apple cheeks and a large, unruly bun of luminous, white hair. It was easy to love her and I knew how lucky I was to be able to count her as a friend.

The Master's family would be there and I was looking forward to seeing Elisha. I was not hoping to see Cassie Taylor and her family, especially since my vivid dream about Cassie and Bruin. It would be nice to have a few words with Bruin, though, because I missed him the most of all.

I shifted about upon the faded powder-blue satin-brocade loveseat. It was fashioned in the French style with curving legs and graceful arms. The same fabric was matched upon two wing-backed chairs that faced me. Charles was proud of these few fine pieces of furniture. They belonged to his mother, and I could understand his feeling of pride whenever Mama's great and wonderful grandfather clock chimed the hour in stately tones. I loved its' polished mahogany, the intricate carving, the delicate porcelain face decorated with golden numerals, multi-colored hand-painted flowers and twisting vines. In a sense, whenever the clock reminded me of the time, both Mama and Papa were here with me.

Last night Charles and I had sat together in the twin oaken rockers before the stone fireplace and shared stories of our childhood. Now when I looked upon the face of Charles' mother, the late Abigail Putnam, who sat framed beside my own portrait of Mama, I would know her to be a softer, more loving woman than the one depicted by the artist in this particular painting.

"You are an artist of unusual sensitivity," Charles had remarked last evening as he gazed up at my painting of Mama. "You see beyond the surface of a person, to reveal a bit of the soul."

The door to Charles' study opened, interrupting my thoughts, and he stepped out into the hall. I rose and faced him. I had been wondering if I was looking my best this morning, but the smile on his face was all the confirmation I needed. I found the look on a man's face to be a more satisfactory mirror than a looking glass.

He stood tall, his hat in his hand, as he beamed at me. "Are you ready, M-My Dear?"

I smiled back at him, faking bravery. "I am ready, Charles," I said, glad I had decided to wear my brown velvet with the russet trim. At least I would be a compliment to the brilliance of the autumn leaves.

As the horses pulled our buggy toward town, I enjoyed the caress of warm October sun upon my back while a cool wind ruffled the trees and bent the bushes like children hard at play. Papa would have said, "This beautiful day calls out to me, Little Mite! It screams, George! Get up off your backside and get going!"

The first person I recognized as we pulled up to the front door of the church was Margaret Taylor. She tugged irritably at the bulging seams of her ill-fitting navy, woolen dress, all the while punctuating her words with the pudgy finger she used to poke her husband, Henry, in the ribs. "Well, they certainly took their time in getting here," she complained in a voice loud enough for me to hear from our buggy."

Mr. Taylor sighed expansively as if he were the weariest put-upon man on God's living earth; and then he reached inside the pocket of his vest to bring forth a large gold watch. "Actually, by my watch, we were early, My Dear," he stated in a colorless voice, "I told you we were much too early."

Early or late, the Taylor's were not the only ones waiting for us on the lawn of the church. As Charles lifted me from my seat and placed me down upon the grass, I peered around him to see if I could find anyone I knew amongst the fast-gathering crowd. Clusters of the regular townsfolk mingled easily with the new arrivals from Boston, as they traded information, and began the business of forming new friendships.

Cassie strolled by and Margaret reached out to grab her arm. She wrinkled her nose and sniffed the air, then leaned close to Cassie's ear, and curling her lip, she spoke in much too loud a tone of voice, "That Jessamyn thinks she's a smart one, arriving just late enough to make a grand entrance."

As Margaret pursed her lips and rolled her eyes, Cassie rudely pushed her mother away. "Stop the shouting, Mother," she whined, clapping her hand over her ear, "You will have me deaf yet. No one cares what Jessamyn does for attention now that she's married."

I was about to fly over there and set both Cassie and her mother straight when Bruin appeared beside me. He looked handsome in his greatcoat and breeches. His tall Beaver hat was set at a fashionable angle and his queue was tied with a thin black ribbon.

We stared at each other for a moment, and for that moment, looking at each other was enough. He cleared his throat to speak and I noticed the tiny lines of tension across his brow. "How are you?" he asked.

I forced myself to smile. "I am well…Charles is kind and prov-ing to be a satisfactory companion. And best of all, he is a kind and patient man."

A light sprang into Bruin's dark eyes. He smiled at me. "Glad to hear that." He said, "I want you to be happy."

My mind raced for the right words to tell him…but as a married woman there were no right words for me to use to describe my feel-ings, or lack thereof. I could only thank him for his concern and slowly die inside.

Cassie darted up beside us and stepped in front of me, pulling rudely at Bruin's coat, chattering, "I have been looking for you, you rascal," she scolded, moving closer to him and tugging at his beard. The tone of her voice hinted at a relationship more deep and intimate than would have been appropriate outside of the bonds of marriage.

I felt short of breath, just as I had on the road when the wagon wheels would kick the dust up into a dark and dirty frenzy, robbing me of my breath, cracking my dignity under the weight of endless layers of gritty filth.

"I was certain I would see you sometime during the past week," she said, a laugh in the musical tones of her voice, "Considering how close we became the last time we saw each other in Marietta…that last wonderful night."

I gasped, feeling suddenly faint. My dream! How could I have known? Was I a witch?

"Jessamyn," Charles spoke near my ear, bracing me with an arm about my waist. "You are trembling. What is wrong, My Dear? Has something, or someone, upset you?"

Bruin and Cassie paused in their flirtation to turn and stare at us. "You worry too much, Charles," I said, faking a smile, "It is a glorious Sunday morning. What could upset me on such a delicious day?"

Cassie clung to Bruin's arm as they strolled down the brick walkway leading to the church. Her bright, light-auburn hair fell down her back, refusing to be tamed by her lace cap. Her dark-green woolen cape set her hair off to its' best advantage. It swung coquettishly against the verdant green covering her shoulders and graceful back as she laughed at everything Bruin said, just as if she had not one brain in her head.

I knew Bruin had every right to keep company with a young lady, but Cassie Taylor was no lady!

We passed a large group of the congregation who stood conversing just outside the main door of the church. I could hear Margaret Taylor's strident voice above all the others and I glanced to see who she might be singling out this time for harsh judgment. "She is much too young for him, you know, Mrs. Compton," Margaret said with a sneer, "Comes from a wild family, too. Her father was an Irishman, if you know what I mean, and her mother was always putting on airs and claiming to be the daughter of a French aristocrat. Not the sort you would want living next door."

I wanted to pull her hair. I wanted to knock her down and watch her roll like a fallen oxen, down the slope of the church lawn to land in a heap beside the dusty road. Charles squeezed my arm and pulled me toward the group. "Sarah," he called to the woman Margaret had addressed as Mrs. Compton, using an authoritative voice that subtly warned us all to behave. "I want you to meet my wife." He turned to me and took my hand, drawing me closer to this small, hostile, old woman. "Jessamyn," he said, "this is Sarah Compton. She practically built this church herself and much of the town too, through persuasion and raw will. I doubt we could survive without her efforts."

Sarah smiled at Charles with genuine affection and took his large hand in both of hers. She was tiny and mean-looking as far as I was concerned, with a long, skinny neck decorated in folds of wrinkled and loose turkey wattle. Her eyes were a bright, piercing blue, as they peered out from under the fringe of pure, white curls that framed her face and fell in tendrils from under her lacy, white cap. She was thin and while not frail, I wondered what great age she had achieved.

"Reverend," she said in the loud voice of the hard of hearing. "I have missed you terribly."

Then she fixed me with an imperious and unfriendly stare, "So this is the young bride you have brought with you all the way from Boston. And someone you barely know if the rumors are accurate."

Charles nudged me forward. "I am fortunate beyond belief to be the husband of this lovely, young, woman, Sarah," he said, raising his voice so she could hear him without difficulty. "She is a talented artist and I know you will put her talents to good use making banners for our next bake sale."

Mrs. Compton's eyes were as cold as her small bony hands. "Since when does a talent for art qualify a woman for the practical tasks of housewifery?"

Margaret Taylor laughed at my startled face, and I would have turned and run away if Charles hadn't held me fast against him with an arm about my waist.

"She is also charming, intelligent, and kind, Sarah," he said, with a gentle tone of admonishment in the rich tones of his voice, "You will see, Jessamyn will be a great asset to me in all things."

Mrs. Compton raised her brows as if she doubted it, but she kept her thoughts to herself. "I wish you all the best, Charles, as always."

I rushed through the expected pleasantries and offered my assistance to the Ladie's Society, but held no hope of being accepted by either Mrs. Compton, or any of the others. If the other women in this town held Mrs. Compton in high regard, as I suspected, I would be a lonely girl indeed.

Charles excused us, and as we walked away, I could hear Sarah's voice, "She certainly is much too young; and a fancy one too. You were right about her, Margaret."

We entered the quiet dimness of Charles's church and the first one I saw was Mrs. Less, sitting in the aisle seat of a pew filled completely with broad shouldered men and pretty women. Several of the women had one child in arms and another, playing on the floor. "Missy," Mrs. Less whispered as I passed, smiling roundly and reaching out to squeeze my hand. "Good morning, Dear. God bless."

I searched the unfamiliar faces in all the pews for Elisha and finally spied the entire Masters family sitting toward the middle of the church on the far side, but Elisha had her head bowed in prayer.

I did not see Veronica Sue Larner and her husband Nat or Little Natty, and I wondered if perhaps she'd had the baby. I whispered my first prayer of the day. "Dear Lord, be with Veronica Sue. Help her to have an easy birth…and a healthy child."

The church was plain and sturdy with a modest steeple. It was devoid of any decoration and hardly seemed like a real church to me without stained-glass windows. We had magnificent ones in our church back home in Boston.

The others filed in and swept down the aisle to find their seats. Charles had put me in the right front pew and I felt very conspicuous. A long, hard bench stretched on beside me and I felt queasy in the pit of my stomach as the realization swept over me that I was expected to fill this pew with endless little Putnams…most likely at the rate of one a year.

Charles reached the lectern and turned toward us. He looked radiant and as close to handsome as he would ever get. "Today is a new day which the Lord hath made. Let us rejoice in it and express our gratitude to Him in song. We will begin with *A Mighty Fortress Is Our God*."

He looked down at old Mrs. Compton who sat across the aisle from me, and nodded, "Sarah, will you please start us off on the right note?"

There was a tittering of comradely laughter as she rose and faced the group. As her hands ascended, the entire congregation followed her lead and stood as one. When we had quieted, Sarah's reedy, but perfectly-pitched soprano rang out, leading us to sing:

"A mighty fortress is our God.

A bulwark never failing.

Our helper, He, amid the flood,

Of mortal ills prevailing."

It felt good to sing, to worship once again in a real church. We were on the second verse of the song when I noticed how close the air in the church had grown. There was a subtle stench of stale perspiration and sour breath in the air. Although characteristic of large gatherings in provincial places, such as Beaver Valley, it was unpleasant nonetheless.

I tried to catch Charles's eye, but he was singing straight up to God and did not see me. I wished someone would have the sense to open several of the windows that lined the right side of the wall. I drew a perfumed hankie from my velvet bag and pressed it to my nose. Far better to pretend a case of the sniffles than to keel over in a faint on my first visit to the rev…to my husband's church.

"Let us bow our heads and give thanks to Almighty God for safely bringing our new friends from Boston home to our church family here in Beaver Valley." Charles said.

As I listened to the comforting rhythms of Charles' gentle voice, I began to relax for the first time in weeks. I still mourned for my papa and for my mama too, but I was lucky to be safely here in Beaver Valley, for there were far worse fates than becoming the wife of a man like Charles Putnam.

His sermon concerned the subject of thankfulness, and I found myself moved to tears when he mentioned the Indian raid and those who had perished, giving special prayers for Adelaide Sullivan, and then, he spoke of Papa, and I had never heard him described so vividly, and with such perception. I wiped tears from my cheeks and glanced back at Ben and Amanda Masters and they caught my eye and nodded. We had loved him…we all would miss him.

Charles ended his sermon with these words, "May we all live in peace and love. And may Almighty God be with us always. Amen."

"Amen," the congregation echoed.

Before I realized Charles expected me to join him in his walk down the aisle, he stood over me and extended his hand. I rose with as little fuss as possible and together we walked down the aisle and out of the church to stand waiting for the others under a massive, twisted oak tree, alive with color, wind, and birdsong.

I glanced up at my husband who beamed down at me from his great height. The vigorous breeze blew the hair across his forehead, and he looked almost boyish, despite the crinkles around his eyes and the deep lines that traced the hollow of each cheek.

"It was a very good sermon…Charles," I said, "You impressed me."

He laughed out loud, startling me with the depth of joy in the sound of it. "Why, thank you, Child," he said, standing even taller in his polished Sunday shoes.

The congregation poured out of the church, chattering like bluejays at a feeder, as they engulfed us in greetings and good wishes. I tried to connect the new names with the new faces, but it was an overwhelming task. Some of the younger people were friendly, but the older members of the church were decidedly cool to me. It got a bit easier when Charles caught on to my struggle and began to call out to each parishioner by name in an attempt to help me.

Then Elisha came by and nearly single-handedly made up for every snub, with her sweet, bubbling good nature. She let go of Cal's arm long enough to dart forward and whisper in my ear, "You look the same, Jessamyn. Do you feel terribly changed?"

I stared at her blushing face and then understood. She was referring to my wedding night. "The reverend is a wise man, Elisha," I whispered back. "He understands I still mourn for Papa and he promises to be patient."

She looked disappointed. "Oh," she said, shrugging, and then giving me a quick hug. "I was hoping to find out what all the fuss is about from you...and I do hope love comes to you both very soon." Her sweet, moist breath was a tickle against my cheek, and then she was gone.

Mrs. Less, Amanda and Ben Masters, and all their other children, surrounded us quickly with their good-will and I was beginning to feel much better about my new role as 'minister's wife,' when Cassie Taylor dragged Bruin over and completely ruined my good mood.

Bruin and Charles exchanged greetings while Cassie turned to me. Grinning evilly, her green eyes mocked me. "Jessamyn," she said, making me hate the sound of my own name, "I just love your gown. A bit extravagant, though, for the taste of most of these modest country people. In fact, I almost expected you to get up after the hymn and treat us all to a dance."

I forced myself to laugh lightly. "Don't be silly, Cassie, this simple frock can hardly be considered a gown, but I can certainly understand your making that mistake." I eyed her woolen dress with what I hoped would be taken for pity and patted her arm in a comforting gesture. "I do appreciate the compliment, though, Dear."

Cassie snatched her arm away as if I'd spilled something nasty on her cloak, and for a brief moment I saw hatred burn in her eyes. "Let us go now, Bruin," she said, tugging at his coat sleeve, and interrupting his conversation with Charles. "You promised me a buggy ride."

Bruin glanced at me and then quickly away as if the sight of my face was painful to him. He scratched his head. "Cassie wants to see the fall foliage," he said, apologetically, "Though the reason why we need to drive around to do it escapes my limited understanding of female logic."

I laughed. "It does seem as if all Cassie has to do is to keep her eyes open and look up in order to see the beautiful leaves all around us. The foliage is everywhere, Cassie. This isn't downtown Boston, you know."

Cassie stamped her foot ineffectively on the grass and pouted prettily. "Stop teasing," she said, "I read about it in a book once, and it was the most romantic notion. All the young people in this little town went off just riding in their buggies, going all about the countryside, sharing long talks, and enjoying the beauty of nature."

"Sounds charming to me, too," Charles said, surreptitiously caressing the back of my hand with the back of his own. "Perhaps Jessamyn and I will follow your lead and do the same thing this afternoon. It won't be too much longer before the weather turns brisk."

We stood watching Bruin and Cassie drive off together in Bruin's wagon. "They make an attractive couple," Charles said, watching my face, "I will not be surprised if we get an invitation to a wedding one day soon."

"That isn't funny, Charles," I said, walking toward our own buggy.

"I had no intention of being funny, Jessamyn," he called after me even as Cassie's shrill laughter floated back to taunt me.

*　　*　　*

I was sad on my seventeenth birthday. So sad that October sixteenth was just another day to me and I missed my parents more than ever.

Lonely and bored, I had not even bothered to mention my birthday to either Charles or to Mrs. Less, and my attempts to ignore the significance of the day only made me feel that much worse.

The Masters lived several miles to the east of our place and due to the distance, Elisha and I weren't as close as we had been on the wagon train. I was a married woman now and my life was dull and restricted by the reality of my situation. I longed for paints and an easel, but Charles was so busy with school, he had no time to take me to Marietta during regular shop hours to purchase them.

Mrs. Less had suggested we make the trip together one clear day, but Charles had balked. "It is not safe for two women to attempt a trip that long and far. I cannot give my permission for such a foolish endeavor."

His permission! I hated the confinement of marriage; hated feeling less than real…as if I had been re-invented by Charles as a creature whose sole purpose it was to compliment his standing as a man and a minister. I cursed my fate, wishing I had been born a man. Longing to be as real and purposeful and important a person as my husband was by the very accident of his birth as a male.

I vowed to try to make some sort of celebration for myself. I packed a lunch of leftovers, including a piece of the apple cake Mrs. Less had made for us several days before, and fixed a fresh jar of mint tea, then headed out with my sketching pad and charcoal for the glen toward the back of our property.

As I left the house, clutching my cloak about me as it whipped about in the sudden gusts of fall wind, I thought I heard the clip-clop of horse's hooves moving along the road toward our house. I peeked around the side of the house and was surprised to see Charles leading the horse and buggy down the drive. Now why was he home at this early hour?

I ducked back inside of the rear door and left the food basket on the kitchen table. Perhaps Charles would have the time to eat with me, or better yet, he would be able to take me to Marietta for my paints and easel.

Eager to ask him, I raced out to the yard and searched about for my husband. The horses and buggy stood abandoned by the side of the house. "Charles," I called, "Where are you?"

I had to fairly shout three times more before I got an answer, "I am here, Child. Come to the glen."

My original destination! What could he possibly be doing back there? I hurried toward the sound of his voice and soon I saw his tall, black hat bobbing toward me through the dense trees and bushes.

We faced each other on the path. Charles grinned at me in a boyish way and removed his hat as if he had just stepped into our sitting room back home in Boston.

"Why are you home at this time of day?" I asked, "I hope the school hasn't burned down."

Charles chuckled and then flushed. "I dismissed the children at noon today…in honor of your birthday."

I rushed forward to hug him. "Oh, Charles, how sweet! I had no idea you even knew!"

He returned my hug, nearly knocking the breath out of me and then grabbed my hand and pulled me along the path back in the direction from which he had just come.

"When we filled out the marriage certificate at the town hall in Marietta, I made note of the date of your birth. I have a present for you, Child, and I hope you like it. I had it made in town and I have been hiding it for more than a week."

I had never seen Charles so excited about anything, and I skipped along behind him, very curious as to what this mysterious present might be. Dare I hope for a new easel and paints? We threaded our way along the overgrown path, toward the wild flower garden nestled on the far side of the glen, on the side near the brook.

Charles pushed the last low hanging tree branches out of our way and there, hanging from an ancient elm, swaying enticingly in the gentle fall wind, was the most glorious swing I had ever seen! I swallowed my disappointment at not finding my art supplies, despite a stab of irritation at the realization he had been to Marietta to have this swing made, and as far as I could see, had completely forgotten how important my art is to my very existence. Still, Mama had raised me to be gracious when given any gift, and the swing was amazing!

It was painted in sunflower yellow and decorated with ivy and bluebells and late blooming roses in shades of red, pink, and coral! I turned to Charles and jumped up to kiss his cheek as I would my own father, had he been the one to gift me with something so charming and so completely unexpected.

"It seems I have made a lucky guess," Charles said, clearing his throat, loosening his collar and fanning his flushed face with his hat. I ran to the swing and sat upon it, feeling like a princess.

"Come, Charles, push me!" I called, pumping my legs and straining to go higher. "I love it, Charles! I cannot thank you enough. You have made me feel special!"

Charles loped toward me, moving more quickly than usual, and soon I was flying through the air, reveling in the movement of the swing, the rush of wind under my skirt and petticoats; loving the sensation of flying up above the trees, the sky, kin to the birds and feeling fine and free.

"You have gone to so much trouble for me," I said, leaning back and smiling at my husband. "And I thought no one cared about my birthday but me. Oh, Charles, if you only knew how lonely I have been."

My swing began to slow to a stop and I realized he had turned away from me. "What is the matter, Charles?" I asked, hurrying to his side. He kept his face turned away from me.

"I am so sorry, Child," he said, "I had no idea you were lonely...and unhappy. I-I have neglected you for my work. I am deeply sorry, Child. I hope you can forgive me."

"Charles," I cried, stepping in front of him. "Look at me. Please look at me." I waited until his eyes met mine. "I am not a child anymore. Why do you insist on calling me one?"

His gray eyes darkened as if storm clouds had moved in to threaten clear skies. My own lips quivered, but I stood my ground. He took a step toward me and his face took on the intense look I found most unsettling. I wanted Charles to see me as a woman and to respect me as such, but I did not wish to anger him. I closed my eyes and willed myself not to cry like a child and ruin my argument to the contrary.

"Open your eyes, Jessamyn," Charles said in the firm tones of a minister, of a man very much in charge...the natural leader I knew him to be."

My eyes flew open and I stared up at my husband. For the first time he was a man to me and not a minister.

"Sweet Jessamyn," he whispered, trembling, yet looking almost fierce.

I drew my breath in sharply and waited. Slowly, Charles lowered his lips toward mine. And when he kissed me, I felt a fire inside...and I found myself responding without thought to the consequences. As his arms tightened around me, I held on for dear life and kissed him back freeing all of the frustrations I had struggled with during these difficult weeks.

We swayed together, lost in our kisses, and then I felt the unfamiliar touch of a hand on my breast. I panicked, and tried to rear back, but Charles appeared unable to stop, and he pressed his face against my cheek, my hair, and then, very gently, he kissed the hollow of my throat. I shuddered, struggling with a new rush of intense unexpected feelings!

His hot breath was against my ear again! I gulped fresh air, whispering his name. Curious and afraid, I closed my eyes and clung to him, no longer able to stand on my own, and I waited to see what would happen next.

The last wild flowers of the season exuded a heady perfume, intoxi-cating us, coaxing us. Together we sank down to the grassy knoll. Charles covered my body with his own and kissed me deeply. Smothered by his weight, I gasped, and then his tongue entered my mouth. I squealed, surprised to find he would do such a thing! Who would want to do such a strange thing! I pushed against his chest, fighting for a breath of fresh air.

Vibrating with the powerful emotions we had stirred within each other, Charles sprang away from me and covered his face with his hands. "Forgive me, Jessamyn," he whispered, "I promised you I would wait…and wait I will. I swear I will."

I hugged my knees to my breasts and rocked from side to side. I had never been this confused in all my seventeen years. "Do not blame yourself, Charles," I said, finally, "I am as much to blame, if blame is even the appropriate word."

He reached for my hand, drew it to him, and kissed it with great emotion. "You need more time. I must control myself. Perhaps I should move into the guest room for a while."

"Oh, no!" I said, before I had given it any real thought. "Please don't feel you have to do that."

Charles smiled, looking much relieved. "I'll stay if you really want me to."

I nodded, feeling my cheeks go hot again. At least this had not been the usual boring day I was so used to having here in Beaver Valley. I had learned something new on my birthday. I had learned a bit of what love-making was all about. I felt a thrill surge through me as I was more curious about it all than ever before. And the most curious part of all was the disturbing fact that I had been nearly willing to make love without first falling in love. What kind of a woman was I turning into? And I, the wife of a minister!

*   *   *

Charles and I were shy with each other during dinner. I kept my eyes on my plate and although Mrs. Less had made us a wonder-ful meal of roast pork with applesauce and browned potatoes along with a mix of fall vegetables, a rainbow of color upon our dinner plates, I had trouble swallowing my food.

Would Charles resent me for making him forget his promise to me? Would he see me as a threat to his self-control?

I was grateful when someone knocked at our front door. "I'll get it," I called back, as I ran out of the dining room, not waiting for a reply or a protest.

I threw open the door and found Bruin! "Come in! You are just in time for dinner!" I threw my arms around him and kissed his cheek. He smelled of warm meadow grass and the odor called up memories of my afternoon's adventure…or near adventure.

"I have already eaten, Jessie," he said, his handsome face glowing. "But I will join you in a piece of birthday cake since that is the purpose of my visit." He ducked outside onto the porch and came back with a huge be-ribboned parcel.

"You are a sweet old bear!" I said, "I should have known you would never forget my birthday! It can't be another doll in that package, it's much too large!"

Bruin chuckled at me. Back during the days of our mother's close friendship, he had given me a china doll each year on my birthday. "Let us join Charles now, so you can find out exactly what is in this package. He'll wonder what has happened to keep you at the door for so long a time."

Charles and Bruin seemed glad to see each other and I eyed my present while they went through the ritual greetings and small talk expected of them.

Finally, unable to wait a moment longer, I grabbed up my present. "I am opening it now, Bruin!" I declared, un-tying the ribbon and ripping the paper away.

Canvases! And my beloved oil paints in every color! Sable brushes! And a new drawing tablet, charcoal and a full set of pastels! I covered my face with my hands and wept in pure joy!

"Oh, Bruin!" I sobbed, "Thank you! My dear, dear friend…this is what I wanted more than anything else in the entire world; more than jewels and furs and a castle in France!"

Bruin laughed at me. "Don't cry, Jessie, you'll make your nose all wet and red," he said gently, "You are supposed to smile on your birthday! I never meant to make you cry!"

I wiped at my face and then beamed at the two men. "I will do a painting for you, Bruin," I said, "I shall start it tomorrow. Something you will love…something suitable to hang above your mantle."

"In that case, I had better give you the rest of your gift." He said, striding back toward the front door.

Charles was suddenly frowning at me. "I should have known to give you the paints and canvases," he said quietly.

I didn't know what to say to him. I agreed totally with that assessment. "I do love the swing, Charles," I said, in too happy a state to risk spoiling this wondrous evening with conflict of any kind.

He stared at me, as hopeful as a young boy seeking the approval of his mother. "Do you? I am glad."

Bruin came back into the room and presented me with a beautifully crafted easel. "I made it myself," he said, "Is it the proper height for you? I can adjust it."

Slightly dizzy with emotion, I stood before the easel and declared it perfect for me. "It's so beautiful! Just perfect! Look, Charles, Bruin has carved my name here."

I ran my hands over the polished oak and felt well blessed. "This has been a wonderful birthday," I said, "thanks to my two favorite men!"

This silence in the room grew thick, and when I looked up again, I could only wonder what was passing between Bruin and Charles as they stood staring gravely into each other's eyes.

*   *   *

The night turned cold, much colder than I would have expected for mid-October. The wind shrieked and moaned outside, rattling our windows and creeping inside the house with a pervasive chill that told me Ohio was as cold a place as I had expected.

Bruin left soon after we had the cake in front of the fire and I felt sorry for him as he walked slowly toward his horse. He seemed lonely, and I worried what would become of him in this low state of mind. It was not easy for a young man to live alone in the wilderness after a lifetime of city activity and family closeness. Even when he thought he had gotten exactly what he wanted.

Bruin mounted his horse then spun around to see if I was still watching him. We raised our arms in a silent salute, and then he was gone at a gallop. I listened to the pounding of his horse's hooves as I latched the heavy front door, then rushed to the window to see whether he pointed his horse in the of his farm, or in the direction of town and Cassie Taylor.

With a stone in my heart, I turned back to the cozy comfort of the fire, and took my seat beside my husband in my rocker, the twin of his own. "Bruin is headed toward town," I said.

Charles sipped at his tea, and then placed the china cup on the small table beside him. The lamp shook as his hand brushed against it, and the amber oil shimmered in the glowing half-light.

"Cassie Taylor," he said, "Bruin is most likely stopping by the Taylor's on his way home." Charles looked oddly pleased at the thought.

"But the Taylor place isn't on his way home, Charles," I pointed out, "It is in the completely opposite direction."

Charles chuckled. "Close enough, all the same, Child."

I sprang to my feet and made a show of poking up the fire, then fanning the last log to flame with the old, cracked-leather bellows. I felt restless, too full of spirit to face a chilly night in that big, old bed upstairs.

Charles stood and adjusted the damper, then pushed the screen more securely against the darkened stone. "Let us retire for the evening, Child," he said, avoiding my eyes, and busying himself with winding Mama's clock. The scrinch, scrinch of the clock key plucked at the cord of my spine and I hurried toward the stairway.

Charles, lamp in hand, checked the front door locks and bolts; then turned to face me where I stood on the bottom step. "I must check the back door and windows," he said, "Take your time, Child."

He was referring to my toilet…as Mama used to say. He was gallantly giving me some privacy so I could wash and dress for bed in blessed solitude. He did this most every evening and on those rare occasions when he was too tired to go through these polite delaying gestures, I undressed and washed behind the screen he had provided for me.

I lifted my skirts and ascended into the darkness above. At first I did not know what was causing the eerie light emanating from our bedroom, but upon entering, it became apparent the full moon was responsible for the strange glow. It appeared to hang like a vigilant spy in the black night, huge and unapproachable, just outside our window.

I shivered as I undressed in haste, hoping Charles would think to fill the bed warmer with hot coals from the fire. This cold was the punishing kind…a trip to the outhouse was more than I could face, and I was glad to use the chamber pot behind my screen and to wriggle as quickly as a hare into my white linen nightdress. I chose the one with the lace trim, and as I sat before my dressing table, brushing my thick hair, and then wrestling it into the partial submission of a fat, twisted braid that ended in one of the new birthday ribbons from Mrs. Less, I deliberately left the top four buttons of my nightdress undone. Then I dabbed rose-water between my breasts, inhaled the sweet scent, and shivered again at the cold assault.

Dressing my wild hair had made me think of Cassie's full, ringlets, curls of a softer nature in a more pleasing shade of light-auburn, and I wondered if Bruin had indeed stopped in at the Taylor home. Was he sitting with that vixen upon a loveseat at this very moment, toasting his cold feet before a roaring fire; warming the chill from his fingers against Cassie Taylor's hot, bare flesh.

I threw my hairbrush into the corner and cursed the skinny witch under my breath. Bruin deserved better…Bruin the fool…as well as my dearest friend.

Charles came through the door, carrying the red-hot bed warmer by its' long handle. "Step aside," he cautioned, as I drew the quilts down to the foot of the bed and he began to move the bed warmer between the sheets. "Now draw the quilts up, Child," he instructed.

I stood back once again, as Charles moved the warmer between quilt and sheet; vibrating with the cold and wondering how we'd survive January if October was this brutal.

"Is it always this cold?" I asked.

"Not always."

He placed the bed warmer on the hearth of the fireplace and threw two more logs upon the fire while I climbed up onto the massive oaken bed, snuggling down into the feathered mattress, drawing the quilts up to my chin, and wishing I was sleepy enough to lose myself in dreams.

Charles extinguished the lamp, then poured his own bowl of wash water and retired behind the screen. I turned away from him to gaze out at the frigid view. Nearly all of the leaves had been shaken loose from the spidery tree branches in the unleashed Autumn winds, and the dark, thin shapes twisted about in the bright light of the moon, throwing shadows across our bed. I closed my eyes and tried to sleep.

I caught his now familiar scent of musty old books, and slightly stale perspiration, and was glad he had not attempted to kiss me goodnight. My new husband confused me; challenging my senses in so many ways.

He was snoring within minutes, and still my mind raced with thoughts; regrets. All the while my heart ached with emptiness.

I thought again of Bruin in town with Cassie and tears soon soaked my pillow slip, while I prayed to God for guidance. I was so confused, so heartsick at the death of my papa and the shock of my sudden marriage to Charles; I didn't know how I truly felt about anything.

Charles shifted in his sleep and threw his arm over his head. He growled again, and mumbled in an urgent way. His head whipped back and forth upon his pillow. I turned toward him, watching him struggle with some secret demon in the shadow land of sleep.

"Sweet, sweet Jesss…" he whispered, then moaned and lurched over, throwing his arm across my middle. His large, long-fingered hand moved up and down the side of my body, grasping, searching, causing shocks of sensation to rock me, to tease me in a new and somewhat terrifying way.

"Soooo soft," he breathed, nuzzling my ear and then burying his face against my neck and shoulder.

"Reverend," I said, my breath coming so quickly, I feared I might faint.

"Whaa? What?" he mumbled, starting awake and rearing. His own breath, irregular; he clutched at his chest, his clear, gray eyes wide and confused. "I…what have I?"

"You have done nothing, Charles," I assured him, touching his arm gently. "You were having a nightmare, I think. You appeared to be in some sort of distress. Are you in pain?"

"No…no, of course not," he whispered, running his hands through his long, pale hair. There was a misting of perspiration across his forehead despite the chill in the room. "I burned like the fires of hell. Everywhere I touched your flesh I…I" He swallowed hard, and swung his legs over the side of the bed.

"Wait, Charles," I said, reaching out to him, but he shook his head and stood back from the bed.

"I cannot sleep now, Child." His voice so gentle, his eyes old and weary in this dim light; the hollows of his cheeks more pronounced as he turned away from me. "I will sit by the window and read *The Bible* for a while."

I leaned back against my pillow and gazed out at the moon. Charles sat in the ladder-backed chair to the right of the window. The moon shone in over his left shoulder and he did not seem to need the light of a lamp to read. The firelight threw long shadows across his face, but his hair caught the light pleasingly and turned to gold. I breathed deeply and savored the scent of wood-smoke and my own lingering scent of rose-water.

"I cannot sleep either, Charles," I said, "Would you mind reading aloud? It might soothe us both."

He nodded curtly; then began:

> "It is not good to eat much honey, so be sparing of complimen-
> tary words. A man without self-control is like a city broken into
> and left without walls. Like snow in summer or rain in harvest,
> so honor is not fitting for a fool. Like a sparrow in its' flitting, like
> a swallow in its' flying, a curse that is causeless does not alight.
> A whip for a horse, a bridle for the ass, and a rod for the backs
> of fools. Answer not a fool according to his folly, lest you be like
> him yourself. Answer a fool according to his folly, lest he be wise
> in his own eyes."

He paused and I said, "I am not familiar with that passage, Charles. Where is it from?"

"Proverbs; I usually find that when I need an answer I find it here with little effort."

"Mama always said the same thing…" I murmured; then fell into my own dreams.

*   *   *

I relaxed against the sofa and closed my eyes for a moment as the emotion of the day caught up with me.

I heard Alexander draw a deep sigh and just as I was thinking he sounded as worn out as I felt, he spoke.

"That poor bastard," he said curtly, then he stood up and walked toward his room and not once did he look back at me.